Michelle Smart's love affair with books started when she was a baby and would cuddle them in her cot. A voracious reader of all genres, she found her love of romance established when she stumbled across her first Mills & Boon book at the age of twelve. She's been reading them—and writing them—ever since. Michelle lives in Northamptonshire, England, with her husband and two young Smarties.

USA TODAY bestselling, RITA®-nominated, and critically acclaimed author **Caitlin Crews** has written more than 100 books and counting. She has a Master's and a PhD in English Literature, thinks everyone should read more category romance, and is always available to discuss her beloved alpha heroes. Just ask. She lives in the Pacific Northwest with her comic book artist husband, she is always planning her next trip, and she will never, ever, read all the books in her 'to-be-read' pile. Thank goodness.

UNWRAPPED BY HER ITALIAN BOSS

MICHELLE SMART

THE BRIDE HE STOLE FOR CHRISTMAS

CAITLIN CREWS

MILLS & BOON

First Published in Great Britain 2021
by Mills & Boon, an imprint of HarperCollins*Publishers* Ltd,
1 London Bridge Street, London, SE1 9GF

www.harpercollins.co.uk

HarperCollins*Publishers*
1st Floor, Watermarque Building,
Ringsend Road, Dublin 4, Ireland

Unwrapped by Her Italian Boss © 2021 Michelle Smart

The Bride He Stole for Christmas © 2021 Caitlin Crews

ISBN: 978-0-263-28267-2

10/21

MIX
Paper from
responsible sources
FSC® C007454

This book is produced from independently certified FSC™ paper
to ensure responsible forest management.
For more information visit www.harpercollins.co.uk/green.

Printed and bound in Spain using 100% Renewable Electricity
at CPI Blackprint (Barcelona)

UNWRAPPED
BY HER
ITALIAN BOSS

MICHELLE SMART

MILLS & BOON

To my partner-in-crime Louise.

Thanks for making our second duet
as great a joy as our first. x

CHAPTER ONE

MERRY INGLES STOMPED her way through the freshly laid snow from her chalet, tugging her woolly hat over the cold lobes of her ears as she went. The thick clouds that had obscured the stars overnight had cleared, leaving the skies above the Swiss Alps crisp and blue and with a sharp chill that fogged the breath. Further up the mountain, the Hotel Haensli rose like a beautiful majestic overlord peering down on its minions. In three years of working and living there, Merry had never lost the awe of her daily morning glimpse.

Ten minutes after setting out, and looking forward to the hot chocolate that would warm her frozen cheeks, she spotted a porter wrestling a huge netted Christmas tree that would be added to the twenty-four ornately decorated trees already placed throughout the hotel's ground floor.

'Want a hand?' she called, upping her pace.

Johann, one of the groundsmen who'd been tasked with chopping the huge Nordmann Firs the hotel grew specially for the festive period, put the base of the tree down and waited for her to catch up, a relieved smile on his face.

'You are a lifesaver,' he said. 'I need to get this to the spa lounge before it opens to the guests. Ricardo was supposed to help me.'

Up close, Merry's practised eye estimated the tree to

be a good fifteen foot. Her nose wrinkled as she contemplated it.

They agreed that Johann would lead the way and in unison lifted the tree onto their shoulders. It was much lighter than she'd expected but the foot in height difference between them meant it slanted at a steep angle. Although her gloves prevented the stray pine needles poking through the netting from scratching her hands, to keep it stable she pressed her cheek to it and tried to ignore the scratching against her cheek and spectacles.

More through blind luck—and blind really was the operative word as Merry's hat sloped down and dislodged her glasses and she couldn't see anything past a blurry Johann—they manoeuvred the tree through the double doors of the staff entrance at the rear. Pausing to stamp snow off their boots and readjust their load, they then navigated their way down the long, wide corridor running the other side of the hotel's huge reception. By the time they reached the double doors that led into the spa, Merry's glasses had fallen down her nose again and were in danger of falling off her face.

'Hold on a sec,' she said, resting the base of the tree down. Hugging it tightly with one arm, she shoved her glasses back up with her free hand and tugged the zip of her snow jacket down a little. Wrapped up as she was, the hotel's warmth was stifling. Not wanting pine needles stuck in her hair, she kept her hat on.

'Ready?' Johann asked.

'Ready.'

'One, two, three...'

They lifted it back onto their shoulders. Johann opened the door. As he did, he twisted his body, forcing Merry to twist too, to keep the tree stable. She had no idea anyone was behind her until she felt a thud followed by a gasp of pain.

'Sugar! I'm sorry!' Setting the tree's base back on the floor, she turned to apologise to her victim, praying it was a member of staff she'd just accidentally bashed.

The tall man in an obviously bespoke navy-blue suit, handsome face wincing in pain as he rubbed his shoulder, was most definitely not staff.

'I'm so sorry,' she said, mortified at what she'd done. 'Are you badly hurt?'

Furious dark blue eyes ringed with dark lashes she'd give a kidney for set above cheekbones she'd give the other kidney for were fixed on her.

Repeating herself in German, she braced herself. There would be hell to pay for this. Only the super-rich and powerful could afford to stay at Hotel Haensli, and in exchange for the astronomical sums they paid for the privilege of staying in such a luxurious setting with some of the best views in the whole of Switzerland, they expected exemplary service. They did not expect to be clouted by a Christmas tree.

Giovanni Cannavaro stared at the horrified bright red face half hidden by a thick scarf, glasses askew and topped with the most ridiculous hat he'd ever seen worn by an adult. His flare of anger at being hit by a hated Christmas tree dissolved as he found himself smothering an extremely rare and extremely unexpected bubble of mirth.

It was also an extremely short bubble of mirth.

He stepped towards the woman. 'Move.'

'What?'

'I will carry it for you.'

'But…but…you can't.'

'You hit me and now you tell me what I can do?'

What he could see of the tiny woman's red face instinctively recoiled in alarm at his words.

'I didn't…'

He pointed with his thumb to where the front of the tree was trapped in the door.

'You get the door,' he said, overriding her protest before nodding at the groundsman he suspected was trying to make himself invisible. 'I am tall, like him. Is easier. And safer,' he added pointedly.

She scuttled to open the door and pressed herself tightly against the wall as the two men carried it past her.

'All done,' Giovanni said when they'd placed it in the stand and the netting had been removed. He flicked stray pine needles from his shoulders and nodded at the two hotel employees. 'Next time, more careful, *si*?'

Then, in need of food and a cappuccino before he solved the mess that had seen him fly to Switzerland in the early hours, Giovanni strode to the breakfast room.

'Sorry I'm late,' Merry said as she hurried into the office she shared with her boss and Sasha, the other member of the hospitality team, only to find the room empty.

While she waited for Katja to come back from wherever she was—her computer was on, so she'd obviously been in—Merry put a hot chocolate pod in the snazzy machine and booted her computer up.

Where the rest of the hotel had been transformed into a Christmas wonderland, their office was devoid of decoration. Mostly. Merry had stuck a small plastic tree filled with tiny baubles on the corner of her desk and wrapped her monitor in tinsel. Katja had rolled her eyes at it, just as she'd rolled them when she'd seen Merry in her red woolly hat that had Rudolph the Red-Nosed Reindeer knitted into it.

She was finishing her hot chocolate and replying to emails when Katja finally hurried through the door, her face creased with worry. 'There you are. You're needed in the meeting room. We have a situation.'

Merry jumped to her feet. 'What kind of situation?'

'Everything will be explained… What's wrong with your face? Have you scratched it?'

'Pine needles. I helped Johann carry a Christmas tree to the spa.' She felt her scratched cheeks flame again, remembering how she'd accidentally bashed one of their esteemed guests with it. Another roll of dread played in her belly. The guest had taken it relatively well, all things considered, but she'd known staff to be sacked for less, and thought it best not to mention the incident to her boss.

That didn't stop the image of the guest's handsome face pinging back into her mind. He truly was gorgeous. Greek god handsome. Hair so dark it was almost black. Long straight nose. Chiselled jaw. And those lashes. Those *cheekbones*…

'That's why I was late. I couldn't let him struggle on his own,' she added as they strode down the corridor and she shoved Cheekbones from her mind. With any luck, she'd be able to avoid him for the rest of his stay there.

'I know,' Katja said tightly. 'You like to help people. That's why I chose you, remember?'

Merry had spent her first two years in Switzerland working as a waitress at Hotel Haensli, thrilled to have landed such a prestigious job in one of the world's top hotels. A year ago she'd been summoned by the management. Terrified she was about to be fired, she'd almost fallen off her chair when Katja, the Head of Hospitality, announced she was in need of a new assistant and wanted to offer Merry the role. Katja had read through the hotel guest book and online reviews and been impressed at how many times Merry's name was mentioned in them as someone who went above and beyond her duties. Returning guests often insisted she serve their table.

Overnight, Merry went from split shifts of six a.m. starts and midnight finishes to eight a.m. starts and, unless they had special evening events on, four p.m. finishes for double her waitressing salary. The job even came with its own two-bed chalet. No more sharing staff quarters with fifteen others! A career path had opened up for her and she was delighted to follow it.

The woman who'd made all this happen for her, Katja, hesitated at the staff meeting room door. 'Just…just think what this could do for your future, okay?'

And with those enigmatic words, Katja opened the door.

Seated at the oval table was Hotel Haensli's elderly owner, Wolfgang Merkel. The automatic smile of greeting on Merry's face froze when she saw the man beside him.

It was Cheekbones. The man she'd clobbered with the Christmas tree.

Heat flushed through her body like a wave. White noise filled her ears.

She, Merry, was the situation and she was about to be fired.

The noise in her head was so deafening that when Cheekbones rose from his chair and extended his hand to her, it took an embarrassingly long time for it to penetrate her brain that Katja had introduced him and she'd not heard a word of it.

Tremors raced through her fingers as she reached her hand across the table to her executioner.

It was the clumsy lady with the crazy hat. Giovanni, heart sinking, recognised her immediately. The large tortoise-shell spectacles gave her away. So did the horrified, gorm-less expression on her face.

A small hand and short fingers folded around his just long enough for a brisk shake that sent an unexpected flash of heat through his skin. Disconcerted, he observed the movement of her slender throat, the flash of baby blue behind the spectacles and the flush of colour staining her rounded cheeks, and cast an idle sweep of his eyes over a body no longer bundled up in outdoor clothing.

Petite. A trim figure hidden beneath the hotel's standard black administrative uniform. Golden hair scraped back in a neat bun. Clear complexion. No make-up. Reasonably attractive without the stupid hat. How ridiculous had that been? He was quite sure Sofia, the younger of his sisters, had worn a similar one when she'd been a child.

Which of the Fates, he wondered grimly, had he angered that they would task this woman with rescuing the project he'd spent three years of hard work and planning on? The whole things was a cigarette paper away from being ruined and his hard-won reputation with it.

Twelve years ago, when his world had collapsed, Giovanni had left Italy and ended up in this very hotel. He'd worked as a porter until, months after starting there, the hotel owner had sought him out and, after a long chat, offered him a job as his assistant.

Overnight he'd become Wolfgang Merkel's protégé, had soaked up the man's knowledge of luxury and refinement and the art of giving the rich exactly what they wanted so they kept returning year after year. A year later, he'd received a small bequest from his grandfather's will and, with Wolfgang's blessing and good wishes, had left to form his own company, Cannavaro Travel.

In the decade since, his business had gone from strength to strength and Giovanni had joined that elite class, amassing riches beyond his wildest dreams. Luxury cruises, private yacht hire, private plane hire, road trips across continents, sumptuous hotels…his company specialised in all those things. Cannavaro Travel had become a byword for excellence and, with Wolfgang's wise words forever playing in his ear, he never let standards drop for a second.

He'd never doubted his mentor's judgement before but, staring at the woman Wolfgang considered capable of stepping in and saving the day, he worried for his old friend's mental faculties.

He waited until she'd taken the chair next to Katja before addressing her. 'Katja has explained the situation?'

She shook her head.

'Gerhard was taken to hospital last night. He has the...' He scrambled for the English word.

'Appendicitis,' Katja supplied.

Merry's hand was tingling so much from Cheekbones' handshake that she had to clamp her other one over it to muffle the sensation.

'Gerhard...?' The name rang a bell in her flushed mind and she tried hard to bring herself back to the present.

'Gerhard Klose. The man I've been training to run hospitality for the Meravaro Odyssey,' Katja explained.

Comprehension flooded her and she practically sagged with relief.

Cheekbones wasn't here to get her fired. He must be part of Cannavaro Travel.

He looked at her unsmiling. 'Now you understand the situation, *si*?'

Oh, yes, she understood.

Wolfgang Merkel had agreed to a collaboration with his good friend, the luxury travel specialist Giovanni Cannavaro. The two men, under Giovanni's direction, had spent the past three years partnering on a brand-new train service, one that would take their guests through Europe's most picturesque cities and landscapes directly to the train station a few miles from the hotel. The maiden journey departed in three days.

This wasn't just a maiden voyage. This was the social event of the year. Eighty of the world's richest and most powerful people would board the Meravaro Odyssey in Paris for a festive voyage of unsurpassed splendour. When, after two nights of glamour on board, the train the world's press were chomping at the bit to review finally arrived at Klosters train station, horse-drawn carriages would take its passengers to the hotel, giving them two days to luxuriate before the annual Hotel Haensli Christmas party. The party the world's elite would sell their kidneys for a ticket to.

As Katja had spent a decade working on the luxury train that had been made eternally famous in an enduringly popular crime book, she'd been tasked with imparting her wealth of knowledge to the gentleman hired to run hospitality on the Cannavaro Odyssey: the appendicitis-struck Gerhard. The role was simple—to ensure all guests had the experience of their lives and that all their whims, reasonable or otherwise, were catered for.

For Katja, training Gerhard had been a nightmare. Giovanni Cannavaro had insisted on frequent detailed reports about Gerhard's progress. Katja had been under no illusion that if the man failed in any way, her own head would be for the chopping block.

'Are you stepping in for Gerhard?' Merry asked her immediate boss, a wave of sympathy rushing through her for being shoehorned into a temporary role that might be a poisoned chalice.

Katja shook her head. 'Angie's on a week-long business trip in Frankfurt.' Angie was Katja's wife. They had a six-year-old daughter.

'Sasha?'

'She needs to be here for the Voegel wedding.' Katja's eyes were wide with apology. 'I'm sorry, Merry, but you're going to have to step in. There's no one else.'

Her chest turned cold. The white noise that had filled her ears at the sight of Cheekbones was now replaced with the drumbeats of doom.

Merry was working over Christmas and the New Year. Her new sister-in-law, determined to bring the Ingles family together, had insisted on hosting an early Christmas dinner for them to celebrate together. That dinner was in two days. Merry was flying home to England for it tomorrow.

No wonder Katja had been so uptight when she'd brought her into the meeting room. Katja knew all this. Knew how hard Merry had worked to ensure her diary was clear for her visit home.

It was ironic, really, considering Merry had been dreading going home. Thanks to her brother's hatred of it, the Ingles had barely marked the Christmas period since Merry was eight, but now he wanted to make his new wife happy and had badgered and bullied and emotionally blackmailed Merry for weeks, until she'd submitted and agreed to go.

On top of that, the day after the dinner her oldest and closest friend Santa was flying back to Switzerland with her for a long-planned stay in Merry's cabin.

She couldn't do it. Couldn't let her sister-in-law down. Couldn't let Santa down.

'You'll fly to Paris first thing in the morning,' Katja said, breaking the tense silence. 'The guests aren't due to board for three days, so you'll have two full days to iron out any potential issues and get to know the staff and the workings and everything.'

Wolfgang finally spoke, the first time in three years he'd addressed Merry directly. 'Katja tells me you are supposed to be on leave tomorrow. You will receive an extra paid week's leave in the New Year to make up for the time you are missing.'

This was a done deal, Merry realised with rising trepidation. No wonder Katja had warned her to consider her future before they entered the room.

Wolfgang Merkel paid generously, and gave perks that far exceeded the industry norm, but in return he expected complete dedication. He expected his staff to rally together in a time of crisis. The man was generous, but ruthless.

As Merry didn't have a six-year-old child who'd be left without care like Katja did, she had no reasonable excuse to say no. Saying, *But I haven't seen my family in six months and, much as the thought of spending a day with them creating a fake early Christmas fills me with dread, I've made a promise*, would cut no ice but would certainly affect her future.

Even if she'd wanted to say any of those words, the moment was lost when Wolfgang groped for his walking stick and got to his feet. 'Now that everything is in hand, I will leave you to sort the details.'

Katja did likewise, minus the walking stick. Her stare was full of sympathy. 'I'll transfer the files to you while you two get acquainted.'

And then, while Merry was still trying to think of a way to get out of this emergency role without losing her job, she was left in the meeting room with Cheekbones and his piercing, astute stare.

'You not want the job, lady?' he asked coolly.

Feeling sick from the mingling dread and panic, she rubbed her face and managed a wan smile. 'I don't think whether I want it or not matters.' Then, fearing she sounded disloyal—if Cheekbones worked for Cannavaro Travel he would undoubtedly be reporting to Giovanni Cannavaro himself, whose reputation as a taskmaster was on a par with Wolfgang's. 'But I know how important this maiden voyage is, so I'll give it my best shot.'

What choice did she have? Accept the last-minute secondment or lose her job. Those were the only choices. If she lost her job, what would happen to her? She'd be forced to return to England while she sought another job. Forced to live in the bleak, unhappy home of her childhood. All the joy and light she'd experienced these past three years would be gone and she'd return to grey.

'What role do you play in it all?' she asked into the silence.

He raised a thick black eyebrow.

'Are you part of Cannavaro Travel?' she queried. 'Sorry, my mind went blank when we were introduced.'

The other eyebrow rose.

A tiny dart of amusement at his expression—it was definitely the expression of someone outragedly thinking, *How can you not know who I am?*—cut through Merry's guilt and anguish. The guilt came from having spent two months praying for the forthcoming trip home to be cancelled. The anguish came from her having to be the one to do it, and with just two days' notice. The early Christmas dinner her sister-in-law had spent weeks and weeks planning had all been for nothing.

Her brother was going to kill her.

The only good thing she had to hold on to was that she hadn't clobbered an actual guest with the Christmas tree, although, judging by the cut of his suit, Cheekbones was on a huge salary, so must be high up in Cannavaro Travel, and all the signs were that he had an ego to match that salary.

She'd get this meeting over and done with and then she'd call Martin.

With that set in her mind, she relaxed her chest with an exhale. 'Your role?' she asked again.

Dark blue eyes glittered. Tingles laced her spine and spread through her skin.

Cheekbones folded his hands together on the table. 'My role...? Think of me as the boss.'

His deep, musical accent set more tingles off in her. Crossing her legs, thankful that she'd come to her senses before mouthing off about being forced into a temporary job she'd rather eat fetid fruit than do, Merry made a mark in her notebook. 'I report to you?'

'*Si.*'

'Are you going on the train ride?'

Strong nostrils flared with distaste. 'It is no "train ride", lady.'

'You know what I mean.' She laughed. She couldn't help it. Something about his presence unnerved her. Greek god looks clashing with a glacial demeanour, warmed up again by the sexiest Italian accent she'd ever heard.

'I know what you mean and, *si*, I will be on the voyage.'

Unnerved further by the swoop of her belly at this, she made another nonsense mark in her book before looking back up at him and smiling ruefully. 'In that case, I should confess that I didn't catch your name. I'm Merry,' she added, so he wouldn't have any excuse to keep addressing her as 'lady'.

His fingers drummed on the table. 'I know your name, lady. *I* pay attention.'

For some unfathomable reason, this tickled her. 'Well done. Go to the top of the class. And your name?'

'Giovanni Cannavaro.'

All the blood in Merry's head pooled down to her feet in one strong gush.

He rose to his feet and stared imperiously at her. With ice-cool precision, he said, 'You have much to do. You will start by reading the files. We will meet later to discuss details and I will decide then if are you up to the job... Or not.'

He left the meeting room without another word.

CHAPTER TWO

'THAT WAS QUICK!' Katja said when Merry stepped back in the office.

Quick? Merry had spent five minutes alone in the meeting room, clutching her mortified face, then another ten minutes talking to her sister-in-law after not being able to reach her brother. Kelly had taken the news of Merry's sudden cancellation with surprising sweetness. Martin, she was sure, would not be so understanding. For once, she wouldn't even blame him.

'How did you get on?'

'Terribly,' she moaned, before confessing, 'I hit him with a Christmas tree earlier—'

'You did *what*?'

'It was an accident,' Merry stressed miserably. 'And now I've made it worse. I didn't hear his name when we were introduced, so I didn't know who he was until right at the end. He thinks I'm useless.' Overcome by fresh mortification, she flopped into her seat and cradled her head.

'He said that?'

'He said he needs to decide if I'm up to the job.' She'd seen it in his eyes too. Such beautiful eyes. Such a beautiful man. Such a powerful, contemptuous man.

And he thought she was an idiot.

'Well, you're going to have to prove him wrong or we're both going to suffer for it,' Katja told her furiously. 'How could you not know who he is? I've been dealing with him for months.' And had muttered numerous murderous complaints about him.

'I've never met him before!' Merry defended herself.

She'd met so many rich and famous people in her three years at the hotel that her curiosity about them had long ebbed. Until that day, Giovanni Cannavaro had been a name amongst many, albeit one punctuated with curses from Katja. Merry had imagined he was elderly, like his good friend Wolfgang.

'You never said he was young and gorgeous,' she added accusingly.

Katja's arched brow instantly reminded Merry of the way Giovanni's brow had risen.

'Merry, I'm married to a woman.'

'So what? That doesn't mean you can't appreciate a good-looking man.'

'It does when he's an arrogant…' Katja's eyes narrowed. 'You don't fancy him, do you?'

The question made her squirm. 'Of course not. I was just stating a fact.'

'Don't fancy him. He has a terrible reputation.'

'With women?'

'Yes. I would give you the details, but as you don't fancy him I won't bother. And, while we're on the subject, I thought I told you to read the business pages? The face you don't fancy is always in them.'

The hotel had a delivery of Europe's most highbrow newspapers delivered early every morning.

'I tried, but they're boring. I'll make it right,' she promised, fearing Katja's dark red face was gearing up to explode.

'You'd better. Giovanni is to Wolfgang what you are to me. His protégé.'

'You've never mentioned that before!'

'I told you they were close friends! If you'd read the damned business pages, like I told you to, you would know this. It's often mentioned. Their collaboration for the Meravaro Odyssey has been written about numerous times. Wolfgang trusts Giovanni implicitly. If you screw this up...' She shook her head, muttering under her breath. 'Why did Angie have to go away now? *I* should be taking this trip.' Her glare fixed back on Merry. 'One bad word from Giovanni to Wolfgang and you'll be fired, and I'll probably lose my job too.'

Merry knocked on the door, her heart racing in the same heavy, painful canter it had thudded with since a note had been passed to her by one of the hotel's reception staff saying she was to meet Giovanni Cannavaro in the Haensli Suite at twelve-thirty p.m.

Mere seconds passed before the door was opened by its appointed butler.

Located on the top floor, the Haensli Suite was the largest and most opulent of the hotel's rooms. Under normal circumstances she'd be thrilled to see its interior, would marvel at its size—her cabin would fit in its living area—but her nerves were too ragged to appreciate any of it.

Led to a set of leather armchairs beside a huge open fire, she accepted the butler's offer of a pot of tea and carefully placed her laptop, notebook and phone on the curved oak coffee table. To her right were huge French doors that led to a large private balcony. In the distance, she could see the hotel's private ski-lifts in motion and experienced a pang that she wouldn't be able to hit the slopes again for a while. If she mucked this up she probably wouldn't hit the slopes here ever again.

'You are here. Good.'

Not having heard him approach, Merry jumped in nervous fright and turned her head in the direction of Giovanni's voice. He was stepping across the threshold of the door that must lead into the sleeping quarters. Her heart started to thump erratically and she wiped her suddenly clammy hands on her skirt.

He took the seat across from hers, his black hair bouncing with the motion. He'd removed the suit jacket and tie he'd been wearing earlier and opened the top two buttons of his white shirt. It didn't appear to have a single crease in it.

She discreetly wiped her hands again. She'd never felt so jittery in her life.

The butler returned, carrying a tray of drinks for them. After he'd poured Merry's tea and Giovanni's coffee, he said, 'Do you still wish for lunch to be served in thirty minutes?'

'*Per favore,*' Giovanni replied. Once the butler disappeared, he got straight to business. 'We have much to discuss so will work through lunch.'

Her throat moved and her lips pulled together. She cleared her throat. 'Before we start, I would like to apologise for my behaviour earlier. You must think I'm incredibly rude. I should have paid greater attention. I give you my word it won't happen again.'

'What won't happen again? Hitting me with a Christmas tree? Wearing that stupid hat? Failing to pay attention?'

Her neck and cheeks turned crimson. Her mouth opened and closed a number of times, but before she could get any words out, a saccharine Christmas song suddenly blasted out. She snatched her phone off the table and quickly declined the call.

'Sorry.' She looked back at him and visibly forced her plump lips into a smile. 'Shall we get started?'

He didn't return the smile. 'You have read the files?'

'Most of them.' She swallowed. 'I'll finish them as soon as we're done here.'

'Make sure you do,' he said sardonically. 'This trip is important. My guests expect the best of everything. One bad experience and my reputation goes...' He held her stare as he snapped his fingers to accentuate his meaning.

Her eyes widened behind the large frames. Her voice sounded dry when she replied. 'I promise I'll be up to speed on everything before I go to bed tonight.'

The Christmas song blasted out again. Her hand shook so hard when she reached for her phone that she knocked it off the table onto the floor.

Giovanni winced at her gaucheness.

Only deep respect for Wolfgang had stopped him going straight to his mentor earlier and telling him that Merry Ingles was too much of a liability to be of any help. For Wolfgang's sake, he would give her until the end of lunch to prove herself, but he was far from convinced she had what it took. He didn't have time to waste if she was incapable of doing the job. If he had to do it himself then so be it. He'd put too much time, effort and money into the project to let it fail.

'Turn that off so we are not disturbed again,' he instructed when she put the phone back on the table.

'Okay.' In her haste to grab hold of it, she almost sent it flying onto the floor again.

To his astonishment, she pressed its side button. 'Seriously, lady? You go into a man's suite alone and turn your phone off? What is wrong with you?'

Panicking eyes met his. 'But you said—'

'I meant turn the sound off.'

'I thought you meant for me to turn it off altogether.'

Gritting his teeth, he said, 'If I tell you to stand on balcony with no clothes on for an hour, you do that too?'

Her demeanour changed in an instant. She stilled. Her eyes widened. Something flared in them. Then he caught a slight flare of her little nostrils and her plump lips twitched.

'Only if I was allowed to turn the balcony heater on.'

Taken aback at her retort, he watched as she calmly turned her phone back on, switched the sound off, placed it on the table, opened her laptop and then rested her notebook on her lap.

Pen poised in her hand, she met his stare. 'Ready?'

By the time the butler entered the suite, pushing a trolley with their lunch, Merry's insides had settled enough for her to keep control of her limbs and string a sentence together that didn't make her sound like a gibbering idiot.

She'd *behaved* like a gibbering idiot. Only the contempt on Giovanni's face when he'd suggested she stand on the balcony naked had snapped her out of it. Unfathomably, it had tickled her funny bone. How she hadn't snorted with laughter she would never know. She'd only just got away with her quip back at him.

Once the dining table was laid, Giovanni led the way and sat down, indicating for her to follow suit.

An array of food had been artfully spread out for them.

Taking the seat opposite him, she placed her notebook and phone beside a glass of water and helped herself to a little each of the burrata, served on a bed of tomatoes, pesto and pine nuts, the lobster in mango and iceberg lettuce, and the fries covered with melted gruyere cheese.

'You do not want caviar?' he asked, indicating the blinis piled with it.

'I'm good, thank you,' she answered politely.

'You do not like it?'

She scrambled for a diplomatic answer. 'It's an acquired taste.'

A black eyebrow rose.

'Okay, I think it tastes awful,' she admitted. 'And the texture… Yuck.'

'You know how much "yuck" costs?'

'Way too much.'

A sudden glimmer of something caught life in the dark blue eyes staring at her, sending darts of awareness firing through her veins. He really was incredibly gorgeous. Suddenly realising her eyes hadn't left his face long enough for her to even look at the food she'd piled on her plate, she quickly dragged her gaze to her notebook, opened it, and began firing questions at him while they ate.

Whatever the glimmer had been, she sensed a slight easing in the tension he carried with him.

The food was, as expected, delicious, and she forced as much as she could into her acrobatically dancing stomach.

It was those eyes… Every time they locked on hers, her belly flipped violently.

With every bite of food she ate, every note she wrote in her jotter, she was aware of him. Not aware as in the usual sense of her eyes and ears telling her that Giovanni was sitting across the table from her, but more as an internal feeling. Everything inside her felt shaky and a little bit nauseous…but not how she normally knew nausea, as a prelude to sickness, but more as a continual churn of butterflies. Her skin prickled. Every time he spoke tingles laced her spine.

Her plate still half full, she could manage no more and pushed it aside.

When Merry had been a waitress there, she'd particularly loved working the lunch and evening shifts. If the head chef deemed any plate of food to be unacceptable in any way, shape or form, another plate would be cooked from scratch. The waiter or waitress who managed to rescue the rejected plate before its contents could be thrown into the scraps bucket had a treat to look forward to when their shift ended.

She had never left any food made in this hotel on her plate before.

Swallowing back all the strange things happening inside her, she forced her mind to concentrate on the job in hand. Giovanni might have loosened up a tiny bit, but she was well aware he was assessing her capabilities and quite certain that she was in the last chance saloon with him. As a result, she ignored the incessant muted string of messages flashing on the screen of her phone from her brother and ignored the three calls he made. Even if she'd felt comfortable enough to ask for five minutes to accept a personal call, no way would she subject herself to a tongue-lashing from Martin when she had Cheekbones around to witness it.

If there was one thing Merry hated, it was crying and losing her temper in front of people, and no one could make her cry and rage more easily than her brother. It was a gift he'd had since she was a toddler.

She was writing another note in her jotter—so far she'd filled around a dozen pages…anything to keep her gaze off Giovanni's far too gorgeous face—when her phone flashed its notification of another call.

She ran her fingers over her lips before flicking her stare to Giovanni. 'Do you mind if I take this?' she asked cautiously. 'It's a client.'

To her relief, he gave a *Be my guest* gesture.

Giovanni watched Merry stride back to her laptop at the coffee table.

She didn't need to put the caller on loudspeaker for him to hear the loud, brash voice shouting at her. She barely winced at the damage it must be causing her eardrums.

After responding to the caller with friendly politeness, she said, 'You beat me to it. I was going to call you later…

Absolutely.' She clicked on her laptop's mousepad. 'Yes...
Of course... That isn't a problem at all... Can you send me
a link and I'll colour-match it...? I'll supervise the decorating personally.'

Giovanni continued to eavesdrop. He knew all about
difficult clients. Working in this hotel had taught him how
to deal with them, something he'd taken and enhanced
with his own business.

'Okay,' she said, 'but before you go the reason I was
going to call was to give you the good news that the fondue gondolas will be installed in time for the wedding...
I know how keen your daughter was for them so I pes-
tered the company until they gave in and moved us up
the diary...'

He heard a bellow of laughter ring out from the caller.

Leaning back in his chair, Giovanni folded his arms
around his chest, half listening, half thinking.

Her earlier retort and subsequent poise had made him
think Merry Ingles might—just might—have something
about her after all, but until she'd taken the brash client's
call he'd still been undecided whether to keep her or let
her go. She asked astute questions but seemed incapable
of maintaining eye contact. How could he take a proper
measure of someone who wouldn't look him in the eye?

Watching and listening to her now, he grudgingly accepted that she was a damn sight better at her job than he'd
assumed. To get such a brash, belligerent customer going
from shouting to laughing in mere minutes required skills
most people didn't possess.

'If your daughter wants to dip marshmallows in it then
marshmallows she shall have...' She laughed. 'Nothing's
too much trouble... It's her big day, and it's natural she
wants it to be special.'

Two minutes later, after warning the client that she'd
be unavailable for the next five days rather than the three

she'd originally told him about, and reminding him of the details of colleagues who could assist in an emergency, she was done.

'Sorry about that,' she said, her stare darting from her laptop to him and then back to the laptop. 'My client's daughter's getting married here next month.'

'No sorry needed. It seems your client is now a happy man.'

A faint smile played on her lips. 'Until the next crisis.'

Knowing exactly what she meant, he felt his lips curve into a faint smile in response.

Okay, she wasn't a complete liability. She could stay.

'What was that about fondue gondolas?' he asked curiously.

'They're refurbished gondolas we're having installed. We're positioning them to overlook the lake and the town. Guests can hire them to share fondue with complete privacy.'

'I remember fondue being a favourite of the guests when I worked here.'

'I think it's the evocation of skiing and Switzerland. Like going to France and having to try snails and frogs' legs.' She gave a sudden start and her gaze shot back to him. 'Did you say you used to work here?'

'*Si*. Twelve years ago. I started as a lowly porter.'

'Seriously?'

'You do not believe me?'

'I'm just surprised I've never heard about it before.'

'It was a long time ago. Not many staff are still here from my time.'

'You went from a porter to this...' she waved her hand around '...in twelve years?'

He inclined his head.

Her gaze stayed on him, frank admiration radiating off her. Giovanni was so used to admiration he rarely noticed it any more, often rolled his eyes at the way success made people react around him. People could be such butt-kissers. But there was something about Merry's expression that made his chest puff up.

Dimples suddenly appeared in her rounded cheeks. 'In that case,' she said, 'we should crack on with the business in hand before we run out of hours to discuss everything and your reputation goes down the pan and you're forced to eke out an existence as a lowly porter again.'

Giovanni had no idea where it came from, but a great roll of laughter burst out of his throat.

It was the first time he'd laughed out loud since he'd been informed of Gerhard's appendicitis.

Actually, now he thought about it, he couldn't remember the last time he'd laughed at all.

It was late afternoon when Merry left Giovanni's suite. She walked briskly to the elevator, punched the button, waited, stepped inside, punched the button for the ground floor, exited, and walked briskly to her office, calling cheerful greetings to the staff and guests she passed.

In her empty office, she closed the door firmly behind her and, finally alone, sat on her chair, slumped over her desk and buried her burning face in her arms.

That had been the most excruciating six hours of her life.

Once their lunch had been done with, Giovanni's attitude towards her had changed, a thawing that had become more evident as the meeting had gone on. And while she felt a great deal of relief at this, and relief that she could actually work with him and relief that he wasn't a pompous ass like so many rich men were, she couldn't help wishing he *was* a pompous ass so she could have a legitimate reason to dislike him.

She'd thought her day couldn't get any worse. Such naivety!

What could be worse than an overwhelming attraction to the man who was your temporary boss and the last person on earth you'd choose to fancy?

It was that short burst of laughter that had done it. The way his glacial features had melted. Oh, but he was *beautiful* when he laughed.

As hard as she'd tried down to clamp down on all the tempestuous internal reactions to him, they'd become more pronounced as the afternoon had gone on and it had taken more control than she'd believed she possessed to stop herself from continually staring at him.

It had been a long time since she'd felt even a flicker of attraction for a man. If there was one thing Merry had learned from her time at Hotel Haensli it was that rich men were to be avoided. She'd lost count of the times she'd been propositioned by rich guests, especially in her waitressing days. It came with the territory. Once alcohol had been imbibed, the beer goggles went on and even her unremarkable features blurred and she became ravishing to their eyes. She'd turned knocking them back without knocking their ego into an art form. It was safer that way. But whether they came from humble beginnings or from inherited wealth, their sense of entitlement was always the same.

She'd be more likely to find a unicorn than a faithful rich man, so why her stupid body had decided Cheekbones was a man to salivate over was beyond her. She hadn't needed Katja's warning about his reputation. You only had to look at him to know he was a player. It wasn't just his Greek god looks but the way he carried himself. And players like Giovanni didn't look twice at women like her. Not without their beer goggles on.

But this was all moot because she didn't *want* him to look twice at her.

All Merry wanted was to get through the next five days without screwing up and putting her job in jeopardy.

CHAPTER THREE

FAT SNOWFLAKES WERE falling in the dark sky when Merry wheeled her suitcase out of her chalet. It was so early the sun wasn't even hinting at making an appearance. Pulling her hat lower around her ears, she set off to the hotel, her way lit by pretty solar lights.

Other than the concierge working the nightshift, the hotel foyer was empty. Carefully draping the wrapped dress she'd borrowed from Katja over her suitcase, and sticking her hat on top of that, she helped herself to a hot chocolate from the machine and hugged it in her gloved hands close to the foyer's open fire. She'd had only a few hours' sleep but the blood in her veins buzzed.

Once she'd pulled herself together in the office, she'd notified all her clients to let them know she'd be away for five days, rather than her scheduled three, and called Santa with the bad news that she'd have to fly to Switzerland on her own and that she'd have Merry's cabin to herself for the first couple of days of her stay.

It had been late when she'd finally made it to her cabin and called her brother back. One screaming match later, in which Martin had called her every name under the sun, her brain had been frazzled.

How she wished Santa was here already. There was no one on this earth who provided a more sympathetic ear or more comforting shoulder to cry on. The two girls had grown up together, next-door neighbours in a tiny Oxfordshire village, which had automatically made them playmates despite Merry being two years older. The fact that they'd both lost their mothers in early childhood and turned to each other for support had forged a tight bond between them that neither time nor distance could break. Santa was the sister Merry had always longed for, the only person from England she'd missed in her time in Switzerland.

The comfort she would have taken from Santa was not something she could have asked from Katja when she turned up at the cabin holding her daughter's hand and a wrapped dress. She would need the dress, she'd told Merry, for the Meravaro Odyssey '1940s Hollywood Glamour' theme Christmas party.

Merry had accepted the dress without bothering to unwrap it and see it for herself. There was no point. Katja was the same size as her so it would fit. If it wasn't to Merry's taste then tough—she had nothing suitable in her own wardrobe to replace it, a fact the glamorous Katja knew perfectly well.

A rifle through her wardrobe told Merry she had nothing suitable to pack for the rest of the voyage either. It essentially consisted of jeans, tops and thick jumpers.

All the administrative staff at the hotel were provided with two standard black skirts or pairs of trousers, four smart black shirts with the hotel's logo embroidered on them, and two black blazers. Deciding she'd have to stick to her work skirts, she'd packed a few of her more sedate tops and jumpers, figured she'd probably be given a uniform to wear on board anyway, read through the files again for luck, then climbed, exhausted, into bed.

Her exhaustion hadn't counted for anything. She'd been too wired to fall straight to sleep. The day had been a rollercoaster with no time to properly think, and so all the thoughts had crammed in her head and fought for attention.

Giovanni. Her brother. Giovanni. Her father. Giovanni. Santa. Giovanni.

Giovanni had been the first thought in her head too when her alarm had woken her, and with it the immediate knowledge that she'd be spending the next five days working closely with him. Nerves and anticipation had duelled inside her ever since.

Movement at the far end of the foyer caught her attention.

Her heart began to thud. A spring released in her belly as the figure of Giovanni Cannavaro emerged, striding towards her.

Giovanni hated the month of December. If he could strike the entire month from the calendar, he would. He usually spent those long thirty-one days trying not to take the darkness of his mood out on everyone else. Gerhard's appendicitis had only added to his gloom and he'd flown to Switzerland with a foul taste in his mouth and an acrid churn in his guts. Realising the clumsy lady with the crazy hat had been tasked with saving his pet project from disaster had come close to pushing him over the edge.

He wasn't entirely convinced she was the saviour of the project Wolfgang and Katja had promised, but his confidence in her had grown as their meeting in his suite had gone on. His confidence that they could work well together had grown too—anyone who could make him laugh under such tense circumstances must have something about them, and Merry had a definite spark about her. By the time their meeting had ended, the foul taste on his tongue had disappeared and he'd been glad he hadn't dismissed her.

Now, seeing her at the other end of the foyer waiting for him, he was surprised to find his mood lift a little.

'*Ciao*, lady,' he said.

A straight row of pretty white teeth flashed at him. 'Good morning.'

For a moment he found himself struck by the heightened colour of her rounded cheeks and the way her plump lips pulled together. Her lips were a beautiful colour, he noted, like ripe raspberries…

Blinking the strange thought away, he noticed the woolly hat resting on her suitcase. 'You are not planning to wear that stupid hat?'

Her mouth dropped open. For a long moment she did nothing but stare at him.

Giovanni experienced a sliver of anticipation. Would she do what he imagined most employees would do in response to such a comment and quickly throw the offending hat on the log fire and promise to never wear such a garment again?

He'd never commented on any member of staff's personal attire before, wasn't quite sure where the comment had come from, knew only that his curiosity was roused as to how she would respond.

And then her dimples popped. 'My hat's not stupid.'

If he'd had dimples of his own, he thought they might just have popped too. 'It is.'

'Isn't.'

'I am the boss. If I say it is stupid, it is stupid.'

'If you think it's stupid, you should see my matching gloves.'

He looked at her hands. They were enveloped in black leather gloves.

Amusement danced behind the large frames. 'You're safe,' she said. 'I lost one of the Rudolph ones so now I have to wear these boring things.'

'With luck you lose crazy hat too,' he said, then shook his head as he noticed the skirt she was wearing. 'Why are you wearing hotel uniform?'

'It's just the skirt.' She unzipped her huge, puffed winter coat to reveal a plain black top beneath it.

He pulled a face. 'I hope you packed better clothes than that.'

'Katja said I had to look smart. I've packed the smartest clothes I own.'

'Smart, not boring.' All their discussion the previous day had been about the train itself and the passengers who would be travelling with them. He'd left the personal stuff for Katja to deal with. 'You will be the face of Odyssey. Our guests do not want to see you dressed like a waitress.'

Her shoulders rose in an apologetic shrug. 'Everything else I have is too casual. Anyway, won't I have to wear one of the train's uniforms?'

'Not for your role—your job is to make sure guests have a great time. They react better if you are dressed well. But it is not a problem. You can buy new clothes in Paris, *si*?'

Great, Merry thought. Not only had she ruined her family's plans, lost precious days with Santa and was suffering from the most improbable attraction for a man who was literally the worst person in the world for her to fancy, but now she needed to splurge hard-earned cash on clothes she would only wear once.

With any luck, she'd be able to recoup the cost on expenses.

Nonetheless, she smiled and said, 'Yes, Boss.'

A black eyebrow rose. The glimmer of a smile played on his lips. '*Eccellente*. You know the order of things.'

'You boss, me underling?' she queried drily.

Now the smile broke out completely, and the triple flip in Merry's belly came within a whisker of turning her back into the gibbering wreck she'd been in his suite.

'You have everything?' he asked.

'Yes.'

'Then it is time we go, lady. Our car is waiting for us.'

* * *

The thickening snow meant the drive to the airport took almost an hour. There was never any doubt they would arrive safely—all the hotel's luxury chauffeur-driven cars were built or modified to withstand Swiss weather and the luxurious vehicle transporting them was no exception.

It would have been a dream drive if she'd shared it with anyone but Giovanni. Being in an enclosed space with him and spending an hour inhaling his freshly showered scent and freshly applied cologne had been a minor form of torture. She hadn't really noticed it before they'd got in the car, but once she did notice it the scent consumed her attention. It engulfed her.

The only way to handle it had been to open her laptop and pretend to engage in work. Thankfully, Giovani was engaged with his own laptop, but that hour crawled at the speed of a sleepy tortoise.

At the airport though, things moved swiftly. In no time at all Merry was following Giovanni up the metal steps and into the sumptuous interior of his private plane.

'Very nice,' she said admiringly as she fastened the seatbelt on a cream leather seat that had the comfort of an armchair. This certainly beat flying cattle class.

Giovanni, who'd taken the seat opposite her, gave a half-smile. 'Not bad for a lowly porter, eh?'

'Gives one hope,' she answered lightly. She was determined to keep things light. She would not allow her internal turbulence to affect her outwardly again. She'd keep a handle on herself if it killed her.

Once they'd taken off, an array of breakfast foods were served. Merry, her stomach hurting with hunger from her half-eaten lunch and skipped evening meal, joined him at the highly polished dining table.

Thankfully, she was able to manage eating around him this time, and after happily demolishing a tongue-meltingly delicious *pain au chocolat* decided to bite the bullet and ask one of the many questions about him that had been playing on her mind.

'How long did you work as a porter at the hotel for?'

He didn't look in the least surprised that she'd asked. 'Two months. I helped clean up after staff meeting. Wolfgang came in to talk to me and ask questions about me. Then he offered me a job as his assistant.'

As Merry's experience of Wolfgang was of a man who rarely bothered with his underlings, preferring to send his edicts down through the hotel's chain of command, this astounded her. 'Wow. I wonder what it was about you that caught his interest enough to talk to you.'

'He read my résumé and was curious about me.'

'He read your résumé?'

He gave a pointed look. 'Wolfgang reads *all* staff résumés.'

This unexpected piece of information almost found her lost for words. The hotel employed hundreds of staff. 'I didn't know that.'

His eyes glimmered with the amusement she kept catching. 'Now you do.'

'What was it about your résumé that caught his attention? Did he say?'

'He wanted to know why I quit my economics degree in the final year.'

'You were doing an economics degree?' she clarified.

He inclined his head.

While there was no disputing that Giovanni was wildly successful, their short time together had formed the impression of someone who'd become successful on instinct, someone with a natural flair for business. All the economists Merry had met had as much flair as a cabbage. And as much personality.

At the start of each year, the world's leading economists

flocked to Hotel Haensli and the town's other opulent hotels with world leaders and the richest of businessmen for a four-day forum to 'meld minds over the world's economic and business challenges.' Or, as Merry privately liked to think, they came to network. While many of the hotel's staff got a buzz out of the event, Merry found the self-importance of it too tedious to be enjoyable. It was like having a bunch of silverbacks descending on the town with their egos puffed up to ten on the Richter scale. You could practically taste the pomposity in the air. Her brain just could not square Giovanni as having once taken a path that would make him one of those people.

Not wanting to insult him by saying that, she opted for asking, 'Why *did* you quit?'

'Personal reasons,' he replied, with a finality that made it clear she was not to ask anything more about it.

Despite her curiosity being piqued, Merry knew a warning when she heard one and stifled her tongue.

'How long have you worked at the hotel?' he asked, turning the tables on her.

'Three years. I started as a waitress. Katja headhunted me to work for her a year ago.'

'I did not know that.'

'Now you do.'

Giovanni couldn't help the smile that formed at her impudence. 'How old were you when you came to Switzerland?'

'Nineteen.'

Interesting, he thought. He'd been trying to work out how old she was. Her fresh-faced looks suggested someone in her late teens, but her position at the hotel suggested someone older.

Twenty-two. Eleven years younger than him. Too young?

He gave himself a mental slap at the inappropriate and highly unexpected thought.

It was the after-effects from the drive to the airport, he concluded. Being in a confined space with Merry had done the strangest things to his concentration. Her legs were so short that she'd been able to comfortably stretch them out and he'd found his eyes constantly drawn to them, which was a joke as they were clad in thick black tights—and he would bet his Lamborghini they were tights and not stockings—and on her feet were perhaps the most unsexy flat black ankle boots in God's creation.

Ugly tights and boots or not, he'd kept finding his gaze on them and then had to keep reminding himself to keep his eyes to himself. Merry was an employee. Okay, a borrowed employee.

Proper employee or borrowed employee made no difference. Merry was not his type. He supposed she was pretty in her own plain way. Other than her voice being musically soothing and her laugh being surprisingly sexy, she was too clean cut for him. Too pure.

He looked at her now, took in the plain rounded face all scrubbed clean, not a scrap of make-up on it, and the blonde hair neatly scraped back into a bun. She even wore her work skirt at the knee-length it was designed to be worn, when half the female administrative staff rolled theirs up.

He'd bet his Ferrari that she'd had had fewer lovers than he had thumbs. When it came to women, he'd become an expert at reading them, and women like Merry always looked for long-term. Nothing wrong with that, but Giovanni didn't do relationships.

Why was he even thinking of Merry as potential lover material? he wondered, shocked at his own thoughts.

Had he turned into one of those men who couldn't look at a woman without imagining her in his bed? No, he defended himself. A high percentage of the employees he worked most closely with within his business were female and he'd never allowed his mind to cross that line with any of them.

Besides, even if he did allow his mind to cross that line, Merry already had a lover. A jealous, possessive lover judging from the number of times he'd seen the name 'Martin' flash on the screen of her phone during their meeting in his suite. She'd ignored every one of his calls. The only calls she'd answered had been work-related.

'What made you choose Switzerland?' he asked, keen to keep the conversation going and stop his mind meandering.

'The snow.'

He pulled a disbelieving face.

She laughed. 'It's true! I went to university to study German but, like you, I quit. Unlike you, I didn't even last a term. I hated it. I only went to university to get away from my family—nothing traumatic, just disparate characters who can't live together—so once I decided to quit I figured I would go somewhere with lots of snow, and here I am.'

The coincidence pierced him. Both had quit university, although for very different reasons, and both had found themselves in Switzerland working in relatively lowly roles in the same hotel over a decade apart. Both had something in them recognised by those with influence and been head-hunted to better things.

'Why did you choose Switzerland?' she asked.

'Fate chose it.'

'Eh?'

'When I left Italy, I let fate choose for me. I bought a ticket for the first international coach out of Rome. It took me to a town close to Klosters. I asked at all hotels for a job. Hotel Haensli give me one.'

The pain-filled months leading up to that coach trip were days Giovanni never allowed himself to think of.

He'd sat on that coach watching Rome and then Italy itself disappear behind him, wondering what the point of anything was. What was the point in following the path he'd set on if Monica wasn't there to walk it with him?

When he'd first arrived at the Hotel Haensli, the only thing that had burned in him had been the need to escape and forget. Wolfgang's tutorage had ignited the burn of his ambition. It was a fuel that had driven him ever since.

The Meravaro Odyssey sat proudly on the track at the Paris train station. A black-and-gold engine with the train's name beautifully embossed on it pulled twenty individually named deep red carriages. To Merry's eyes it was stunning, like something from a bygone age.

The doors slid open and, with a fluttering heart, she followed Giovanni on board.

All her reservations about taking this last-minute secondment had been dispelled on the journey to Paris. This was the opportunity of a lifetime, something to tell her grandchildren about…that's if she ever had children, of course. Having children required finding a partner, and as she thought this she found her gaze sweeping over Giovanni's handsome face.

He was a man who'd make gorgeous babies, she thought with an internal sigh, before reminding herself that he was also a billionaire who walked with a wreckage of broken hearts in his trail.

How could any woman find emotional security and safety in the arms of a man like him? And that, more than anything, was what she craved, the thing she'd lost when her mother died. Emotional security.

They stepped into the first of what the train's blueprints had told her were three lounges.

'You have a notepad?' he asked.

She patted her oversized bag, in which she'd placed her laptop and notebook. Her suitcase had been taken to the hotel they'd be staying in for the next two nights. Their task for today was to inspect every inch of the train, another last-minute task she'd been seconded to as Giovanni's PA's flight from Rome had been delayed by heavy snow.

Giovanni walked the length of his latest acquisition casting a critical eye over every aspect. Everything from the dining tables to the mahogany panelling to the glass cabinets in the bars was hand-crafted. It had all been signed off by Quality Control but, perfectionist that he was, he needed to satisfy himself that nothing had been missed. Upholsterers, carpenters and other craftspeople were already in Paris, ready to touch up any defects he spotted.

In the second bar, which doubled as a casino, he carefully rotated the table-top to reveal the roulette wheel on the other side. Perfect. Turning it back to its original position, he used a handkerchief to remove his finger-marks from the gleaming wood and moved to the next table. This one transformed into a blackjack table.

He was inspecting the first of the dining carriages when Merry, who'd followed silently in his wake with her notepad in hand, spoke for the first time since they'd set off on the inspection.

'The screws on this panel aren't aligned.'

He looked at her sharply, then back-stepped to the panel in question, which he'd already inspected. She was right. It was only a slight misalignment, but Giovanni sold perfection to his clients and that meant *everything* had to be perfect, right down to the smallest detail.

Impressed, he raised his stare from the panel and nodded his approval. 'Make a note of it.'

She scribbled on the notepad.

They didn't speak again until they were in the third bar. He liked that she didn't feel the need to fill the silence, that she understood his inspection required concentration without him having to tell her so. She stood in front of the Christmas tree, and something in the way her nose wrinkled caught his attention.

'What is wrong?' he asked, standing beside her.

His question made her cheeks redden. 'Nothing.'

'If something is wrong, I need to know,' he told her. 'Tell me and I fix it.'

'There's nothing to fix. It's elegant and sophisticated.'

'Then why do you look at it like it offends you?'

Her still-flaming face scrunched as she clearly sought a diplomatic explanation. 'I just find it…boring.'

If there was one thing Giovanni hated, it was 'boring'. To be boring was to be bland and uninspiring. His life had been bland and uninspiring once. Safe and cosy. Boring. His sister and his parents were happy to live their lives in banality, but not him. All 'boring' gave you was a false sense of security that could be ripped from you without notice, opening a man to a pain that tore the soul in two. Better to take risks and live life to its fullest.

'A professional decorated it!'

'And they did an excellent job,' she said with a shrug. 'I happen to prefer a splash of colour, but I'm not your audience—your guests are.'

He looked more closely at it. The tree was decorated with pale blue and silver tinsel and crystal baubles shaped like stars, snowflakes and bells. It was extremely tasteful, if you liked that kind of thing. Which he didn't. He didn't like anything to do with Christmas. If the festive season wasn't such a lucrative time of year for his business he would hibernate in one of his wine cellars for the period.

The scent of tinsel mingled with fragrant pine breezed into his airwaves and he automatically recoiled.

'Did you decorate the trees at the hotel?' he asked, blocking the scent of the tree from his senses with much-practised precision. He'd heard a few comments from guests there about how beautiful the Christmas trees were.

'It was a collaboration, but I oversaw it.'

'You were in charge?'

'Yes.'

He thought hard, wondering if the risk he was tempted to make would be the first mistake of his career. But then, his entire career was built on taking risks. Look at this train. When word had first got out about Giovanni and Wolfgang's collaboration on a new breed of luxury train travel, the general consensus of opinion had been that they were throwing their money away. He'd been undeterred, convinced that what they were doing would prove a success. And look at them now, two days from the maiden voyage for which the exorbitantly priced tickets had sold out in under an hour. Speculation in the media had risen to fever-pitch. All the speculation was of the excited and positive variety.

'Okay, lady,' he said decisively. 'Call the people in Paris and tell them what decorations you want. They will deliver them in the morning for you.'

She looked stunned. 'I can redecorate it?'

Giovanni was as astounded at this turn of events as she was. In twenty-four hours he'd gone from thinking her useless to putting her in charge of redecorating the main festive feature of the voyage. Justifying it to himself, he reasoned that Merry might have terrible taste in clothes but she was proving to have an eye for detail.

'No one likes "boring",' he answered.

Her face lit up. 'Is there a theme or anything you'd like me to…?'

'Do what you like to it,' he cut in.

She tilted her head. 'Don't you like Christmas?'

Surprised at her astuteness—he'd perfected the mask he needed to get through the period as openly loathing Christmas was not a good look for someone who earned a fortune off the back of selling 'that Christmas feeling'—he answered shortly, 'No. It is only good for making money.'

To show the topic was not up for discussion, and wanting to be away from the tree, he turned his back on it and stepped over to examine the upholstery of the lounge sofas. At the fourth one, he spotted a tiny piece of thread poking out along the seam and called Merry over.

Her head bowed as she made careful note of it.

The late-afternoon sun streamed through the window and danced on her golden hair. Idly, he wondered if the colour was natural. She raised her head and, with the sun still shining its spotlight on her, he saw through the thick lenses of her glasses to the soft baby blue colour of her big eyes.

A weird, fluttery sensation was set off in his stomach. Lower down, a tightness tingled and sharpened until he dragged his stare from her.

Shaking the sensation off and putting it down to his stomach needing food—it had been at least four hours since he'd eaten—he continued with the inspection.

CHAPTER FOUR

AFTER ANOTHER FOUR hours of close inspection, broken only for a brief lunch, only fourteen further defects were spotted. To Merry's great relief, the inspection was over, and she followed Giovanni into the chauffeured car that would drive them to the hotel they'd be staying at for the next two nights.

It wasn't the inspection job itself she was relieved to be done with, but having to work at such close quarters with Giovanni. It would be much easier to work with him if he'd put a bag over his head. And maybe if he stopped showering.

Now all she had to do was get through the drive to the hotel and she'd be able to escape him for a while.

The deeper the inspection had gone, the more she'd come to appreciate just how magnificent the Meravaro Odyssey actually was. Every aspect, every detail, had been thought out carefully, every inch of space maximised to its fullest potential. The super-deluxe suites, with their king-size beds and separate living areas, were frankly spectacular. She'd managed to refrain from squealing when Giovanni had nonchalantly told her that as a perk of her job she'd been appointed her own junior suite.

All the craftsmen and tradespeople who'd fix the defects were in Paris, waiting for notification of what needed to be done. When the car was set in motion, she said to Giovanni, 'Do you want me to make the calls?'

'Veronica can do that. She is at the hotel, waiting for us.'

Veronica was Giovanni's PA, she of the delayed flight.

'I don't mind,' Merry said. 'I'm sure you two have other work you need to be getting on with.'

He gave her a curious look. 'You have the numbers?'

'They're on the files. I'll call them as soon as we get to the hotel.' Her phone buzzed. She pulled it out of her bag. Martin. Swiping to send it to voicemail, she dropped it back.

'You not going to answer that?'

'It's personal. I'll call him back later in my own time.' No doubt Martin was gearing up for round two of the sport known as Shouting at Merry.

'We are not working. You can call back now if you want.'

'He knows better than to call me in work time.'

'If he is being the pain in the butt, tell him to get lost.'

His comment was so unexpected she gave a bark of laughter.

She would gladly tell her brother to get lost if it would make an ounce of difference. She'd lost count of the number of times she'd told Martin to stay out of her life, to stop interfering, to stop putting everything wrong with their family on her shoulders. Everything that was wrong with their family went back fourteen years, to when their mother had died. Death pulled many families together. It had ripped hers apart. If she hadn't had Santa to hold on to...

Sugar! She'd forgotten to leave the cabin key for her.

'Do you mind if I call Katja? There's something I forgot to do.'

'What did I just say?' he chided.

She met his stare with a wry grin and felt her belly

loosen. It was something that happened every time she caught his gaze and the sensation was getting worse.

Twisting her body away from him, she made the call.

'Can you do me a favour?' she asked Katja after they'd greeted each other. 'I forgot to leave my key for the cabin with Reception. Can you ask them to put the spare one aside for Santa, please?'

Giovanni's ears pricked up. Merry was due a visitor? Was that what her leave had been for? Not a romantic rendezvous with the pathetically persistent Martin but with a man named Santos?

How many lovers did this seemingly pure woman have?

'In two days, yes,' she said into the phone. 'You're a lifesaver. Thank you!'

Blowing out a puff of air, she dropped her phone back into her bag and rested her head back.

'Personal problem?' he asked.

'Nothing I can't handle,' she muttered.

A sudden vision of her handling *him* floated in Giovanni's mind. A frisson raced through him at the thought, its strength enough to make him blink with shock.

He looked at her. Took in the thick glasses. The clear complexion. The prim hairstyle. The trim but ordinary figure. The plump lips that suggested sensuality.

Was he attracted to her? Or was it the notion that she had a secret exotic sex life piquing his interest?

As if sensing his scrutiny, she turned her face to him. The blue eyes behind the thick lenses locked on his and, for the first time since early on in their meeting in his suite, held them instead of immediately darting away. Her throat moved. Colour spread over her cheeks...

That disturbing fluttery sensation in his stomach set off again, and with it a tightening in his loins.

Rarely did Giovanni find himself lost for words, but in that moment, and in that locking of eyes, the words needed to defuse the strange tension building between them refused to form.

It was with much relief that he felt the car come to a stop.

They'd arrived at the hotel.

Merry scrambled out of the car, certain her insides had just spontaneously combusted. She barely registered the chill in the air. Her senses seemed to have heightened too, to such an extent that it was as if she could *feel* Giovanni's movements as he followed her out, her ears alert to the crunch of his foot as he stepped on the pavement, her skin vibrating at his nearness.

From the corner of her eye she watched him adjust the sleeves of his shirt beneath his suit jacket, straighten his shoulders and then turn to her. 'We are here, lady,' he said, before his long legs propelled him inside.

The swoop of her belly as she took in the hard leanness of the body beneath the immaculate tailored suit rooted her to the ground.

The concierge discreetly coughed for her attention.

Blinking, she quickly gathered her wits and hurried inside.

The hotel that was to be their base for the next two nights had a gorgeous, romantic bohemian flair to it that evoked thoughts of the Moulin Rouge, and made Merry feel she was walking through a Toulouse-Lautrec painting.

A severe-looking and impeccably presented woman of around seventy mercifully joined them the moment Merry reached Giovanni in the foyer. It was Giovanni's PA, Veronica.

'Your room is ready for you,' Veronica said briskly after they'd been introduced. She held a key card out to her. 'I've arranged a breakfast meeting in Signor Cannavaro's suite for eight tomorrow morning. Food will be served. Let me know immediately if you have any dietary requirements. Dinner's served in the restaurant from seven, your bill will be added to Cannavaro Travel's tab.' Then she held another card out for her and without pausing for breath, added, 'My number. Call me immediately if you have any problems.'

'I will, thank you,' Merry murmured, taken aback by her brusqueness.

She almost stumbled in shock at the conspiratorial wink Giovanni gave her.

Praying the heat rising in her stomach didn't show on her face, she excused herself, saying, 'I'll get those calls made.'

She was so busy concentrating on not giving in to the temptation to turn her head for one more glance at Giovanni's gorgeous face that when her phone rang she made the fatal mistake of answering it without looking at the name flashing on the screen.

Hiding behind a pillar across from the elevators, she leaned against it and closed her eyes as Martin laid into her for being unable to tell him when she would next come home.

'You are unbelievable,' he ranted. 'It's all me, me, me.'

'That's not fair,' she finally snapped back. 'I told you I'd confirm the date when I get back to Switzerland. You having a go at me isn't going to make that happen any quicker. Now, excuse me, but I've got work to do.'

'Oh, that's right, use your work as an excuse like you always—'

She disconnected the call and threw her phone in the bag she'd laid at her feet.

'More personal problems?' a deeply accented voice said from the other side of the pillar, making her jump.

A moment later Giovanni's face appeared, followed by his long, lean body.

'Were you eavesdropping on me?' she accused, too cross and shaken to moderate her tone.

'I was going to the elevator and heard shouting. Everything okay?'

'Everything's fine,' she muttered.

He raised an eyebrow at her obvious lie. 'Anything I can help with?'

Touched at his offer and surprised at the gentleness in his tone, she leaned her head back against the pillar. 'Thank you but it's family stuff. My brother.'

'Your brother was shouting at you?'

She nodded morosely. 'Martin's an expert at shouting at me.'

It had never crossed Giovanni's mind that the persistent Martin could be a family member, and relief washed through him.

He was Italian. Shouting was the preferred means of communication in his family but it was good-natured. The tone of shouting he'd heard directed at Merry, assuming it came from a lover, had raised his hackles.

'He is the one who keeps bothering you?'

She nodded.

'Why?'

'He's peed off with me because I didn't go home.'

There was a sinking feeling in his stomach. 'That is what your leave was for?'

She closed her eyes and sighed again. 'Yes.'

'Working for me has got you in trouble with your family?' She'd already mentioned that she'd escaped to Switzerland to get away from her family, but a pang still thumped in his chest.

Giovanni's business kept him too busy to see much of his family, but they made up for it with plenty of video calls. The time they did spend together was always quality time. Old bonds ran deep.

'I'm *always* in trouble with them… Well, with Martin.' Her eyes opened and locked onto his. 'We've never got on.'

Disconcerted again at the fresh fluttery sensations being trapped in her gaze caused, he dropped his stare at the same moment she took a deep breath and her chest rose. For that brief moment her breasts lifted and pushed out against her plain top.

His blood heated. Thickened. Pulsed heavily through his arteries and veins and through to the skin he suddenly felt the weight of over his bones. When he lifted his gaze back to her face he was taken with the wild urge to discover if those raspberry-coloured plump lips tasted as good as they looked...

Their eyes locked again. Colour slowly crawled over her cheeks.

Just as a warning voice was making itself heard in Giovanni's head, telling him to move back, Merry pushed herself off the pillar and side-stepped him to pick her coat and bag up off the floor.

When she next looked at him, a wide smile was fixed to her face. 'That's enough talk about my brother. Any more and I'll get all angry, and probably cry, and flood the foyer with my tears, so I'd best get to my room and get those calls made.'

Only the unsteadiness of her short walk to the elevator proved the brightness of her swiftly delivered speech to be a mask.

And only once the elevator doors had closed on her did Giovanni manage to expel the breath he'd been holding.

Only by gritting his teeth and with the utmost concentration did he keep his own steps to the elevator steady.

Too relieved at the respite from being in Giovanni's orbit and having to deal with her body still running riot from that brief moment locked in his gaze to pay much attention to her hotel room, Merry went straight to her desk and turned her laptop on. Locating the file with all the tradesmen and craftspeople who, together, had built and fitted and decorated the Meravaro Odyssey, she got to work.

Making the calls was the perfect distraction from all the funny feelings rampaging through her, and from the strange ache in her heart at Giovanni's unexpected concern.

She'd studied German at school, so had had a good grasp of the language when she'd started at Hotel Haensli. Her three years there had seen that grasp become fluency, and the international flavour of their guests had found her gaining proficiency in French and Italian too. The craftspeople, all on standby, ready for immediate deployment to the train station, were mostly French and, though she was confident she'd relayed her instructions well enough to be understood, she followed all the calls with an email to confirm.

She was in the middle of writing the last email when her room phone rang.

Her heart was thumping before she lifted the receiver. 'Hello?'

'Hey, lady,' said the deep voice her sixth sense had told her would be on the end of the receiver. 'How is your room?'

Dear God, his voice was even sexier down a phone than in person, and she pressed the tops of her thighs together and concentrated on not thinking about how it had felt when their eyes had locked together, and on making her voice sound normal and not all breathless.

'Very nice, thank you.' Now she looked properly at it, it was more than very nice. Like the rest of this old but expensive Parisian hotel, her room had a bohemian romantic feel. 'How's yours?'

'Not as good as the Haensli Suite, but is okay. How are you feeling now?'

Touched at the question, she paused before answering. 'Fine.'

'You sure?'

'Honestly, I'm fine. Dramas are par for the course in my family, but thank you for asking.'

'No worry. You finished?'

'Nearly.'

'Any problems?'

'No.'

'How long will you be?'

'Ten, twenty minutes… Why?' she added cautiously.

'There is a boutique here you can get clothes in. Meet me in Reception when you finish.'

The clunk of the receiver being hung up resounded in her ear.

Merry sighed and rubbed her forehead. She'd really hoped to avoid Giovanni for the rest of the day. She was coming to like his company a little more than was healthy. The imperious man she'd met barely thirty-six hours ago was rapidly disappearing, emerging in his place was a more relaxed, easy-going man. A man with unexpected empathy. A man with a sense of humour that, when it poked out, tickled her funny bone.

Bad enough that she fancied him. She didn't want to actually *like* him too. That really would be dangerous.

And now there was this new issue of the boutique he wanted her to shop in. A boutique in one of Paris's most expensive hotels. She fervently hoped she could find something cheap enough that her credit card didn't laugh at her for trying to use it.

Last email sent, and feeling grubby and out of sorts, she had a shower, then pulled on a pair of jeans and, after only a moment of hesitation, a soft red jumper with a smiling snowman knitted on it. Then she quickly redid her bun, slung her handbag over her shoulder and went off to meet Giovanni.

Her heart was already thudding weightily before she

found him, seated on a deep burgundy armchair, his ankle hooked on a thigh, scrolling through his phone. Like her, he'd changed, now wearing black jeans, a black T-shirt and a snazzy charcoal blazer.

He stood as soon as he spotted her and looked her up and down. He rolled his eyes and shook his head. 'Crazy jumper, lady.'

She decided to take this as the compliment she knew perfectly well it hadn't been. 'Thank you.'

'You should wear a coat.'

'We're going out? I thought the boutique was in the hotel?'

Not a muscle moved on his deadpan face. 'No, you should wear a coat to cover that thing. I not want people to see me with you wearing it.'

Her funny bone tickled, Merry kept her own face straight. 'That would be awful. They might think I work for you or something.'

His lips twitched. 'Big disaster.'

Biting her cheeks to stop the laughter escaping, she said, 'Rather than go back to my room for my coat, why don't I walk three paces behind you to the boutique like a good underling?'

He pulled a musing face. 'That could work.'

'Better still, why don't I go on my own?'

'No way, lady. I have seen the crazy things you wear. I need to supervise.' Giovanni clicked his fingers. 'Come, Underling.'

She saluted. 'Yes, Boss.'

His grin made her already squidgy belly flip.

Blanking out the huge, extravagantly decorated Christmas tree they passed and the lobby pianist tinkling out Christmas carols, Giovanni led the way to the boutique. It astounded him how amusing he found Merry's crazy jumper. How amusing he was coming to find her.

And how sexy…

No sexy thoughts, Cannavaro, he told himself sternly.

It was something he'd told himself numerous times in his suite.

This trip to the boutique was for professional purposes only. He didn't trust Merry's definition of smart clothes and needed to ensure she looked the part for the role she was taking. It was also a way to say thank-you. Merry was giving up family time to save his and Wolfgang's butts and reputations, and making herself a target for her brother's wrath. Giovanni didn't understand why this bothered him so much, but he preferred to think about that than allow his mind go back over that moment when he'd felt the compulsion to kiss her. That had been as crazy as her jumper!

The craziest thing, though, had been while he was going through work emails in his suite, when he'd found himself idly speculating about poaching her from Wolfgang permanently. Like Veronica, his ultra-efficient PA, Merry had an eye for detail. Unlike Veronica, she was personable too.

It was a turnaround of opinion that could give a man whiplash. For sure, his admiration for her had grown during the train inspection—she'd spotted a further five defects that he'd missed—and his confidence she would do the job well had grown too. His worries about her capabilities had been eradicated. Eradicated enough that his mood was lighter than he'd ever known it to be during this dark month in twelve years.

But to go from thinking Merry a probable liability to potential permanent employee in the space of a day? *Molto pazza!*

The manager of the boutique approached them as they entered.

Giovanni quickly explained what they were in need of. 'She needs to look professional, but not boardroom. *Si?*'

The manager nodded, knowing exactly what he meant, and, after instructing one of her assistants to make him a drink, she whisked Merry off.

The clothes in this specialist designer boutique were so beautiful that Merry feared her eyes might pop out. When she caught sight of the price tags, she feared her brain might pop out too. These prices were on a par with the designer boutiques that filled Hotel Haensli's local town. She'd long stopped browsing in them. The temptation to load her credit card had often been overwhelming.

'Here,' said the manager, plucking another pair of slim trousers off the rack and handing them to the assistant she'd ordered to accompany them, and whose arms were now laden with clothes. 'Now shoes.'

'I don't need shoes,' Merry insisted. She had a pair of simple black heels that went with any outfit, the black ankle boots she was currently wearing, and her snow boots, which she'd packed just in case.

Her protest was ignored, and as she was led to the shoe section at other end of the boutique she passed Giovanni, seated on a red velvet armchair, drinking what looked like Scotch. Their eyes met briefly. Her belly made its familiar flip and she hurriedly focused on the array of beautiful shoes lined up before her, all of which seemed to be squealing, *Buy me!*

But not even the gorgeous footwear could hold her attention. Not when a turn of her head would put Giovanni back in her eyeline. She sensed him watching her. It was the strangest of sensations, unnerving and thrilling all at the same time.

'What about these?' the manager asked, holding up a pair of black heels that were similar to her own heels and yet a thousand miles apart in the quality and beauty stakes.

Merry darted a quick glance at Giovanni. She was right. He *was* watching her.

'Yes, fine,' she said quickly, suddenly desperate to escape the heat he was evoking in her with his stare. 'I'd like to try these on now.'

In the privacy of the changing room, Merry pressed her forehead to the mirror in a futile attempt to cool her flushed skin.

It was getting worse. Her crush. There was not a cell in her body that didn't react to him and she needed to find a way to stop it in its tracks, and fast.

This felt so different from her schoolgirl crush. Michael had been the object of obsessive daydreaming and future happy family fantasies. This was chemical. Physical. A burning attraction she had no control over.

But she had control over her actions, just as she'd had with Michael. Shyness and a fear of rejection had stopped her declaring her feelings to him. Looking back, she thought she must have had a sixth sense that her feelings for him couldn't be reciprocated, because when they were seventeen he'd come out as gay. Just as well, really, as her brother would have made his life a misery if her feelings had been reciprocated.

Something about the way Giovanni kept looking at her told her she didn't have to fear rejection from him. And that scared her almost as much as her desire for him.

CHAPTER FIVE

MERRY TUGGED THE black cigarette trousers up her thighs and looked directly at her reflection.

This had to stop.

Why couldn't she just enjoy the experience of working on what was possibly the world's most luxurious train with the additional perk of Giovanni's handsome face to privately sigh over? If he was attracted to her, it was only because of their close proximity. Merry was not a woman who inspired passion in men unless they'd been drinking.

Selecting which items to buy caused its own headache. Everything fitted. Not just fit but enhanced. Foolishly, she'd tried the shoes on too. Her feet had never been in anything so fabulous. But her credit card had a maximum limit and she needed to choose carefully. Imagine it being rejected! The humiliation!

Wishing she could buy the lot, she chose two outfits and crossed her fingers that they'd pass the credit card test.

Giovanni's heart thumped against his ribs when Merry emerged from the changing room.

He'd spent the time she'd been in there doing his utmost not to think of her stripping to her underwear. It had been a nightmare ask, just as it had been when she'd stood in front of the rows of shoes and his mind had mischievously imagined her wearing a pair of blood-red stilettos and nothing else, before he'd reminded himself of his vow of no sexy thoughts.

'That is all you get?' he asked, joining her, determined not to allow his imagination to get the better of him. The huge pile of clothing she'd taken in had reduced considerably, and the assistant carrying them to the counter was not struggling in the slightest.

Her smile was faint, and in an embarrassed undertone she quietly said, 'That's all I can afford.'

He stared at her blushing face with disbelief. 'You are not paying, lady. *I* am paying.'

'Don't be silly,' she protested.

'Who is the boss?'

'You.'

'And who is the underling?' An excellent word. He'd never heard it before Merry had said it, but it was one he fully intended to use in future to employees who kissed his butt a little too hard.

'Me. But—'

'You need clothes to do the job for me, so it is right I pay.' Stepping away from her, he strode to the assistant and told her to pack all the rejected items.

He felt a tug on his jacket. Turning, he almost bumped into Merry.

She took a hasty step back, eyed the assistant hurrying to the counter with the rejected clothes, and hissed, 'It's too much. We're only on the train for two days, so I only need two outfits.'

He closed the gap. 'Four outfits. The voyage is for two days and two nights, remember? And you work for me tomorrow too. An outfit for each day.'

'That's more than four outfits—'

Impulse made him place a finger to her lips. 'No arguing with me, Underling.'

The plump lips immediately stilled.

Dio, they were softer than he'd imagined. Like pressing into velvet. Did her clear skin have the same velvety texture…?

Her wide eyes locked onto his. Was he imagining the hitch of her breath?

He leaned in a little closer and caught her clean fruity scent. No trace of perfume. Moisture filled his mouth. No perfume needed. She was intoxicating enough without it.

This woman, this plain, almost mousy woman, was intoxicating *him*. How else to explain how he, a man who chose his lovers with the utmost care, was standing in a hotel boutique with his finger on an employee's lips, his own lips itching to replace the finger, close enough to feel the heat of her body and with a stirring in his loins that would have him arrested if he didn't get it under control.

The same employee he'd spent a couple of hours earlier debating in his head about poaching and making a permanent employee in his own workforce.

The same employee he was finding it increasingly hard to stop his imagination running riot over.

Dio, she did something to him.

And he did something to her. He could see it in her face and feel it in the excitement vibrating through her heated skin.

One small step closer and their bodies would be flush together…

Move back now.

Allowing this attraction to develop was a recipe for disaster.

Breathing deeply, Giovanni dropped his finger from her velvet-soft lips and stepped back.

Other than the widening of her eyes, Merry hadn't moved a muscle. But her cheeks were saturated with colour. He wondered if it was the colour they went when she climaxed…

Enough! Mind over matter, Cannavaro.

Mind over matter was one of his many strengths. It had never failed him.

Folding his arms tightly around his chest, he fixed her with a stern stare and spoke in his sternest voice. 'You will take the clothes. Think them a thank-you for giving up your leave for me.'

She blinked, and blinked again. Then she visibly pulled herself together, standing straighter, and cleared her throat. 'When you put it like that...'

'I do,' he insisted firmly, relieved that she seemed as willing as him to pretend that nothing had almost happened between them. 'No more excuses for you to wear crazy clothes.'

She jutted her chin with mock primness. 'I like crazy clothes.'

'Not when you are with me. I have reputation, lady.'

'You certainly have.'

'What do you mean by that?'

'You're a clever man. I'm sure you can work it out.'

To his amazement, she winked boldly, then strode away to the counter.

Merry had no idea how she was able to put one foot in front of the other. She had no idea how she'd just been able to string a sentence together, never mind make a wisecrack at him.

Everything inside her had melted. Her lips throbbed. Her skin felt taut. Sensitised. One touch and now she could only walk, talk and breathe by using complete concentration.

Giovanni's reputation with women was something she must keep reminding herself of. Katja wasn't someone who gossiped. She wouldn't say something like that without foundation.

All Giovanni had to offer was fleeting pleasure...

A deep throb in her most feminine parts almost had her tripping over her own feet just to imagine it.

The frustration was enough to make her want to stamp her feet. Three years in Switzerland, hoping to meet someone who made her feel like this, and finally, *finally*, she'd found it. She'd met someone she was attracted to, who made her laugh, who was great company, and it was a ruddy billionaire playboy, and her temporary boss at that.

It would be easier if the attraction was all her own but, inexperienced though she was, she wasn't completely naïve. If she'd received the same kind of signals from Michael all those years ago that she was receiving from Giovanni now, she would have taken the plunge and told him how she felt.

Merry didn't have the experience to play with fire with a man like Giovanni and hope to escape without being burned. She didn't want to play with fire at all.

'Are you hungry, lady?' Giovanni asked when her new clothes had been expertly packed into beautiful boxes.

'Why?' she asked, sensing what was about to follow and already knowing she absolutely did not want to spend another minute with him, while at the same time knowing she absolutely did not want to leave his side.

Her feelings were *hopeless*.

'I am hungry.'

Merry's belly was too busy doing somersaults at his close proximity for hunger to get a look-in.

He turned to the manager. 'You will take Miss Ingles' clothes to her room?'

'Of course.'

'*Grazie.*' And then he strode out of the boutique. 'We will go to restaurant,' he announced as they stepped back into the hotel's atrium.

'I'm actually feeling pretty tired,' Merry lied. Truth was, she was buzzing. Her entire body was wired. Sensitised. 'I think I'll eat in my room and watch some mindless television.'

He widened his eyes in a puppy-like fashion. 'You would make me eat alone?'

'Can't Veronica eat with you?'

'She sleeping in her coffin.'

She gave a bark of joyous laughter. Oh, why couldn't Giovanni be pig ugly, so she could just enjoy his company without lusting after him? 'She can't be that bad.'

'She is awful. Drains the blood of anyone who does wrong.'

'Then why employ her?'

'Because she is excellent at her job and never kiss my butt.'

Merry stopped walking. While they'd been sparring, Giovanni had steered her to the hotel restaurant.

She had no choice but to brazen it out.

She ignored the voice in her head, telling her that she *did* have a choice and she was about to make the wrong one.

'If I eat with you, you'll have to put up with my crazy jumper,' she warned him. 'People will see you with me. They might think we're together. Your reputation could be destroyed by the time you've finished your starter.'

He shrugged, but his dark blue eyes gleamed. 'Is okay. The restaurant is dark. I will blow table candle out so no one see us.'

Giovanni's insistence that Merry eat with him was a test to himself to prove that his attraction to her wasn't as strong as suggested by the fleeting moment in the boutique...and by the pillar near the elevator...and that moment in the car... And that, even if it was, he could control it. It was also an excellent opportunity to get a better feel for her suitability as an employee of Cannavaro Travel.

He couldn't have her in his bed and in his boardroom. It had to be one or the other. He wasn't going to throw away a potential company asset just because he had the temporary hots for her.

Lust and attraction were only ever temporary. That was all he'd allow them to be.

He kept the conversation professional. Not once did he allow his mind to wander anywhere he deemed forbidden. And as he finished his main course he congratulated himself on his self-control. Not one suggestive comment or look had been exchanged between them. *Eccellente*.

The first time they strayed into personal territory was when she finally checked her phone. It had buzzed in the bag she'd placed on the floor between them intermittently throughout their meal.

'Your brother?' he asked.

She grimaced as she fired off a quick response. 'Mostly.'

His mind finally broke from the constraints he'd placed on it and he thought about Santos, the man who would be making himself at home in Merry's cabin in two days' time.

Maybe Santos would break a leg skiing before she got back.

It was a thought that cheered him hugely and then disturbed him.

Why would he wish ill on a man he'd never met?

She put her phone back in her bag, picked up her wine glass and cut through his disconcerting thoughts with, 'Have you got any brothers or sisters?'

Giovanni had a large drink of his wine and nodded. 'Two sisters. Sofia and Carla. Both older than me.'

'Do you get on with them?'

'Better than you get on with your brother,' he observed drily.

'That's not difficult.'

'But they are very bossy. They still think I am ten.'

She sniggered into her wine glass. 'Poor you.'

'*Si*. Poor me,' he agreed solemnly.

The waiter arrived and cleared the table, reappearing moments later with dessert menus.

Giovanni read through his, amused to find Merry poring over hers with eyes that would be drooling if eyes could drool.

'What are you having?' she asked.

'Lemon tart. You?'

'Probably nothing. It all looks wonderful, though.'

'Have it all, then.'

She grinned. 'I wish. My belly's so full I don't think I could fit anything else in, but it's all so tempting.'

Not as tempting as her...

Damn it!

Before he could castigate himself for this wayward thought, the waiter came back to their table.

As Merry was still dithering over whether to order anything or not, Giovanni gave his order first, adding a coffee to it.

The waiter looked at Merry.

She snapped her menu shut and raised her shoulders. 'Pistachio ice cream, please.'

Giovanni smothered a laugh. She'd decided she could make room after all.

'And a hot chocolate,' she finished.

The moment the waiter was out of earshot, Giovanni leaned across the table. 'Ice cream and hot chocolate? Are you five, lady?'

'Only when it comes to pudding, Cheekbones,' Merry shot back before she could stop herself, and immediately covered her mouth.

He stared at her, his eyes widening with astonishment. '*Cheekbones?*'

Despite her horror at the faux pas, laughter rose up her throat. It was the expression on his face that did it. She tried so hard to fight it tears leaked from her eyes and she lifted her glasses to wipe them.

'*Cheekbones?*' Giovanni repeated.

Merry's obvious struggle not to laugh tickled him as much as the name she'd called him. Her shoulders were jiggling, her hand covering her bright red face.

She lowered her hand enough to say, in a voice choked with laughter, 'You can cut diamonds on them.'

He experienced a sudden urge to grab hold of that crazy jumper, yank her to him and kiss the laughter from those fabulous, plump, twitching lips.

Dio, this woman. What was she doing to him? He'd never met anyone like her before, someone who made him want to laugh out loud and take her over the table at the same time…

He was doing it again!

Breathing deeply through his nose, he leaned back and rubbed his cheekbones musingly. 'My sister say she kill me for them.'

'Bit drastic,' she laughed.

'That is what I say.'

Her lips pulled in, then out, her rounded cheeks sucking in as she looked at him. 'Personally,' she deadpanned, 'I'd kill you for your eyelashes.'

'Is that why you hide your eyes behind those big glasses? Ashamed you have no lashes?'

'That's definitely the reason,' she agreed with straight-faced solemnity. 'Definitely not because I'm blind as a bat without them.'

'Is that why you hide your hair too? You have a bald patch under your bun?'

'Have you been spying on me?' Merry asked with mock

horror, before covering her mouth to stop her laughter ricocheting around the room.

He opened his mouth, no doubt to give another riposte, but then something caught his eye and his features darkened. Before she knew what he was doing, he'd shot off his chair opposite her and onto the one next to her.

'What are you doing?' she asked, bemused.

He leaned into her, arm brushing against arm, and spoke in an undertone. 'The King of Monte Cleure has been taken to table across room. I do not want him to see me.'

Trying to ignore the thrills of excitement rampaging through her at his unexpected closeness, she managed to keep her voice evenly modulated. 'Why?'

'Because he is a giant pain in the butt.'

She would have laughed if the thrills hadn't started to burn. The cologne that had come close to overwhelming her on their journey to the airport and in the boutique had filled her senses again.

Swallowing, she crossed her legs away from him and gripped the stem of her wine glass tightly. 'Isn't he coming on the train ride?' She'd done a double take when she'd seen the title on the guest list.

His grimace turned into a mischievous grin that made her heart flip. He nudged her with his shoulder. 'He is so awful I made him pay twice what everyone else pay.'

For the first time since she'd met him, Merry had to force her laughter.

She had a drink of her wine, consuming more in one large swallow than she had over the duration of their meal.

Never in her entire life had she experienced such heat or such awareness of either another person or herself. It was as if all the sensations she'd experienced around him these last two days had coalesced and ripped through her in one huge shot. Her pulses were racing. Her skin felt as if it had come to tingling life all the way to her toes. And her pelvis was *squirming*. The two years of maths lessons during which she'd sat next to Michael filled with lovelorn awareness felt utterly tepid in comparison.

She could have cried with gratitude when their desserts were brought to the table.

On the pretext of needing more arm-space, she shifted her chair away from Giovanni and, with a hand whose tremors she could barely conceal, dipped her spoon into her ice cream.

Its creamy chilliness did nothing to mask the burn inside her.

'Is good?' Giovanni asked after he'd eaten half his tart.

A strange tension had formed between them, a tension it felt increasingly imperative he dispel.

He'd moved next to Merry without thinking, his body propelling itself on instinct. He'd seen the King of Monte Cleure, a boorish man he despised, and had swiftly moved seats before the King could notice him.

The end result was that he'd escaped the King's notice—for now—but had inadvertently engineered an intimacy between himself and Merry. And now his entire body vibrated with awareness and he was having to fight its straining to shift closer to her and having to fight an arousal that had no place in polite society.

Dio, he was a fully grown man, not an adolescent. Why the hell had he leaned into her? Allowed himself to catch that fruity scent he reacted to so viscerally?

The fixed, mechanical way Merry was spooning her ice-cream between her raspberry-coloured lips told him quite clearly that he wasn't the only one dealing with this tempest of unwanted desire.

Mind over matter, Cannavaro, he reminded himself grimly, and resisted stealing a spoonful of her ice-cream to cool his ardour.

She swallowed her mouthful and nodded without meeting his stare. 'And yours?'

'Is perfect,' he lied. Truth was, he hadn't tasted a speck of it.

She drank some of her hot chocolate. After she'd put the glass cup back on the table, she dug her spoon into her ice cream again, inhaled deeply, and casually said, 'Going to tell me why the King is a giant pain in the butt?'

Relieved at the direction she'd steered their conversation in—if such a deed wasn't so dangerous, he'd kiss her for it—Giovanni immediately launched into tales of the King's outrageous entitled behaviour, some of which he knew first-hand, most of which was from gossip rife in his circles. A steady flow of talk prevented dangerous silences.

He finished by saying, 'If he gives you trouble on Odyssey you tell me, and I will push him out of window.'

For the first time since he'd made the impulsive move to the seat next to her Merry's laughter had a genuine ring to it, and amusement sparkled again in her eyes. Her laughter, though, dived straight into his loins. It was just so damn *sexy*.

Determined that this time he would keep his loins in check, Giovanni drained his coffee and rose to his feet.

'Time to go, Underling.'

Time for a cold shower.

The elevator doors closed. Merry's lungs closed with them. They didn't open again until the elevator reached her floor.

How was it possible for time to become elastic? For an elevator ride that took seconds to stretch so? And how was it possible for the beats of a heart to deafen?

'I will walk you to your room,' Giovanni announced, stepping onto the narrow corridor behind her.

'Yes, Boss.' Her voice was nowhere near as light as

she would have liked. Everything in her felt so heavy.
And tingly.

'Room number?'

'Three one two.'

He marched briskly towards it, beating her by three
paces. He stood back while she unlocked it, then gave a
nod as brisk as his stride.

'All safe. *Buona notte*, lady.'

His long legs were carrying him back to the elevator
before she could wish a good night back to him.

CHAPTER SIX

GIOVANNI STRAIGHTENED HIS tie in the mirror then slipped his arms through his suit jacket. In the living area of his suite hotel staff under Veronica's direction were setting up the meeting he'd be hosting shortly. The day would be exceptionally busy. This was the last day before the Meravaro Odyssey set off on its maiden voyage and, along with ensuring everything on board was perfect and that the staff were fully primed and prepared, he also had conference calls with the management team of his cruise liners and with his American lawyer.

Striding into the living area, he nodded his approval at the plates of pastries and fruit and jugs of water and fruit juice set out on the dining table, then helped himself to a fresh coffee from the cafetière.

The Meravaro Odyssey's head chef and chief steward were the first to arrive, quickly followed by the restaurant manager, the bar manager and the shop manager.

With only five minutes to go until the meeting officially started, the only person missing was Merry.

A good night's sleep and Giovanni felt much better about the situation with her. There was no situation! She was a temporary employee he was increasingly inclined to make a permanent employee—Wolfgang would forgive his poaching—and someone he was coming to like immensely. She would be a good fit for Cannavaro Travel.

Yes, he was attracted to her, but it was nothing he couldn't manage. Those few 'moments' between them yesterday were mere blips. Hadn't he walked her to her room and wished her a good night without any awkwardness? There had been no lingering, not of speech nor eyes. *Eccellente.*

He was pouring his second coffee when Merry arrived.

He only just had enough wits about him to stop himself from doing a double take.

She didn't look any different from when he'd wished her a good night. Her hair was still pulled into a neat bun, her tortoiseshell glasses still covered half her unadorned face. Her only jewellery was a pair of tiny gold ear studs and a thin, ancient-looking silver watch.

And yet there *was* something different about her. The clothes. They were exactly the professional-but-not-boardroom he'd stipulated. Black, textured, slim-fitting trousers that cut off snugly at the ankles. A cream silk top that formed a thin V to just above the line of her cleavage. Unbuttoned blue blazer. Black heels…

That was the difference, he thought dazedly. The heels. He'd only seen her in flats or utilitarian boots before. The heels elongated her figure. The cut of the blazer worked for her too, enhancing curves he'd never noticed before.

Damn but she looked sophisticated. Sexy. *Molto sexy.*

'Morning,' she said, smiling brightly as she walked towards him, eyes flickering to the seated attendees. 'I'm not late, am I?'

Although he knew without looking that she'd made it with two minutes to spare, he took the opportunity to drag his gaze from her to his watch. He snatched a breath before flashing his teeth at her. 'Not at all. Take a seat. Eat.'

She smiled again and made her way to the table. Francois, his head steward, jumped to his feet and pulled out the spare seat next to him. Before she sat, she removed the blazer and hung it on the back of her chair.

Mamma mia, the soft curves didn't come from the cut of the cloth. They were all her own. He'd just never noticed them before under the shapeless, unflattering clothing she'd worn.

Giovanni rubbed the back of his neck. It felt hot to his touch. The beats of his heart had become weighty. There was a sensation in his loins.

Gritting his teeth, he carried his coffee to the table and took his place at the head.

He pointed to Merry, who'd piled her plate with *pains au chocolat* and fruit. 'Before we start, this is Merry. She is the lady stepping in for Gerhard while he is sick.'

Merry experienced a huge jolt at hearing Giovanni say her actual name for the first time. Part of her had been convinced he'd forgotten it.

'Merry?' said the woman sat to her left. 'An unusual name.'

'It's short for Meredith,' she explained. 'But no one calls me that.'

Apart from her brother.

A pang rent her belly as she remembered that, if Gerhard hadn't got appendicitis, she would now be eating an awkward muted breakfast with her father and gearing herself up for spending a day of fake festivity with him, her brother and her sister-in-law.

It was done. No point regretting something she couldn't change.

She found her gaze darting to Giovanni. He looked gorgeous today, somehow more gorgeous than normal. Swoon-worthy. It was taking all her willpower not to keep her stare fixed on him. Just to walk into this suite and lock eyes with him had made her pulses quicken. And they'd already been racing in anticipation of seeing him again.

Once everyone had introduced themselves, the meeting got started.

The aim of it, she quickly realised, was to ensure everyone was singing from the same hymn sheet. Their passengers were some of the world's richest and most powerful... and also some of the fussiest people ever created. Their dietary requirements alone took thirty minutes of the allotted meeting time. Then there was the bedding issue. They had almost as many individual requests for specific sheets and pillows as they had passengers. All the whims had been catered for, passengers and whims matched and prepared, and now it was a case of being prepared for the additional whims that were bound to follow. Every eventuality needed to be catered and prepared for.

Merry concentrated hard, making copious notes in her jotter. Not only did she need to learn and remember by the end of the day the stuff these people had spent months preparing for, but making notes proved she was listening and meant she didn't have to keep looking at Giovanni whenever he spoke.

Every small gaze she cast at him was followed by a battle to tear her eyes away. Every small gaze sent her heart thumping.

For his part, he didn't look at her or talk to her any differently than he looked at or spoke to anyone else. She was just another employee.

Of *course* she was just another employee. He hadn't whisked her to Paris on a whim. He hadn't bought her an array of beautiful clothes because he'd felt like being nice. He'd bought them because he'd determined them necessary for the way he wished her to present herself for his guests.

Whatever undercurrents ran between them were nothing to do with the job she'd been tasked to do.

Or had she imagined the undercurrents?

The man running this meeting was very different from the man who'd revealed himself yesterday. This man was serious and focussed, far more like the Giovanni she'd first met.

Not one person there was unaware of the exact role they were being employed for or what Giovanni's expectations were. The team he'd formed to run the Meravaro Odyssey, she came to realise as the meeting went on, had been individually selected not just for their talents in their particular field but for how well they'd gel together. This was a team that, once the maiden voyage was over and Giovanni was no longer micro-managing things, would work in harmony.

By mid-morning, they were done. As everyone filed out of his suite he stood at the door and shook each person's hand, thanking them for coming in so early. When it was her turn, she held her breath as she extended her hand towards his.

Long, warm fingers wrapped around hers. Thrills raced through her skin. Their eyes met. There was the faintest squeeze of his hand against hers and then he released it with a nod and said, 'Any problem, call Veronica.'

'Are you not coming with us?' she asked before she could stop herself.

A couple of cars had been arranged to transport them all to the train station, so they could get going on the final day's preparations.

'I have other business to do. I will be there later.'

Smiling to cover the fact that her heart had sunk at his words, she murmured, 'See you later, then,' and strode out of the suite.

It took everything she had not to look back at him.

By the time Giovanni made it to the train station late that afternoon, the Meravaro Odyssey was a hub of energy. His first task was to check that the defects he and Merry had found had been fixed. He made his way through the carriages carefully, nodding greetings at the staff doing the final polish and vacuum and clean of the windows.

He'd gone through numerous carriages before he reached the third bar. Merry had taken him at his word. The Christmas tree had been transformed. Not only did it dazzle with sparkle and colour, but carefully laid beneath it were dozens and dozens of beautifully wrapped presents.

Crouching down, he picked one up with a frown. It felt like there was something contained within it.

'You're here!'

He turned his head to find Merry approaching him, her arms full with more boxed presents. Red tinsel was draped around her neck. She'd lost her heels, her feet bare.

'What is this?' he demanded to know.

The smile on her face dimmed a touch at his tone. Placing the boxes on the nearest table, she replied, 'Presents for the passengers. Now, I know you hate Christmas, so before you get cross hear me out.'

He got to his feet and folded his arms around his chest. 'I am listening.'

'This whole voyage is geared around the Christmas season, and it seemed to me that not having presents for the passengers was missing a trick—even rich people like Christmas presents. It's just a gesture, that's all. I got them from the onboard gift shop. Don't be angry with Claude about it, I insisted. Bracelets for the women and cufflinks for the men. I would have cleared it with you, but Veronica said you were on a conference call so I made an executive decision.'

He raised an eyebrow.

She held her ground. 'If I'd waited for the okay from you I'd have been up until midnight wrapping them all, so I figured it was easier to get wrapping and hope you'd say yes. If you think it's a terrible idea then that's not a problem at all. I'll just unwrap them and put them back in the shop and you can deduct the cost of the gift-wrap from my wages. No harm will have been done. I've been wrapping them in my cabin, so I haven't made any mess that needs to be cleaned up.'

Although Merry forced herself not to cower, beneath her nonchalant façade her heart was beating hard. She'd taken a calculated risk with these presents, especially when she'd seen the fear in Claude the shop manager's eyes when she'd told him of her plans. She already knew Giovanni liked to micro-manage things—it was one of the things about him that had driven Katja mad—but she'd considered it a risk worth taking.

His eyes narrowed.

She tried to hide her automatic gulp.

She could have fainted with relief when the corners of his mouth twitched. 'How much notice do you have to give Wolfgang?'

'What for?'

'Your contract with the hotel. How much notice to leave must you give?'

Not at all sure where he was going with this, she hesitated before answering, 'A month.'

He nodded. '*Eccellente.* You give notice and come work for me.'

'You what?'

'I will pay you much more than you get from Wolfgang.'

Not sure how to respond, not sure if he was even being serious, she decided to play it safe. 'Does this mean you're okay with the presents?'

'Is a good idea.'

A very good idea. One he should have thought of himself. Giovanni supposed it was because he avoided anything to do with Christmas on a personal basis. His family were long used to him not celebrating it, and knew not to buy him presents or expect to receive them. He made up for it with their birthdays. They understood his reasons, knew that Christmas Day for him would be spent alone.

But he wondered why none of his other talented staff had thought of giving presents to their guests.

Making a mental note to contact the management teams at his luxury resorts around the world and other associated businesses and tell them to get gift wrapping, he added, 'You show good initiative. I like that.'

The smile that lit her face made his chest expand and then contract. The urge to lean in and discover if her skin still smelled of fruit was so strong he took a step back.

'Go finish wrapping,' he ordered.

Get away before I do something I regret. Like pinning you to the wall and helping myself to a taste of your delectable lips.

With another smile and a nod, she turned and padded back through the carriage.

A lump formed in his throat as he watched her go. It sharpened when she turned back to look at him.

Their eyes met. Her chest rose.

A beat later, she turned her face away and quickened her pace.

Giovanni rubbed the back of his neck. Like earlier, it felt hot to the touch.

Much as he enjoyed her company, his accelerating reactions to her made it clear that when Merry came to work for him he would have to find a role for her that limited their interaction together.

Mind over matter wasn't working.

There was only one thing for it. From now on he would have to ensure they were never alone together again.

The next morning, the platform heaved with Meravaro Odyssey staff dressed in their livery of black trousers and gold-piped deep red overcoats, loading boxes and crates of perishables through the open windows to their colleagues.

On the train itself, nervous and excited staff crowded together. Giovanni shook each person's hand, greeting them like old friends. This, Merry knew, was the first time the vast majority had met their ultimate boss, and she was impressed with how at ease he put them all.

After he'd delivered a rousing speech that made it clear each had been selected to work on the Meravaro Odyssey because of their individual reputations for excellence, and emphasised the need to maintain that excellence, the staff dispersed and Giovanni indicated for Merry to follow him off the train.

The train now loaded, staff began to line the platform in preparation for greeting their guests.

Merry was checking her watch when Francois, the head steward, hurried over to her. 'Where is Mr Cannavaro?'

'On a call with Veronica.'

She turned her head, trying to spot him. Giovanni's PA had flown back to Rome first thing that morning. Having dined with Veronica and Giovanni last night in the hotel restaurant, Merry now understood why he thought it best to keep her away from the paying guests. She really was terrifying. Merry had spent most of the meal suppressing giggles whenever she'd caught Giovanni's amused eye.

As scary as his PA was, it had been a relief to have her dining with them. It was getting harder and harder to keep a lid on her feelings when she was alone with him. All her internal reactions accelerated and heightened. She just became so *aware* that they were alone, that there was nothing and no one there between them.

For some reason, Veronica's departure meant the staff all assumed Merry was now second in command.

'What's the problem?' she asked.

'There's a broken window in the junior suite allocated to the Bussons.'

She cursed under her breath. 'Have you got Thibault to look at it?' she asked, referring to the Odyssey's maintenance man.

'Yes. The pane needs replacing.'

'Do we have a replacement?'

'No.'

This time she cursed openly, especially when she saw that the first passengers had arrived on the platform.

No way on earth could they put the Bussons in a suite with a broken window. Unfortunately, every single suite had been allocated.

'Give them my suite,' she said, thinking quickly. She'd just have to squash into one of the staff cabins that slept four people each. 'I need to stay here and greet guests, so get someone to take my case and stick it somewhere out of sight. I haven't unpacked or touched anything but the table in the suite, but double check for finger-marks, then make sure everyone knows where the Bussons have been moved to... Oh, and run a vacuum cleaner around it. There might be some bits of gift wrapping around.'

Francois nodded and hurried off.

Not having time to wallow in disappointment that she wouldn't be sleeping in the beautifully appointed luxurious junior suite after all, Merry summoned her friendliest smile and strode over to welcome their guests.

The passengers were in high spirits, Giovanni noted with gratification. All had been shown to their suites and given the grand tour, and all the noises he'd heard thus far had been appreciative.

The whistle blew. Champagne flutes were held aloft and cheers rang out as, three years after he'd approached Wolfgang Merkel with his idea for a collaboration, the Mera-varo Odyssey departed on its maiden voyage.

This was a moment that should induce great satisfaction, but the usual sense of elation he felt when a project came to fruition was muted.

He knew it was the Christmas feeling causing his dark mood. The maiden voyage had been promoted as a festive delight. Indeed, tomorrow morning they would arrive in Vienna, and Giovanni and the passengers would spend the day at one of the city's most beautiful palaces, enjoying a festive meal and a private indoor Christmas market.

While he'd trained himself to be immune to festive preparations, he hadn't taken part in any actual festivities since Monica's death. He remembered how much she'd looked forward to them spending Christmas together. Their families had planned a huge joint celebration so no one would be left out.

Giovanni had looked forward to it too, had counted the days off on the wall planner he'd pinned to the tiny room of the student house he'd shared. His housemates had thought him an idiot for tying himself down at such a young age, but he'd been smug about it. Why jump from bed to bed with strangers when you had the woman you intended to spend the rest of your life with waiting for you?

He hadn't thought of himself as missing out. He'd mapped his life out and followed that path with pride, right until the moment he'd returned to his family home from a Christmas shopping trip and absorbed his parents' and sisters' white faces. He'd known before his father had staggered to him and pulled him into a tight embrace that it was Monica.

The Christmas gifts he'd spent hours selecting had remained in their shopping bags until someone—he'd never known who—had removed them. He'd never asked what had become of those gifts. Those days remained nothing but a blur to him. The days after her funeral were clearer in his memories, but still a void. A void filled with agony.

He'd told Merry that he'd quit university, but now he remembered that he'd never actively made that choice. He'd just never returned. He hadn't been capable of making that decision. He hadn't been capable of making the decision to leave Rome either. That had come from his father, two months after the funeral. The gentle suggestion of a change of scene.

Neither of them had known the change of scene would be permanent.

Merry came into his line of sight. His chest lightened.

She had her tablet in front of her and was searching for something on it for the wife of the boss of a fashion house. He watched her plump lips move as she spoke, noted the way they frequently curved upwards, noted the way she managed to give her undivided attention to the woman without encroaching on her personal space *and* indicate to the couple who were hovering close to her that she'd seen them and would attend to them soon, without being distracted from her immediate task.

All the women on board could afford the best clothes, surgeons and beauticians that money could buy. Yet Merry, with her hair tied back in her faithful bun and her face unadorned by cosmetics, outshone them all. Today she wore a pair of black and white checked fitted trousers that clung to the curve of her bottom, matched with a deep green silk shirt, and those heels that elongated her sexy body.

Dio, he desired her. It was impossible to look at her and not envisage himself removing those tortoiseshell glasses, releasing that prim bun, and pulling her face to his for a deeply erotic kiss while her unconfined hair tumbled over them. How long was her hair? Shoulder-length? What was its texture? Was its blondeness matched by…?

Her gaze suddenly flickered to him.

Their eyes locked together. Barely a second did the lock between them hold, but it was long enough for his lungs to deflate and his heart to kick against his ribcage.

He should not want her like this.

Since making his vow, he'd avoided being alone with her. He'd forced his vampire PA to dine with them, figuring a scary chaperone would prove an excellent antidote to desire, but her presence had had the opposite effect, casting him and Merry as conspirators against the stern headmistress.

He'd ached to drag her to his suite and kiss the shared secret humour from her lips.

He broke the stare with a blink and a jerk of his head.

It was imperative he stop thinking of Merry like this. Bad enough that he ached so badly for her, but to have her consuming the entirety of his thoughts was far more dangerous.

Putting his brain back in gear, he straightened his shoulders and set about mingling with his guests.

CHAPTER SEVEN

HOURS AFTER THE Meravaro Odyssey departed, one of the female guests had an issue she insisted only Merry could deal with. A *personal* issue, Merry had been informed in hushed tones by the guest's cabin steward.

Heading off to the sleeping carriages, she found herself struggling to keep her balance. She thought it would be easier to manage without her shoes on, but if that was the case how on earth did the female passengers manage when half of them were wearing heels twice the height of hers? And how on earth did the waiting staff manage to carry trays of champagne?

She'd just reached the first restaurant carriage when the train must have taken a gentle bend, because she completely lost her balance and bashed into one of the dining tables.

'You okay?'

How could a heart soar and sink at the same time? she wondered as she lifted her head to see Giovanni stride through the doors at the other end of the carriage.

'I'm fine.' She rubbed her smarting thigh and strove hard to keep her voice its normal tone and tempo. Being unexpectedly alone in a carriage with Giovanni threatened to unravel her composure more than any bash to her leg could.

Her pulses had accelerated from low to high with a

speed faster than the train was carrying them, and her belly and abdomen were a sudden quivering wreck.

'Just lost my balance.' Could he hear the strain in her voice? She prayed not. Prayed the burn scorching her skin wasn't visible on her face. 'I'm sure I'll get the hang of walking on a moving train soon.'

He raised a brow. 'No one tell you to waddle?'

'Waddle?'

'Like a duck. Like this, see?'

He showed what he meant in exaggerated movements that had her covering her mouth to smother a laugh. Despite her best efforts, it sneaked out through her fingers, and the sound must have triggered something in Giovanni because his handsome face creased in a grin that sent her heart soaring.

Dark blue eyes clashed with her. Locked. Held. The smile on his face dissolved. The momentary lightness between them dissolved with it. The beats of Merry's soaring heart turned into heavy thumps that rippled through her.

His eyes darkened. Strong throat moved. Broad chest rose slowly but raggedly.

He took a step closer. Then another.

The roar of blood in her ears was deafening. Breathing had become impossible. She could no longer feel the individual beats of her heart.

The tingles dancing over her skin pooled between her legs, and suddenly all she could see was Giovanni's sensuous mouth moving closer to her. Dark, anticipatory heat rose inside her. Her lips were prickling…

He was going to kiss her…

Finally…

How Giovanni pulled himself out of the spell that had seen him come within an inch of kissing Merry was a question he'd never be able to answer. He had no recollection of positioning his body close enough *to* kiss her.

Hunger burned him. Hunger for Merry.

He would not—could not—satisfy it.

Stepping back from the danger zone, and tearing his gaze away from the rapidly blinking eyes and rounded cheeks awash with colour, he swallowed to get moisture into his mouth.

'It is the best way for balance,' he said, as if he hadn't been a breath away from kissing her.

Her stare, which he allowed himself only the lightest of skims over, was blank. The colour washing over her cheeks was the darkest he'd ever seen.

'Oh?'

He gripped the table he'd backed onto. 'Duck waddle,' he reminded her. 'All guests are shown by their cabin steward.'

'Oh,' she repeated. Then she seemed to pull herself back into focus, straightening and rubbing her arm before airily saying, 'That'll be why I wasn't told. And, speaking of cabins, one of our lady passengers is waiting for me in hers, so I'd better go before she thinks I've forgotten about her.'

'Is there a problem?' Why was he asking? Why, when he'd only just pulled back from the precipice, and after all the talking-tos he'd given himself these last few days, was he reluctant to let her go?

'Reluctant' was too mild a word for it.

'I don't think so. From what her steward told me it's a personal problem, so probably something female-related.'

'Then you are the best person to help her.'

Her dimples popped briefly before she bowed her head and then, with a murmured, 'See you later...' headed off.

'Hey, lady,' he said, before he could stop himself.

She stopped mid-stride and turned her head. More colour stained her face.

'We talk later about how the first day has gone, *si*?'

The dimples popped again. 'Yes, Cheekbones.'

* * *

As daft an idea as it sounded, waddling like a duck really did help. By the time Merry had dealt with the guest's issue, and was walking back through the narrow mahogany panelled corridors of the sleeping carriages to the main hospitality section, it felt as if she'd spent her life walking on moving trains.

In the piano bar, she caught a glimpse of Giovanni weaving through the crowd to exit the carriage. There was nothing inelegant in the way he waddled. His long legs carried him with the same elegance he had when he strode on *terra firma*, and she felt the familiar loosening in her belly and a rush of the tingles that had swept through her when, for that heart-stopping moment, she'd thought he was going to kiss her.

He *had* been going to kiss her. She hadn't imagined it. She could scarcely believe the disappointment that had ripped through her when he'd pulled back from it. She should be relieved, not feel all hollow and yet so heavy inside.

Much against her better judgement, late last night, alone in her hotel room, she'd finally given in to temptation and searched his name on the internet, specifically his romantic history. There was nothing romantic about it. Giovanni had been linked to so many women that her eyes had blurred skimming their names and faces.

But she'd already known that. Katja had warned her. It hadn't stopped Merry developing a crush on him. It hadn't stopped the crush accelerating. It hadn't stopped fantasies enveloping her.

Was this why he'd pulled back from kissing her? Did he sense the depth of her attraction? Did she exude a virgin neediness that made him want to run?

Why should she even *care* that he was fighting the attraction when so much of her energy was taken in fighting it too? She should be grateful.

Only two more nights to go, she reminded herself. Two more sleeps and then she'd return to her life at the hotel in Switzerland, and Giovanni Cannavaro would become a fading memory and all the feelings he induced in her would fade with it.

Soon the crowded bars and lounges thinned as the guests went off to their cabins to prepare for dinner. The dress code for the duration of the voyage was smart, and Merry looked forward to seeing the finery on display that night. She especially looked forward to tomorrow night's '1940s Hollywood Glamour' theme Christmas party, which reminded her that she really should try Katja's dress on in case she needed to make any last-minute alterations to it. Which in turn reminded her that she had nowhere to try the dress on or, for that matter, anywhere to sleep.

As things were quieter for the staff for now, Merry sought out Francois, finding him by the housekeeping stores carriage, deep in conversation with Giovanni.

Of *course* he was with Giovanni. Giovanni appeared like a spectre everywhere she went, taunting her with his continual presence, never giving her pulses time to settle.

Not wanting to interrupt, she kept her distance, wishing for the ability to become invisible and, resolutely keeping her eyes anywhere but on him, replied to Santa's latest text message. Only two more days and she'd be with her best friend, a hugely cheering thought.

She longed to confide her feelings for Giovanni to someone, felt as if she might explode from all she was having to keep contained within her.

As she hit 'send', another message came through, this one from her brother.

Hope you're enjoying yourself. Dad's in pieces because of you.

She took a deep breath and put her phone in her back pocket without replying, then looked up to find Giovanni's eyes on her.

He stepped over to her. 'Something the matter?'

Pasting a smile to her face, she shook her head. 'I'm waiting for Francois. Don't let me interrupt.'

'We are finished.'

Francois joined them at the mention of his name. 'What can I help you with?'

'I just wondered if you've thought of a place where I can get my head down tonight?' At the confusion on his face, she clarified, 'Somewhere for me to sleep.'

Comprehension dawned. 'I'm sorry, I forgot all about it.'

'Don't be sorry, you've eighty guests to look after,' she chided. 'I'd forgotten too.'

'What is going on?' Giovanni asked.

'A crack was found in the window of the suite allocated to the Bussons in the final inspection. Merry gave up her cabin for them,' Francois informed him, swiping at the tablet in his hand.

'Why was I not told about this?'

'It was discovered literally as the first passengers arrived on the platform,' Merry explained. 'We've been so busy since then that I forgot all about it.'

'You gave them your cabin?'

'There was nowhere else to put them,' she said with a shrug. 'All the others are allocated. It was pure luck I had the same cabin as them, so they're none the wiser.'

Francois peered closely at the tablet screen in front of him and rubbed his forehead.

'No spare beds in the staff carriages?' Merry guessed.

'No…' He sighed.

'I thought not. Never mind, let's think out of the box. There must be a space somewhere where I can make a nest for myself.'

An idea came to her and she stepped over to the house-keeping carriage and pushed the door open.

'This will work.'

Francois peered over her shoulder. 'There's enough space on the floor for one of the spare mattresses—'

'No.' Giovanni's bluntness interrupted his flow.

'Why not?' Merry asked, surprised.

'Staff come in and out of here all the time.'

'Where else can I go?' Another answer came to her. 'I'll sleep in one of the lounges. I'm only little. I'll fit on one of the sofas, no problem.'

'Out of question. You will not sleep in space where guests can see you or be squashed in a space where you get stepped on. You are not an animal. You will share my suite.'

'You what?'

Ignoring her, he spoke to Francois. 'Take Merry's stuff and show her to my suite. Make it with two beds.'

His long legs had carried him away before Francois could acknowledge the instruction and before Merry could close her shocked open mouth.

Merry hesitated before following Francois, who'd insisted on carrying her luggage, into Giovanni's super-deluxe suite. A couple of stewards were in the process of turning the huge bed into two large single beds separated by barely a foot of carpet.

She couldn't look at them. She didn't dare.

After thanking Francois, she sat at the small table at the other side of the suite and checked her emails on her phone, trying to make herself look busy, trying to affect nonchalance that she, an ordinary employee, was being moved into the big boss's suite.

The stewards finished making the beds with the unob-trusive efficiency she'd already come to expect from the staff working on the Odyssey and then she was alone. In Giovanni's suite.

She felt sick, but not in a nauseous way.

The handle of the door turned.

Her heart punched against her ribs, then set off at a canter.

Giovanni appeared. He closed the door and leaned against it. His chest rose slowly before the heart-breaking grin she was coming to adore spread across his face.

'Okay, lady, we are roommates now. You not snore, no?'

She expelled the air she'd been holding, relieved he was taking a this-isn't-the-slightest-bit-awkward tack. 'I hope not,' she murmured.

She hadn't imagined the angry tension in his demeanour when he'd strolled off after decreeing that she share his suite. He'd clearly felt compelled to offer his spare bed to her, but it was an unwanted compulsion.

He wanted *her*, of that she had no doubt. She also had no doubt that he didn't want to want her. She thought that more humiliating than if he didn't want her at all, a thought she was painfully aware was contrary, considering she didn't want to want *him*. But she didn't want to want him because he was everything she didn't want in a lover. Desiring a billionaire playboy was a fast track to heartache. There would be no safety in Giovanni's arms.

What possible threat did she pose to him? Giovanni's track record proved how easily he separated desire from emotions.

'*Bene*. Which bed do you want?'

The mere mention of the word made her belly flip.

The thrills racing through her blood just at being in an enclosed space alone with him accelerated.

Forcing her voice to adopt the same nothing-to-see-here tone as his, she said, 'It's your suite, you choose.'

He peeled away from the door and patted the nearest

bed. 'I will have this one. If any intruder comes in, lady, I will be close enough to bash them and save you.'

'How gallant of you, Cheekbones.'

He winked. 'Is my middle name. I will take a shower now. There is room in the wardrobe for your clothes.'

He closed the bathroom door firmly behind him. The lock clicked into place.

Alone, Merry removed her glasses and rubbed her eyes.

The camaraderie they'd both forced just then had been *too* forced. Draining.

She had no idea how she was going to get through the next two nights, with the man she wanted with a hunger she'd never known she could feel sleeping in a bed only an arm's length away.

Giovanni stood beneath the powerful shower spray and vigorously lathered shampoo into his hair.

He must have angered *all* the Fates. They were forcing him to take the chivalrous route and have Merry share his suite. But what else could he have done? He could not allow an employee to sleep on a floor in a store cupboard, and as for her idea of sleeping on one of the lounge sofas… What kind of impression would that make to their nocturnal guests?

And now he was stuck sharing his suite with the woman he desired more than he could remember ever desiring anyone.

It caused a wrench in his chest to acknowledge that this included Monica.

Giovanni liked to bed beautiful women who lit a flame in his loins but left his heart cold and his brain bored. He would never marry. This was nothing to do with misplaced loyalty to Monica's memory. Monica was dead. She wouldn't know. If by chance there was a heaven and she was sitting up there in it, watching him, she wouldn't expect him to spend his life pining for her. Monica would want him to live his life.

To marry, though, meant making a lifetime commitment to one woman. It was a commitment that should only be made if you loved that person and couldn't imagine yourself without them. That was how it had been with Monica. And then she'd died and ripped a hole in his heart so big and painful that he would never put himself in a position to feel that way again.

It had taken the move to Switzerland for him to reach the point of living again. The career path he'd then embarked on had opened the doors on a new future, one he'd enthusiastically embraced. He travelled the world making pots of money, ate the best food, drank the best drink, and bedded the most beautiful women. He woke every morning raring to go. He took risks. Listened to his gut rather than to his advisors—Wolfgang excepted. He lived his life on his terms and under his own control.

So why could he not control his desire for Merry?

And why, when he knew how damned imperative it was to prevent himself being alone with her, had he invited her to share his suite? He wouldn't have made the invitation to anyone else.

Only once he'd dried himself did he realise that in his haste to escape her presence he'd locked himself in the bathroom without a change of clothes.

He cursed. Clothes were a barrier he needed around Merry Ingles as much as he needed distance.

Securing the towel around his waist, he took a deep breath and unlocked the door.

The suite was empty.

'Time for a debrief, lady. Drink?'

Merry, who'd been chatting to the bar manager, turned

to Giovanni and pretended she hadn't been hyper-aware of his approach.

She'd been hyper aware of every movement he'd made during the evening.

Her nerves had slowly shredded as the guests had eaten dinner and then steadily retired to their suites as the evening had passed, the knowledge that soon she would be retiring to Giovanni's suite *with* Giovanni fixed in great big neon letters in her head.

Tempting though it was to ask for a bucket of Scotch to knock her out, she played safe and asked for an Irish cream liqueur.

Drinks poured, she followed him to a table and stretched her legs out, careful to avoid Giovanni's much longer ones.

'How do you think it went today?' he asked after he'd swirled some Scotch in his mouth.

Feeling ridiculously, painfully, terrifyingly happy to be with him, she sipped her own drink and said, 'I think it went brilliantly. The only complaint came from the King of Monte Cleure.' She dropped her voice and leaned forward to speak in an undertone. 'You were right about him being a giant pain in the butt. He complained the poker cards were rigged.'

'How much did he lose?'

'Tens of thousands.'

Straight white teeth flashed. *'Eccellente.'*

'I thought that would please you. He's a terrible player. Got the worst poker face going.'

'Do you play?'

'No, but even a novice like me knows that if you've got a good hand, the last thing you should do is sit there looking all smug about it.'

He sniggered. 'Did you sort the hat issue for the Pernices?'

Mrs Pernice had left her hatbox in her car in Paris.

'Yes. It was delivered when we made the short stop in Belgium.'

Giovanni continued peppering her with questions about the various issues—passenger whims mostly—that had arisen throughout the day. He knew perfectly well that he was playing for time.

When they rose from this table it would be to retire for the night. Together. Within the same four walls. His heart hadn't beat in a normal rhythm since he'd commanded it.

Nothing was going to happen. He would keep control if it killed him.

Thoughts of a similar hue must have been going through Merry's head too, for the bright conversation they'd been forcing tapered away into an awkward silence.

'Another?' he asked, nodding at her empty glass.

She hesitated, then shook her head, no longer meeting his stare. 'If you're going to have another, would you mind if I go to the suite and have a shower before I get some sleep?'

'No, no. I'll stay here. Message me when you are done, okay?'

She nodded and shifted over. As she moved to slide out from her seat, her calf brushed against his.

Their eyes met one last time before she was on her feet and walking away from him.

Walking to the suite he would shortly be joining her in.

CHAPTER EIGHT

MERRY HAD BEEN cocooned in the softest yet crispest bed-sheets imaginable for only a few minutes when there was a gentle tap on the door. A beat later and it opened. Giovanni's face appeared.

'Am I okay to come in?' He looked straight ahead rather than in the direction of the beds.

She cleared her throat and burrowed deeper under the covers. 'I'm decent.'

Door closed, he opened the wardrobe and rummaged in it. 'You sure you are finished in the bathroom?' he asked with his back to her.

'Yes.'

Still not looking at her, he disappeared into it.

Merry swallowed in a vain attempt to still the thuds of her heart and tried to catch her breath. There was not a cell of her body not on heightened alert.

She rolled onto her side, facing the wall, and closed her eyes, then prayed for sleep to come quickly. Her eyes refused to obey and kept flickering open.

She should be exhausted. She'd been on the go since seven a.m. and it was now close to midnight.

Her breath caught in her throat again when the bathroom door opened and the suite was engulfed with the scent of fresh, masculine shower gel and toothpaste.

She heard footsteps pad through the suite, then squeezed

her eyes shut and held her breath even tighter when those same footsteps neared her. Bedsheets rustled. She sensed rather than heard the mattress dip. Sensed because the thuds of her heart were deafening.

Then the light went out and they were plunged into darkness.

Time crawled slowly. Only the fact that she hadn't passed out from lack of oxygen proved she was still able to take air in.

She was certain Giovanni was awake too, though not a sound came from his bed.

If her phone hadn't suddenly buzzed loudly on the narrow bedside table between her bed and the wall, she was quite sure she would have stayed in that suspended animation the whole night long.

'Sorry,' she muttered, grabbing hold of it. 'I'll turn it off.'

As she swiped to mute it, she grimaced to see the message she'd been sent.

'Your brother?' Giovanni guessed from the sharp intake of breath she'd made when the cabin had been briefly illuminated by the screen of her phone.

'Yes.'

He rolled onto his back and arched an arm above his head. 'What his problem now?'

She took so long to answer he thought she was ignoring his question.

'He's still angry with me for not going home.'

'Still?'

He heard her roll over too. He wondered if she was staring at the ceiling the same as he was.

'He got married six months ago. Kelly, his wife, wanted us to celebrate Christmas together, but I'm working over the period so we were going to have an early celebration today.'

'No wonder he is cross if you pulled out at last minute.'

A hint of defensiveness came into her voice. 'We haven't celebrated Christmas as a family properly in fourteen years.'

Giovanni hadn't celebrated Christmas in almost that long either.

'It's not fair,' she blurted, suddenly impassioned. 'Martin *hates* Christmas, and has spent most of my life making sure everyone knows how much he hates it, and Dad...' She sucked in a breath and lowered her voice. 'Martin messaged me saying Dad was in pieces because I'm not there, but that's just a fat lie. Dad couldn't care less, not about me *or* Christmas. He'd go through the motions on the day itself, and cook Christmas dinner, but there were never any decorations or crackers or the silly games we used to play when Mum was alive. Martin would spend the day acting like a brat, sneering that it was all consumerist rubbish and then hiding in his bedroom. But now he's got married and wants to make his wife happy and suddenly Christmas is a big deal and I'm the bad guy when I spent years begging and pleading for us to celebrate it properly, to celebrate *anything* as a family properly. He doesn't want me there any more than Dad does—he just wants to make Kelly happy. I bet he hasn't told her how he's spent his life tormenting me, and I bet she doesn't know I moved to Switzerland because I was sick to death of him thinking he could bully and control me.'

Finally, she paused for breath. Giovanni tried to take this barrage of confidences in. There were a lot of things to sift through.

'Your *mamma* died when you were a child?'

'When I was eight. Breast cancer.'

He sucked in a breath. 'I am sorry. That must be very hard.'

Her voice softened. 'It was.' She sighed. 'And *I'm* sorry. I don't know why I just dumped all that on you.'

And he didn't know why her confidences had settled like a boulder in his chest. 'Is okay.'

He heard her move. Turning his face to her, he saw through the darkness that she'd rolled back onto her side, away from him.

They lapsed into another silence. Giovanni knew he should shut his eyes, but found himself unable to tear them away from her still form beside him. She was so close he could hear the faint sound of her stilted breathing. Never in his life had such awareness for another filled him. Taking a cold shower before bed had done nothing to lessen the heat coursing through his veins.

Merry forced her eyes and mouth to stay shut. She had no idea where her outburst had just come from. Frustration, she supposed. She'd spent a lifetime dealing with her brother's dictatorial attitude towards her and her father's apathy.

Her mother's death had shattered their family unit. The roles they'd all played before her death had become entrenched. The siblings who'd barely tolerated each other had embarked on open warfare. The father who'd never been demonstrative with his affections had turned into a shell of a man, there in presence but not in spirit.

She knew her father couldn't have cared less if she'd gone home. Knew too that Martin's anger was just an excuse he needed to pick up the stick and beat her with it, but that didn't stop the guilt. It sat inside her, fighting for dominance over the maelstrom of emotions consuming her over Giovanni.

And *how* they consumed her. Especially now, here, alone in the dark, all her nerves straining, her pelvis aching, the beats of her racing heart rippling through her.

Just go to sleep, she begged her sensitised body. *Sleep. Fall into the rhythm of the train. When you wake up, the night will be over...*

Giovanni's deep, musical voice suddenly cut through her increasingly despairing thoughts. 'I have not celebrated Christmas in twelve years.'

Her eyes sprang open and she rolled over before she could stop herself. All she could see through the darkness was the outline of his body and the whites of his eyes staring at her.

'My fiancée,' he said quietly. 'She died a week before Christmas. Was hit by a car.'

It felt like a brick had been thrown at her belly. Air expelled from her lungs in a slow wheeze. 'That's awful,' she whispered.

'We were together a long time. Five years. We got together at school. We were going to marry when I finished university. She was training to be a hat maker. We had it all planned. Where we were going to marry. Where we would live. The children we would have…she wanted four.'

Her head spun. Never would she have imagined Giovanni, the great Lothario, had come close to marrying. She'd imagined he'd always lived a charmed life, a man with the Midas touch, had imagined him breaking hearts before he was out of nappies. With his looks and personality he'd have had the pick of girls from a young age.

It had never crossed her mind that he'd suffered heartbreak, and it made her heart squeeze into a tight ball to think of the pain he must have gone through.

Using only a few words, he'd painted a picture of the life he'd once had too. A life of stability. Two teenagers who'd fallen in love, grown together and planned a future together. And then it had all been ripped away from him.

Giovanni could sense Merry's mind whirling with questions, and as suddenly as the compulsion to share something of himself as she had shared something of herself had risen in him, the compulsion to put things back in their rightful place smothered it.

The atmosphere in the suite had become too charged to breathe. He needed to lighten it before a spark caught.

'Is late, so no more talking,' he said in a much firmer voice. 'I need beauty sleep.'

It worked. After a beat, he heard a soft, if tentative, giggle. 'Did you remember to moisturise your eyelashes?'

'Most important part of my routine. *Buona notte*, lady.'

'Goodnight, Cheekbones.'

Grinning in the darkness, he rolled so his back was to her.

In seconds the grin had fallen and he found himself pressing his lips together to stop his tongue getting the air it needed to make more conversation, then squeezing his eyes shut and gripping the pillow to stop his mind from imagining the nightwear she was wearing.

Pyjamas? Nightdress? A slip? Lingerie…?

Mind over matter, Cannavaro. Mind over matter.

He was still telling himself that a long time later.

Darkness had been replaced by duskiness when Giovanni opened his eyes. Once he'd fallen asleep, the rhythmic motion of the train had helped to keep him unconscious.

Stretching, he turned over and his heart stopped.

Merry lay on her belly, close to the edge of her bed, face turned to him, bare arm overhanging, fingers skimming the carpeted floor. Her blonde hair spilled all around her, some hanging like a waterfall over her arm. Unimaginably long. Unimaginably silky.

Unthinkingly, he shuffled to the edge of his bed, reached out and lightly stroked it. It was even silkier to touch.

Reluctantly, he withdrew his hand and soaked in her sleeping face. He'd never seen Merry without her glasses on before, had never realised how much of her face they disguised. Disguised the fact that, far from being ordinarily pretty, Merry was extraordinarily beautiful.

And then she opened her eyes and stared straight at him, and his heart kick-started back to life, rising up his throat to choke him.

Dio, her eyes…

He'd always assumed the thick lenses of her glasses magnified them, but they were huge in their own right. Beautiful.

She blinked. Blinked again. Then the plump lips that had somehow become even more kissable overnight curved at the sides, and she lifted her hand off the floor and tucked it beneath her heart-shaped chin.

'Good morning,' she whispered.

It took more effort than he could have imagined to get his throat working. *'Buongiorno,'* he said huskily. Any moisture in his mouth had vanished. 'Sleep well?'

She smiled ruefully in reply and covered her mouth with the back of her hand to hide a wide yawn. Holding the sheets carefully to her chest, she sat up. 'What time is it?'

He looked at his watch. 'Seven.'

She yawned again. 'I should get ready. Do you want to use the bathroom before I shower? I don't mind going second.'

'Go ahead.'

She pushed the covers off and twisted round to put her feet on the floor.

He tried not to look, but his eyes were too greedy to obey his brain's command and with lungs that forgot how to inhale he stared at her. *Dio*, her body…*incredibile*. Lightly golden lithe legs, respectably covered in blue mid-thigh-length cotton pyjama shorts, trim waist, and a white vest that didn't show an inch of cleavage…

But he could see the shape of her unbound breasts clearly beneath it. Perfectly round. Perfectly plump. The outline of her nipples were a shadow of darkness beneath the lightness of the thin cotton.

His greedy stare took less than a second, but it was possibly the longest second of his life and he had to wrench his gaze away before she noticed.

She rose to her feet, and that was when he saw the nasty bruise on the side of her thigh.

As unthinkingly as when he'd touched her hair, he reached out and gently put the tips of his fingers to the bruise. 'You are hurt.'

Merry had woken from the most wonderfully vivid dream in which Giovanni had been touching her hair knowing instantly where she was. The joy that had bloomed in her to open her eyes and see his face right there, watching her, had been as shocking as it had been incredible. Her eyesight was too bad to read the look in his eyes. but the charge coming from him had been unmistakable and it had flown into her veins like an electric pulse.

It had taken what felt like an age to compose herself enough to speak, to realise that, however powerful the charge flowing between them, he wouldn't act on it, didn't *want* to act on it, and to know that if she didn't hide away until she had more control over herself she was liable to do something she'd regret. Like throw herself at him.

Because she *did* want to act on it.

Because Giovanni hadn't been the only one to watch the other sleep.

Merry had woken in the early hours and, too restless to fall straight back to sleep, had sat up and gazed at his sleeping form, sitting on her hands to stop them reaching for him.

She'd come close to crying. Was she destined to remain a virgin her whole life? Now that she knew what true desire felt like, how could she settle for anything less? What were the chances of experiencing all these wonderful, heady, sicky feelings for anyone else when she'd spent the first twenty-two years of her life unaware such feelings existed? How could she give herself to a man who didn't make her feel as if she'd give a decade of her life for just one touch?

And now he *was* touching her, and she was unable to stop the tremor that ripped through her at the shock of it, and she lost her balance, stumbling forward and landing with a flump on him, feet still on the floor but her breasts crushed against his chest and her face in his neck.

Neither of them moved.

Time stopped. Stretched. Became elastic.

The beats of Merry's heart slowed to a dull thud as her senses sharpened and heightened. The musky scent of Giovanni's skin flowed into her airwaves and triggered a rush of warmth that pooled between her legs and made her breath catch. She could feel the hitch of his ragged breaths and the strong pulse at the base of his smooth, strong neck against the base of *her* neck, while the heavy beats of his heart thumped against breasts that had, in a moment, become thrillingly sensitised.

She tried to breathe. Tried to summon the strength to pull herself up and get away.

It seemed to take for ever before her frozen yet burning body obeyed her brain's increasingly frantic commands. Hands flat on his pillow, Merry dragged her unwilling face out of the crook of Giovanni's neck and levered herself up until her face hovered over his and then all the sense she'd managed to summon scurried away as she found herself helplessly caught in his stare.

Her heart ballooned as she read the stark hunger contained in his gaze and saw the rapid flare of his nostrils.

She held her breath as he lifted his hand. Gently, he skimmed the back of a finger over her cheek. She shivered as electricity zipped pleasurably through her, the shivers turning into quivers when he slowly brushed fallen strands of hair from her face and cupped her cheek with the whole of his hand, lifting his head as he pulled her to him.

Their lips brushed together. Held. He pulled away and stared again into her eyes, before pressing his lips harder to hers and breathing deeply as their mouths fused.

Everything in her melted.

And then his mouth moved against hers with an almost lazy intensity that would have weakened her knees if she'd been standing. The hand against her cheek skimmed her hair, dived through it and clasped the back of her head. The kiss deepened. His tongue danced into her mouth, shocking her with the thrill of desire it provoked and filling her already overloaded senses with his dark taste.

Giovanni gave up. He didn't want to fight any more. He didn't think he *could* fight. It was too late for him. He'd lost. His hunger for Merry was too strong. Containing it was impossible. The taste of her mouth was an aphrodisiac he craved to get his fill of, and the deeper their kisses, the hungrier he became.

Her pyjama vest had ridden up, and when he put his hand on her back the feel of her silky warm skin sent another jolt of electricity racing through him.

Not breaking the fusion of their mouths, he tightened his hold around her and used his strength to lift her wholly on top of him, then rolled her over so she lay beneath him.

Smoothing the hair off her face, he gazed into her eyes. What he saw ringing back at him stole what little breath he had left. Merry was as intoxicated with the moment as he was.

Languidly, he kissed her again, and shivered when she wound her arm around his back and, tentatively at first, dragged her fingers over his skin, marking his flesh with the burn of her touch while her other hand cupped the back of his head.

Only the need to taste her flesh had the power to break

him away from the taste of her mouth. Feeling as if he was in the midst of a drug-induced fever, Giovanni pressed kisses down her arched throat, licking the silky skin when he reached the swan of her neck, as drunk on its texture as he was on the texture of her lips.

Barely breaking the contact between their bodies, he gathered her pyjama vest up and pulled it over her breasts. Giving him the dreamiest of smiles, she lifted her arms. The moment he'd pulled it over her head he was so desperate to touch her again that he released the vest immediately and cupped her cheeks for another deeply passionate kiss, experiencing a powerful jolt when her naked breasts crushed against his chest.

Slowly, he traced his lips back down her neck, his hands exploring her soft contours as he kissed his way down to her breasts. He took a dark, puckered nipple into his mouth and closed his eyes tightly in an attempt to steady the heady thrills burning in him.

Merry was utterly lost to everything but this moment. Tiny yet violent darts of pleasure ravaged every part of her.

What did it matter if Giovanni didn't want to want her? He wanted her, and in this heavenly moment that was enough. And what did it matter if he was a heartbreaker? She'd pay the price of a dozen broken hearts if this glorious sensory explosion was the reward.

That sensory explosion only built as he trailed gentle kisses over her belly, his hands incessant in their caresses until they pinched the top of her shorts. Chin on her abdomen, he looked at her with the stare of a man unwrapping a gift he'd spent a lifetime waiting for.

She felt like she'd waited a lifetime for *this*. For him.

Shaking, she skimmed the tips of her fingers over his forehead, saw him shudder at the effect of this tiny touch, then fluttered her eyes shut as her shorts were drawn down her thighs, followed by the trail of his tongue all the way down to the tips of her toes.

There was a vague awareness of him removing the underwear he'd slept in, and then he kissed his way up to the arch of her thighs, turning her skin to lava and sending blood pumping ferociously through her body, roaring in her head. When he pressed his mouth right in the heart of her femininity, a jolt of electricity flew through her veins and out of her throat in a gasp that turned into a sigh as he gently opened her up to him and his tongue found the nub of her pleasure.

It was *all* pleasure. The most incredible, mind-altering pleasure that seeped into her every pore and carried her to a secret place filled with wanton, erotic treasure.

Falling deeper into a pleasure-induced stupor, she dimly recognised the change in Giovanni's breathing, heard the heavy raggedness of it, felt the thrilling bite of his fingers into her hips. Her anticipation fizzed when he grazed his lips back up to her mouth and covered her with his body.

She put her hand to his neck and gazed into his eyes. Wondrously, she couldn't just see the hungry passion coming from them, but feel it too.

His lips brushed over hers. He pulled away to stare at her again. Kissed her. Pulled away. Then he kissed her with such potency she moaned into his mouth and arched into him, spreading her thighs further as the burning need for consummation overrode everything.

A thick weight pressed against her. She sucked in a breath at the wanton pulse that ripped through her. He used his hand to guide himself and then clasped her hand. Eyes locked with hers, his mouth skimming lightly against hers, he inched slowly inside her. There was a brief moment of discomfort as her body adjusted to the newness, but the steadying of his hand holding hers, and the tenderness of his lips against hers, and all the heady feelings that had built inside her and brought her to this point converged to clear her mind of everything but this.

Giovanni inside her. Making love to her. Filling her head and her heart as much as he filled her femininity. Filling her. All of her.

Tightening her hold on his neck, squeezing her fingers tightly against his, Merry closed her eyes and sank into the saturating pleasure.

Giovanni had never known sensation like this…there in every cell of his body, enflaming him. Every slow thrust inside her threatened release but he fought against it, needing to savour every incredible moment. He wanted it to last for ever, for the last place he would be on this earth to be here, in the tight—*Dio*, he'd never known it could be so tight—velvet heart of Merry, and for the last sound he heard to be the breathy sighs falling from her lips.

Passion heightened the colour on her cheeks. Her sighs deepened as she rocked into him until her breaths shortened and quickened, then her legs wrapped tightly around his waist, her mouth pressed into his neck and he felt her thicken around him. The sensations that erupted through him as he was pulled deeper inside her were too much, and his release burst out of him like a pent-up tsunami as she clung to him, shuddering violently with soft mews of pleasure while he finally let go and drowned in the wave engulfing them both.

CHAPTER NINE

IT TOOK A long time for Merry to float back to earth. Even then, she was too dazed for her thoughts to do more than form cloud-like in her mind. She was still clinging to Giovanni. Their hands were still clasped. That was the delicious weight of his body slumped on top of her, his ragged heart beating against her skin and his mouth breathing so heavily into her neck. He was still inside her…

The magnitude of what she'd just done slammed into her like a bucket of ice.

'Giovanni?' she whispered, trying not to panic.

'Si?' he answered, voice muffled.

'Did you…did we…use protection?'

His head turned slowly and he lifted himself to look at her. His eyes were wide and horror-struck and gave her the answer in an instant.

He gave a short shake of his head and swallowed. 'Are you…?'

She gave her own frightened shake of the head.

Giovanni closed his eyes and muttered a curse under his breath, and a louder curse in his head. How could he have not used protection? What had he been *thinking*? The answer was obvious. He hadn't been thinking. He'd been doing the thing he'd sworn never to do again and feeling.

He forced himself to think now, even as he gently pulled out of her and shifted over, so his weight no longer squashed her, even as a wave of wonder engulfed him at what he'd just found in her arms.

It had been the most incredible experience of his life, too incredible for him to castigate himself for allowing it to happen. The desire between them had taken a life of its own. But he could castigate himself for not using protection. For that failure there was no excuse.

Pulling the bedsheets over them, and resting his head next to hers so he could gaze at her, he stroked her hair and said, 'Where are you in lady times?'

He was surprised to see her blush.

'Are you talking about my…er…?'

'Period?' he supplied.

She nodded, the blush deepening. 'It's due in a couple of days.'

He breathed a little easier. 'Then we should be okay.'

She didn't look convinced. 'Really?'

'I have two big sisters who thought it their duty to teach me in horrible detail how women's bodies work.'

They'd both been evilly determined about it and, as much as it had grossed him out when he'd been younger, it meant that as an adult he was comfortable and familiar with this kind of conversation. Merry, he could see, was not.

'We will play safe and check with Dr Internet, okay?' He grimaced. This was a problem he'd never encountered before, and he cursed himself again for his slip into insanity.

Giovanni had slept with countless women over the years and always been scrupulous about protection. He was one hundred per cent confident there were no mini Giovanni Cannavaros roaming around anywhere, and until a few minutes ago had been one hundred per cent confident there never would be.

Something told him this would not be an appropriate

topic for discussion with the woman staring at him with eyes begging for reassurance.

He kissed the tip of her cute little nose. 'No need to worry. We will make sure it is all okay…okay?'

She nodded and gave a tentative smile.

'Why do you not use protection?' he asked curiously, slowly dragging his fingers from her hair to graze them over her cheek. 'You are such a sensible—'

His words were cut off at the look she gave him. It was one of the strangest he'd ever been on the receiving end of, and suddenly he got it.

If he hadn't been so lost in the moment they'd just shared he'd have got it straight away.

Heart pounding, he raised his head to look at her more clearly. 'Was I your first?'

Her lips pulled in together and she nodded.

He rubbed his mouth, gazing at her blushing face. 'You were a virgin?'

'*Yes,*' she hissed.

'How?'

'How do you think?'

'But what about Santos?'

'Who?'

'Your lover. The man waiting in your cabin for you.'

She blinked. 'Oh, you mean Santa.'

'Santa? What name is Santa?'

'My best friend's name. She lives next door to me in England. She's flying over tomorrow to stay with me for two weeks.'

Giovanni laid his head down and rolled onto his back, trying not to allow the strange burst of emotions playing out inside him show on his face.

Damn it all to hell. He wouldn't have made love to Merry if he'd thought for even a second that she was a virgin.

He acknowledged to himself grimly that it was only

when he'd imagined her having lovers beating a path to her door that he'd started seeing her as a sexual being. He'd hidden it from himself up to that point. Refused to acknowledge that he was attracted to her. Lied to himself.

He supposed this was a punishment for making assumptions about her lovers. There were no lovers. There was her brother and her female best friend.

Had he made assumptions because he'd needed, even then, to excuse his own behaviour in desiring her?

But why had she waited? Twenty-two was pretty old to be a virgin.

Although he'd not been much younger his first time.

Monica had been deeply religious and had wanted them to wait until they were married. He'd been deeply in love with her and content to wait until she deemed them ready. He'd been twenty-one when she died. An inexperienced virgin.

His arrival at Hotel Haensli, where no one knew about his devastation, had suddenly found him on the receiving end of female attention. His looks and single status had attracted women like a magnet, and once his virginity had been taken care of, courtesy of a rich, older woman who'd seduced him in her hotel room, there had been no stopping him.

But he was always careful with the lovers he chose, preferring older, divorced women who wanted to use him for his body as much as he wanted to use them for theirs. The single women he bedded he chose with even greater care, preferring narcissistic ones who were too attached to themselves to form an attachment to him. Never virgins.

Had Merry been waiting for the 'right' man? *Dio*, he hoped not, hoped like hell she didn't have romantic notions about a future with him.

'Are you okay?' she whispered cautiously.

He took a deep breath and slipped an arm around her,

pulling her to him so her cheek rested on his chest. Whatever the reasons for his assumptions, they were on him, not her, and she didn't deserve for him to take his inner turmoil out on her.

The feel of her soft, warm body pressed against his miraculously soothed him. Hardly any time had passed since they'd made love and yet, despite all the shocks that had filled that limited time, his body stirred at their physical closeness.

'Just thinking,' he said, although he had no intention of telling her his thoughts. 'You have a best friend called Santa? And your name is Merry? It is strange you both have Christmas names.'

'Well, neither of us have, not really. Santa's real name is Santina but I always knew her as Santa. When we were little, I thought Santa was her real name and was really jealous and wanted a Christmas name too. I actually squealed when my mum pointed out that Meredith could be shortened to Merry. After that, I refused to answer unless people called me Merry.'

The tightness in his chest had loosened considerably at her melodious words. Her voice was as soothing as the closeness of her body…even if that closeness was rekindling flames not long spent.

'How old were you?'

She shuffled up and lifted her head. 'Six or seven.'

He smiled to imagine it, but then caught the narrowing of her eyes. 'What?' he asked.

'How did you know about Santa? I don't remember mentioning her to you.'

'I earwig when you called Katja the other day.'

The other day? Merry thought in wonder. The last few days had passed on turbo charge, and now, having shared what they'd just shared, 'the other day' felt like it belonged to someone else.

She grinned at his shameless admission. She couldn't believe she was *smiling*. Shouldn't she be angry with herself and frightened at the possible consequences?

She refused to be angry. She'd made her choice. Passion had trumped sanity and it had been too glorious for regrets. As for the possible consequences, Giovanni's practical attitude had eased her panic before it took full hold. In the security of his arms, and with her mind a little clearer, she was now certain she was far too late in her cycle for conception to take place. She was as regular as clockwork and always knew when she was ovulating—thank you, tender breasts—which had been two weeks ago.

As all these thoughts ran through her mind, she noticed the tightening of Giovanni's features. A stab of anxiety plunged through her. She'd been so busy dissecting her own lack of regrets that she'd not thought about his.

Giovanni hadn't wanted this to happen.

'Are you sure you're okay?' she asked.

Mouth curving a little, he swept his whole hand over her cheek. 'I am sure.'

She gazed into his eyes. Her chest filled with so much emotion it almost choked her. She needed to get ready for work, but the thought of leaving this warm bed and the warmth of Giovanni's arms made her want to wail.

He stared right back at her. Slowly, the tightness of his features softened. His throat moved, eyes darkening and pulsing. Another sensation began to fill her...

Suddenly breathless, Merry swallowed, frantically reminding herself that she had a job to do, and attempted to disentangle herself from his arms. As her hand brushed over his stomach it thumped against something huge and hard.

'I...' She swallowed again, clenching her hand into a fist so she could fight the temptation to take hold of it. She could scarcely believe such pulsating heat could be coursing through her veins so soon. 'I should shower.'

He raised his face closer to her. 'Should you?' he whispered huskily.

'I've got to work.'

He'd flipped her on her back before she could take a breath. His lips grazed against hers. 'Who is the boss?'

Her insides melted. 'You.'

He kissed her. 'And who is the underling?'

'Me...' she breathed into his mouth.

'If the boss orders the underling to be late...?'

She wrapped her legs around his waist and arched into him. 'Then the underling must obey.'

The Meravaro Odyssey sat in the Viennese train station steadily turning white under the falling snow. Giovanni finished reading through his emails, then checked the time.

The passengers had long since disembarked and gone off in the chauffeured cars taking them to one of Vienna's most beautiful palaces, where they would be enjoying a private, luxury indoor Christmas market, with items for sale including Fabergé eggs, followed by an exquisite seven-course meal that he would join them for.

If he wanted to make it to the palace in time for the meal he would have to leave soon. Time to call a management meeting.

With no passengers to take care of, the management team arrived promptly.

After reiterating, again, the importance of that evening's party, he double checked that everyone was prepared and that no issues were unresolved. This party would be the voyage's highlight, a glamorous festive delight as the Odyssey made its steady way into the Austrian Alps. If it didn't make the passengers feel festive, then nothing would.

If he could think of a way to get out of attending the

party himself, he would. He would just have to grin and bear it.

Tomorrow they would wake in Switzerland, and by lunchtime the voyage would be over. The guests would be transported by horse and carriage to Hotel Haensli for two days of luxury and skiing, before enjoying a very different, much less intimate party at the hotel.

Giovanni's own journey terminated at the Swiss train station. He would be driven to the airport and from there would fly to Miami, far from snow and anything even remotely connected to Christmas.

Until he took that flight he would keep his work head on. This was *his* train. Tonight's party was *his* function. And if it went badly, it was *his* reputation that would take the hit.

It would not go badly. Not with Merry acting the role of hostess alongside him.

As the meeting went on, he found himself struggling not to address everything to her. Whenever their eyes met her dimples would pop in an adorable mix of knowing and shyness, before she hastily looked to the ground. Even with her eyes hidden behind the huge frames of the glasses she'd put on before leaving his suite, he saw them. Saw the soft baby blue properly. They shone brightly enough to eliminate the need for sunlight.

How had he been so blind as not to see those eyes clearly before?

He was glad she wasn't standing close to him. Since she'd left his suite, freshly showered in a cloud of soft fruity scent, he'd been unable to get her out of his head. His loins kept stirring as images of the sensory pleasure they'd shared sprang unbidden into his mind, as did the discovery of her virginity. The more he thought about the latter, the more it troubled him. It was a subject he was in no hurry to broach.

He wouldn't broach it at all, he decided, after their eyes had locked again and the thumps in his heart had deepened. It was a topic that would only lead to the exchange of more confidences. He didn't want Merry getting the wrong idea that what they'd shared would lead to anything after they left this train. He wanted her to work for him, knew she could be a real asset to his company, and had a couple of roles in mind that would suit her all-round talents perfectly. But that would be the extent of any future between them.

They had one more night together, and he wasn't deluded enough to think they could share the suite without anything happening. *Dio*, just standing here, surrounded by staff as they were, he could taste the chemistry swirling between them.

One more night of perfect sex and then they would part company on good terms, with Merry's future as a member of Cannavaro Travel sewn up. He would make no promises, nor even allude to this…*thing*…continuing.

When the meeting was over the management team filed out of the carriage…all except for Merry.

'Everything okay, lady?' he asked, finally allowing his eyes to luxuriate in a long sweep over her beautiful body.

A shy blush coloured her cheeks. Idly, he considered dragging her back to the suite, locking the door and spending the rest of the day devouring her again…

He firmly pushed the thought away. It was one thing to make love at night. The fact that he was even tempted to scrap his visit to the palace set an alarm ringing in his head. Not only were the passengers of the Meravaro Odyssey attending the dinner, but many of Austria's most illustrious people, whom he intended to court for his business.

The mere thought of making love to her again, though, made his loins burn.

The lips he'd devoured such a short time ago pulled together before she said, 'I just came to say goodbye. I've got to meet the company delivering the decorations for tonight's party.'

'You are not going to the Christmas market?' Some of the staff were taking advantage of the passenger-free day and, providing their duties were taken care of, taking the shuttles he'd provided for them to Vienna's vast number of famed Christmas markets.

'I won't have time. There's too much to sort out for tonight.'

'You have a few hours, surely?'

'Not really. I love Christmas markets, so going there would probably distract me, and I'd lose track of time and then you'd have to send a search party out for me.'

'Is a shame for you to miss it.' Merry obviously adored Christmas.

She shrugged. 'There will be other Christmas markets.'

'You have a good attitude.'

And the most fantastic body...

The navy dress she wore was stylishly respectable, falling to just above her knees, not revealing an inch of excess flesh, but the silk moved fluidly against her skin, subtly showcasing her soft contours.

Dio, he was getting hard just looking at her.

'I try,' she said, with a smile that filled his head anew with remembrances of all the erotic delights they'd shared and sent another hot spear of lust firing through his loins. 'Anyway...'

Her voice trailed off and her eyes darkened as if she'd read the direction of his thoughts.

He took a step towards her. 'You need to go?' he supplied in a husky murmur.

She nodded and took a half-hearted step back. Her chest was rising and falling rapidly, eyes pulsing.

Fully hard, and with his own breaths shortening, he took another step closer. 'You should go now.'

Her chin lifted. He recognised the colour heightening her cheeks. It was the colour of her desire...

'Should I?'

Giovanni had her pinned to the wall in a hot, passionate kiss before he was fully aware of it.

If Merry's response hadn't been so wantonly immediate and so immediately intoxicating it might have ended there, before he hitched her dress up to her waist and before her greedy hands could undo his trousers.

He only just found enough sense to stretch an arm out to lock the door before lifting her up and yanking her underwear and tights down. Merry impatiently kicked them off with her shoes, and he thrust deep inside her. Legs wrapped tightly around his waist, arms wrapped tightly around his neck, and her gasps and moans of pleasure fired his desire until the moment he felt her thicken around him. Burying his mouth in her hair to smother his groan, his climax burst free in long, glorious shudders.

Merry's soft giggle into his neck brought him back to the present, and Giovanni suddenly realised where they were.

He blinked a number of times to clear his dazed head. That had never happened before. Losing control like that.

She lifted her face from his neck. One look at her kiss-bruised lips and pleasure-saturated cheeks was enough to douse the kernel of disquiet at his out-of-character behaviour.

At some point her glasses her fallen off. Gently dropping her back to her feet, he smothered his own bubble of laughter at the heady absurdity of what they'd just shared by kissing her again.

Working quickly, they rearranged their clothing.

To his disappointment, she redid her bun—the strands

that had come free were wantonly adorable—and said, 'If I'm late it's your fault.'

'No, is *your* fault for being so sexy.' Then he strode to the door and dropped her a wink. '*Ciao*, sexy lady.'

Merry unpacked the boxes piled carefully and examined the contents. These were gold decorations specifically for tonight's party, ordered long before she'd been shoehorned into working here. There were black and white photos of old Hollywood icons in their heyday set in gilded frames, and a host of other adornments she would supervise the placement of.

As hard as she tried to concentrate on ticking the items off her list and passing them on to the staff designated to help, her thoughts never strayed far from Giovanni.

She'd never imagined he would be such a tender lover. It made her go all squidgy inside to remember how wonderful it had been. How beautiful it had been.

Her body still hummed from that sudden burst of passion that had exploded between them in the staff carriage. She hugged it to her like a delicious secret.

She sliced open another box, then put down the knife she was using and closed her eyes as another wave of memories of the night they'd shared washed through her.

Maybe if it had been rubbish, like everyone said the first time usually was, she wouldn't be feeling so melancholic. Wouldn't be hoping—however foolishly—that when the Meravaro Odyssey terminated in Switzerland, it wouldn't be the termination of *them*.

Giovanni gritted his teeth and forced a smile at the King of Monte Cleure's latest offensive opinion. He had definitely annoyed the Fates to be stuck next to this oaf.

Everything had been going so well. He should be in excellent spirits. He'd timed his arrival at the palace perfectly. He'd been escorted through the great halls just as his passengers and the other guests were being led into the banquet room, meaning he'd missed the private Christmas market the rest had been treated to.

Despite this, his mood was as dark as if he'd been forced to spend a week submerged in saccharine Christmas sweetness. Darkness always shrouded him like a cloud in the Christmas season. There was nothing sweet about any of it to him.

And, *Dio*, he was bored out of his skull. He should have brought Merry with him. At least he would have something to feast his eyes on. At least she knew how to have a conversation about something other than money.

He wondered what she would be like if she earned herself a fortune. Would it change her like it changed so many others? Like it had changed him…?

No, he dismissed. His fortune hadn't changed him. Monica's death had. He didn't suffer fools not because he was rich, but because life was too short to bother dealing with them.

Mercifully, the final course was cleared away and everyone rose to circulate. The Ambassador in attendance made a beeline to talk to him. Despite it being a conversation that could be lucrative to Giovanni's business, he found his mind wandering. Back to Merry.

How was she getting on? He'd checked his phone a few times but she'd not messaged him, so he'd assumed there either weren't any problems with the party preparations or she was dealing with them. To be sure, he'd thought it prudent to call her. Those had been purely business calls. Both times she'd assured him that all was well.

He considered calling her again, then thought better of it. He would hate her to get the wrong idea and think he was calling so often because he wanted to hear her voice play in his ears. That would be ludicrous. This function would be over soon, and then Giovanni and his passengers would return to the Meravaro Odyssey in good time to get ready for the evening's party and the second and final leg of their voyage.

There was no need to call her again. No need at all.

CHAPTER TEN

MERRY STARED AT her reflection. Other than her bare arms, Katja's dress showed little in the way of flesh. The neckline wrapped around her throat choker-style, the silver lace clung to the waist and then splayed out to the ankles. It was easily the most beautiful and glamorous item of clothing she'd ever worn. And the most sensuous.

She was glad she hadn't taken it out of its wrapping sooner. Only a few days ago, wearing something as sensuous as this would have frightened the life out of her. Merry chose clothes for comfort or for their ability to make her smile. Safe clothes. An outward projection of the safety she craved.

She wrinkled her nose at the rest of her appearance. Her glasses looked totally out of place with the outfit, as did her usual bun.

Her bun, she now saw, wasn't just a convenient style to maintain and keep the hair out of her eyes but another safety mechanism. When she'd been a little girl her hair had been much lighter, almost white. Every night before bed her mother would brush it with long and steady gentle strokes, and tell Merry what beautiful hair she had, 'Like a fairy.'

Her mother had scolded her when necessary—she'd never taken any nonsense—but her touch had always been gentle. Always loving.

In those days Merry had always worn her hair loose. Martin had liked to pull it, she remembered. She would clout him back. But never tie it up. She'd been proud of her hair. Her mother had instilled that pride in her, not just with her hair but with everything.

Having to wear glasses… 'They make you look as clever as you are,' her mum had said.

Her early terror of swimming… She thought that might have had something to do with Martin pushing her in the deep end of a pool when she'd been a toddler. She'd been wearing armbands, but fear had rooted in her, and when she'd been taken to her first swimming lesson she'd screamed her head off rather than get in the pool. But her mum's unwavering belief that Merry did have the courage to do it had infused her, and she'd soon pushed through the fear and learned to swim.

A year later her mother had died. Merry had rarely worn her hair loose since.

She hadn't worn it loose at all since moving to Switzerland.

Her mother's death hadn't just shattered the family, but ripped Merry's safety net from her. She'd been adrift and seeking safety ever since, and it terrified her to remember the feeling of safety she'd experienced in Giovanni's arms.

But, as terrifying and irrational as it was, it had been real. That feeling of safety. He'd made her feel beautiful and special too. He'd made her feel so much.

She wasn't gullible enough to expect anything more than what they were sharing here on this voyage. She'd made her peace with that before they'd made love. But Giovanni had unwittingly pushed her out of the rigid safety zone she'd imposed on herself. Now it was time for her to push herself a little further too.

Each suite on the Meravaro Odyssey had its own top-of-the-range hairstyling products. The onboard hairdressers and beauticians wouldn't be able to fit her in, even if it was appropriate for her to ask, which it definitely wasn't, but she could work on herself.

Working quickly, she heated the curlers and let her hair loose, then found an online tutorial to follow. After twenty minutes of fiddling she was pleased with the result, and turned her attention to rooting through her suitcase for the contact lenses she'd thrown into it at the last minute. As a rule, she preferred wearing glasses, as she never found contacts particularly comfortable to wear, but on this occasion…to hell with comfort! This would be her last night here, so it would be sacrilege not to make the most of it.

She'd just finished applying mascara from a three-year-old wand and a layer of equally old coral lipstick when the suite door opened.

Her heart leapt with joy.

She'd only seen Giovanni to exchange a secret smile with him since his return from the palace an hour ago. As she was the official party hostess that night she needed to be ready to welcome the guests, and so had taken herself off to the suite while Giovanni was having his ear chewed off by a tipsy media mogul.

'What a nightmare that man…'

Giovanni's complaint about the King of Monte Cleure, who had sought Giovanni out again as he'd made his way down the sleeping carriages to his suite, was forgotten as his eyes locked on Merry.

He swallowed hard, trying to clear airwaves that had closed in on themselves. His heart bashed in thumping pulses through his chest.

His determination to play it cool with her was as forgotten as his complaint.

'*Sei bellissima…*' he breathed.

He didn't think he'd ever seen anything more beautiful. He'd only seen Merry's face naked with the curtains drawn and the suite dusky, only seen her hair loose after being slept on. What she'd done to her hair…gathering it all together into giant ringlets swept over her right shoulder, the colour like spun gold…

A blush spread over her cheeks as slowly as the smile forming on her lips. 'You were saying?' she prompted, feigning a nonchalance that didn't fool him for a second. The breathless quality of her words was the giveaway.

His legs carried him to her as if being drawn by a magnet. He cupped her neck gently, being careful not to mess up her hair. It was the first time he'd touched her since they'd said goodbye after that burst of passion in the staff carriage that morning, and it sent a charge racing through him to feel her quiver.

'Only that the King of Monte Cleure is buffoon.'

She gazed up at him. 'Nothing new there, then. How was the palace?'

'Boring.'

But the darkness that had cloaked him there had lifted at an astounding speed, and suddenly it came to him that he hadn't experienced any of his usual gloom on the Odyssey itself since its departure. Whether that was because he'd spent the journey concentrating on not concentrating on Merry, or if it was something more intricately linked to her, he couldn't say. All he knew for certain was that he didn't have to hide the December Darkness with her. Because with her, the darkness didn't exist.

'Poor you,' she teased.

'*Si*. Poor me. Would have been more fun to feast on you…' He slowly dragged his fingers down to the tiny diamond-shaped exposure of skin just below the base of her throat. 'I could eat you whole.'

Her eyes widened. He might have been as good as his word if there hadn't been a sharp rap on the door.

He loved it that her eyes squeezed shut in obvious disappointment.

Unable to resist, he bent his head and brushed a kiss into her neck before stepping away from her.

'Come,' he called.

It was Francois. He needed Merry.

Not as much as I need her, Giovanni thought, as he watched her attempt to slip her feet into high heels. It took her a few goes but she got there, holding onto the wall for support. Then she visibly pulled herself together, threw him a rueful smile over her shoulder, and left the suite.

Giovanni took a moment to gather himself too, before stripping his clothes and taking a shower.

Physically need. That was what his unbidden thought had meant. That was all he needed her for. To slake this physical ache in his loins. An ache that had only formed because of their proximity to each other.

Dressing in his tuxedo, he quickly styled his hair and laced his buffed brogues. One final look in the mirror to satisfy himself that he looked presentable, and a glance out of the window at the falling snow they were travelling through, and then he left the suite, ready for the party that would make or break this entire voyage.

As he made his way towards the lounge and bar carriages where the party was being hosted he passed through the onboard gift shop. He'd just made it through the doors to the next carriage when his feet came to an abrupt stop and his body turned itself around.

'Is everything ready?' Giovanni asked Merry when he joined her in the first bar, where she was helping to pour champagne into flutes for the waiting staff to circulate.

To his trained eye, everything looked perfect. The party carriages had been adorned with gold tinsel and other decorations, and adornments that glittered with the exact Hollywood vibe he'd specified. In the second lounge the pianist had already started playing jazzed-up Christmas carols.

When the Meravaro Odyssey made its other voyages, the parties on it would be exactly like this but without the Christmas theme. It had to go well. Knowing the biggest danger for failure was dissatisfied guests, he had every confidence it would be a success. How could it fail with Merry as the chief hostess?

'As ready as we'll ever be,' she answered with a smile. 'What do you think? Happy with it all?'

'Is perfect,' he admitted.

He'd dreaded this party. He'd imagined himself having to give his practised fake smiles and make forced conversation and spend the evening counting the minutes until the guests all retired to their suites.

Now, he surprised himself by feeling something that felt a lot like excitement.

Her eyes sparkled. 'Good!'

He waited until she'd finished pouring from the champagne bottle she was holding before leaning in to speak in her ear. 'Come with me.'

Dio, the urge to take hold of her hand was strong.

This was not a date for heaven's sake. This was an official function. What he was about to give her was only an adornment for the costume she was wearing in her role as hostess, no different from the clothing he'd bought her, which she wore to do her job.

Why he felt the need to give it to her privately was a question he stubbornly ignored.

'I have something for you.'

'Oh?'

He reached into his back pocket, pulled out the square velvet black box and thrust it in her hand.

A furrow formed in her brow.

'Open it,' he ordered.

Merry stared at the contents and gasped. Nestled within the box was a pair of pear-shaped diamond earrings.

'These are for me?' she asked in disbelief.

She was no jewellery expert—the only item of value she had was her mother's engagement ring, which she kept in her Swiss cabin's safe—but even she could see the extravagant quality of them.

'To go with your dress,' he confirmed. 'Our guests expect you to look the part, remember?'

She could almost feel herself salivating over them, so it was with real reluctance that she closed the lid of the box with the initials of the Meravaro Odyssey set in an elaborate flourish on it, and handed the box back to him.

'They're beautiful but I can't wear them, Giovanni. You can't return worn earrings. It's not hygienic.'

He ignored the box and folded his arms. 'You will keep them.'

'I can't,' she refuted, aghast. 'They must have cost a fortune!'

'*Si*, but is *my* fortune, so not a problem. Is a gift.'

A gift wrapped up as a work adornment…

The expansion of her heart filled her throat and she had to swallow hard to speak. 'Thank you.'

He winked. 'Is nothing, lady. Now, put them on—our guests are arriving.'

Giovanni left Merry to put the earrings on, and as he walked back into the bar swiped a flute of champagne and downed it in one swallow.

Why the hell had he told her the earrings were a gift? Of course she was right that they couldn't be returned once worn, but he hadn't needed to say that when he'd already explained his reasons for giving them to her.

He caught her sashaying into the room, a welcoming smile on her face as she headed straight to the nearest guests. For one brief moment their eyes met. A bolt of desire shot through him. *Dio*, he wanted her so badly...

He smiled, his sudden burst of self-recrimination gone. He had to stop overthinking things. So what if he'd told her the earrings were a gift? It had been a slip of the tongue; nothing to beat himself up about.

They had one more night together. He intended to enjoy every minute of it.

Merry enjoyed the party hugely. It helped that the guests had all had a marvellous time at the palace and returned to the Odyssey slightly tipsy and ready to party. As a result they were in excellent spirits, even the ghastly King.

It amazed her how a glitzy dress could make an ordinary-looking woman beautiful and a tuxedo make an average man handsome.

None of the men were a patch on Giovanni. His gorgeous looks outshone everyone.

She touched the earrings again. She still couldn't get over him giving them to her.

Their respective roles as hosts meant they spent little time together that evening, but their gazes were never far from each other. Somehow they both seemed to gravitate to the same carriage. Whenever they passed each other their fingers would stretch out to brush the other's. It never failed to send a thrill of electricity through her skin.

The carriage that had been turned into a nightclub pulsed with bodies dancing. A deep ache to be enfolded in Giovanni's arms in an intimate dance ran through her... and then all her nerves tingled as she turned her head to find him standing beside her.

'Enjoying the party, sexy lady?' he asked in an undertone.

'I'd enjoy it more if I could dance with you,' she said boldly, before fluttering her eyelashes. 'But dancing on duty is not appropriate for underlings.'

His eyes shone with lust and amusement, and he dipped his head to speak into her ear. 'It is appropriate if your boss says so.'

She shivered at the feel of his breath, thrillingly warm against her skin.

His tongue darted out to lick her earlobe. 'But not appropriate for the boss to ravish the underling in front of guests because the boss cannot control his desire.'

Her legs weakened with longing. Instinctively, she grabbed his tuxedo jacket and fisted it.

'Soon, lady, we can both lose control.'

His teeth nipped the rim of her ear and then, with a smile full of sensuality, he moved away from her to talk to an approaching guest, leaving Merry with jellified legs and a pelvis that throbbed so deeply it was its own kind of heady rush.

Somehow she managed to pull herself together enough to do her job, but the time that had been passing at an even pace suddenly slowed, every minute until she could be in Giovanni's arms again dragging interminably.

Finally, the midnight hour approached, and so did Giovanni, weaving his way to her carrying two flutes of champagne.

'For you.' His eyes gleamed. 'You are now off duty, Underling.'

'Whatever you say, Boss,' she murmured.

Their fingers brushed as she took the flute from him. Their eyes locked again.

He put a hand on her hip and whispered into her ear, 'You have been magnificent tonight. All guests have had a fantastic time. No problems at all. Unheard of.'

Delicious shivers laced her spine, both from his words and from the fresh effect of his breath blowing warm against her skin. Before she could unfreeze her brain enough to respond, he added, 'You *must* work for me. Name your price.'

She tilted her head to meet his stare.

His deep blue eyes bored into hers. 'I will have you, lady.'

She sucked in a breath as a swirl of heat loosened in her abdomen and thanked God the guests were too busy laughing and singing to take any notice of her. The pianist had spent the past hour taking requests, which had turned into an upper-class version of Christmas karaoke. To see the glossily immaculate head of a luxury make-up brand singing along at the top of her lungs to 'Winter Wonderland' was a sight—and sound—Merry would never forget.

She wouldn't forget *any* of it. Whatever happened between her and Giovanni in the future, the memories of her time on the Meravaro Odyssey would stay with her for ever.

Eyes sparkling with the same intensity as the champagne in his hand, he tipped the golden liquid down his throat and indicated for her to do the same.

Done, he inclined his head to the door and set off towards it, swiping two more glasses of champagne for them as he went.

Exquisite anticipation rampaging through her, Merry followed him the length of the train. 'Where are we going?' she asked when he carried on past their suite.

He turned his head and gave a secretive smile. 'I have surprise for you.'

Only when he reached the final carriage, the secret carriage known only to the most elite of their elite guests, did he stop walking. He passed a flute of champagne to her, then opened the door.

She stepped inside and gasped.

The viewing carriage differed from all the others, being almost entirely constructed from glass, giving an almost complete panoramic view. She'd been in it only once, during the train inspection, when the view had been the Parisian station. That view hadn't made her gasp.

'You like?' Giovanni murmured, pressing his solid form into her back and slipping an arm around her waist.

She sighed with pleasure and leaned into him. 'It's the most beautiful sight I have ever seen.'

They must have just ridden through an Alpine town as the rear view showed it in the distance, illuminated by the night sky. To their left a lake surrounded by thick trees rippled. To their right were the Alps in all their glory. Best of all, snow was falling upon it all.

It was the most magical of dreamscapes. Christmas brought to life. All it needed was for Father Christmas to ride his sleigh over the town and the dreamscape would be complete.

Giovanni rubbed his nose into her silky hair, thinking *she* was the most beautiful sight he'd ever seen. 'I knew it would please you.'

It had been while arranging the earrings for Merry that he'd remembered the shop manager had previously worked on a train line that travelled across Bavaria and asked him to recommend a specific location that would delight a winter-lover in the viewing carriage. This location had been the answer.

A quick chat with the driver about timings, followed by a notice to all staff that guests must be refused entry into the carriage in the hour up to midnight, and it had been done.

'You have not had a chance to enjoy any of the views,' he explained, tightening his hold around her.

'That's because I've been working.'

'Working hard. No complaints.' Even though she'd been unable to attend the Christmas market that would have given her much joy.

A long time passed while she said nothing, just leaned into his strength and enjoyed a view even Giovanni could appreciate would seem magical to her.

Then she had a drink of her champagne and tilted her head back to look at him with a dreamy smile. 'Thank you.'

'My pleasure.' He cupped a plump breast and pressed his arousal into her lower back. 'Let me know when you are ready to go to bed,' he murmured sensually.

She turned and wound an arm around his neck. Her baby blue eyes were dense with desire. 'I'm ready now.'

CHAPTER ELEVEN

GIOVANNI LOCKED THE suite door and gazed at the woman whose beauty stole his breath.

'Why do you always hide your hair?' he murmured as he dragged his fingers through the silky strands, delighting at her shiver.

'I don't hide it.'

'Liar.' He smothered her protest with a kiss. 'Your hair is beautiful. *You* are beautiful.'

Her arms wound around his neck, her lips parted, and she was kissing him back with an uncontained hunger that matched his own, her tongue sliding into his mouth to infuse his senses with a sweet taste uniquely Merry.

He found the hidden clasp in the material of her dress around her neck and undid it. Immediately it fell down, exposing her naked breasts.

Dropping to his knees, he took one in his mouth, and then the other, his hand sliding around her back to tug the zipper of her dress and bring it tumbling to her feet.

He pressed his mouth to her smooth, adorably rounded belly and looked up at her. *'Sei bellissima.'*

Her shoulders rose in a slow inhale before they fell again and she reached a hand to run her fingers through his hair.

Her touch was electrifying.

Rising back to his feet, he was about to lift her into his arms when her fingers went to his bow tie. Eyes holding his with a look as wantonly electrifying as her touch, she stripped him slowly, peeling the jacket from his arms, unbuttoning the shirt and then sliding that off him too.

She stared at his bare chest, then back at his face. He didn't think he'd ever seen such unashamed hunger before. Hunger for him. It filled him with...

He didn't know the word in any language. Whatever it was, it made every vein in his body pump thickly and every cell strain and pulse for her. When she pressed her lips to his nipple he could do nothing to stop the groan escaping his mouth.

When she kissed his other nipple, and then slowly kissed and licked her way down his abdomen, he felt like he was on fire. The first time he was conscious of her undoing his trousers was when she tentatively took hold of his excitement and pulled him free, and the inferno that charged through him almost knocked him off his feet.

He really was magnificent, Merry thought dreamily as she tugged Giovanni's trousers and underwear down to his ankles. Perfect. Perfectly toned chest with dark hair that lightly covered his chest and thickened as it met his perfectly hard abdomen. Perfectly muscular thighs. Perfect arms.

He made her wish she could paint portraits and commit every inch of his perfection to canvas.

On her knees before him, she took his perfectly huge, smooth excitement into her hand for the second time. It throbbed at her touch. The rush of power that filled her blood was dizzying.

This perfect, magnificent man wanted her just as much as she wanted him.

She didn't hesitate to take him into her mouth. The need to give him pleasure overrode any shyness she might have expected to feel at performing such an act for the first time.

Giovanni's low groans and the fist he made in her hair told her she was doing it right.

She ran her tongue the length of him. Felt him root his feet more firmly to the floor. After encircling the head with her tongue, she enveloped it with her lips and gripped the base with her hand, then slid her other hand around him to clasp a tight, perfect buttock.

'Ahh…' He rocked into her, just a little deeper.

Sticky heat bubbled like a cauldron deep in her femininity at the pleasure she was so clearly giving him and, emboldened, she began to slide her mouth up and down the length.

'*Dio*…' Giovanni groaned, tightening his fist of her hair, fingers scraping into her head. '*Dio*. Merry…'

He had never felt *anything* like this.

Merry's soft, greedy moans as she made love to him with her mouth only fuelled the inferno. But, much as he wanted to climax, he wanted to bury himself deep inside her tight heat and feel her orgasm thicken around him more, and so, having to use all the strength he possessed, he pulled away from her and hauled her into his arms.

In three quick strides he had her on the bed, and then he was parting her legs and raising her thighs, and then, finally, deliciously, he plunged inside her.

Her legs wrapped around his waist and she grabbed his buttocks to pull him deeper, biting into his neck, moaning her pleasure.

In and out he thrust, deeper and harder into her velvet heat, tighter the fingers on his buttocks, louder the moans in his ear that turned into pleas as she urged him on, begging him until her words became breaths that shortened and she let out one last, everlasting cry as she thickened around him and her spasms pushed him over the edge and, with a drawn-out cry of his own, he thrust into her one final, glorious time.

* * *

Giovanni's heart beat so hard and so fast he feared it would burst its way through his ribcage. He'd never known an experience like it. Nothing had come close. Nothing. Not ever.

Dio, he could stay here, in this moment, for ever…

What in *hell*?

'You okay?' she asked softly.

Was she a mind-reader?

'I'm great,' he lied, rolling off her and pulling her with him.

After they'd slept together that morning, he'd put the unusually high dose of euphoria down to the days of pent-up, suppressed desire he'd put himself through. He'd told himself the same thing after their burst of passion in the carriage.

Sex should be a nice physical exchange that left you feeling happy and sated. The euphoria should last a short period, after which you'd put your clothes back on—or the lady in question would put *her* clothes back on—and you'd bid each other goodbye.

There was little in the way of euphoria thrashing through him right then. The beats of his heart were too weighty. The sensations still vibrating through his skin and veins too…*present*. Too real.

Too much.

Far too much.

It was just sex, he reminded himself, dropping a kiss into her hair. Sex with a woman he happened to find excellent company. These feelings would pass, he assured himself.

A sharp rap on the door interrupted his thoughts.

He sat up sharply. 'Who is it?'

'Francois,' came the muffled reply.

Cursing, he swung his legs off the bed. 'One minute,' he called.

Merry raised her head so she could admire Giovanni's perfect naked form as he strode across the suite to the bathroom.

What they'd just shared had been perfect. Wanton. Hedonistic. Liberating. The connection between them had blown her mind as much as the lovemaking had.

Her vision of perfection was hindered by Giovanni shrugging his arms into a robe and tying the sash tightly before answering the door.

She wriggled under the sheets and hoped Francois wouldn't notice the other bed hadn't been used.

Their voices were too low and she was buried too deeply under the covers for Merry to hear, but Giovanni's tone was enough for her to know it was bad news.

Conversation finished, he shut the door and faced her.

No longer having to hide in embarrassment in case Francois realised she was naked, Merry sat up. 'What's wrong?'

'There's been an avalanche the other side of Innsbruck. Thirty feet of snow on the track. Means we have to stop at Innsbruck and wait. It could take a day to clear.'

The joy that burst through Merry's heart at this information was so strong and pure it left her speechless.

Giovanni looked at Merry's dumbstruck face and nodded his taut agreement. '*Si*. Is a nightmare. Our guests will not be happy.'

She smiled in sympathy. 'They'll expect you to buy a humungous bulldozer to clear it.'

'They will want me to dig with my own hands.'

'It'll be fine,' she said. 'It's not as if we're going to be stuck in the middle of nowhere. By all accounts, Innsbruck is beautiful. I'm sure we can arrange transport there for them. And also, none of them have to be anywhere specific, do they? They're all going on to the hotel. So long as they're there in good time for the party, they'll have nothing to complain about.' Her nose wrinkled. 'Okay, of course they're going to complain! But we'll have everything in hand. We've plenty of time to make sure we have transport to take us to the hotel if it seems the avalanche won't be cleared in good time. We can get the contingencies rolling.'

See, this was why he wanted her to work for him. No wasting time bemoaning the situation for Merry, just an immediate focus on finding solutions, looking ahead to potential knock-on effects and finding solutions for them too. Employing her was a certainty that had only grown. The way she'd handled the guests that night, blending in, always there if needed, never breaching the line between personal and professional with them, endlessly patient, quick-thinking... Her list of qualities was endless.

He dragged his fingers through his hair and gazed at her. He needed to touch her again. With her hair all tousled, colour high in her cheeks and lips plumper than ever, she looked ravishing.

Sliding back under the sheets, he pinned her hands above her head and feasted his eyes on her beautiful face.

An extra day and night with Merry?

Maybe he was back in the Fates' good books.

It was still dark when Merry opened her eyes. It took a few moments for her to realise the train had stopped moving. That was probably what had woken her.

Moving carefully so as not to disturb Giovanni, who was sleeping soundly, she climbed off the bed and scooped up the robe he'd worn when opening the door to Francois. She padded to the living area for a bottle of water. After drinking some, she knelt on the sofa and peeked through the curtains. Through the falling snow she could see they were at a train station. They must be at Innsbruck.

Giovanni's sleepy voice cut through the silence. 'Why are you awake?'

'I couldn't get back to sleep,' she whispered. 'Sorry for waking you.'

'It's okay. Come back to bed.'

'In a minute.'

'What are you doing?'

'Watching the snow.'

A long time passed before she heard him sit up. 'Why are you watching snow?'

'I like watching it, especially at night. The flakes seem alive.'

'You are crazy, lady.'

'So you've said. I just know the things that make me happy.'

'Watching snow makes you happy?'

'It reminds me of my mother. The winter before she died, we had so much of it. Masses! I was so little it came up to my thighs. She took me and my brother sledging, and we built the most enormous snowman. Living in the Swiss Alps…when I get up in the morning and step out onto the snow I always get a hit of that feeling of wonder and happiness I had that day. It takes me right back and I can see my mum so clearly.'

Giovanni, who'd been gazing at her silhouette, awed at how the sliver of light coming in from the curtain she was peering through had turned Merry into a silvery, shining goddess, swallowed the lump forming in his throat. 'You do not find that painful?'

She sighed and pressed her forehead to the window pane. 'It's a sweet pain. It's why I love Christmas so much, too. It keeps her alive in my heart and makes me feel closer to her. I *like* remembering the happy times, because God knows there weren't any after she'd gone.'

He felt a huge tug in his heart and lay back down. He

didn't want this conversation to continue, sensed it would lead down a path he didn't want to follow. The only path he wanted to follow with Merry involved sensory delights.

But he'd never thought of it like that before. That there could be sweetness in the pain of memories.

Squeezing his eyes shut against the memories trying to push at him, he didn't hear Merry come back to the bed until she slipped under the covers and snuggled up to him.

'What do you do at Christmas?'

He caught the hand she'd placed on his chest and wound his fingers through hers. 'I go somewhere with hot sun and cocktails and no stupid Christmas trees.'

'Do your family come with you?'

'No. They are like you. They love Christmas.'

His mother especially. Every year she would turn their living room into a huge Nativity. The feasting would go on for days, with all the traditions and religious observations catered for.

He'd loved it once too.

'They must miss you being there.'

'They used to it.' He tried not to sound defensive, unsure why he was even feeling defensive. His family understood his feelings. 'My sisters, they have husbands and children. They all get together at my parents' home. My *mamma* and sisters take over the kitchen and cook feasts for everyone.'

'I thought your sisters were feminists?'

'They are. That is why they get the men to do all the cleaning up. They make a *lot* of mess.'

She laughed softly but with a tinge of sadness. Her warm breath brushed against his chest.

'It is a big deal for them,' he said, even as he wondered why he was revealing all this to her. 'They do not want me there spoiling it, like your brother spoiled yours when you were children.'

'Martin spoiled it because he's selfish and because he

knew how much *I* wanted to celebrate it.' She hesitated before asking, 'Don't you miss being part of it?'

'I want nothing to do with it.'

Her fingers squeezed against his. 'How sad.'

'If memories hurt, why feed them?'

'I suppose there's logic in there somewhere,' she said doubtfully.

'Much logic. Is your brother's logic, *si*?' At the tilting of her chin to look at his face, he elaborated. 'Christmas reminds him of pain. He does not want pain, so he does not celebrate.'

'He could have let *me* celebrate,' she muttered. 'I wasn't allowed to do anything. I remember making paperchain decorations at school and putting them up in the kitchen. He ripped them down and stamped on them. His attitude is—*was* until he married Kelly—that if he hates Christmas then no one can celebrate. At least you let your family get on with it without spoiling it for them.'

'How old is your brother?'

'Twenty-five.'

'So he was a boy when your *mamma* die?'

Her brow furrowed.

He stroked a strand of hair off her cheek. 'I was twenty-one when Monica died. A man. I make the choice of not celebrating and let my family have fun without me. Your brother was a child. He was not able to make the choice to leave.'

'He could have made the choice not to let me suffer for it.'

'He was a child,' he repeated. 'No maturity. Your papa was the adult. What did he do about it?'

'Not a lot. He hates confrontation. Anything for a quiet life. When Martin and I were screaming at each other he'd go off to another room until we'd stopped.'

'He was like that before your *mamma* died?'

'Yes. He left all the discipline to her. I don't remember him ever telling either of us off.'

'Then your anger is at the wrong person.'

'If you mean that I should be angry with my dad rather than Martin, I can assure you I'm angry with them both.'

Her mother was the parent who had died but her father had been the ghost, Merry thought. The taciturn man had turned even more inward after his wife's death, his face mostly hidden behind a newspaper or a book, even at the dinner table, deaf to the screaming rages between his two children. Sometimes she wondered if she would recognise him or he her if they passed in the street.

'Long-term anger is not healthy.'

'Nor is using grief as a weapon,' she retorted hotly. 'Martin has tormented me my entire life and Dad has let him get away with it. As kids he picked on me, like all big brothers do, but after Mum died it stopped being just a mean big brother thing. He turned into a tyrant, on at me all the time about every little thing. Want to know why I was still a virgin?'

She didn't wait for an answer. If she had, the answer from Giovanni would have been a resounding no.

'It was because Martin policed my every move,' she explained bitterly. 'Everywhere I went, he turned up. It took me two years to realise he was tracking my phone. I had no chance of finding a boyfriend with PC Ingles threatening any boy who looked at me.'

Giovanni had no idea how this subject had started, but wished to God it would end. He didn't want to think of Merry as a bereaved daughter or a neglected daughter or a tyrannised sister. He wanted to think of her only as the clever, funny, sexy woman he was sharing a bed with for a couple of nights and as a future employee.

'Maybe he thinks he needs to be your father as your papa wouldn't be.'

Dio, he couldn't help himself. His mouth needed zipping.

'Are you making *excuses* for him? You have no idea... *none.*'

'I do not make excuses, but you said he was a normal brother before she died. I try to think of his reasons. You should too. He is your brother. Your family. Family is important.'

'Says the man who hasn't spent a Christmas with his family in twelve years?'

'I did not run away from my family.'

'But you did run away?'

'No,' he stated flatly, trying his hardest not to let the anger her words were provoking show in his voice. He didn't argue with his lovers. He didn't get angry with them. He didn't get to know them well enough for arguments and anger.

He hadn't run away from his family like Merry had run from hers. He'd always intended to go back...to begin with, in any case. And then he'd found himself taking a new path from the one that had been mapped out when he'd thought he would marry, a path that had left all the pain of the past behind. They were entirely different situations.

'I love them, and they love me, and they understand that Monica dying was the worst pain I will ever feel. I will not feed the pain. They know that. They understand. I look forward, not back. I enjoy life. I take care of my family and I do not break promises to them.'

'That's not fair,' she whispered furiously. 'This is the only promise I've ever broken, and you know as well as I do that Wolfgang would have sacked me if I hadn't agreed to this secondment.'

'You did not even try to explain the situation to him.'

'I wasn't given a chance.'

'You could have made a chance.'

She tugged her hand out of his hold. Her hair tickled

across his chest as she sat up. Through the growing duskiness, he saw her eyes on him. Saw the bewilderment.

'Why are you being like this? Blaming everything on me? You know who that reminds me of? Martin.'

A stab of guilt pierced his chest. 'I am not blaming you,' he lied.

He *had* been blaming her. Goading her. Trying to push her away. She was getting too, too close.

The guilt grew. His sense of being suffocated by the weight of emotions she brought out in him was not Merry's fault. It was all on him, for letting it get this far. All the warning signs had been there and he'd made excuse after excuse to ignore them.

Grabbing her hand, he brought it to his mouth and grazed his lips across her knuckles. 'All I think is that you should talk to him. You are an adult now. He is an adult too, a married man. Maybe he is so angry about you not going home because *he* was wanting you there?'

She snorted.

'I am serious.' He waited until she looked back at him before continuing. 'My sisters still talk to me like I'm ten sometimes. It is like a default setting, *si*?'

He saw her eyes cloud with confusion and knew he was getting through to her. He kissed her knuckles again.

'You left England before you could find your adult relationship with him. Talk to him. Tell him how you feel. Get him to tell you how he feels. If he does not want to know then you can say you tried. Okay?'

She stared at him, inhaling slowly through her nose, holding the breath for a long time. And then she exhaled, closed her eyes and nodded.

Lying back down, she wrapped her arms around him and kissed his shoulder.

They didn't speak, just held each other as Giovanni drifted into uneasy sleep.

CHAPTER TWELVE

MERRY CLOSED HER laptop, drained the last of her hot chocolate, and finally allowed herself a moment to breathe.

The passengers had reacted as expected to the situation. With complaints. Complaints she'd overridden before they could pick up steam by announcing the new itinerary that she, a handful of the other staff, plus Veronica and the team Veronica had pulled together in Rome, had spent two hours arranging before the passengers had even risen for breakfast.

Those who wanted to, could ski. Ski-hire, ski clothing and ski passes had been taken care of. Or they could visit one of Innsbruck's Christmas markets. Complimentary afternoon tea had also been arranged in one of its most luxurious hotels. Or they could stay on board the Meravaro Odyssey and take advantage of the free bar and sumptuous treats the kitchen staff would be creating for them.

It never ceased to amaze her how much rich people liked the word 'free'. She supposed that was why they were rich. Still, if it made them happy, she wasn't going to complain. The vast majority had taken advantage of the complimentary transport, and those who'd stayed behind were mercifully the least fussy of their passengers.

'All done?'

Her heart sighed with pleasure as she looked up and found Giovanni propped against the doorway.

While Merry had worked in one of the staff carriages with the others, he'd had work to deal with regarding his business.

How could his gorgeous face look so fresh when they'd had so little sleep? But then, he'd had a little more than she had. After their talk in the early hours she'd lain awake, thinking of everything they'd talked about. About his family. Her family. Monica.

When she'd drifted into sleep in his arms, the imaginary picture she'd created of the woman who'd died so tragically young had been the last image in her head... And the mourning Giovanni who'd never got over her death.

How wonderful it had been, sharing this whole experience with him, but how sad that a tragedy had closed his heart to the one time of year in which magic happened. How could he ever move on if his heart remained locked in the past? Locked on Monica.

She had to accept that he hated Christmas and all its associations, just as her brother had done...

How could she hope for a future with Giovanni if he was so bound by his past? She didn't dare hope for a future with him, but every erratic beat of her heart when she was around him told her how deeply her feelings ran.

The cramps she'd been experiencing since her morning shower had flattened her spirits further. It was a relief to have it confirmed that she wasn't pregnant—she hadn't really thought she could be—but it had drained her already depleted energy.

None of this stopped her heart expanding and her veins buzzing to see him, or stopped her smile from forming. 'Yes. All done. The emergency transport in case we're still stuck here tomorrow has been taken care of too.'

His eyes sparkled. 'Good work, lady.'

Her heart expanded even further, rising up through her throat. 'Thank you...'

Giovanni noticed the way she chewed on her bottom lip. 'Something you want to tell me?'

Colour flamed over her cheeks. 'Yes. Just…er…that I've started my…er…'

'Lady times?' he guessed.

He also guessed why she found it so embarrassing to talk about. From what she'd told him about her family, he doubted her father had sat her down and told her the facts of life.

He didn't want to imagine how difficult it had been for an adolescent girl without a mother, nor imagine her trying frantically to hide the evidence of a normal bodily function for fear of being teased by her brother.

She nodded.

'That is good.'

Extremely good. He hadn't thought there was much risk of pregnancy, but to have it confirmed filled him with relief… And, strangely, a tinge of disappointment.

Disappointment?

No, that tinge must be a different, unquantifiable emotion that was the opposite of disappointment.

It did mean, though, that he could fly away from Europe without even the tiny possibility of pregnancy hanging over his head.

'You feeling okay? Need painkillers?'

Merry couldn't help but smile. His sisters had trained him well. 'I've had some, but thank you.'

He inclined his head and propped his backside on the table beside her. 'As most of the passengers have gone out and you missed the Christmas market in Vienna, I have arranged for us to visit one here in Innsbruck.'

She stared at him, dumbstruck, uncertain she'd heard correctly.

Had he just said, 'us' and 'Christmas market' in the same sentence?

His brow furrowed at her silence. 'You do not want to go?'

She pulled herself together. 'I'd *love* to go, thank you.'

But had he really said *us*? Was he really intending to go with her?

He grinned. 'I knew it. Go put some snow clothes on. I have call to make, then I will change too.'

He *was* intending to go with her! If her smile widened any further it would reach her ears.

'Well?' He tutted, tapping at his watch. 'Get changed.'

She saluted. 'Yes, Boss.'

Merry practically danced out of the carriage with hope nudging and bouncing its way through her heart.

A blanket of snow covered Innsbruck's old town, giving a magical quality to the snow-topped medieval buildings lining the pretty streets. There was far more to see and do than Merry had anticipated, and people bustling and dawdling, all making their way through the sparkling market stalls and amusements put on for their entertainment. Christmas music filled the air, Christmas scents filled her senses, and the magic of it all seeped into her already elevated spirits.

Having Giovanni at her side made her feel she was walking on air.

They spent a wonderful few hours exploring the craft stalls, nibbling on cinnamon-flavoured cookies, roasted chestnuts and the endless array of free samples being handed out. They talked endlessly, discussing early childhood japes and older siblings who liked to torment, before moving on to their favourite films—romances for Merry, thrillers for Giovanni.

Not a single word about the Meravaro Odyssey or work in general passed their lips.

How lucky was she to be here, experiencing this? And

with *Giovanni*? He'd pushed aside his hatred of Christmas for *her*, just as her brother had done for the love of his wife.

Every time she thought this, her heart would jolt sharply. Was it possible that Giovanni was unbinding himself from the past? She didn't dare allow herself to hope what that might mean.

If fate hadn't stepped in, in the form of Gerhard's appendicitis, she would be back working at the hotel, having flown in from England yesterday with Santa. She'd be recovering from a tense couple of days with her family. No doubt she would have spent the flight crying on Santa's shoulder.

She always saved her tears for her, and Santa did the same. They'd lost their mothers within months of each other, two tiny girls finding comfort and solace for their grief in each other.

They were at a stall filled with hand-blown glass baubles and figurines. Merry was asking his opinion on which of the ice skater figures she should buy for Santa, when Giovanni pulled his hand free from hers.

'I'm going to get us a drink,' he said. 'Hot chocolate?'

'Yes, please. Shall I come—?'

'No need. You look happy here. I not be long.'

As Giovanni strode to the closest drinks stall, he dug his hand in his pocket and pulled out his phone.

He'd known he'd made a mistake the moment the scent of roasting chestnuts had filled his nostrils. But, strangely, it wasn't the setting so much as Merry's joy at it all.

For the first time in twelve years Giovanni had walked into a Christmas scene from fairy tales and not felt even an echo of the expected pain that usually chewed him up and spat him out as a hollow shell of the man he'd once been.

He'd first thought this bonus day and night with Merry had been the Fates conspiring in his favour. Now he feared they were really conspiring in anger against him.

That morning, while alone in his suite, he'd distracted himself from his work by thinking of something special he could do on this bonus day with her, something that would show his gratitude for all she'd done for him: stepping in at the last minute and giving up her family time to save his and Wolfgang's butts, working her own butt off to familiarise herself with everything, working her butt off to keep their guests happy. For being the first person to make him laugh—truly laugh—in a long, long time. For making this voyage bearable. More than bearable.

Of all the things he could do to say thank you, he'd known a Christmas market was the thing she would love the most. He'd pushed aside his violent aversion to it and set the wheels in motion.

The smile on her face when he'd announced his plans had been the first warning that he'd made an error.

The swelling of his chest as the day had gone on, the pleasure he was taking in Merry's pleasure in it all, the plummeting of his mood the few times she'd excused herself to use the bathroom followed by the immediate uplift when she'd returned…

And then she'd asked his opinion on a gift for her friend and a burst of jealousy had ripped through him at the monopoly on Merry's time her friend would have for the next couple of weeks.

That was when the real alarm bells had hollered at him.

He was starting to crave her in a way that far exceeded sexual desire.

'Veronica,' he said without preamble when his PA answered. 'I need you to make arrangements for me to leave Austria today… Yes. Today… As soon as possible.'

Giovanni's call over and the drinks purchased, he rolled his neck and took a deep breath before carrying them back to Merry. Her back was turned, and that ridiculous, crazy hat was bobbing on her head as she spoke to the seller.

How could a *hat* make him feel so tight inside?

Just from her stance, he knew she was smiling.

How could he *know* that?

It was for that reason he had to leave.

He was in trouble. Real trouble. He knew it. All the guards he'd placed around himself were being dismantled at an accelerating rate.

Because the swelling in his chest wasn't the only thing that had grown as the day had passed. The taste of guilt on his tongue had grown too.

Guilt that the passion he felt for Merry was stronger and more consuming than anything he'd felt before.

Fear of what that meant.

He'd never pressured Monica. He'd respected her wish for them to wait.

But he couldn't shake the feeling that the teenage Giovanni would have marched Merry to the nearest church the moment they came of age just so he could consummate things between them.

And that killed him.

The sooner Veronica arranged his transport out of Austria, the better. She was working on it, but it wasn't looking good. A blizzard in Switzerland, where his private plane was waiting for him, had grounded flights.

After putting her purchases securely into her bag, Merry's heart flip to find Giovanni back with their drinks. Sliding her arm through his elbow, they set off again to explore the rest of the Christmas market delights.

'Did I tell you Santa's an ice skater?' she asked as they passed an ice rink filled with families, groups of teenagers and young couples.

'No.'

'She's incredibly talented. Honestly, it's amazing to

watch her. And the *hours* she puts into it! When I passed my driving test, I used to take her to her lessons and practices. I think I enjoyed it more than she did! Seriously, she has the potential to be the best ice skater in the world.'

'Will you be there to cheer her when that happens?' Giovanni asked, his stomach churning at the animation in her voice.

She was a good person and a good friend. Supportive. Enthusiastic. Merry was a friend anyone would wish for. If not for the chemistry, he would want her as a friend for himself.

But their chemistry was too strong for that. It was doing things to him. Making him behave in uncharacteristic ways. Making him feel things that, if they got any stronger, would have the power to control him.

Never again. He would not go through that again. Never.

'Of course!' she replied. 'I'll have a ringside seat.'

Then she craned her neck at something she'd spotted in the distance.

He followed her gaze.

She faced him, eyes alight. 'Can we go on the Ferris Wheel?'

'This is your day, remember? We do what you like.'

She beamed, grabbed hold of his hand and led the way, weaving nimbly through the growing crowds.

The queue wasn't too bad, he was relieved to find, and as they joined it his phone buzzed. He checked the message and was further relieved to learn that Veronica had pulled a rabbit out of a hat and booked him onto a commercial flight.

He hadn't flown by commercial travel for many years but all his planes were contracted or too far away to get to him speedily, or, in the case of his personal jet, grounded in a blizzard. And he wanted to be gone. It felt more imperative with every passing minute. A car would collect him in two hours.

Work had barely crossed his thoughts since they'd arrived at the Christmas market, but now the countdown had started.

'Let us talk about you working for me,' he said.

Her nose wrinkled adorably. 'You really are serious about it?'

'Have I not said so a hundred times?'

'A slight exaggeration.'

He put his thumb and forefinger together and winked. 'A little.'

She sniggered. 'Do you have a role in mind?'

'Head of Customer Relations for Cannavaro Travel Cruises.'

Her mouth dropped open in surprise. 'Seriously?'

'*Si*.' And then he explained what the job entailed, and finished by saying that if she was as good at the role as he expected, she could expect promotion to Head of Customer Relations for the whole of Cannavaro Travel within two years.

It was nothing less than she deserved. A woman of her talents shouldn't be hemmed in by a hotel where any prospects were limited. She deserved the opportunity to spread her wings and learn to fly.

They'd reached the front of the queue.

Merry stepped onto their gondola, feeling she could burst with happiness. Giovanni's offer sounded so tempting. If she took the job it would be the equivalent of her being on the second to bottom rung of the career ladder and taking an almighty jump to the second from the top.

The temptation to say yes!

But was the temptation to do with the coup of landing an excellent job with a correspondingly excellent salary or to do with continuing this thing with Giovanni? This romance.

She wanted it to continue. Every weighty beat of her heart told her that.

She lightly touched one of the earrings he'd given her, which she hadn't taken off, and felt her heart sigh.

Their gondola began to rise just as fat snowflakes began to fall. The early setting sun added another layer of magic to the experience. The Christmas lights covering the city had brightened, the colours becoming more defined. The humungous Christmas tree she'd admired earlier now shone so brightly it must be seen for miles.

She stuck her tongue out to catch one of the falling snowflakes and giggled for the sheer joy of it all.

'You are crazy, lady,' Giovanni said.

His amusement at her antics was accompanied by a wrench that made all his internal organs cramp tightly.

She beamed and snuggled closer to him.

For the first time he didn't welcome her touch. He wanted to sit as far from her as possible.

The temperature was dropping at a much faster rate than the ride was taking, and he took advantage of it to hug his arms around his chest.

Merry noticed. 'Want to wear my hat?' she asked cheekily.

'I rather get frostbite.'

'You really hate the cold, don't you?'

'Si.'

She laughed. 'How ever did you cope working in Switzerland?'

'Badly. If Wolfgang had not made me his assistant I would have quit and got a job in the Caribbean.'

She laughed again, then stuck her tongue out to catch another snowflake.

This time Giovanni hardened his heart against the

wrench at this amusing antic. Getting onto this Ferris Wheel had been a mistake. Staying at the Christmas market with her once he'd realised what a mistake it was had been the biggest mistake.

As soon as they were at the bottom he jumped out, helped Merry down, and rammed his hands into his overcoat pocket.

No more touching her.

It was time to end things.

He made a beeline for the smart café with outdoor, heated seating that he'd spotted earlier. The snow was piling down harder, turning the roads and pavements to slush.

'Mulled wine?' he asked, once they'd taken their seats and he'd shaken the snow from his hair.

He wanted them to part on good terms. Excellent terms. There was no reason they should part on any other terms.

She wrinkled her nose mischievously. Adorably. If he had the capacity in him to give his heart, that nose wrinkle would have taken it.

'Hot chocolate?'

'This is a public café. I have a reputation, remember?'

A wide grin broke out on her beautiful face. 'How could I forget?'

Despite his steeling of all internal emotion, a surge of heat zinged through his loins and almost had him leaning over the table to kiss her senseless.

He took a long, deep inhalation.

He would never kiss her again.

He waited until their mulled wine had been brought to the table before getting down to business. 'What we talked about earlier. About you working for me. Do you have any questions?'

'Only one. Where would I be based?'

'Is up to you. I will get Veronica to send you list of our

administration offices. We do not have one in Switzerland, but if you want snow Canada is an option. So…shall I get contract process rolling?'

Merry cupped her drink in her gloved hands. It smelt heavenly. One sip told her it tasted just as good. The heat of the spiced aromatic liquid warmed her throat and belly and made her sigh with pleasure.

Staring at Giovanni was even more pleasurable.

It was wonderful to know she *could* stare at him, stare to her heart's content. Even wrapped for the cold weather in a long navy lambswool overcoat and a thick scarf wrapped snugly around his neck to nestle against his chin, there was no denying his Adonis-like handsomeness. She didn't have to look around to know most of the females in the vicinity were surreptitiously ogling him.

A week ago she had been so sure a man like him could never find a woman as plain as her attractive.

He made her feel beautiful. Worshipped.

She was falling in love with this man and there was nothing she could do about it.

But her future was something within her control.

She could take the safe route and stay in Switzerland, spend another three years, ten years, for ever, safe and secure in her job and her life.

Or she could take the risky route and take a chance on life. And love.

Maybe the future wouldn't work out for them, but she would never know if she didn't try.

Giovanni's wonderful gift of this day was proof that he'd taken the first step in releasing the ghosts of his past. Now it was time for Merry to release hers too.

'Yes.'

'Yes?' he echoed.

'Yes.' She had another sip of mulled wine and beamed, a burst of happiness gushing through her now the decision had been made. 'Yes, I will come and work for you. Get the contract rolling.'

His mouth curved with approval as he held his glass mug out to her. 'Welcome to the team.'

'A bit premature, seeing as I've not handed my notice in yet, but…' She chinked her mug to it.

'When will you give notice?'

'After I've signed the contract.'

'Then I shall make sure the contract is done as priority.' Giovanni finished his mulled wine, put the mug on the table, checked his watch and rubbed his hands together.

Thank God that was done.

'And now that it is agreed, it is time for me to go.'

'Go where?' she asked, brow furrowing.

'I have important meeting tomorrow I cannot miss. Veronica has arranged a flight for me.'

'You mean…you're *leaving*? But…' She shook her head as if in disbelief. 'I thought you were staying on?'

Giovanni kept a tight check on his emotions. He would not feel guilt. If not for the avalanche, they would have said goodbye hours ago.

'No. Me staying was never possible,' he lied, before pushing his chair back and getting to his feet.

He pulled some cash out of his wallet to pay for their drinks, and the card with the number of the driver who'd brought them to the Christmas market, and said, 'Call him when you are ready to go back to the train.'

She just stared at him.

'Thank you for all your hard work, lady.' Maintaining a cheerful tone was difficult with those big eyes behind the tortoiseshell frames staring at him in such stark bewilderment, but he forced it. 'It has been a pleasure.'

The biggest pleasure of his life.

And now it was over.

He winked at her and saluted. '*Ciao*, lady.'

With one final nod at her ashen face, Giovanni ducked under the lip of the canopy, straightened his frame, and strode briskly away.

CHAPTER THIRTEEN

MERRY SAT THERE frozen. All the warmth had left her body. She couldn't move.

'Are you okay?'

She blinked, and the waitress who'd taken their order came into focus. Merry tried to speak but no words would form in her constricted throat.

Her glass mug was still tightly clasped in her hand. Moving as if in sluggish slow motion, she placed it on the table next to Giovanni's empty one.

The punch that landed in her stomach made her gasp.

The person who'd thrown it had disappeared in the crowd.

She shoved her chair back and stood clumsily, banging into the table. She barely felt it.

Her legs began to move. She had no conscious thought of where they were taking her.

'Excuse me, miss?' The voice was right behind her.

Turning, she found the concerned waitress there. She had Merry's bag in her hand.

Feeling that she was in the midst of a dream, she took it from her and slowly hooked it over her shoulder.

Someone jostled into her. Apologies were shouted to her in German. She opened her mouth to thank the waitress for her kindness, but she'd disappeared too.

Suddenly feeling very lost and very alone, Merry spun

around. All the people surrounding her, walking in all directions, couples, families, parents holding tightly to small children's hands, dawdling teenagers eating, drinking and laughing…a crying toddler…

The *noise*.

She covered her ears against it and felt another punch land in her stomach. This one doubled her over.

Hand pressed tightly to her nauseous stomach, her legs set off again, propelling her blindly through the crowd, moving faster and faster until she was running and *she* was the one jostling into people.

And then she saw him.

He was approaching the main road.

She saw the gleaming car with its lights on parked illegally, knew it was for him.

She reached it before the driver could close the door after him. Not anticipating a petite woman with hair streaming in all directions racing at him full pelt, then barging past him and throwing herself into the back with his client, the driver was powerless to stop her.

Giovanni closed his eyes before addressing the breathless Merry who'd appeared from nowhere. He must act as if this was an expected development. Hopefully, she just had something about the contract she wanted to ask before he left.

He didn't believe that hope for a second.

'Is there something you forget to ask me about the job, lady?' he asked.

There was a long silence before she said, 'Are you *finishing* with me?'

He wished he could close his ears as effectively as his eyes. Then he wouldn't have to hear the pain and bewilderment in her voice.

He attempted to summon the barricade around his heart that had enabled him to walk away from her without a backward glance. Every step taken had chipped at it, until he'd reached the car feeling quite queasy.

He faced her.

She was gazing at him, her throat moving, chin wobbling. Snowflakes clung to her hair and her puffed winter coat.

She'd lost her crazy hat...

Giovanni forced the barricade back in place and, emotionally detaching himself, raised a brow, as if he were surprised at her question. 'That is a dramatic way of putting it,' he said lightly.

The driver's voice came through the speaker. 'What do you want me to do, sir?'

'One moment.' He looked again at Merry and held his palms out, as if bemused. 'I need to go. My flight leaves in an hour.'

She raised her wobbling chin and folded her arms across her chest.

Sighing as if this were all a complete waste of time, he spoke into the microphone. 'Just drive.'

'Yes, sir.'

Giovanni muted the intercom and the car set off. 'Looks like you are coming to airport with me, lady.'

'But not to wherever you're flying to,' she whispered.

He winked. 'That would be crazy—you have passengers to look after.'

Her face seemed to crumple. 'Will you *stop* acting like this and talk to me? Please?' she begged. 'You can't just leave like this, not after everything.'

'There is nothing to talk about. We had fun, but all good thing come to an end, lady.'

She covered her ears. 'Stop calling me that! You always call me that when you're making light of something, but you can't make light of this. If you're finishing with me the least you can do is show me some courtesy instead of pretending it's some kind of game we've been playing.'

'Not a game, no,' he said steadily, 'but it was never serious. Just fun.'

'How can you *say* that?'

'I speak the truth. I am sorry if you thought we would still have fun together when the voyage end, but I never said anything to make you think it.'

On that, he was clear. He had been scrupulous about it. Giovanni did not make false promises.

Not verbally, the sly voice in his head whispered.

He batted the voice away and fought to hold on to his detachment.

He could have left without saying goodbye but he'd done the right thing when he'd never bothered to go out of his way to say goodbye to any lover before. Why she was acting so upset was beyond him.

Liar.

She swallowed hard and took a deep breath. The look she gave him could have speared a dragon dead.

'Is it because of my *lady times*?' she mimicked bitterly. 'Now that you know you can't have *fun* with me tonight, you've decided to hot-foot it away from me?'

The detachment slipped. A burst of emotion poured out and flooded his veins, angering him almost as much as her words had just done.

'That is offensive,' he said tightly.

'*You're* offensive,' she shot back.

'Why? Because you were virgin you think that means you are special and I should treat you different to my other lovers?'

'No!'

He wouldn't let her cut in, continuing furiously, 'I never lied to you. I do not do relationships. You know that. You were warned. I know you were. The things you said told me that. If you made love to me with your eyes closed then that is your problem.'

'I gave far more than my virginity to you!' she cried. 'I gave you *everything*. And you gave me more than sex too, don't you deny it. You let me get close to you and yes, we had fun… God, Gio, you make me laugh more than anyone in the world… But it was much more than that, and now you're severing everything we shared with no discussion and no warning—'

'What is this if not discussion?'

'This is me forcing you to talk. Remember the advice you gave me about talking to my brother? Well, that's what I'm making *you* do. Did you seriously think I would be satisfied with you dumping me with a plaudit of the time we had together being *a pleasure*?'

'It was a pleasure, but now it is over. I wanted us to part on good terms, but I was always going home today.'

'Home? What home? You don't *have* a home. You ran away from it, just like you're running from me.'

'No, Merry, I'm not the one who runs away—that is *you*. You ran from your living family to chase the ghost of your mother.'

'At least I accept that and never pretend otherwise!'

'I do not pretend. I left because I look forward, not back.'

'Codswallop! You're completely stuck in the past. I chase my mother's ghost because feeling her alive in my heart makes me remember that I was loved. I was prepared to leave the place where her ghost most comes alive for me because, for the first time since she died, I felt the stirrings of love from someone else. But now I realise those stirrings will never come to anything because you won't let go of Monica.'

The barrage of words she'd thrown at him landed with punches into Giovanni's guts, making his heart thump so painfully its marks bruised his chest.

He was losing his grip, holding on to his temper and the

emotions boiling in him like a tempest by a thread. 'Don't you dare bring Monica into this.'

'Why not, when she's the reason for it all? How can you say you look forward when you won't even try to deal with the past? You've slammed a door on it. I might hate my brother, but at least he's found the courage to move on—at least he's willing to make changes to his behaviour out of love. You will never be able to move on until you accept the pain of losing her.'

The thread snapped.

Grabbing the sleeve of Merry's coat, he tugged her to him. 'I accept the pain. Don't you understand that?' he snarled in her face. 'I know she is gone and she is never coming back. That is something I made peace with a long time ago, but what I will not do is open myself up to pain like that again. Not ever. Do you understand?'

All the fight in Merry was expelled in a puff.

The expression on Giovanni's face was both terrifying and heart-breaking.

For the longest time nothing was said as they gazed into each other's eyes with all the hate and the loss consuming them both. The only sound was the heaviness of their breaths.

Slowly, he unpeeled his fingers from her sleeve and leaned back. Eyes still holding hers, he unmuted the speaker between the passengers and the driver. Only then did Merry realise they'd arrived at the airport.

Still staring at her, he spoke into it. 'I am ready. When you have removed my luggage, take Miss Ingles to the train station.'

'Yes, sir.'

Then he backed slowly towards the door.

The driver opened it.

The locked gaze between them was severed for the final time.

Giovanni unfurled himself and got out of the car.

The last thing she saw of him was the back of his legs before the door shut firmly and Merry was alone with nothing but the last vestiges of his cologne before that vanished too.

Merry stepped through the Hotel Haensli staff entrance with Santa. Keeping up a flow of light-hearted chatter, the pair of them stamped snow off their boots before hurrying to the staffroom to hang their coats, change into their party shoes and check the hoods worn to protect their hair from the snow during the walk from her cabin hadn't ruined them.

'Will we do?' Merry asked, after they'd carefully examined each other.

The pair of them had spent the afternoon dolling themselves up, turning two little girls who'd always been happy caked in mud into princesses. Well, they had turned Santa into a princess. She looked utterly, glamorously divine in a purple floor-length ballgown.

Merry had borrowed another dress from Katja, insisting on something far less sensuous than the one she'd worn on the Meravaro Odyssey. But, compared to Santa's sparkling diamond, Merry felt like a flat piece of costume jewellery.

Santa pretended to ponder. 'I think so.'

They both laughed, but it had none of the force their laughter usually contained. The short time they'd spent together since Merry's return from the Meravaro Odyssey had seen conversation between them far more stilted than it usually was. Merry blamed herself for this. It grieved her that, far from confiding all that had happened with Giovanni to her best friend, she'd kept it to herself.

She didn't dare talk about it. Didn't trust that once the tears started they would ever stop.

Having Santa in the cabin was a comfort, though, and it was a comfort having her here at the party too.

At the door of the ballroom, they pulled each other in

for a tight embrace. It was a comfort that came close to making Merry weep.

Sensing Santa's rising nerves, she whispered, 'You don't have to hide in the shadows. Stay with me as much as you want.'

Poor darling Santa always got jittery in big crowds. A hang-up, Merry suspected, from their schooldays, when she'd been horrendously bullied, something Merry, as much as she had tried, hadn't always been there to protect her from.

Was she imagining that Santa seemed more jittery than normal?

'Don't you worry about me,' Santa said, with what was clearly fake brightness. 'Get to work before you get into trouble.'

For the first time the thought of getting into trouble didn't strike fear in her. It made Merry blink to realise she no longer cared if she was sacked.

Had it really only been two weeks since the thought of losing her job and having to return home had terrified her so?

What had changed?

Giovanni.

His name whispered in her head.

It always whispered in her head.

She pushed him out with all the mental force she could summon.

As Katja was speeding her way over, Merry brushed her cheek to Santa's and joined her boss for the final ball-room inspection. Together, their practised eyes ran over every last detail.

It was all perfect. Giovanni would approve...

Don't think of him.

The waiting staff were lined up, ready to circulate with champagne and canapés the second the guests made their entrance. The musicians were tuned and primed to play their opening number. The singers were in a separate room, doing their vocal exercises. The Christmas trees and all the plentiful decorations glowed and sparkled. The chocolate fountain poured its silken contents like a never-ending waterfall.

In all, the room was a festive sparkling delight that couldn't fail to make their illustrious guests feel smugly special to be there.

Merry remembered her first Christmas working at the hotel. She'd been given the job of circulating miniature orange and chocolate brioche canapés at the Christmas party and had loved every minute of it. Her senses had been overloaded by Christmas. It had been the most amazing night of her life. Up to that point any way.

Tonight, she didn't even get a rush from the scent of pine and tinsel. She had no urge to pull one of the giant gold Christmas crackers artfully placed around the room. The only urge she had was to go to bed and sleep for days.

The first guests entered the ballroom.

Shaking off her maudlin thoughts, she curved her mouth into a welcoming smile and strode over to greet them.

The evening passed in glamorous fabulousness. The noise level alone was a good indication of how much everyone was enjoying themselves. Merry found herself much sought after by many of the guests who'd been on the Meravaro Odyssey, some of whom acted as if she were a personal friend rather than an employee. She winced every time one of them asked where Giovanni was.

Had they all guessed they'd become lovers?

She'd thought they'd been discrete. The staff knew better than to talk about the sleeping arrangements so there was no reason any of the passengers would know of it.

So had her feelings for him been obvious?

Had his feelings for *her* been obvious?

And why was she torturing herself with all these thoughts about him?

Whatever feelings Giovanni had for her, he didn't want them. And hadn't she always known that? Hadn't she known that he didn't want to want her?

And yet she'd still made love to him.

She'd made love to him knowing he would break her heart.

She had no one to blame but herself.

What she hadn't known was just how painful a broken heart could be. She'd assumed that the grief she'd experienced when losing her mother would prepare her for it, had naively thought it would have immunised her.

She could never have guessed the pain of a broken heart would be so physical. That it would hurt to breathe. That it would hurt to eat. That her bones would ache. That it would feel like she'd been smashed in the chest by a wrecking ball.

Giovanni rubbed his eyes for the tenth time in as many minutes and tried, again, to read through the purchase contract Veronica had printed for him rather than look out of the window and gaze at the blue Miami sky. This was a major food contract for his cruise ships. Any contract above a certain amount had to be approved by him, and his team were waiting for his go-ahead.

He needed sleep, he thought grimly. Usually he was a sound sleeper, but these last seven nights had seen him tossing and turning until the early hours.

Veronica stepped into the office with a coffee for him.

'Are you going to sign that?' she asked in her usual no-nonsense manner. 'Only, I have a flight to catch, a home to get to, and Christmas preparations to make.'

He didn't.

That was a question that had kept running over and

over in his head. Where was his home? He had so many
houses and villas and apartments all over the world, but
which one did he think of as home?

The answer was none of them. He had his family in
Rome. His headquarters were in Rome. He rarely slept a
night under Roman skies.

'Have you read the contract?' he asked Veronica.

'Of course.'

'And?'

'It all seems in order.'

'Then that's good enough for me.' He turned the contract to the last page, signed his name and handed it to her
with a smile. 'Merry Christmas.'

She merely raised a brow.

As she was about to leave, the question he'd been biting back all week spoke itself. 'Has she signed the contract yet?'

'Miss Ingles?'

He nodded.

'No. Want me to chase her?'

He gave a grim smile. 'Wait until after Christmas. Go
on. Get out.'

She nearly smiled. 'Merry Christmas, Giovanni.'

Alone in the office, he bowed his head and forced air
into his cramped lungs. He'd been struggling to breathe
for the last week, had wondered if he'd caught an airborne
virus while on the Odyssey. He should see a doctor. If it
was viral, he should notify Merry.

His lungs tightened again. The cramping in his stomach that had also bothered him all week doubled him over.

Why hadn't she signed the contract? He didn't deny that
they had ended on the bad terms he'd wanted to avoid. How
could he deny it when the pain written all over her face
had haunted his fractured sleep all week? But that didn't
alter the fact that she would be an asset for his company.

To hell with it.

He scrolled through his phone, found her number and dialled. Immediately he received a message saying the number was unavailable.

Strange.

He tried the Hotel Haensli.

'Merry Ingles, please,' he said, when the call was answered.

'I'm sorry, sir, but Ms Ingles no longer works here.'

'Since when?'

'I'm sorry, sir, but I cannot divulge that information.'

'Put me through to Katja.'

'I'm sorry, sir, but she has finished for the day.'

'Is anyone in the hospitality team in?'

'I'm sorry, sir, but it's eleven o'clock in the evening.'

He hung up and cradled his head over the desk again. The time difference between Miami and Switzerland hadn't even occurred to him.

Not until he lifted his head from his desk did he find that the paperwork strewn over it was wet with his tears.

When Merry had left home at nineteen it was because she'd had enough of being miserable. She'd wanted to escape her brother's bullying and her father's indifference and find some happiness, a safe niche to call home. She'd always believed she'd found that in Switzerland, but now, as she knocked on her brother's front door, she knew the truth was more complicated than that.

Her brother yanked it open, yelling something over his shoulder that was cut off from his lips when he saw her standing there.

'Meredith?'

'Hello, Martin,' she whispered. And then she burst into tears.

* * *

He couldn't do this any more. Go without sleep. Without hope. Without life.

He made the call.

'Veronica, I need to fly to England... Yes, I know you're on leave... Okay... Yes... Tickets to Broadway whenever you want them... Yes, best seats in the house...' Whatever she wanted. He'd throw in a car if she asked for one. 'Today... As soon as possible. Just get me to England.'

Get me to Merry.

It was too late for him.

All the things he'd spent twelve years running and hiding from had caught him, ensnared him in a trap, and the harder he'd tried to escape from it, the tighter it had bound him.

Love had found him.

He couldn't live another day without her.

CHAPTER FOURTEEN

MERRY LAY IN her childhood bed with the ache in her heart and the sick feeling in her stomach that had become a permanent part of her.

Her first thought on waking was, as always, of Giovanni.

Where was he? The Caribbean? Florida? Wherever he was, the sun would be hot and there wouldn't be so much as a speck of tinsel.

How could she still miss him?

Why did the world feel so colourless and lonely without him?

How could it still hurt so badly?

She closed her eyes and let the tears fall onto her pillow. No point fighting it. She'd learned that the hard way. One day her heart would accept that their time together had been limited for a reason and that that time had run out.

She let the tears run dry before peeking out of the window, and found a smile when she saw it wasn't raining.

Downstairs, she found her father reading the paper at the kitchen table. Considering there were no Christmas Day newspaper deliveries, it must be an old one.

'Merry Christmas, Merry,' he said, without looking up at her.

'Merry Christmas, Dad.'

He turned the page and continued to read.

For the first time in her life, it didn't bother her.

'I'm going to make a cup of tea before I get ready. Want one?'

'Yes please, love.'

When she laid the cup in front of him, he finally peered up at her. 'Your present is under the tree.'

She smiled and dashed off to get it.

When she'd ripped it open, the tears she'd thought spent started again. It was a framed family picture, taken, she guessed, only months before her mother had died. He must have had it worked on, because it was as crisp and clear a photograph as any modern camera would take.

She wiped the tears away and studied it carefully. It had been taken on the beach. She thought it might have been in Bournemouth. Her mum had an arm each around Merry and Martin. Their father was standing slightly apart from them, but judging by the angle of his arm, he was resting his hand on her mother's bottom. All four of them had enormous happy grins on their faces.

She wished she could get in touch with Giovanni and thank him, but knew to do that would be to add to the bruising of her battered heart. One day, when it wasn't all so raw and debilitatingly painful, she would write to him. Taking his advice about talking to her brother had had much better results than she could have dreamed.

Much better results than the hate fest she and Giovanni had shared.

The past had come back to her remastered, much like this photo.

Her father, she now knew, was on the autistic spectrum. Her mother had been the disciplinarian because he just hadn't been able to cope with it. He would shut himself away in his own head rather than deal with it. Her death had destroyed what few social functioning skills he'd had. They only knew this because Martin had insisted he be tested for it that year. Martin had been so angry about

Merry not coming home in part because he'd wanted to share the diagnosis with her in person.

If only their father had been tested and given the support he needed decades ago, how very different all their lives might have been.

And if she hadn't run away Martin would not have had to bear the burden of it alone. No, she reminded herself. Not alone. He had Kelly now.

In the future, he would have her too. Their splintered family was going to knit itself back together into a solid unit.

After wiping her tears one more time, she kissed the frame and carried it up to her bedroom so she could get ready for Christmas dinner at her tormentor's house. Martin. The brother who had, as Giovanni suspected, taken up the mantle of parent to her. The one who'd made sure she got ready for school on time. The one who'd shouted at her if she was late back. The one who'd shouted at her for trying to sneak out of the house with make-up on...

But he'd been her protector too. And a child.

Being a child herself, she just hadn't recognised it.

Giovanni looked at the ordinary white door of the ordinary terraced house, took a deep breath and rapped sharply on it.

An obviously pregnant woman wearing a too-tight Christmas jumper and a yellow Christmas cracker hat opened it to reveal a narrow hallway. In the background he could hear a song that had played on the radio at this time of year all over the world since his childhood.

'Can I help you?' she asked, obviously confused to find a stranger on her doorstep on Christmas Day.

'I'm looking for Merry Ingles. Is she here?'

Please let her be here.

A quick chat with Wolfgang had made the Hotel Haensli administrative staff more amenable to giving him Merry's next of kin details, but there had been no one home in the pretty cottage in the tiny village. More calls had followed. He had many contacts, including in telecom companies. A few bribes—always welcome for the poor souls forced to work on Christmas Day—and after a two-hour wait he'd been given Martin Ingles address.

If she wasn't here...

He didn't know what he would do other than keep trying.

He would knock on every door in England if he had to.

The woman's eyes narrowed with suspicion. 'Who are you?'

'A friend.'

Her arms folded around her ripe belly. 'You wouldn't be called Giovanni, would you?'

'Yes.' Fearing she was about to slam the door in his face, he put his foot in the doorway. 'Please, I just want to talk to her.'

'It's Christmas Day,' she hissed. 'And, believe me, you're the last person she wants to see.'

'I know.' He swallowed back the bitterness rising up his throat. 'But please...ask her. If she says no, I will leave.'

Face pinched, she stared at him some more, then turned on her heel and walked back towards the noise.

A moment later he heard a glass smash, and the next thing he knew a short, stocky man with brown spiky hair and a rounded face came charging down the hallway. He shoved Giovanni in the chest so hard he fell back, landing on his backside on the cold pavement.

'She doesn't want to see you,' he snarled, looming over him, waving his fist in Giovanni's face. 'Now, get lost.'

'I just want to talk to her.'

The fist would have connected with his face if a firm hand hadn't gripped it and pulled it back.

'Martin, no!'

His heart soared to hear Merry's voice. She manoeuvred her brother out of the way, then stepped in front of him to form a barrier between the two men. Only then did she look down on Giovanni.

Her face was expressionless.

After it seemed an age had passed, she extended a hand to him.

He stared at it, shocked that she would offer to help him. And then he stared at her. The tightness in his chest that had finally forced him to see his doctor loosened for the first time in nine days.

Her beautiful hair was loose over her shoulders, and her beautiful eyes were hidden by the tortoiseshell frames he'd grown to love so much. She wore a pair of slim jeans and the most ludicrous garish jumper with a sequinned Christmas tree on it, so ludicrous that he found a smile forming for the first time since he'd left her in the car at the airport.

'Crazy jumper, lady,' he said shakily, from his vantage point on the pavement.

A flicker of something finally appeared in her eyes. A hint of her dimples flashed on her cheeks—thinner, he was certain, than since he'd last seen her—then disappeared.

'Are you going to take my hand or not?' she said, no longer looking at him, her tone indicating she couldn't care less.

If he hadn't seen the tremor in her hand, he would have believed it.

'If you want to spend Christmas on the pavement, that's fine, but I need to go back in. My dinner's getting cold.'

He swallowed and took her hand. The soft comfort filled him and he closed his eyes before rising. Instead of getting to his feet, though, he rocked onto his knees.

Merry's resolve nearly crumbled.

When she'd heard the knock on the door, some unknown sixth sense had made the hairs on the nape of her neck stand to attention. She hadn't even realised she'd risen from her seat at the table until she'd dropped her glass when Kelly had come in and said his name.

If Martin hadn't gone all Protective Big Brother, she might still be standing there, rooted to the floor with the world spinning around her, but she'd acted instinctively.

Somehow, from somewhere, she'd found the strength to look Giovanni in the eye and close in on herself. Her own form of self-protection. And now her hand was enveloped in his, and the pain and the longing were fighting through her control.

Looking over his head, she said in a voice that was a little less clear than a moment ago, 'What are you doing?'

'Merry, look at me,' he begged.

But she was too frightened to look. Suddenly the magnitude of what was happening hit her and she realised that it was Giovanni's warm hand wrapped around hers and her whole body began to shake.

He had come to her. On Christmas Day. Oh, God, what did he want with her? She didn't dare hope…

He didn't *deserve* her hope. He deserved nothing from her, not even her time.

About to snatch her hand away and tell him, coldly, to leave, she made the fatal of error of looking at him again without placing the barrier back over her heart.

The tears rolled down her face before she could even begin fighting them.

He inched closer to her and took her other hand, drawing them together and clasping them both as if in prayer to his chest.

'I am sorry,' he said brokenly, staring up at her with bloodshot eyes. 'All those thing I said. Leaving you like I did. Forgive me, please. I beg you. Forgive me.'

Through the falling tears she began to notice other little things. The deep circles beneath his eyes. The crumpled appearance of his suit that looked like he'd spent days sleeping in it. The mass of stubble over his usually clean-shaven jaw...

'Say something,' he beseeched. 'Do something. Tell me you hate me. Call me bastard. Hit me. Anything. I deserve it. I deserve your hate. I hate myself only a little less than I love you.'

Her heart bashed so hard its echoes racked her already shaking body.

The clasp on her hands tightened. 'I love you, Merry. So, so much. Everything about you. Look at me; I am *nothing* without you. I spent so many years running—you are right, I was not looking forward, I was running from the past. I did not want to feel the pain I felt with Monica again. And I was right, because this pain I feel now is killing me, and it kills me that I made you cry and hurt you. Tell me what I must do to make you love me again, please, and I swear I will never hurt you. Please, Merry, be my lady again, be my lady for ever. Let me try. I will do anything. *Anything.*'

The sickness in Giovanni's guts threatened to spill over when she slipped her hands from his hold, the anguish hitting him so hard that at first he didn't feel the gentle touch on his hair... Not until her fingers threaded through the strands and slowly caressed down to his forehead. Not until she was cupping his cheeks and her face was right before his.

Her glasses had slipped down her nose and she moved a hand from his face to take them off, carelessly discarding them before putting her palm back to his cheek.

And then she kissed him. A long, drawn-out sigh of a kiss that deepened as her hands moved to wind around his neck, and his arms wound around her, until they were clinging together as if they would never let go.

'You being here...' she whispered when they came up

for air. 'Today…? Oh, Giovanni, this is the best Christmas present I could have wished for. I didn't dare to dream it but you're *here*. You're here! Oh, I love you. So, so much. I've *missed* you. I love you.'

And then she kissed him again. And again. And again.

The joy and love ripping through the despair of the past ten days was incredible to feel. It seeped into every crevice of his body.

Only when he'd finally got back to his feet and pulled Merry tight to his chest did he notice their audience.

The pregnant woman—Merry's sister-in-law, he guessed—elbowed the human cannonball who'd sent him flying.

The human cannonball coughed. 'Does this mean we need to get another plate out?'

Giovanni looked at the woman he loved.

The dimples on her face popped and she leaned up to kiss him again.

EPILOGUE

'WILL YOU TWO pack it in?' Merry sternly told her two small children, who'd just started clouting each other.

Her inappropriately named six-year-old daughter Grace scowled. 'He started it!'

'Did not!' four-year-old Luca shouted.

'Did too!'

Merry gave them what Giovanni called her Death Stare until the pair of them quietened.

'That's better,' she said. 'There's no need to fight over Christmas decorations. I'll put them at exactly the same height, okay?'

They looked only slightly mollified.

First she put the woolly snowman Grace had made at school on the tree, and then, on a branch of the same height and with the same prominence, she hung Luca's semi-carefully painted wooden Rudolph the Red-Nosed Reindeer.

Those two decorations had been the most painstakingly packed items when they'd travelled from their English home to their home in Rome for the Christmas holiday.

'Can we put the angel on the tree now, Mummy?' Grace asked.

Just as she replied, 'That's Papa's job,' the front door opened and the kids went rushing off to greet him.

It was only because her children were whirling dervishes that they beat Merry to him. Even after eight years of marriage she still missed him terribly when they were parted, even if it was only for a half-day of Christmas shopping.

'I hear it's angel time,' Giovanni said, after he'd put his bags and bags of gifts in the reception room, hugged his children and pulled his wife into his arms for a kiss that made his youngest child giggle and his eldest pretend to vomit.

Merry, her arms looped around his neck, smiled. 'Yep. Angel time.'

He kissed her again, then picked up the silver angel that never failed to remind him of that night on the Meravaro Odyssey, when the snowy moonlight had turned Merry into a silvery goddess, climbed up the stepladder, and placed it on the top of the Christmas tree.

'Everybody ready?' he asked a moment later, when Merry had turned the living room lights off.

'Ready!' the children shouted.

'Three, two, one...' He pressed the button and the Christmas lights came on, and their home was filled with the sparkling, bright festive colours his wife so adored.

Later, when the children had gone to bed and Merry was taking a bath, Giovanni gazed at the tree with a heart full of joy and gratitude.

He loved his family all year round, but Christmas... Christmas was when magic happened.

Grinning broadly, he descended to the wine cellar for bottles of his wife's favourite red, so it could warm before both their families arrived the next day. Then he poured himself a measure of Scotch, a more generous measure of Irish cream liqueur for his lady, and carried them upstairs to join her in the bath...

* * * * *

THE BRIDE
HE STOLE
FOR CHRISTMAS

CAITLIN CREWS

MILLS & BOON

CHAPTER ONE

HAD TIMONEY GEORGE not felt dead inside, she might almost have enjoyed this lavish dinner the night before her farce of a wedding.

Almost.

It was merry enough, as suited a pre-wedding gathering on Christmas Eve. The guests were well-heeled and far too well-bred to speak directly of the many unfortunate undercurrents flowing up from the old stones all around them. The groom was well-liked in this particular circle, having considered himself a scion thereof for many decades. Two of his previous wives had been great favorites here as each had been part and parcel of this same crowd, as likely to claim power in Whitehall and international stock exchanges as in the titles so many had inherited.

Everything tonight was the height of sophistication, in deference to both her uncle's self-regard and his bottomless ambition. To say nothing of the groom's.

Too bad about the tart of a bride, Timoney thought from her position at her uncle's right, with a glimmer of her former wry humor.

But she locked it away. Because she didn't feel things anymore. She'd already had her fill.

Timoney looked around the hall instead. Her childhood home, entailed away to her uncle after her father's death, was done up like a stately Christmas card. Aunt Hermione was renowned for her joylessness in all things, which Timoney suspected was directly related to her endless pursuit of the skeletal figure she liked to coldly tell her rather softer and rounder teen daughters was the height of elegance. True enough, as collarbones like hers essentially acted as clothes hangers for couture. And yet despite the iron self-control and what had to be a lifetime of gnawing hunger, the woman was possessed of an excellent eye for decoration.

If Timoney had been of a more poetic bent, she might have indulged herself with imagining that tricking out the old family hall was how Hermione expressed herself in ways otherwise unavailable to her as the thin-lipped, thinner-hipped, and much younger wife of Timoney's loathsome uncle Oliver.

But poetry was far too emotional. Aunt Hermione was likely good at decorating because she was, herself, a decoration. And like all the other trophy wives here tonight, her true vocation was in making her husband happy—likely so he'd go off and be happy elsewhere and leave her to her poinsettias and evergreen boughs.

You would do well to learn a little something from Hermione, Timoney told herself, bracingly. After all, she was staring down a future as a trophy herself.

Though a rather tarnished one, as her uncle never hesitated to remind her.

She slid her gaze toward her groom and was pleased to find that even tonight, one more sleepless night before the wedding, she felt the same wealth of nothing she'd felt since her uncle had announced that Timoney's choices were stark. Either marry his business associate, Julian Browning-Case, or be cut off from the family forever.

It wasn't that Timoney liked her extended family all that much that the loss of them would be devastating in any way. But after losing her parents—and afterward, losing what was left of her heart so wholly and irrevocably—she didn't have it in her to walk away from what she had left. She also knew that her parents would have hated it if she had. They had always told her that Oliver might have faults, but it was better to believe that he was doing the best he could.

Timoney had seen no evidence of that. But really, it was the least she could do after her scandalous behavior had, according to her uncle, blackened the family name forever.

She was well aware that her uncle's real concern had nothing to do with the family's reputation. It was her reputation, not the family's, and why would anyone care what the orphaned daughter of the former heir got up to? The Georges had old money and unlike some, had held on to it. And every family with a drop of noble blood in England had at least one embarrassing member. Especially among the younger generations, who tended to perform for the pages of

Tatler—especially if it horrified their parents. It was an excuse for her uncle to flex his power as the head of the family, that was all.

But none of that mattered any longer. Julian Browning-Case, while not what Timoney would describe as *doting* in any way, was not openly vicious. He was three times her age, had not insulted her even when her uncle did, and was shaped like a man who could look forward to future heart trouble. To that end, the kindest advice her aunt had ever given her—moments before entering the engagement party a month ago that Timoney had worked to pretend wasn't happening as it did—was a pointed reminder that the Browning-Cases were not known for being particularly long-lived.

Hermione had seen Timoney balk, just outside the doors of the hall. And because Oliver had not, it had likely felt safe for her to lean in and offer a dollop of her own brand of wisdom.

For those of us who make practical instead of romantic marriages, Hermione had said with a curious expression on her face—as if, Timoney had reflected from the usual distance from which she observed anything these days, seeing her niece for the very first time. *Perspective is everything. One must always weigh one's—ah—expected future solitude against the manifold joys of one's actual marriage while it exists in its current form. It is a delicate math.*

That was the closest Hermione had ever come to any kind of surrogate maternal expression. That, too, was just as well.

Because Timoney did not wish to think too much about her parents—or her actual, horribly missed mother. It was too hard. Too painful, though it was nearly three years ago now. The two of them had been gone so quickly, so suddenly. And then everything had changed so rapidly. One terrible, irrevocable event after another so that Timoney rather thought that if she had the capacity to feel anything inside any longer, anything at all, a night like this might have wrecked her.

For surely it ought to be painful to be back here in this house where she had once been so happy. When joy had been at the heart of everything, waiting around every corner, filling all of these ancient rooms. Some of her fondest memories were of running through these halls that had seemed far lighter then, lit up with her parents' love for each other. And their boundless delight in her.

She had been on the verge of her twentieth birthday when she'd gotten the call that an icy road on a cold March evening had taken away the two people dearest to her. Mere miles from this old manor house, hidden away in hedges and stone.

Uncle Oliver had wasted no time. As the new head of the family, he was in charge of the George fortune—and Timoney's trust—until her twenty-eighth birthday. But he hadn't wished to trouble himself with paying for her until then. He had yanked her out of her beloved finishing school in the French Alps two weeks after her parents' funeral. Once she'd come back to the house he'd already claimed as his, he had informed her that for the next eight years she was to do as he bid her because, as far as he was concerned, she was a charity case. And it was too bad for Timoney that he was no fan of charity.

Even then, he had offered her choices, such as they were. She was to marry to suit him—because she would be a useless drain on him for nearly a decade aside from her ability to please his rich friends and access their wealth and favor—or she was welcome to make her own way in the world.

Timoney wet her lips with the wine on the table before her, an easy way to check to make sure her mouth was in the polite near-smile shape that was expected of her. And she nodded along, pretending to listen as the swell of conversation went on all around her.

Something in her shifted, almost unpleasantly, as she thought of the girl she'd been back then. Puffed up with outrage and grief. Filled with a deep loathing of her evil uncle and appalled at his demands. Did he really think he could treat her like a *chattel*? She was newly twenty then, and modern—not a medieval twelve.

She'd told him where he could go, she'd swanned off to London, and she'd taken the first job she could find. It turned out she was an excellent fit to do a bit of PR for a corporation she'd never heard of and didn't care to learn much about. But that was the benefit of her brand of public relations. Timoney didn't need to move the product—she threw the parties. She already had the kind of connections businessmen in suits were always gasping to exploit, so it mattered little that she knew nothing at all about the things they got up to in their endless meetings. All that mattered was that she was blonde and could get certain names to turn up, which guaranteed press.

And for a good eighteen months she'd had a lovely time. She'd shared a flat in Central London—it was more a house, really, but they all called it a flat because that felt more career-girls-in-the-Smoke—with a few girls she knew from school. All of them had been in the same sort of purgatory, cast out into the world by the heads of their families with vague expectations that they should prove they weren't entirely useless—even though everyone knew that in five years or ten or so the trust funds would start kicking in and all the proof would be pointless. They'd all been playing the same sort of waiting game in those years, trading this party for that in all the trendiest corners of giddy London, all of them counting down the days until they could stop pretending.

It would be better, Timoney had often thought back then, not to know that there was a future, fixed date upon which one would never have to worry about paying a bill again. Especially when she couldn't go beg Daddy to do it for her like her friends.

Then she'd met Crete Asgar and she'd stopped thinking of any future that didn't involve him.

Even thinking his name here, now, at a table filled with the kind of braying toffs he disdained, made her fight back a deep shiver.

There was a straight line between that fateful night and this one. It had all been headed for disaster from the start—though she hadn't known that then. She hadn't known, or wanted to know, a thing but Crete.

And Timoney was pleased that her heart had been ripped out and trampled, because it no longer beat too hard. It no longer threatened to burst. She could stand here, on the night before her wedding to another man she hardly knew, and congratulate herself on feeling very little at all.

Because after a whirlwind six months as Crete's mistress, he had finished with her two months ago. Brutally.

She felt proud that she could think of it that way. Such a quiet little sentence. *He had finished with her.* Such bloodless words to describe that scene in that penthouse of his, all modern angles and cold lines set up there above the Thames, where he'd taken everything that Timoney was, shredded it, then set it all on fire.

It's better this way, she assured herself. *There's nothing left to worry about losing.*

She heard her uncle's voice from beside her and snapped back into the here and now, at this holiday dinner party that was supposedly in her honor.

"I hope you aren't lapsing off into any unfortunate second thoughts," Uncle Oliver said coldly at her elbow. Timoney had no memory of the rest of the party rising from the banquet table, but they must have done. For now she could see straight across to her favorite tapestry on the far wall, though staring about the brightly lit, festive room didn't warm her as it might have once. It could have been ash for all she cared.

Maybe it was.

"I don't have thoughts, Uncle," she replied coolly. "Second or otherwise. You have forbidden it."

His hand was on her elbow then, and he squeezed far too hard, but she did not give him the satisfaction of wincing. No, indeed. She felt the pain of it, and some part of it thrilled her. That she could feel even a sensation like that, her uncle's brand of quietly sadistic violence, and react not at all.

"Julian tells me that you declined his offer of a drink last night," her uncle hissed into her ear. "I thought we were agreed on our course of action." Meaning he'd ordered her to offer the groom a preview of what he was purchasing.

"I will be marrying Julian soon enough," Timoney said, turning her gaze toward her uncle. And maybe it wasn't entirely true to say she felt nothing. Only that she showed nothing. Because, she could admit, she took no little pleasure in the way she gazed dispassionately at this man whose distaste for her seemed to bounce off her now. Like rubber. She especially liked that it clearly enraged him. "So no reason to rush into it."

"What sudden preciousness is this?" her uncle snarled. He leaned in closer, across the corner of the table they shared. "You're damaged goods, Timoney. That cretin's fingerprints are all over you. You flaunted yourself on his arm and he made no secret of the base physicality of your union in every photograph taken by the baying press. Yet you dare pull on a cloak of false modesty?"

Timoney pointedly tugged her elbow out of his grasp. "It's not modesty, Uncle. It's strategy. Why give myself away for free with the wedding so soon? What if he was disappointed?" She shrugged as if they were discussing livestock. Well. She supposed they were. "Damaged goods or not, why would a man pay full price for something when he'd already had it at a discount?"

If she wasn't already ruined—and not in the way her uncle imagined—this would destroy her, she was sure. This cold, dispassionate discussion of the marital rights she'd be expected to perform tomorrow.

Said marital rights that were, she was well aware, something her elderly husband was eagerly awaiting. Julian had made his interest in her clear since the moment he'd laid eyes on her here at one of her uncle's dreadful soirees not long after she'd slunk back to the ancestral pile in shame, still licking her wounds.

Though it was more accurate to say that she wasn't so much *licking wounds* as she was attempting to… pretend that she was still a person. Instead of the tiny little pile of crushed-out cinders that Crete had left behind him that night.

It had taken her uncle only a few weeks to talk her into this marriage that benefited him the most. He had ranted on about the shame she'd brought on the family. About the stain of it that would cling to his own three daughters if Timoney was allowed to continue her downward spiral.

By his reckoning, having been sullied and discarded by the likes of Crete Asgar—as infamous for his entirely self-made wealth as for his contempt of the sort of hereditary riches that Oliver now possessed—Timoney was no better than the sorts of addicts one could find cluttering up the streets. Oliver did not view such addictions as diseases. They were choices, he liked to declare. For it was one thing to genteelly pop painkillers like all the women in Oliver's circles did to survive their practical marriages. It was something else again to allow one's weaknesses to be so *visible*, and Timoney was already on the wrong side of that equation.

For she had appeared in too many papers Oliver's friends actually read, clearly in thrall to her unacceptable lover.

What next? he had thundered at a family dinner a week or so after she'd returned. Would she turn to modeling—which, in his mind, was merely prostitution by another name.

I will take that as a compliment, Uncle, Timoney had replied over her chilled soup with a flash of her former defiance. *I had no idea you rated my looks so highly.*

That had gotten her a slap.

More than that, it had gotten her uncle thinking about how best he could use her looks to his advantage.

You're the spitting image of your mother, he had said not long after. Timoney knew this was true, and it was one more thing painful for her to try not to think about. She grew more like her mother every day. The blond hair, the wide smile, the pointed chin. So similar, and yet Crete had seen to it that there was nothing resembling the spark of joy in her that had always brightened her mother's gaze.

It was better not to think of such things. It only made her sad.

Beside her, her uncle seemed to still be turning over the notion that Timoney might actually have acted strategically in his interest. But she knew it wouldn't last. She had only to inhale too loudly to agitate him anew.

"On that note," she said now, "I believe I will call it a night. I expect tomorrow will be long." And arduous in more ways than one.

"You and Julian will be staying in his guest suite tomorrow night," her uncle told her coldly. "He does not wish to travel after the reception. And I had better not hear of any impediment to a swift and comprehensive consummation of your union."

"What a pity we can't gather everyone round for viewing of the marital sheets," Timoney said drily.

Uncle Oliver's gaze was scathing. "To what end? That is a ceremony for virgins. I think we both know that there is not an unspoiled inch on your body, girl. Not after letting that animal rut all over you."

Timoney couldn't keep herself from thinking about the way he'd said that as she left her own party, smiling distantly at the assembled guests, all of them cold like Aunt Hermione, cruel like her uncle, or simply self-satisfied like her husband-to-be. They would go on, no doubt toasting their own wealth and consequence, well into the wee hours.

Maybe there would be so much toasting it would stave off the worst of any *comprehensive consummating*.

"Tomorrow, my dear," said Julian when she crossed his path, his creased and reddened face perhaps a shade too jolly for her liking.

"Tomorrow," she agreed, and had to force the ends of her mouth to curve.

Soon enough, she told herself harshly as she took herself out of the grand hall, she would be lying beneath that man. Far more intimately acquainted with his brand of jolly than she liked. It was not a pleasant thought. It had been better in the abstract, when the wedding was *someday*, not soon. Not tomorrow.

Timoney stopped at the foot of the stairs that led up toward the bedchambers. She looked toward the banquet hall she'd just left. Then, following an urge she could hardly name, she turned and fled out into the cold gardens.

Because Timoney knew full well that she would do as women always had. Or she hoped she would. She would lie back, close her eyes, and think not of England, but of the man who had imprinted himself upon her so completely that it was not clear to her that she would ever take another breath without feeling him somehow inside her all over again.

She was glad she'd thought to grab her cloak on her way outside, for the night was cold. A mist made the winter garden mysterious, especially when the moon shone through.

It was a silent night indeed.

And if Timoney had let herself feel, all the things that moved inside her then might have taken her to her knees. Right there where the flowers would bloom again in spring, long after she had calcified and died anew inside this marriage of hers. Long after Julian carried her off to his estate, sampled her, and then added her to his collection of stodgy statuary that was often written up in guidebooks, or so he claimed.

She didn't buckle or fall over. She drew the warm cloak around her and sank down on the first stone bench she found, letting her eyes fall shut.

And she worked so hard to keep herself from thinking about Crete or that last night with him too closely. But tonight was the last time she would be able to think about him as a singular event in her life. In her body.

From tomorrow forward, Crete would be the gold standard—but there would be Julian, too. And here, in the privacy of this frozen garden, she allowed herself to take a peek at all the things she truly felt about that notion.

Shock. Despair. Horror.

And a kind of resolute acceptance, because there was no changing this.

Crete Asgar had swept into her life like a wildfire, burned her to a crisp, then had left nothing in his wake save charred ground.

She could remember each and every moment with

such distinct and spectacular detail it was like punishing herself. Every touch of his hand. The first, life-altering curve of his hard mouth. The kiss that had knocked her sideways and stolen her heart.

She had given him her innocence and in return, he had taken her apart.

He had made her body feel and do things she had not believed could be real. She still woke in the night, her body electric and alive, her heart pounding so hard it hurt and his taste in her mouth.

Sometimes she would dream that she was still living with him, the heat of his possession making the whole of that penthouse glow, all its hard angles and edges softened by the fire in the way he looked at her. The way he held her. And how all-encompassing it was between them.

You are a terrible distraction, he had told her once and, foolish girl that she was, she had thought of that as a compliment.

To be able to distract a man of his singular focus. A man who had established himself with his single-mindedness. A man who had been flung out of his father's family the moment he was of age and left to fend for himself—because he was a bastard, evidence of an affair, and soundly unwanted.

Crete Asgar had not cared who wanted him. What he wanted was power.

It had taken him five years to make his first fortune. And then he had made so many subsequent fortunes that it had become something of an international sport to guess his net worth.

She should have known better than to imagine a man like that would ever welcome too many distractions.

Timoney stayed there on her cold bench, her eyes screwed shut as her heart began pounding again.

If she let herself, she could almost imagine that the Christmas Eve air was thick with the tension that had always hummed between the two of them. Only between them, and obvious from the start. She had looked up from her mobile, there outside a club in London so trendy it had already disappeared before that weekend had ended, checking in big names to another party. She couldn't remember the supposed purpose of that particular evening.

What she could remember in stark detail was lifting up her gaze from the screen of her mobile when she'd sensed the man standing before her.

She could remember her first sight of him so clearly. His dark black hair. The gleaming arrogance of his shocking blue gaze. He was tall and perfectly built, though she spent her life around men who could claim the same. Yet there was something about Crete Asgar. He was bolder. Wilder. It was as if he carried a storm with him, and it was evident in the width of his shoulders, the hard planes of his face. He was a perfect combination of his Greek mother and Scandinavian father, and it was easy to imagine him as some kind of Spartan warrior, prepared to storm the gates of Valhalla if he wished.

Looking at him had felt like an ancient ritual, sparked with drums deep within her and ecstatic dancing beneath the hidden moon. Timoney had felt as if the act of locking gazes with him was something like…obscene. Too precious and private to be happening out on a London street.

She'd seen a pulse beat in his neck. She'd seen a kind of recognition flaring his gaze.

He'd reached out his hand to slide it over her jaw, as if to test whether she was real, and she'd been lost.

It was possible she had never been found.

Crete had muttered a curse. He'd taken her hand, then led her away from her post and into the party.

She remembered the heaving club as if it was a part of him, of them, of that mad current that had flared between them from the start. She had felt it between her legs. She'd felt it all over her skin, like a terrible tattoo.

Terrible and wonderful, and then he had drawn her behind him into what she realized, only much later, was a cloakroom.

Who are you? he'd asked, breathing her in, and then his mouth had been upon her.

She liked to think that she had found herself again at the stamp of his hard possession, the slide of his tongue against hers.

Crete had not so much kissed her as taken her, stormed her, claimed her forever.

And later, she would learn the details that made what happened there marginally less sordid—not that she had cared at the time. That his security detail had paid off the cloakroom worker and stood sentry at the door, so there was no possibility that anyone would walk in on them.

But Timoney hadn't known that then. She had only been swept away. The fire between them so intense, so overwhelming, that her only choice had not been whether or not to surrender, but only how. Or how much.

She told herself to recast the scene in her mind, now, all these bitter months later. She told herself it had been a sickness on her part that had led her to tear her mouth from his to follow a spark of feminine intuition she couldn't possibly have named when she had so little experience to her name. Still, she'd sunk down onto her knees before him, because she'd wanted nothing more than to worship at the altar of... Whatever this was. Whatever he was.

Whoever he was.

She'd never done such a thing in her life. She had never *wanted* to do such a thing, but her hands had seemed to find the fly of his trousers of their own accord. Timoney had wrenched the zipper down, finding him huge and hot and pushing out to meet her.

And then she taught herself what it was to worship a man, there on her knees with the music lighting her up, the drums deep within, and a need so profound it made her sway her hips back and forth as she knelt there and took him deep into her mouth.

She followed instincts she hadn't known she possessed, running her tongue up the length of him, then sucking him deep. Out here in a cold Christmas Eve, she told herself she should be ashamed.

That she should feel wretched that she had esteemed herself so little, that she had debased herself like that, losing herself completely in the slide and the stretch of him inside her mouth.

But try as she might, that wasn't how she remembered it.

It was never how she remembered it.

For Timoney had never felt so alive, so powerful. She knew his strength by the way his hands gripped her hair, taking control of her, guiding her head, and then, as everything seemed to brighten, to get bolder, to crystallize into something—

He had pulled her away and stared down the length of his body, his chest moving and his face so intense with need and hunger that he had seemed nearly cruel.

But the kind of cruelty she wanted to wrap herself around and writhe against.

Have you ever done this before?

It had been a low, rough whisper.

And it had felt like a sacrament as she'd knelt and beheld him. A quiet, sacred moment, all theirs.

Timoney had been lying to her friends for years, pretending she possessed the casualness and sophistication they all seemed to exude so effortlessly. They had assumed she had partaken of the same experiences they did, and she had never corrected that impression. But she couldn't lie to the stranger. To him.

She had shaken her head, *no.*

And an expression she could not possibly have read had flickered across the carved sculpture of his face.

He had tucked himself away, wincing slightly, and had pulled her to her feet.

Have you ever done any of this before? he had asked.

She'd shaken her head again.

Tell me, he had ordered her. *Tell me what you've done.*

Nothing, she had confessed. *I've only been kissed once before, and not like that. And you're the only man I ever...*

Her voice had betrayed her, but she would have betrayed herself a thousand times again for the look on his face then.

So possessive. So deeply male it hurt.

Tell me your name, he had ordered her. *And then tell me what it will take to make you mine.*

She shuddered at that, here on her frigid bench on this lonely Christmas Eve, her body as alive and greedy as she had been that night.

And Timoney wanted to scream out all the anguish, all the artless fury that he'd left her with. His betrayal so absolute that it had taken her whole months to fully comprehend exactly what he'd done. Chucked her out. Forgotten her name. Washed his hands of her completely.

Yet tonight, when she should have been reveling in exactly how cold and dead inside she'd become, it was as if he was here. A ghostly presence in the mist, and it seemed deeply unfair that any ghost could fill a cold garden the way he had always overwhelmed a room.

She blew out a breath and told herself not to be such a fool. For once.

Crete was immovable. A terrible wall of stone and silence, and some part of her had known that from the start.

And still she had run straight for all that brick and smashed herself apart.

"Have you fallen asleep, Timoney?" came the terrible, wonderful, familiar voice.

Timoney wrenched open her eyes, and as she did, the moon came out from behind the clouds.

And it was impossible, but Crete was there. He stood before her looking beautiful and dangerous, as ever. He was sheer male glory in his typical uniform, one of those dark, bespoke suits that made love to his body in all the ways she longed to do.

It was not possible, and yet every hair on her body seemed to stand on end, so she knew that it was real. That this was no dream.

That somehow, Crete Asgar was stood in the remains of the garden while her uncle and her husband-to-be carried on toasting the wedding up in the manor house.

"Crete…" she whispered.

And all the feelings she'd been holding at bay slammed back into her, and worse, were lit up with hope.

Because he had finished with her because she'd committed the cardinal sin of telling him she loved him. Why would he be here, on the night before her wedding no less, unless he was finally ready to admit what she had always suspected, that he loved her, too? What else could bring him out on Christmas Eve?

"You can't possibly marry that old man in the morning," he told her, and he did not sound like a man tortured by love. He did not sound tortured at all. Or in love. If anything, Crete sounded impatient. "I have standards, Timoney. Obviously any lover after me will be a downgrade. But this verges on an insult."

CHAPTER TWO

CRETE ASGAR DID not chase women before he went to bed with them.

He certainly did not chase them afterward.

There was absolutely no reason he should have found himself in a frozen garden on Christmas Eve, no matter who his former mistress was marrying.

It was a matter of no little astonishment that he was even aware of Timoney's betrothal. He supposed it was possible that all of the women he had once claimed as his for a time had moved on into matrimony, but it was of no matter to him, as he could barely recall any of them.

And yet he felt as if he'd been assaulted by Timoney's engagement from the start. All the tabloids that had taken such delight in chasing the two of them all over London while they were together had taken an equal delight in arch commentary regarding Timoney's new choice of man. He hadn't gone looking for these accounts—and yet, it had seemed as if he could not avoid them.

Crete was not normally one to heed or even notice the opinions of others, so he had dismissed each and every article that had flashed at him from newsstands. For the whole month since her engagement announcement—a mere two months since the end of his relationship with her, not that he had counted—he had tended to his usual business affairs and told himself it was no matter to him what his former lover did.

He told himself this repeatedly, because it was usually true. If she chose to shackle herself to some old man, what was it to him?

As it turned out, Crete cared a great deal.

Far more than he would have liked.

And yet, having never chased a woman in his life, he had found himself…at something of a loss. Or as close to as he was capable of coming to such a state, given that he did not lose. As a matter of preference, will, and precedent.

He had never visited Timoney's family home. Having been ejected from what passed for his own family twice—first as a toddler and then again when he was a young man—Crete had never found himself particularly interested in the familial institution. He had made his fortune with no help from anyone and disdained these English notions of blood and honor as a matter of course. He also could not recall Timoney ever speaking too much about the people she came from—but then, they had never done much in the way of talking.

But it had still been easy enough to find his way to this rambling estate in the quiet of the countryside, far enough outside town that London seemed like it belonged in a different lifetime altogether. That was the thing with these English landowners. The houses themselves had names and everyone knew how to find them.

When he'd set out from London tonight, Crete had told himself he was only going for a drive. Then, as he found that he was inexorably winding his way into Oxfordshire, he told himself that he would stop by to see her, that was all. Have a lovely cup of tea, the English answer to any awkward moment, and be on his way again.

That it was Christmas Eve hadn't really occurred to him. But if it had, it wouldn't have stopped him. He had about as much use for Christmas as he did for families.

The real question was why he thought it necessary that he see her at all.

For Crete never returned to scenes of crimes, passion, or pain. Ever. He did not look back, for his life was about new horizons. He had always had a terrible hunger that he preferred to slake as often as possible, which was why he kept mistresses. He liked his sex consistent, constant, and without all the games involved in meeting a new woman. And when they claimed they'd fallen in love with him, as they often did when they sensed his interest was waning, he simply moved on.

Though another truth was that after separating from Timoney, Crete had found his typical hunger… changed. Not muted or removed, but somehow, though two months had passed, he had not yet slaked his thirst.

And he had told himself a hundred stories to explain that bizarre lapse in his usual habits, but the truth was before him now.

Timoney, with her hair like spun gold flowing down her back tonight, catching the moonlight and gleaming brighter. Timoney, wrapped in a cloak that looked thick against the cold night air, but did nothing to disguise the lush ripeness of her figure. Perhaps it was that he recalled it too well.

And maybe it was the Greek in him who could never get enough of her eyes, as blue as the Mediterranean, even in the shadows of this cold winter garden.

"What are you doing here?" she asked him, staring up at him as if he was a ghost.

It was possible that Crete had entertained the notion that merely glancing upon him would wake her up from whatever spell she was laboring under. It was possible that he'd expected her to fly into his arms, the way she always had while they were together.

He scowled when she did not. "Surely that should be obvious."

She did not look chastened. Her blue eyes blazed. Her chin tilted upward. "I can think of no reason."

Something sparked in him, and it surprised him. For she was as beautiful as ever, that was true. And God knew, he was a man who not only appreciated beautiful things, but had appreciated her beauty in particular. Moreover, there were certain brands of fire that she'd shared with him and he had greatly enjoyed the flames of each.

But this was different.

Because for once, Timoney was not looking at him with her customary awe and emotion.

In fact, to his astonishment, she appeared to be glaring at him. At *him*.

With what he could only call hostility.

He would not say he was *disconcerted*, per se. But only because he did not get disconcerted. His scowl deepened. "I was in the neighborhood."

"Crete Asgar himself? Roaming about England's greenest hills? Surely not." He was sure he had to be mistaken, but she sounded…mocking. Sharply amused, when he could see no call for amusement. "You were always at pains to tell me that the countryside held no allure for you. What could a man who owns his own Mediterranean islands want with rainy hedgerows and stodgy Georgian facades?"

"And yet here I am. In the neighborhood. As you see."

Crete had the strangest sensation then, when all she did was gaze back at him. And not as if she was transported by his glory as in simpler times. He could not even name the sensation, it was so foreign. And then, as she made no move toward him, he belatedly understood. He had never seen her look at him like this before.

As if she did not want him.

As if she did not want him, which was impossible.

It was unthinkable.

"You must know that I'm getting married in the morning," was what she said. Eventually. In a tone he did not like. "Have you come to wish me well? Perhaps you needed my registry details?"

Crete took that in, aware that a different kind of heat was humming in him. His months with Timoney had been lush. Sweet. From their explosive first moments in that ridiculous club straight through to the inevitable finish. He sometimes thought that had she not so foolishly fallen in love with him, they might still be together—though he very rarely kept a mistress for more than a few months. She had been that delectable.

What she had never been was sardonic.

He couldn't deny that it surprised him. But it also made him hard, so there was that.

Crete had deeply appreciated her sweetness. Yet deep down, he was a man who appreciated a fight. It was hard not to appreciate the only thing he had ever known.

"Did you grow a backbone, little one?" he asked quietly, letting the hunger and the need wash over him. Through him, like a baptism, out in the dark and cold with the mist and the moon and no more stories to explain the truth away. He wanted her. "I think perhaps it suits you."

"Maybe it's a backbone." But she sniffed. "Or maybe it's that I'm wearing another man's ring. Either way, there's nothing here for you, Crete. You made that clear."

She had not fought with him that night. That was what he had found himself brooding over in the days, the weeks, the two long months since. She had cried out her love. He had shared his philosophy with her and then, to prevent any misunderstandings, he had ordered her to go.

Standard practice, really.

Normally, the kind of women who dared tell him that they loved him were outraged at that point. They would scream at him, berate him, prove to him beyond any shadow of a doubt that their love was more squarely focused on his bank details than anything else.

But Timoney had only stared at him, tears rolling down her perfect cheeks, her soft lips parted as if she found it hard to breathe.

He hated to admit how many times that image had distracted him as he went about his business.

And now she was sitting there on the little bench before him, staring up at him like he was a stranger. He couldn't bear it. So he reached out to fit his palm to her cheek as he had a thousand times before—

But unlike before, she knocked his hand away.

And then surged to her feet. "You don't get to show up here in the middle of the night and just…touch me whenever you feel like it."

"Do you not wish for me to touch you?" He let his hand fall back to his side. "I think you are a liar, Timoney."

"If you wished to touch me, you shouldn't have tossed me aside like so much trash," she threw back at him. "Should you?"

"It wasn't the touching I had an issue with."

He thought she might shout at him, and he couldn't decide if he would find that exciting—or if it would once again make her seem like a stranger to him.

But she didn't.

Her chest was rising and falling rapidly, the cloak spilling out all around her, a deep red. She put him in mind of some kind of fairy tale, out here in the misty moonlight, when he had as little use for children's stories as he did for Christmas Eve.

Crete was not one for holidays in general, but especially not this holiday. It seemed a part and parcel of that kind of home and hearth, overtly familial notion he had never really experienced. But Timoney in a red cloak had him feeling the closest to festive he'd felt in a long time.

Maybe ever.

"Why are you here, Crete?" she asked, her voice even. When the Timoney he knew had never seemed to have herself in control. She'd never indicated she wanted to try to keep herself in control. "You made it clear to me that you don't care about me. Crystal clear. So why should it matter to you who I marry?"

He let out a bark of disbelief. "You cannot marry this man. To begin with, he is ancient."

"Some would say he must be filled with wisdom, then." Her smile seemed sharp. "What luck."

"He cannot possibly satisfy you, Timoney." Crete studied her. "I could barely keep up with you."

There was a telltale bloom of color in her cheeks, but all she did was square her shoulders. "That remains to be seen. My previous experience left much to be desired."

He laughed. "We both know that is a lie."

"Yes, Crete. We had chemistry. But I can't say

I have much admiration for the way it ended." She crossed her arms before her, as if she was warding him off. And she frowned at him. At *him*. "And here's what I know about Julian. He will not leave me. He will not cruelly cast me aside if I say the wrong thing. He will honor the promises he makes me tomorrow. Any way I look at it, marrying him seems like a good bargain."

"You cannot be serious."

Crete moved closer to her. And he, who prided himself on his iron self-control to match his will of steel, had no idea how his hands rose to grip her slender shoulders. Only that they did, and that holding her made him…feel.

He concentrated on the part he understood. The heat. And the faint scent of her, teasing him on the cold breeze like a memory.

"Let me assure you of something," she whispered, her chin still high and her arms still crossed. "Unlike some people standing in this garden, I do not take relationships lightly. But I certainly do not take the prospect of marriage lightly, either. You can be certain that whatever else I might be in regard to my wedding tomorrow, I am deadly serious."

Crete zeroed in on the most egregious part of that little speech. "You think I took our relationship lightly?"

She scowled at him, another first. Then she lifted her hands as if to knock his grip off her shoulders. But instead, her fingers braceleted his wrists, not quite managing to close, and stayed there.

And he had the notion that she could feel the way

his blood pumped in his veins. That she could feel it in her, too. That their bodies were still that connected, that attuned.

The song of it seemed to pool in his sex, then beat hard, like a drum.

"The only thing you take seriously is your money," she threw at him.

And she clearly meant it to wound.

But Crete only laughed and pulled her closer, because he could smell that wildflower honey scent of her everywhere. And he could feel the heat of that in his blood, too, because everything about Timoney was heat and honey, longing and that need so deep, it felt like it was in his bones.

"Yes, I care about my money," he confessed. He laughed again. "I think you'll find it comes as a habit to those who remember having none." He jerked his chin at the sprawling mansion behind her and the extensive grounds. It had been a ten-minute drive in from the lane to find the house. "Not all of us grew up surrounded by such finery."

"I think you'll find that the rags-to-riches tale is more relatable after your first fortune," Timoney retorted. "Not so much your tenth. Or is it your twentieth by now?" Her eyes were bright with a new kind of fire, and it took him long moments to understand that it was temper. Why did he want to drown himself in her—temper and all? "I have all of seventy pounds to my name at present, Crete. Tell me which one of us is privileged?"

"Seventy pounds, a rich fiancé, and a fortune to

come." He shook his head at her. "You're not exactly the Little Match Girl yourself, are you?"

"What I am or am not is none of your concern," she threw at him. "You still haven't told me what you're doing here. Did you pop round to infuriate me?"

"That is but a happy side effect."

"I would have thought you'd be thrilled to find that I was getting married." Her eyes flashed. "No need to worry about scraping me off your boot heel if I'm someone else's problem, isn't that right?"

He didn't think he'd said precisely that to her, though Crete knew that it aligned perhaps too closely with his feelings on the topic. For it was a fact that he had always been delighted when—if—he heard that his former mistresses had moved on. There was far less chance that they would hang about making things tedious that way.

But this was Timoney.

And nothing about her was tedious.

And he was *here*, wasn't he? It spoke volumes.

"Very well," she was saying, in that bristling British way. "I can see that you really did come here just to be difficult."

"Some would argue that I do this without even trying."

"Here's the great news, Crete," she said, and he felt certain that he would not find whatever news she was about to share at all great. "When I was your mistress, it fell to me to try to keep you happy. And I failed at that. I failed at it so completely that you not only finished things, but ordered me to move out immediately—then made sure your security detail saw to it that I did."

"That is not entirely true." But it was close enough to make him uncomfortable, he was forced to acknowledge.

"Whatever it is you want tonight, both you and I already know that I don't have what it takes to please you," Timoney said. Not as if she was apologizing or even particularly broken up about it. She inclined her head. "So perhaps you'd best move along."

It was an order, clearly. But against his will, all he could think about was all the ways she really had made him happy.

Again and again and again.

He had moved her into his flat within a week of meeting her—and with only the most superficial vetting—because once he'd tasted her, he couldn't bear to have a single free moment and not indulge himself with more of her. His craving for her had been so intense that he'd reasoned the only way to handle it was to immerse himself.

Completely.

And still it hadn't been enough.

For the first time, he admitted that maybe, just maybe, there had been some small part of him that had been relieved when she'd crossed his uncrossable line that night. When she'd spilled over with those words she should never have said.

Especially when he was not the least bit tired with her yet.

Because he had spent whole months consumed

with her, and maybe, just maybe, he had been grateful to get his head back.

But he realized now, as the mist swirled around between them and her blue eyes glistened in the dark, that he'd only been fooling himself.

"You cannot marry that man," he growled at her.

"Why not?" she tossed back at him. "It seems to me that Julian is as good as anyone else. Better than most."

"He is neither. He is a cretinous gasbag who sheds wives—"

"The way you shed mistresses?"

He didn't care for that. "There are no similarities between us."

"That's why I agreed to marry him in the first place," she snapped. "I understand his expectations of me, Crete. There's no pretense."

"Your body. Your soul. Your life."

Timoney laughed at that, but the sound was bitter, and he hated that. She had been so joyful. So bright. He hated that he had rendered her something less than that. That he had taken it along with her innocence.

Maybe he truly was the monster his father's wife had always maintained he was.

All evidence suggested it.

"Imagine that," Timoney said when she stopped laughing, and her blue eyes shone cold. "Julian wants the same things from me that you did. But look at all he's willing to offer me in return. His name. Children, if I wish it. Primarily my body, yes, but the difference between the two of you is that he's not afraid to sweeten the pot. Nor will he cast me aside if I displease him, unlike his former wives. Divorce would be far too expensive. My uncle has seen to it."

That she was comparing him to the likes of Julian Browning-Case was insult enough. That he was losing by her reckoning was insupportable.

"You cannot marry him," Crete said again, while a terrible storm wailed in him as he pictured, against his will, what she was describing. Surrendering herself. Selling herself. Giving the decrepit old man that body of hers that Crete understood, with a certain resignation, he had long since considered only and ever his.

It turned out that he was not prepared to share.

"Why not?" she demanded. Her hands turned to fists and she knocked them into his chest. "Give me one good reason why I shouldn't?"

He welcomed the faint kiss of her fists. He welcomed any touch from her at all, and what did it say that he'd fallen so far? But there was no arguing with the truth. There was only accepting it and moving forward.

Crete had built his life on exactly this premise.

And he was more than happy to provide her with all the reasons she needed to see this truth as he had. Surely that, in the end, was why he'd come here.

Surely that was what mattered.

"Because, little one," he growled at her, "you have belonged to me since the moment we met. You still do."

And then Crete proved it the way he always had, by crushing his mouth to hers.

CHAPTER THREE

TIMONEY HAD THOUGHT this would never happen again.

She'd been sure. He'd made certain she was sure.

But now he was kissing her again, as if there had been no separation. She was kissing him back as if her heart had never been crushed. And all her dreams, all her memories, faded away as the searingly beautiful reality of it took hold, sweeping through her and lighting her up as if she had never dimmed.

As if there had never been the faintest hint of darkness.

The taste of him. The heat. The way a kiss from this man was nothing so simple as the word implied. There was no fairy tale here. There was no swelling soundtrack in the distance with magic all around. It was too intense for any of that. Too wild.

Too much.

And even though Timoney knew better now, even though he had taught her too well that the abandon she felt when she was close to him was a lie—

How could any of that matter when his mouth was on hers again?

When finally—*finally*—she felt alive again?

As she always had, Timoney melted into him, and that, too, was an opportunity for more intensity. Because the wall of his chest was hard and hot, and far better than she remembered it. When she had remembered it in excruciating detail. And it was this particular stone, this wall of toned muscle, that she had tried so hard to shatter herself against, hadn't she?

And had. Over and over again.

Like every kiss, it was like the first.

Unlike so many others, Timoney knew, now, that it could also be the last.

But the mad storm of sensation washed over her and through her, and it didn't matter that now, she knew this would end.

It didn't matter because it was too much in all the ways she'd grown to adore. It was too wicked, too impossible, too good.

Crete's tongue found hers and once again, he led her on that ancient dance that he had taught her.

And she knew each and every one of the steps by now. The angle of his jaw, the low, distant growling sound he made that had always made her shudder. It did again.

Deeper. Wilder.

It seemed preordained that he should have found her tonight, in this barren garden while seasons of flowers slumbered beneath their feet. It seemed right, somehow, that he would appear like one of her dreams and kiss her like this, making the choice before her—

the choice she had already made, though her memories had plagued her—so stark. So desperate.

So unfair.

It was that last thought that had her pulling her mouth from his, so that their breath sawed out at once and made their own clouds.

But for once, she felt as if her own mind was remarkably clear where he was concerned. Though to make sure, she stepped back and put some space between their bodies. Better not to put her yearning for him to the test.

"This is wrong." Timoney was surprised that she could use her mouth to speak when what she wanted to do was curl into a ball and cry. Or pound actual stones to sand. Maybe both at once. "I'm engaged to marry Julian."

Crete's hard mouth curved. She would not call it a smile. "I hardly think that counts."

"How liberal you are," she replied, doing absolutely nothing to hide the bite in her voice. It felt like a weapon. Maybe the only one she could muster. "I hope you take this same position when, should you ever condescend to marry, you find your betrothed in another's arms only hours before the ceremony. Somehow I do not think you will."

"It does not count, little one, because you did not choose to marry him." That impossible dark blue gaze of his seemed to pin her back down to the stone bench behind her. "Did you?"

"Of course I had a choice." She should have left it at that. But instead, her mouth kept moving, and not in the right direction. "It might not have been a choice I liked, but I chose it. I chose Julian."

Maybe if she said it enough it would feel more like a gift and less like a noose.

"Did you indeed? Out of all the men in the world, you looked around and selected him?" Again, that curve in his mouth. That too-sharp amusement in his gaze. She wanted to claw at his face—but her hands couldn't be trusted to stick with violence. Crete continued as if she'd answered him. "Or was he rather chosen for you? Presented to you as the only option, to better serve your uncle's interests?"

"I'm astounded that you know Julian exists in the first place," she managed to say. "Or that my uncle does, for that matter. And I'm awash in pure astonishment that you have ever bothered to consider the business interests of men you so clearly disdain."

"I know other people exist, Timoney." His arrogant expression intensified. "I don't care that they exist. There's a difference."

"Only if you're a raging narcissist."

He shrugged, looking wholly unbothered by that. "Narcissists claim power that is not theirs and attempt to profit off of it by any means necessary. My power is earned. And it doesn't take more than a cursory examination of the financial pages to know that your uncle has grand ambitions."

In all the intense and heartbreaking dreams and daydreams she'd had since leaving London, Timoney had not thought to imagine what it might be like to finally see Crete again…only to discuss her uncle. Or Julian, for that matter.

She had imagined, fervently, that if he came for her, it would be to declare his undying love at last. To beg for her to come back to him. To tell her that he'd missed her terribly, that he couldn't live without her, that he would do anything if she would only come back to him…

But none of those words seemed to be forthcoming. And the longer she stared up at him, waiting for him to even hint a little in that direction—she had that little pride, apparently—the more arrogant he looked.

And the more a new sort of stone hardened into shape inside her.

"What does it matter?" She shook her head, trying to keep it clear. It didn't matter how he kissed. What mattered was how he'd disposed of her when he was done. She needed to remember it. "The choice was made."

"Unmake it," Crete urged her.

Her heart, her poor heart, broke. Then melted. Then broke anew as he reached over and cupped her face in his hands.

As if this was a romance. As if this was the part where that pretty music rose to a crescendo while the credits rolled and happiness was assured all around.

When she knew better.

"The guests are already here," she told him, furious that it was so hard to keep her voice even. To fight back the emotion that threatened to spill out from her eyes. "The contracts have already been signed."

"And yet we do not live in the Dark Ages, where such things might be considered irrevocable. Do not marry him, Timoney." His thumbs moved against her cheekbones, spreading warmth and heat spiraling through her. Once upon a time, she had confused that for affection. Once, she'd imagined that no matter what he said, moments like this told a different tale. Back then, when he'd told her he could not love, she'd been so sure that she knew better. Because she had known so much love from her parents, and how could that all have been lost forever? She had been certain she could *show* him. "Come back to London with me. Surely you want that more than this."

And the truth was that Timoney wanted nothing else.

In the distance, she could hear music from the house, the piano's sweet melody spilling out into the dark. Silent night. Holy night. Yet all was not calm. She had felt nothing for so long that it was like being much too cold only to leap into hot water. Everything tingled, so sharp it was very nearly painful.

In some ways, it was worse than pain. Pain would have taken over and blocked out everything else.

She was entirely too aware of the things she felt.

Each and every one of the things she felt.

"You don't want me," Timoney said quietly, though she didn't want to. Oh, how she didn't want to. But she couldn't hide behind convenient fictions any longer. If she couldn't tell the truth now, when could she? And if she couldn't tell the truth…who was she? "When you had me in every possible way, you threw me out."

"Timoney—"

"Have you changed your mind, Crete?" she asked him then, cutting off whatever excuse he might have offered. If, indeed, he would have bothered to make any excuses. "Have you come here to tell me that you love me, after all?"

And her curse was that even though she knew he had not—that he could not—she wished he had. That he was about to drop to his knees, make speeches, pull out a ring. Make any or all of the grand gestures she would have sworn she neither wanted nor needed…but, it turned out, she would very much have liked to have experienced. With him, the only man she had ever loved.

The only man you ever will love, a voice within her intoned.

As if her heart wasn't already broken enough.

His face didn't change. And he was such a magnificent specimen of a man. She had never seen his like, his beauty so ferocious it hurt to look upon. Yet once she had, it was impossible to look away. She felt as if he'd burned himself into her, a terrible brand, and yet the fact that she could smell her own charred flesh didn't keep her from tracing her fingers over the marks he'd left.

Again and again and again.

Something softened in his gaze, but his mouth stayed in its usual hard line.

"Come back," he said again, more command than entreaty. "I don't have to tell you how good we were together. You already know. I do not pretend to understand why you would walk willingly into a marriage that can give you nothing you need. Or want. Come back and we need never speak of this chapter again."

The longing was so intense then that surely she should have doubled over. Crumpled to the frozen ground. Cried, at the very least.

Timoney would never know how she remained upright. Her gaze clear. "I will take that as a no. Nothing has changed. Because you can't change, can you?"

She thought she might hate him, then, and that felt like an upgrade from the mess inside her. Because it was easier to be numb. It was far easier to lock up all the things she felt far away, where none of it could torture her. Where she could observe what happened to her from a distance. Where she could feel nothing.

Now she felt everything.

Now she *felt*, and that might have been the most unforgivable thing he'd done yet.

"We don't need to change a thing," Crete said, as if he was warming to the subject. It made her wonder what he'd come here to say, if not this—but she pushed it aside. It didn't matter. None of this mattered. "It can be as it was."

"It can't be as it was." She shook her head at him. "Because I'm in love with you, Crete, and your reaction to my daring to say that out loud was to end everything. On the spot. Why would I sign up for that again?"

His expression hardened, and she knew that look. It was one she'd seen him wear often enough while tending to his many business concerns.

"Surely it is better to be with someone you love than this animated corpse who you will never love at all," he said, mildly enough, though she could see that considering gleam in his gaze.

Timoney wanted to scream at him not to imagine he could handle her the way he handled his legion of underlings.

But screaming would prove to him that she needed handling and kid gloves and all the other things that set her teeth on edge. Or would, if he had ever offered them. He hadn't before.

"On the contrary," she said, with a great, icy calm that she hadn't known she had inside her. "Far better to be in a relationship where I know exactly what I'm getting and what I can expect. Far better that than dying of loneliness with a man who could love me, but refuses. If I'm not to be loved, Crete, I'd rather not pretend. I'd rather immerse myself fully in the lovelessness."

What she didn't say was, *I would rather not break my heart all over again.*

He actually laughed. Timoney felt nothing short of murderous.

"I have never heard anything so absurd," he said. "You cannot mean it. Might as well march yourself off to a stint in a prison, no?"

Timoney did not choose to tell him that her upcoming wedding rather felt like a prison, actually, and that she welcomed it. Better unmistakable iron bars than a touch like fire and that look in his gaze when he was inside her. Better not to avoid confusion.

"Surely you've had other mistresses who moved on to other men," she said, scowling at him. "I don't understand why this is such a surprise to you."

"It is true." Crete shrugged again and looked almost...philosophical. "But they did not love me. Many times they said they did, but it was not so. Not like you. You, Timoney, I believed."

"Your arrogance is breathtaking."

That wasn't hyperbole. She felt as if she'd fallen from a great height and had landed hard on her back, knocking all the air out of her body.

Timoney stepped back even farther, because she didn't want to. She wanted to move closer to him. She wanted to fling herself into his arms and promise him anything at all if he would simply take her back.

Did it matter if he loved her? Surely she could love him enough for the both of them...

But this was the trouble with Crete. He felt like a dream come true, but she knew better. She'd lived it once already. This time, she knew there was no happy ending here. There was only misery—and that dispassionate look on his face gone cruel when he dismissed her.

She couldn't sign up for that again. She wouldn't. "If you've come all this way simply to tell me that you don't like the idea of my marrying Julian, it's a wasted trip. You could have saved yourself the trouble."

"What would make it something other than a waste, then?" he asked, in the silky manner that set off little fires all over her body—and also reminded her that whatever else he was, he was almost supernaturally gifted at making people do as he pleased. It was one of the reasons he had made himself too many fortunes to count.

She had never been any match for him.

But then, Timoney wasn't the same woman he'd met outside that club, was she? She was the woman who'd survived him the only way she knew how.

"You have nothing to offer me," she told him quietly. "It's Christmas Eve, Crete. This is a season of miracles, but you have none on offer. You decided long ago that you are incapable of such things, of any and all human emotion. And once your mind is made up, there's no changing it. I wouldn't dream of trying."

"But you cannot wish for this fate, Timoney," he said, his voice still a rough thread of silk against the night. "Do you think I have forgotten how you came apart in my hands? How you sobbed out my name? How you told me you might die if I did not return to you quickly enough each evening?"

She swayed on her feet, still breathless. And she didn't like him reminding her of those days, those weeks, that life. How desperate she'd been for him, always. How needy.

But he wasn't finished. "And yet you truly plan to shackle yourself to a man who will use your body to pleasure himself? You wish to endure a lifetime of his touch?"

"For all you know Julian is a marvelous lover," she threw at him.

And then, at last, she saw Crete change.

It was instant and overwhelming. As if they'd moved from a bright, sunny summer's day to a howling winter storm in the blink of an eye. He seemed to grow larger, wider.

Darker.

It took her long moments, her heart stuttering in her chest, to recognize that though it felt like he'd gone volcanic—though she could *see* the explosion all around them—he actually hadn't moved at all.

"And have you had many lovers since we parted?" he asked. Softly. So softly.

But the threat there was unmistakable.

Not that he would hurt her with his hands. That would be easier to handle, because if he was that kind of brute, she wouldn't feel so torn by this. By him. Rather that he would make his displeasure known in other ways—and heaven help her, but she didn't think she could survive that again. She wasn't entirely sure she'd survived it the first time.

Her heart was pounding so hard that she hurt. It *hurt*. And she had never been a liar. But she didn't think that any good would come of telling truths here. Not when he looked molten and dangerous, and too likely to express himself with his mouth on her body—

And no matter that her body responded enthusiastically to that notion, she couldn't let that happen. Not because she was so virtuous, but because the only way to live through this was to go cold turkey from Crete and his dangerous, intoxicating touch. That he'd kissed her tonight was bad enough. Anything more and she would be lost.

Julian wasn't anyone's idea of a savior, but there would be safety in marrying him all the same.

"A lady doesn't kiss and tell," she said, lifting her chin.

But Crete only laughed, as he closed the distance between them. "I don't believe you."

"Luckily, I don't require your belief. That's the thing about facts, Crete. They remain facts whether or not you believe in them."

There was a curve to his hard mouth. A gleam far harder in his dark gaze. "I believe in this."

Then he was kissing her again, and this time, it was as if he'd taken all that heat, all that fire, and thrown gas on it.

It was a mad spiral of sensation and need. Timoney could feel him everywhere, swirling around inside her, pooling low in her belly, and making her melt between her legs.

He bent her backward and she arched into him, jubilant and joyful, her blood pumping out a rhythm that sounded like *At last, at last, at last.*

And it was only when a shock of cold hit the heated flesh of her breasts that she remembered herself.

Or tried.

She pushed him away again, unable to tell if she was gasping for breath or sobbing.

More likely, it was something in between. She glanced down at the bodice of the dress she wore, and readjusted it. Then pulled her cloak tight over breasts that ached, because, she knew, all they wanted was more.

All she ever wanted from Crete was more.

And she knew that as long as it was physical, he would give her all the *more* she could possibly want. More than she could handle. Almost more than she could take.

Timoney had lived like that for months. And when he'd taken all that *more* away, with such brutal finality, she'd thought it might kill her. Maybe it had killed her, in a way, because she wasn't who she'd been then. Not anymore. She couldn't pretend that she was.

Somehow, she knew that it was only possible to fall in love so heedlessly once.

Because ever after, it would be impossible to forget what it was like to crash back down to earth.

Or what it was like to live like that, in so many pieces.

She had gathered herself together and loved again after her parents died. But how could she possibly be so reckless again? She couldn't. She wouldn't.

"I can't tell you how many times I dreamed that you would come," she told him softly. "But it makes no difference, in the end. At least I know that now."

She told herself that was a kind of gift. A bit of grace in an otherwise bone-chilling December. Something she would find a way to live with, going forward.

The way he looked at her then was in no way graceful. "I think you will find it a stark difference, indeed, to wake the morning after next to find a man half in the grave heaving away on top of you."

Timoney did not particularly wish to imagine that. Some demon moved in her, however, and she found herself smiling serenely at him as if the image did not bother her at all.

"Crete." She tried to sound something like pitying, because it felt good. To pity someone other than herself. "You're too late."

His hard mouth moved. That was all. Maybe she needed to examine why it was she wanted it to mean more than it did. "That sounds a great deal like a challenge."

"It's really not." She thrust her hands deep into the pockets of her cloak, not sure that she would ever truly be warm again. Not now that he'd reminded her what true heat was like. True fire. "I do appreciate you coming here and reminding me exactly why I'm making the decision that I am."

Crete studied her. The moon came out from behind the clouds again and shone down all around them, making everything feel magical and miraculous—and a great many other things that were not true. She blamed Christmas. And him.

"You're getting married in the morning," he said, after a moment. "That means I have the whole of the night to change your mind."

And like that, she lost the ability to breathe again. "It…absolutely does not mean that."

His eyes glinted with a hint of heat. "I don't mind telling you, little one. I like my chances."

"What do you think will happen? Do you think you're going to so muddle my head with sex that I'll forget what you did to me? That you had me bodily re-moved from your flat?" And she still couldn't breathe, but it turned out, she didn't care about that as much as she could have. As much as she should have. "Because let me assure you, Crete. I won't forget that. Ever."

"Forget or do not forget," he said with a shrug. A *shrug*. "All I ask is that you allow me to remind you of everything else."

Timoney couldn't understand why he wanted to do this. It didn't make sense, not after the night he'd so cruelly tossed her aside. When he'd been brutally clear that there was no future here, no matter what.

She stared at him in the mist and moonlight, that beautiful face of his set and unreadable, the way it always was.

And she reminded herself that she had survived him. She had survived that night, though she'd thought it might kill her. Dead inside though she may have felt, she had not, in fact, died. She wasn't the same woman he'd crushed so easily.

And she was marrying Julian tomorrow, no mat-ter what he did tonight.

If, as she suspected, the light of day would remind Crete how little he wanted the things he seemed to think he wanted here in the dark, that was fine.

What would it hurt to treat this as a little exercise in wish fulfillment until then? She wasn't suscepti-ble to him now—not the way she had been, anyway. She could have lost herself completely in him only moments ago, but she hadn't. She'd found her foot-ing. She'd held it.

And this was the first time she'd been around him for more than a few minutes without the passion between them erupting, rolling on into that same inferno no matter where they were. The cloakroom of a club. Too many vehicles to count. The bathroom at an upscale restaurant with most of fashionable London on the other side of the door.

There you go, she told herself. *It's already different. You're fully clothed.*

She told herself that the heat she felt inside her then was shame. And then felt a tiny ribbon of real shame, because it wasn't.

"You'd better come into the house," Timoney told him, after a moment. After making sure she felt steady enough with the invitation. "But you mustn't be seen."

Then she whirled around and started back up the cold stone path, not checking to see if he followed her.

For she knew that he did.

Like something out of a Greek myth.

Are you afraid that if you look back that he'll be gone? she asked herself as she walked. *Or that he won't?*

She led him to one of the doors on the far side of the manor that led to the conservatory, where no one but Timoney ever seemed to go. Her uncle and his guests had moved into one of the sitting rooms, as she'd seen through the brightly lit windows, and she couldn't think of a reason any of them would venture away from the warmth and the drink to come all the way across into the old part of the house.

It would be safer to take Crete to her bedchamber, where she could lock the door, but she hoped she wasn't quite *that* foolish.

Once inside, she sat down on her favorite settee, where she'd spent hours and hours as a child. And she wasn't prepared for the sight of Crete, then, prowling around this particular room as if he was altering her childhood with every step. He was so male. So reckless and bold in this place she thought of as soft. Sweet.

She told herself it was a rude intrusion, that was all. He didn't belong here. He belonged in that flat of his, sharp and chilly. Not in a room of books and cozy throws, soft woven rugs, and the promise of plants come spring.

Timoney ignored that melting sensation, molten hot between her legs, that suggested she was interested in other intrusions, the ruder the better.

This was for her, she reminded herself sternly. She would indulge Crete, but only to please herself. Because she hadn't imagined she would ever be alone with him again. And this was her opportunity to ask him all the things she'd always wanted to know, but had been too afraid—or perhaps too overawed—to ask while they'd been together.

And this time, he might actually answer.

He might deny it, but she knew that he would leave. Possibly as soon as he realized that she was not the girl he'd known. That he'd made her into the woman she was now, and he might not like what that meant.

But before he understood that shift, he would answer a few questions.

Like the one she'd asked the version of him she carried around in her head every night since she'd last seen him.

"So. Crete." She cleared her throat. "Why are you like this?"

CHAPTER FOUR

IT TOOK CRETE a moment or two to process that question.

He stopped moving around the graceful room she'd led him into. It gave the sense of genteel clutter and faded glory, from the arched glass windows that curved up overhead to the battered old carpets tossed this way and that across the floor. Betraying the sort of carelessness that went along with generational wealth, he thought.

It was only when your great-grandfather had carted that rug back from the mystical lands where he'd found it, and your grandmother had used it in her dressing room, that you might carry on and fling it on the floor beneath a great mess of planters.

Still, he couldn't work up his usual disdain for these people who thought the world had been built for their pleasure. Because the books on the overstuffed shelves that lined the back wall were not the fancy hardbacks with gold embossing on the spines that he always thought looked fake. They seemed to be popular in the supposed libraries a certain sort of man always seemed to have scattered about the old stately home, though Crete had never been able to imagine a person actually using such a place for anything but attempting to intimidate.

But this room was different. It felt like Timoney.

"Is this your room?" he asked, because it had her air, somehow. Did he actually smell wildflower honey, or was he imagining it? All the books on the shelves were well read. He could see the swollen, cracked spines of thick, fat paperbacks. He picked up a battered hardcover at random and found the pages worn from turning.

This was like a view inside of her, and he had avoided that. Had gone out of his way to avoid that, in point of fact. This was an intimacy. And Crete had always preferred that his intimacies remain only and ever physical.

"My mother used to grow her favorite plants here," Timoney told him, a distant sort of look in her eyes, as if she was looking off into a beloved past. That, too, seemed like an intimate moment. Or maybe it was that he, personally, had no experience with any past that wasn't harsh. So much so that, any time she had attempted to talk about the parents she so clearly loved, he had prevented her. Usually by stoking the fires between them as he would have dearly liked to do now. But he did not. Because if she wished to discuss her mother, he would grit his teeth and allow her to make her mother real for him. No matter how uncomfortable it made him. "She was no gardener, but she liked to putter about with the odd herb and an occasional hardy geranium. She would play with potting soil and seeds in the sunlight and I would read."

The look on her face was so open then. So naked. Something seized in his chest at the sight, and he told himself it was concern for her, that was all. That she should show such softness to another. That she would allow herself such recklessness and let it infect the whole of her face.

That she should let anyone see her feelings like this. Even him. *Especially* him.

She sniffed as she regarded him, her expression suddenly much less soft. "You haven't answered the question."

He looked at the shelves of books again, a vast selection of all genres with colorful covers and yellowing pages, trying to imagine Timoney here. As a small child, as young girl, as a sulky teenager. And with a mother who wanted to spend time with her— or, at least, did not actively avoid it.

The notion was like folklore. He dismissed it.

"Why am I like what?" he asked. Coolly.

He turned to face her again, and they were indoors now. This room was far brighter than the moonlight out in the garden. The lamps she'd turned on as she entered, finding them so easily in the dark that he should have known precisely how comfortable she was here, cast a buttery light all around. He had told himself, in that moment before she'd switched on the first light, that the spell would be broken. That the creature he'd seen out there in the dark was not the enchantress she'd seemed in that swirling red cloak, as much mist as moon.

But of course, in the light, it was worse.

She made his mouth go dry.

Timoney still wore her cloak, swirled around her like some kind of blanket. She pulled her feet up beneath her and she should have looked like a child, sitting there on that little couch of hers while she gazed up at him with her blue eyes so solemn.

Almost accusatory.

But she did not look like a little girl at all. Even inside, she looked as if the moon was in her hair. She was elfin, unworldly. Her blond hair was silvery as it fell about her shoulders, cascading down from two pearlescent combs. Her chin was pointed just enough to make her face the shape of a heart. And there was that perfect bow of a mouth of hers, generous and sensual, that he had tasted a thousand times. Yet he still wanted more.

He had accepted that truth, uncomfortable as it was, out there in the dark.

Or he had stopped fighting it. Surely that was the same thing.

"Everybody knows your story," Timoney said after a moment. In a careful sort of way, as if she was choosing her words with precision. As if he required such handling.

He bristled at that notion. "Do they indeed? Am I so easily digested, then?"

"What you tell of your story, anyway," she amended, a considering sort of look on her face.

"Your mother met your father when she was very young and he was on a business trip to Athens."

Crete would never understand why the everyday squalid details of his parents' lives were a subject of such fascination to other people. When what mattered, to his mind, was never the hand he'd been dealt but what games he'd learned to play—and win—with those cards.

"My father had the affair," he said now. Perhaps too brusquely. "He was married. My mother was foolish perhaps, but all she did was follow her heart. She was eighteen. He was thirty-four. I tell you this only because their age gap is always mentioned, as if it alone is what caused all the trouble."

Timoney looked almost dreamy. "I think many people forget that eighteen feels quite worldly and grown up. To the person experiencing it."

Crete found himself leaning back against the nearest bookshelf and thrusting his hands deep in the pockets of his trousers, because it was that hard to keep them to himself. He tried to remember other times that he and Timoney had sat about talking, but none came to mind.

Because when they were in the same room together, it had always been about that passion. About that need. He could feel it inside him, bright and greedy.

Outside, he'd intended to indulge in that passion. That greed. To use it to prove what he already knew. That she was his—whatever that meant. And that whatever happened, she certainly wasn't going to marry a lascivious old tosser like Julian Browning-Case. He had felt certain that the best way to make his point was by reminding her exactly how good it was between them. As acrobatically as possible.

But he hadn't gotten where he was by being unable to read a room. It was obvious to him that Timoney believed he wasn't capable of talking. That this was a challenge.

And Crete had never backed down from a challenge.

He wasn't about to start now.

"I do not disagree with you," he said after a moment. "After all, I was cast out into the world at eighteen myself. No one seemed concerned about whether or not I felt ready. I was expected to be a man, therefore I was." He lifted a shoulder, then dropped it. "But my mother had been very sheltered up until that point. She was not prepared."

He said that with authority, though all he knew about his mother had come to him secondhand. Some of what he knew had come from the very articles he disliked, because his mother's family had allowed reporters access they had always refused him.

Until he became so infamous the world over that they'd changed their tune. Which had allowed him to refuse them all in turn. The circle of life was a circle of spite, he had always believed. And he had never been afraid to prove it.

But somehow he did not want to express it in quite that way to this magical creature, who, unlike everyone else, never looked at him as if he was an alien.

Crete normally did not care how others regarded him. He often encouraged them to imagine he was not quite human.

It was different to imagine Timoney doing the same. The notion made him...*feel*.

And it was an unpleasant feeling. He preferred her to regard him as if he might, in fact, be the sun.

He had come to depend on it.

"You lost her when you were two years old," Timoney said, and though it was a statement, he could see the question in her blue gaze.

"Do you wish to tell me my own story?" he asked her. "Or are you waiting for me to tell you things it seems you already know?"

He hated that her gaze turned...sympathetic. "Do I know the real story, Crete? Does anyone?"

Crete found himself rubbing at his chest, and dropped his hand like it was lit on fire. He didn't understand why he was indulging her like this. A challenge, yes. But as much as he didn't walk away from challenges, he was also justly famous for changing rules he didn't like to suit himself. What he knew was that he didn't want her to marry tomorrow.

But why was he subjecting himself to... this?

It wasn't that he didn't spend his time chatting with women. Crete didn't spend any time chatting. With anyone. At all. He knew that other men had friends. Warmer associations with others. The odd golf buddy. But he had never seen the allure in such connections.

And he didn't particularly care for the fact that this woman had seemed to zero right in on the *why* of it.

Crete had always taken such pride in the idea that nobody knew him at all.

"I don't remember her," he told Timoney now. Because the only thing worse, to his mind, than telling her his personal details was the idea that she might think he was afraid to do it. When he was afraid of nothing. Not even the sad truth of the end of his mother's life. Abandoned by her lover, then her family. Unable to care for her child when she was little more than a child herself. Was it any wonder she had chosen despair and drink? A slower suicide than some, but a suicide all the same. "That seems monstrous, perhaps, but as you say, she died when I was two. Her parents had disowned her when she fell pregnant."

Timoney made a soft noise. It sounded like distress. Possibly…for him?

Crete did not attempt to parse that, or why it echoed in him like a kind of pain. He also did not permit his hand to rise again to his chest. "The legend goes like this. After burying his only daughter, my grandfather took her son to the doorstep of the man he blamed for his daughter's dark spiral, and left him there."

"You mean you," Timoney said softly. "He left you there."

"I am told this is a sad tale, but for me, I have always liked it." Crete shrugged. "It is like the ancient Spartans, is it not? He laid me out to see if the wolves would take me. Perhaps he expected me to die. But instead, I thrived."

As he always did. As he always would.

"Did he really leave you on a doorstep in Oslo?"

"He did." Crete was uncomfortable. Stiff. When he had learned over time that others usually displayed signs of discomfort when he told stories about himself. It was why he'd stopped doing it a long time ago. But she had asked, had she not? Even if she looked… well. Not as uncomfortable as he felt. "Luckily it was summer. My father's wife found me. And who can say how long I was there? I've heard it told many ways. An hour, perhaps, in one reckoning. Overnight, according to another. But however long it was, my father's wife opened the door eventually. And saw before her a toddler with jet black hair and her husband's eyes. She knew at once who I must be. And it would have been so easy to turn away, but she did not. She took me in."

"Who would turn away from an abandoned toddler on their doorstep?" Timoney asked, shaking her head as if he'd said something funny. "I have heard you give this version of events before, you know, and I cannot understand it. As if your father's wife was some kind of saint for…not leaving you to die."

"Was she not? To take in her husband's bastard? Who else would do such a thing?"

"I think it's very human to wish to help a child." Timoney studied him, frowning slightly, and he chose not to wonder what she saw. "And did she actually take you in?"

"That is where I lived for the next sixteen years."

"That is where you lived, yes. And from where you

were summarily ejected on your eighteenth birthday, never to return. Isn't that right?"

He found that his jaw was so tight it actually hurt. "Yes."

Timoney nodded as if he'd confirmed her worst fears. "Did your father's wife take you in out of the goodness of her heart? Because she is some sainted creature? Or did she do it to rub your father's nose in what he did?" When he didn't respond, she blew out a breath. "A less saintly motivation, I think. And not particularly kind to the child caught in the crossfire."

Crete did not often permit himself to descend into memories of his childhood. Because he already knew that nothing good waited there. And perhaps because of that, he had always been focused on the only thing that was ever his. His future.

"What interests me, Timoney," he said now. And with intent. "Is that you asked me to tell you my story, did you not? And yet you are now arguing with me about it."

"I've read great many articles about you." Another woman might have flushed at that admission. But not Timoney. She kept her gaze trained on his in a manner he would have called challenging if it was anyone else. Anyone at all but this woman, who had only ever melted in his arms. He could not quite see her in any other way. He did not wish to. "And they all hit the same notes. Callous grandparents. Lost mother. The long-suffering wife who overlooked her husband's infidelity to raise you almost as her own."

"They all tell that story because it's true." She

didn't shift her gaze away at his fierce tone. Something in him thudded. Hard. "Are you suggesting that I have lied about my own history?"

And it said something—though nothing he wished to acknowledge—that he questioned himself for a moment. That she sat there looking like moonlight and the Mediterranean, and he wondered, if only for a moment, if she knew more about his childhood than he did.

"I don't think you're a liar," she said. "But that doesn't mean I think you're telling the truth, either."

All of this was settling on him in a way Crete could only call uncomfortable. It was because she didn't look dazed or dizzy at the sight of him, the way she always had before. It was because she wasn't flushed and prettily begging for his touch. Nor did she look crushed, the way she had that last night.

Instead, Timoney was looking at him coolly, as if examining a specimen.

He couldn't say he cared for that at all.

And not only because he could not recall anyone looking at him like that in a very long while. Certainly not since he had become the Crete Asgar the world liked to whisper about in tones of awe behind the very hands they held out to him.

"Am I not?" he asked, though he didn't want to know. But he didn't want her to see how very little he wanted to know.

"You are closed off in every way," she replied, her gaze intent and her voice quiet. And had she sat up straighter, like some oracle delivering bad news?

"Locked up tight. If you have any emotions at all, you only let them out by having sex. Everything else is off-limits. You make money and you make love, though I doubt very much you would call it that. And that's it. You act as if there's nothing else to you. And that cannot be, can it? No one is so stark or uncomplicated. Especially those that pretend otherwise."

He found he was more tense than he should have been. When normally he laughed off attempts to attack him or psychoanalyze him in turn, because his foes might as well throw stones at the moon. Yet she was not a foe. And it felt too much like her stones were landing. "You seem to believe that simple truths about me are accusations, Timoney. When perhaps what they are is a bit of wishful thinking on the part of a scorned woman, no?"

That was not exactly the smart way to play this, but the words seemed to come out of him of their own accord. As if he had somehow lost the control that had always defined him.

But instead of reacting badly to being called a scorned woman, Timoney only smiled.

As if she, elfin and unearthly, was the one in control here. An insupportable notion, but Crete did nothing to challenge it. Almost as if he…didn't want to challenge it.

"No one is that compartmentalized," she said after a moment.

As if she, too, expected him to do something. To challenge her, maybe. Or to do what he had always done when she'd lived with him—cross the room and get his hands on her, forestalling any possibility of a discussion. Almost as if he'd done it deliberately.

Had he?

But there was no time to answer that, thankfully, because she was considering him much too closely from her perch on the small sofa. "And if you think that you are, in fact, precisely that uncomplicated, then there's no reason at all for you to be here. Is there? Because interfering in an ex-lover's wedding is, I think you'll find, the very definition of *messy*."

Crete straightened from the bookshelf, but slowly. He did not take his eyes off Timoney, who was still sitting there looking innocent and unruffled as if she hadn't set a trap and walked him right into it.

He really should have been impressed. Instead of…tense.

"I am as possessive of my money as I am about my women," he growled at her. "If that is what you mean."

"We both know *that* is not true." She tilted her head to one side, her eyes bright. Very, very bright. "One thing I think the whole world knows about you and your many women is that you are the very opposite of possessive. Or so a great many of them have complained. In the tabloids. Repeatedly."

"You did not."

"I did not," she agreed.

And he did not care for the solemn way she looked at him then.

Crete wanted to go to her. He wanted to show her exactly how possessive he was of *this* woman, anyway. But there was something in the cool, steady way she was regarding him that told him she expected him to do just that.

And he intensely disliked the idea that he was in any way predictable. Especially to her.

He moved away from the well-loved books toward the selection of colorful pots arranged over a thickly tiled table set before one of the great windows. The pots were all empty and the window was cold enough that he could feel it from several feet away, as if the winter was pressed against the glass. And he could not have said why it was that the sight of so many pots, empty of their supposed herbs and occasional plucky blooms, made him ache.

Crete would have claimed, before tonight, that he was incapable of *aching*.

"Why don't you tell me my story, then," he said, his voice as dark as the thick Christmas Eve outside. Because he could see her reflection in the glass before him, and the ache in him only grew. "You know it better than I do, apparently. But I must warn you, Timoney. When you're finished, I might just return the favor."

"I think you're lonely," she said, and for all her voice was soft, the words still stung. "I think your father's wife made certain you were never comfortable in her home. She made sure you were always made to feel different. Always her charity case. Always expected to be grateful for the crumbs of her affection."

"You are mistaken." His gaze was on the collection of empty pots before him. A blue one in particular, with leftover dirt clinging to the clay. And he reminded himself that he was relaying facts, that was all. Only the facts. "There were no such crumbs. There was no affection."

"She strikes me as a deeply bitter woman who kept you so she might better punish her straying husband. And it's striking to me that you never speak of him. The man who abandoned your mother, did not claim you until he had no other option, and was happy enough to see the back of you when his wife determined that she had done enough of her duty."

"He is a weak man, yes." He ran a finger over the raised edge of the pot's wide mouth. Once. Again. He did not think of his tall, blond, disinterested father. Because what point was there in it? "But surely that goes without saying. Look at what he did."

"But how does it *feel*, Crete?" Timoney asked in the same devastatingly quiet way. "You're a grown man now. You've gone to such trouble to make your way in the world. And I know it's a story you tell, but how does it feel? How did it feel when you were just a kid and treated differently than your half siblings?"

He turned toward her then, incredulous. "What does it matter how it felt? Feelings don't change anything."

They had never changed anything. Not his cold childhood, always given less than his brother and sister. Not nothing, but less. So that no one could ever forget that he was not the same as them.

Their father had never intervened. He had never

spoken to Crete at all, if he could help it. And whatever his wife did or said, he supported it.

Crete had felt a great deal about all of that, at the time. And those feelings had done nothing but make his misery the worse.

It was when he'd ignored what he felt and concentrated on what he could *do* that everything had changed. Not his situation. Not his tormentors. But his reactions to them.

Change yourself and you change the world, he liked to tell himself.

He was living proof.

"Feeling is who we are," Timoney was saying, her voice…intense.

"I prefer facts."

"All facts tell us is what happened," she retorted. "Not what it was like."

"I do not wish to remember what it was like." And the words seemed to come from somewhere inside him he would have sworn wasn't there. Because he'd torn it out a lifetime ago and filled it with other, better things, like the infinite pleasures of the flesh. Still, he kept his distance from Timoney, with her elfin face and too much wisdom in her eyes like the sea. "Why would I want to remember such things? I already lived through it once."

She only waited, and he didn't understand what was happening. The woman he'd taken as his mistress had given him her innocence, and everything after that had been an exercise in yielding. The softness and sweetness of it, all her smiles and surrenders.

Had she always been this way underneath? How had he failed to notice it before now?

Crete wanted to go. Now. If he was king of anything, it was a well-timed retreat before coming back harder. Stronger.

He had the strangest sensation that he was out of his depth here, with her—

But he refused to indulge such nonsense.

He refused to indulge any of this nonsense.

"It is as you say," he told her, his voice rougher than before. "My father's wife used me to bludgeon him. An effective weapon, I think, as there is no evidence he ever strayed again. Meanwhile, my mother's grim legend of a father died when I was ten. And any notion I might have nurtured, that the other members of my mother's family might take a softer approach to my existence, was quickly extinguished. For they blamed me as much for his death as for hers."

She breathed something. He thought it was his name.

"Do you wish me to tell you that it was a bitter childhood? Lonely years spiced up only by disdain and contempt?" He laughed, and jerked his chin to take in this room they stood in, still warm from the very different childhood she'd had. "Unlike you, I have nothing to compare it to. And those years made me who I am today, Timoney. How can I resent them?"

"But you do," she said quietly, frowning at him. "Deeply, I think."

"You're mistaken."

He didn't mean to move. He didn't know it when he did. All Crete knew was that one moment he'd been across the room and the next he stood above her, staring down at where she sat—looking as wildly innocent as the night he'd first touched her.

Maybe he should have known then that she would be a terrible problem.

"This is why I do not tell the real story of how it was," he gritted down at her. At that lovely face of hers that had haunted him across two full months. And half a year before that. "This is what happens. Softhearted, emotional people like yourself imagine that they must infuse it all with pathos. With incurable grief. While for me, those years were an opportunity. A crucible, if you will. I survived them, I became me, and if anything, I am grateful to my father and his wife and even my bitter old grandfather, for making certain that I never, ever succumb to the petty emotions of the human heart."

But as he watched too much emotion fill her blue gaze, then, nothing about it felt petty at all.

"And the only reason you could possibly be here is that you don't like sharing your toys, is that what you're trying to tell me?" Her voice was little more than a whisper, her sea-colored eyes luminous. "That's not a very good reason, is it?"

He wanted to rage at her that she was no toy. That if she was a mere toy, he would have forgotten her as surely and as quickly as the rest.

"We'll get to that in due time," Crete promised

her, grimly. But inside him, a different kind of storm brewed. Electric and more than a little mad. "But first, little one, let us speak of you."

CHAPTER FIVE

"I'M THE ONE asking the questions," Timoney protested, but her words seemed to trail off even as she was speaking them.

Because Crete levered himself down, bracing his hands on the back of the settee, effectively caging her there.

Unless, of course, she wanted to lean forward and—

But no. That would be bad.

Because it would be so good.

And Timoney was unprepared for this, if she was honest. It had been bad enough for him to appear out of the mist, like every dream she'd had since she'd left his flat in London in tears. It had been another to sit on this well-worn couch she loved, to gather her strength around her as securely as she had her cloak and imagine this was some kind of cross-examination.

One she might actually win.

Especially when she'd gotten him to do a thing he'd never, ever done before—talk about himself. Not his businesses, but *him*.

It was a harsh little gift, but a gift all the same.

She had always suspected he was a man who *could* feel deeply. She had always told herself that, secretly, he did. But having heard him actually discuss the cold facts of his stark upbringing, she wasn't at all surprised that he didn't want to.

Timoney felt entirely too much on his behalf.

But now his face was too close to hers. And that same old familiar seismic upheaval that was a hallmark of the Crete Asgar experience rocked through her anew. There was no solid ground. There was only the brilliant dark blue of his eyes, his perfectly sculpted face, and that scraped-raw, hollowed-out-with-longing need for him that she didn't think she would ever be rid of.

No matter what happened tomorrow.

"You were soft and spoiled when I found you," he said, his voice as pitiless as it was rough, and yet she felt it on her skin—all over her skin—like a caress. She had to fight to repress a shudder of reaction. "A ripe little peach, mine for the taking. If it hadn't been me, little one, it could have been anyone. You and those useless friends of yours, careening about London, looking for trouble. Do you know how many girls like you find more trouble than they can handle, year after year?"

"Do *you*?" she retorted, though her heartbeat was heavy in her ears and her skin felt so oversensitive that a glance might make her come apart. "And if you do, it really begs the question—how many young women do you normally pluck up and carry off into coatrooms?"

His mouth curved and it was not a relief. It was too hard for that. Too sardonic.

"Here's what I know about entitled little heiresses like you," he said, his voice a raw thread of dark need inside her. That was the trouble with this man. He had always felt like he was a part of her. "You spin around brightly, then crash. One after the next. Whether it is into sad marriages like the one you plan to enter into tomorrow. Whether it is too much partying, too much exposure, too much glamour, until all you can see is the underside of such things, black and scarred and torn. It all ends in the same dreary way."

"If I'm so interchangeable, there seems even less of a reason that you should find yourself here tonight," she managed to say, somehow getting her chin to lift in at least some small show of defiance. No matter how shaky she felt inside. "Go find another just like me, with my compliments. I'm sure she can tell you exactly what you want to hear. Sooner or later you'll almost certainly find one who won't dare to express emotion in your sterile little apartment no matter the provocation. A match made in heaven."

"This is the point I'm trying to make, little one," he murmured, still much too close. Still too raw, inside and out. Could she feel the heat of his body, blazing into her? Or was it that she wished she could? "Girls like you are used to getting what you desire. You don't even know how to want, not really. The world is simply handed to you on one platter after another, so that you truly believe it's character building to live in Belgravia in a listed house. You may even think you're roughing it when really, all you're doing is playacting until your money comes in."

As that hewed a bit too close to her own thoughts on her tenure as an admittedly silly PR girl, she had no choice but to bristle at hearing *him* say it.

"Thank you for your dissertation on my uselessness," she threw back at him. "But I assure you, no one is more aware of the playacting component than me."

"You should thank me for throwing you out, Timoney." And his dark blue eyes glittered like the night sky. "It looks as if it's given you a little bit of character."

What was funny was that she knew that was meant to be a killing blow. If he had delivered it while they'd been together, it would have destroyed her.

But that was the thing about being wrecked as totally as he had wrecked her. It wasn't possible to be wrecked like that twice.

Or she hoped it wasn't.

So she did the unthinkable. She laughed. "It seems to me that you're indicting yourself," she said. "Maybe it's true that I was an unformed little piece of clay, traipsing about London in search of meaning or a kiln. But it's also true that you were captivated by that particular little lump of earth. Besotted, one might even say. But not in love, of course." And she did nothing to keep that faint note of mockery from her voice. Maybe not so faint. "Because that would be a bridge too far. Did you come here to see if you can erase the damage you did so I can go straight back to being putty in your hands?"

"I would not object."

His gaze dropped to her mouth, then, and try as she might, Timoney couldn't deny the electricity that hummed within her. Maybe she didn't want to deny it.

But whatever backbone she might have gathered on her way out of London, she knew she might as well rip it out and sling it out into the snow if she succumbed to his kisses again.

Twice tonight was already too much. It made her much too weak. Too susceptible.

She ducked under his arm and rolled to her feet, not caring if he knew she was legitimately running away from him. She was.

Because she knew exactly how shaky her foundation was when he was concerned.

"Insulting me isn't going to change the fact that I have more questions for you," she told him when she was standing some distance away. "If that's what you thought."

"I did not intend to insult you. And I've answered your questions. You are the one who has flung herself halfway across the room a great deal, as if you fear something. Is it me, *Timonitsa mou*? Or is it yourself?"

Timonitsa mou. My little Timoney.

"Very well." She could feel herself flushing hot, and knew that it was entirely possible that he could see it. That was unfortunate. But she didn't understand what she could do to stop it, so she simply slipped out of her cloak, and tossed it over the back of the settee, a little shower of bright red fabric to distract them both. "Let us speak of fear. To the casual observer, it would appear that you're the one who's afraid. Of the possibility I might love you. Or is it something more than that? Is it…?" She dared to look back at him then, searching his face and that faintly arrested expression he wore. "Is it more that you're afraid you might actually love me back?"

Timoney couldn't believe she'd dared ask that question.

It was as if all the air in the room was sucked away, and there was nothing but the beat of her heart. And of his, too, though perhaps she only imagined she could hear it. Feel it.

Like he was always going to be a part of her.

She saw his jaw tense. There was a flicker of movement, and she glanced down to see his hands in fists at his sides.

And Timoney couldn't tell in that moment if she wanted to push him further, to see if he would break—

Or if she wanted only to hold him and mend his jagged pieces back together as best as she could, with whatever tools she had to hand—

But there was a sound in the hall outside the conservatory, and to her horror, she realized that she could hear voices.

And worse, they were drawing closer.

"You cannot be found here," she hissed at Crete.

One of his arrogant brows rose and she thought he intended to refuse to hide himself. To stand his ground and face whoever came in the door, and everything inside her...eased, a little, at that notion.

Because if it happens, you will have to choose, won't you? asked a voice inside her. *If it is your uncle, he will know exactly what this means, and he will demand—*

But it didn't matter. Because, perhaps more astonishing than anything that had come before, Crete looked around and then stalked over to that long table where her mother had kept all of her pots. It was sturdy and tiled, and it was impossible to look beneath it, thanks to all the terra-cotta pots still stacked there.

She blinked in astonishment as Crete...disappeared behind it, lowering himself between the table and the window with tremendous, offended dignity.

On any list of things Crete Asgar might do, she would never in her life have included any possibility that he might secrete himself behind a table. For any reason at all.

It made her feel something like dizzy.

Out in the hallway, the voices moved closer. Timoney looked around, snatched a book off the shelf, then retreated to her settee and did her best to look as if she was entrenched in her reading.

Only moments later the door was flung open and a couple came tumbling in, laughing and flushed with as much wine as ardor.

And it was from some great distance inside, some bird's-eye view, that Timoney recognized the pair of them. It was Julian, who was to marry her come the morning. And the young wife of some minor diplomat.

Julian came to a stop. He stared at Timoney, who stared back.

In mute astonishment.

The diplomat's wife took longer, and when she recognized the bride—the reason she was here in this house at all—she only glanced at Julian and quietly excused herself.

After she shut the door behind her, all was silent.

Timoney dared not glance over at her mother's potting table.

"I say, my dear," said Julian in that same voice that he always used, that Timoney liked to tell herself was *courtly*. When she thought the real word to describe it was *condescending*. "I rather thought you'd retired for the evening."

"I like to read each evening before I sleep." She glanced down at the book in her lap and saw that she'd picked out one of her favorite books, a thick volume of children's adventure stories that actually featured girls, not boys.

She wanted to club him with it.

Which was in itself a surprise, as it was the most she'd felt in Julian's presence since they'd met.

Julian studied her for a moment, then smiled in a manner that looked diffident and apologetic. That was, unless she looked at his cold gaze, which was neither.

"I am a man of many needs, my dear," he said then, in the same tone. "A conversation I expected to have after our wedding, not before. But you are a practical girl, are you not? You must be, I think, to marry so quickly after such a scandalous union as the one you had with Asgar. As you know, I have already indicated that I will care for any…unfortunate consequences of that union." He nodded at her belly, as if she might have missed his meaning. "I ask very little in return."

"That *very little* being a blind eye, presumably," she said. "To diplomat's wives and whoever else catches your fancy. Is that it?"

He inclined his head. "I'm of an old school. I will require all the usual marital rights, but in a situation such as ours, where there are no complications involving tender feelings, it can truly harm no one if I slake some of my darker hungers in other places. You may learn to thank me for this, in time." That smile of his deepened, though his gaze seemed harder. "You seem at a loss for words, Timoney."

"It's all so indelicate," she said quietly, like the girl she'd been pretending to be for months. Encased in ice and irritated when anything disturbed her bleakness. But now everything was different. Now she had melted. Still, she tried. "Surely such things are not spoken of. Not like this."

"Now, now," Julian said, with a chuckle that was not in the least bit friendly. "Fewer lessons in decorum from a girl who until recently was nothing but a whore for a mongrel, please."

Her blood pounded so hard in her ears that Timoney was shocked she didn't topple over. It took every bit of willpower she had to keep from whipping her head around to see if Crete was reacting to that *mongrel* comment from his place behind the table.

She wanted to scream.

She wanted to fly at Julian and slap him straight across his red, jowly face.

It was as if she'd emerged from some kind of frigid swamp. She'd thought of it as being frozen solid, but what she felt now was far worse than a simple melting. It threatened to suck her in, this realization of what she'd done. What she'd agreed to when she'd felt nothing.

Had Julian said such things before? Had he expressed his opinion about not only Crete but also Timoney's behavior like this?

She couldn't remember it, because she hadn't cared either way. And yet she knew, suddenly and without doubt, that he had.

And more, that she'd simply sat there like a block of icy wood, too lost in her own misery to care what was said to her or around her.

God help her, but this brutal awakening was not a kindness.

"I see the cat has got your tongue," Julian said with another chuckle. "This pleases me, Timoney. I don't mind telling you, I'm not marrying you for your conversation."

His gaze raked over her then, making her feel stripped naked. And not in a pleasant way. Not the way she felt when Crete looked at her, too much heat in his gaze.

It felt rather more like a threat.

She actually bit her own tongue to keep from speaking any of the words that clambered there, desperate to fall out of her mouth.

Or more likely catapult out and insult this man, who she was only just realizing she didn't know at all.

Not because he hadn't showed himself to her. But because she hadn't been paying attention.

"Enjoy your reading," he told her. "I shall see you in the morning."

Another threat.

Timoney stayed where she was until she heard the faintest sound from behind her, only a breath after the door closed behind Julian.

She turned, almost afraid, so wildly did her heart pound.

For Crete rose from the place where he had concealed himself, a dark movement. And his gaze upon her was like thunder.

She expected him to seethe at her. Possibly even shout. She expected him to storm across the room and grab her, hauling her up against him to argue his case.

And the contrast between the man who had just walked out of this room and Crete there before her was almost too much to bear. Especially when all he did was stand there instead of moving closer, that blue gaze dark and intent on her.

Meaning she could not help but compare the man she loved with the man she would marry.

It was painful.

More than painful. It made her stomach twist viciously, so that she almost doubled over. It made a kind of sick shame wash over her. It made her feet seem to lose their grip on the floor beneath her, like she might tumble off into nothing, and she did not know if she wanted to scream or cry. Or both.

She had known the differences between the two men, of course. It wasn't as if she hadn't noticed them before. How could anyone fail to notice them?

But she had never gazed upon Julian with Crete's taste in her mouth.

"Well?" she demanded, because that was better than the silence. "Will you delight me with more trenchant observations about who I am and why I've made the choices I have?"

His mouth flattened. "I think your choices speak for themselves."

And that was worse.

Timoney's eyes eased closed and she found herself wrapping her arms around her middle, as if that could do something. As if she could hug herself out of this.

"Do you require that I say this again?" came his voice. Dark. Silken and rough at once and worse, inevitable. Irrevocable. "You cannot marry that man, Timoney. You must know this."

Timoney had never known anything more. And she sucked in a breath, prepared to tell him that, no matter how reckless—

But she stopped herself.

Because there were other things she knew.

And one of them was him.

She had long wanted to ask him about his childhood, and while he hadn't told her anything tonight she hadn't known already, that he'd told her anything at all felt like a revolution. Because while he had spent their time together splitting his focus between her and his many businesses, she had done absolutely nothing but study him. It was one more thing she'd beat herself up about once he'd dropped her.

But her studies hadn't been in vain—because he'd shown her that he did feel. As deeply as she'd known he did. She'd heard his battered heart in every gruff word he'd uttered.

Timoney still believed with everything she was, every bone in her body, that he loved her. But so what? What did Crete Asgar know of love?

Not only did she doubt that he could identify his own emotions, she doubted it would matter if he did. If she were to do as he asked, walk away from this wedding, move in with him again, even attempt to hammer out some kind of relationship that was less one-sided than the one they'd had before... What would it accomplish?

There would be more time with him, yes. And that was no small thing. She thought there was a part of her that would gladly sell her own soul for even one day more. At her lowest point, she would have made that bargain for a mere glimpse of him from across a road.

But she already knew how it would end.

And what she'd told him out in the garden had not changed.

It was a shame that she felt alive again, so that the

devil she knew seemed a whole lot more like a demon she hadn't fully comprehended until now.

But Julian had already given her the schematics to the marriage she expected. All she had to do was follow the rules. There would be no emotional cost. Sex would be unpleasant, but then, wasn't that what she wanted? Because she'd already had far too much of the kind of lovemaking that made her soul feel too thin. That had not only taken her apart with pleasure, but had made her wonder how it was possible to exist in a world when she was so profoundly changed.

She had to think it was better for her to subject herself to Julian's attentions rather than go back to Crete only to lose herself, then him, all over again.

Because she also knew that Julian's attentions would also end. The diplomat's wife was young and Timoney would inevitably age out of his interest. Once that happened, she assumed he would be perfectly amenable to living separate lives.

Maybe Crete was right and it was a sad little life. But at least she would be *herself*. Not that mess of raw emotion and no spine to speak of that she became around Crete.

That had to be better. She was sure it was.

"Why are you smiling?" Crete asked her then.

And Timoney might regret what she was about to do. She knew she would. It had been bad enough to look upon the reality of Julian with Crete here in the room. It would be nothing short of a horror to truly let herself experience Crete once more only to walk down the little aisle in the chapel here tomorrow.

But she could handle regret.

Or anyway, she hoped she could.

Hadn't she already?

"Am I yours?" she asked him. "Truly?"

She saw something flare in his gaze, that brilliant shot of heat. And she could feel it inside her, far better than those other feelings of shame or horror.

Or this deep sadness she doubted would ever really leave her.

"You know you are," he said, his voice low.

Thick. Hot.

And threaded through with a hint of deeply male satisfaction. Because, she knew, he thought he'd won.

For there was nothing Crete Asgar loved more than winning.

Especially not her.

But Timoney held out her arms anyway, because this was for her, not him. "Then prove it."

CHAPTER SIX

EVERYTHING INSIDE CRETE shifted into a long, low, simmering beat.

His chest. His temples.

Deep in his sex.

Timoney stood in the center of this curiously welcoming room bathed in buttery light. She was so beautiful it felt like a terrible ache to look upon her, and a greater ache that the man she thought she was going to marry had not seemed to notice.

He had looked at her as if she was a bauble, nothing more.

And Crete had no doubt that Julian intended to glut himself on her, but it was not the need in him it was in Crete.

It couldn't be, or he would not have left her here tonight.

There were a great many things that Crete could have said on the topic of Julian Browning-Case, and surely one of them would have gotten through to her, but nothing as pointless as another man seemed to matter with Timoney's gaze on him.

That endless sea. Enduring. Beckoning. Blue enough to make a man believe in miracles.

He could not resist her. Then again, he did not wish to try.

Crete stalked past her outstretched arms, crossing to the door to make sure that it was locked. That it would admit no further visitors this night—and would not require that he debase himself any further by concealing himself behind the furniture as if he was taking part in some noxious theatrical production of a play he would dislike. When he turned back around, she had dropped her arms and had twisted around to watch him.

With a look on her face that suggested she thought he might have been on his way out.

The way he knew he probably should have been.

But Timoney had haunted him when he had never before believed in ghosts. She'd stayed with him even after he'd scrubbed his home of any stray trace of her presence. She had woken him in the night. She had chased him through his days and all over the world, never giving him a moment's peace.

He could remember, if vaguely, other women he'd been with for a time. He had always, eventually, felt a sense of great calm when away from them. That was usually how he knew that it was time to move on. When even sex could not give him a moment's peace. When leaving their side was far preferable to suffering their presence.

This normally did not take very long. Six weeks at the outside.

But everything with Timoney was inside out. Six weeks had come and gone and turned into six months, and he had still felt undone by her. Tonight he wasn't even touching her. He was gazing at her from across a room, having actually secreted himself behind some old pots so as not to distress her. All *she* was doing was looking at him with the expression he remembered best. The one that haunted him most.

Open and soft. Sweet and yielding.

It felt like peace.

And yet deep within that peace that only came when he was with her, and layered all around it, was this wanting that never seemed to fade.

When he had walked up to the house tonight, he had assured himself that all it would take was a glance in a window and he would feel the fool. That he would feel nothing when he saw her again. That he would melt off back into the night, taking his shameful obsession with her along with him when he left.

Alas, he had found her in the garden instead.

And *foolish* was not at all how he felt.

"Go back and sit on your little couch," he ordered her, in that tone he had always used when he intended to indulge his dark desires.

And like she always had, Timoney shivered. Visibly. He watched with a familiar surge of delight as goose bumps tracked down her neck and over her bare shoulders. His sex was like iron. His mouth watered.

He wanted to taste her more than he wanted his next breath. He would have happily traded it in.

When she did not move as instructed, he only

raised an eyebrow. And Timoney let out a rush of breath. Half a laugh, half a sigh.

A sweet music he had missed.

Then she turned, her dress rustling around her, as she set about obeying him.

"Pull up your skirts," he demanded, his voice darker than before. Hungrier. "I want to see you, Timoney."

She let out her little song again as she settled down onto the settee, the red cloak spread out around her like a scarlet frame.

And she kept her eyes on him as she pulled the skirt up, slowly, teasing them both.

He had taught her that, too.

Her legs were as perfect as he remembered them and he had to forcibly restrain himself from going over and getting his hands on her calves, her knees, her thighs. The hem of her gown skimmed along and then stopped at her thighs. She breathed in a deep, shaky breath.

Crete said nothing. He waited.

She took in another breath, then another, her gaze still locked to his.

He did not have to tell her to continue. And he did not wish to tell her. He wanted her to want him even a quarter as much as he wanted her. Even a sliver.

Timoney sighed a little, again, a soft surrender.

Then she pulled up the remainder of her skirt so that he could see the tiny scrap of fabric covering the V between her thighs.

"Bare yourself to me," he told her, hardly recognizing his own voice.

He could see the way she melted at that, but even if he had somehow missed it, she gave herself away. It was the way her fingers shook as she lifted up her hips and wrestled to pull her panties down, then tossed them aside. And she didn't wait for him to move his finger as he did, commanding her to take her place once more. She lounged back, spreading her legs wide, and holding her skirt up again.

The perfect picture of anticipation and abandon.

All his.

And because it made her shudder, he waited. Even though he was so hard he was surprised his trousers contained him, he waited.

Only when she sighed again, and there was that little catch in the sound, did he move toward her at last.

Crete stalked over to that couch, refusing to admit that he felt something less than solid himself. Something less than sure. Holding her gaze, he sank down to his knees before her, placing himself squarely between her outspread legs.

He leaned in and the scent of her arousal rose between them, that raw, sweet honey.

Another thing that was only and ever his.

He hooked his arms around her thighs, hauling her toward him, then lifted her up before him.

And she melted for him, her body lush and supple and entirely his.

Possibly the only thing in this world that was always and ever his.

Crete could have spent a lifetime watching the way that flush moved over her skin. It reminded him that when she flushed, it went everywhere. Her nipples would become rosier, darker. The hotter she became, the pinker she would grow.

He could have spent still another lifetime cataloging the ways she burned bright, but he wanted her too much.

As he had always wanted her too much.

So he bent forward and put his mouth to the very core of her need.

And felt her as she shattered around him.

But he was only beginning.

Crete licked his way into her, holding her hips where he wanted them no matter how she bucked and moaned. He knew every contour of her. He knew what she liked and what she pretended not to like, but loved. He knew what set her to trembling and what made her sob.

He knew her.

And it was not enough to simply taste her. It was not enough to add one finger, then another, to the rhythm he set.

It was not enough to bring her to the edge then retreat, then throw her over again.

Again and again, just to make sure.

Just to remind them both.

None of it was enough. And he was drunk on her taste, on the sounds she made, on the way she brought her whole body into this. The way her heels drummed against his back and her fingers gripped his hair.

The way she rocked herself against him, greedily. As if she, too, was as much a slave to these fires between them as he was.

Though he knew that couldn't be true.

For he knew that there could be no wanting deeper or wilder than his.

"Please," she cried out, arching up against him again. And then again. "Please, Crete. I need you inside me."

And it all felt preordained. She had always tasted too much like fate. As if he had been heading right here, to her, since before he'd even thought to take a drive this night.

He reached between them, pulling himself out. And there was no fumbling. There was no hesitation. He found his way to her entrance and found her molten.

Always molten hot. Always his.

And he thrust himself deep inside.

Timoney shattered again, this time on a silent scream that still managed to echo around within him.

Filling him. Scalding him.

Changing him, he thought.

He pulled her off her little couch and on top of him, so that she was straddling him where he knelt. Timoney came easily, gracefully. She wrapped her arms around his shoulders and took her time straightening, lifting her head from where it had fallen back.

And he could see the chaos in the blue of her eyes then. He could growl at the way she bit her lip.

"If you want me," he told her, in a low voice, "you must take me, Timoney."

He watched the way all that heat flashed in her eyes. He could feel inside him.

It had always been like this. One fire burning too bright in both of them, consuming everything. Taking them over. Making them ash and cinder, flame and fury.

A more beautiful immolation Crete could not imagine, then or now.

And then he found himself gritting his teeth as she began to move.

He had remembered every inch of her. Every touch committed to memory and trotted out to haunt him each night. Every moment of need and hunger made real since that first kiss. Since she'd lowered herself before him, tipped back her head, and stolen his breath.

Here, now, he could admit—if only to himself—that he had thought of little else since she had quit his flat.

And still, somehow, it was as if he'd forgotten how bright she was, how intense. Or had diluted her effect on him, somehow, in the recollection.

It was the way she lifted herself, pulling away from his length and then dropping herself down again, making them both gasp a little at that slick, hot fit.

She was perfection, taking all of him and gripping him tight.

And she was his.

He had taught her this, this lush and lyrical dance.

He had shown her all the different ways that they could light each other on fire. How to build these flames so that they danced high.

And how to ride them home, again and again.

He had taught her, and this seemed a celebration of that, of them. Her gaze locked to his. The way she rode him with all that artless determination made everything in him tighten as she rocked them closer and closer still.

Too good. Too right.

Too perfect to bear.

And then he could take it no more.

Crete tumbled her down to that soft rug beneath them, rolling her beneath him and placing his hands on either side of her head so he could change that rhythm. He went deeper, harder.

Her heels dug into the backs of his thighs as she met each thrust and everything then was fire.

That glorious fire, the delirious pounding, and when Timoney threw back her head to scream out her pleasure, he covered it with his own.

And only when she stopped shaking did he let go, thrusting jerkily within her until, finally, he surged over the edge at last—her name like a song inside him.

A song he took the time to sing to himself, for some time, while they both fought to find breath again.

It seemed to him a lifetime later when he could finally move. He took his time, rolling over again so that she was no longer beneath him, but instead splayed out across his chest.

And for another long while, another lifetime at least, she rested there, that soft weight Crete had not allowed himself to admit he missed.

More than missed.

"I'm glad we could settle this," he said. Eventually. And it was more than an olive branch. It felt...revealing. "We should head back to London now. We can send for your things in a day or so, when whatever commotion there might be tomorrow has died down."

And it was only when she did not make a happy, joyful sound, or nuzzle her face into the crook of his neck, that something cold moved through him.

"Timoney." His voice hardly sounded like his. "Everything is settled, is it not?"

She pulled away from him and sat up, smoothing her dress down as she went. Then she took a moment to push the masses of her silvery blond hair back.

And when her eyes found his again, they were steady.

Too steady.

It was as if the floor fell out from beneath him when he was lying there upon it.

"Things were not unsettled," she said, as if she was choosing her words carefully. Very carefully, and yet her blue gaze did not waver. "On the contrary, they have felt very settled indeed for some time. Two months, I might even say."

Crete did up his trousers and then jackknifed up. He resented that he had revealed himself at all, while she was apparently more than capable of *steady gazes* and bizarre statements. So bizarre, he assured himself, that it was no wonder they put his back up. "I do not understand you. Not a word you're saying."

Because she could not possibly mean what he thought she did. It was not possible, surely.

"You should return to London, Crete, but I will not be coming with you," she said softly. But directly. "I will be staying here. As I have told you all along, I'm getting married tomorrow."

"Don't be ridiculous." He could hardly get the words out, his jaw was so tight, and it seemed likely that it—that he—might shatter at any moment. "You have been rolling around on the floor with another man. *With me*, Timoney."

"And it is very likely that my husband-to-be might even now be availing himself of the woman he intended to roll around on the floor with in here." She lifted a shoulder, then dropped it, her gaze still offensively, outrageously calm on his. "It appears that I have found myself in a very open kind of arrangement."

"Have you been hit in the head?" he gritted out.

Her gaze cooled. "I have not."

"Because that is the only possible explanation," he continued, despite her reply. "For one thing, you cannot possibly imagine that the likes of Julian Browning-Case, so horrified at my parentage, would ever think that what's good for the gander is good for the goose, or whatever horrifying English phrase might fit."

"Whether it is or isn't, it is certainly no concern of yours."

He rubbed his hands over his head because what he wanted was to put them on her. And conduct another lesson. Maybe this time, it would take. "Timoney. Do you think I can't tell that you violently dislike that man? How can you possibly think you might marry him?"

But she only gazed back at him. Placidly. Even more placidly than before, as if the more he objected the more serene she became. "Because I have agreed to marry him, Crete." She waved her hand at him. "He gave me a ring and I agreed to wear it. More than wear it, I agreed to honor what it represents."

Crete was certain of two things then. One, that he needed to rip that diamond solitaire from her finger and toss it—and soon. And two, that she was taking some kind of perverse pleasure in this. In sitting there, still flushed from his touch, while she discussed her wedding as if it was something she wanted.

He could not believe it was something she wanted.

He did not believe it.

"Setting aside the fact that you looked at him with sheer horror," he managed to get out from between his teeth, "there remains the small issue of the fact that we did not use any protection whatsoever just now."

And he blinked when Timoney only smiled.

As if what he said was amusing, when he had never been less amused in his life. Since when did he forget protection? What madness did this woman stir up in him?

"How can this be?" she asked in mock amazement. "The pathologically overcautious Crete Asgar failing to use protection with a woman? Is this a typical lapse when you engage in one-night stands? Because for the six months we spent together, you never forgot it. Not even once."

"I never forget."

And at some point he was going to have to ask himself why, when that was an ironclad law he had followed for as long as he could recall, he hadn't thought about protection at all tonight. Not once.

But Timoney was only shrugging again, as if it was of no matter either way. "You heard what Julian said. He's prepared to accept any and all consequences of my liaison with you. What did you think he meant?"

Everything inside Crete went still. Like the moment before detonation.

Or the moment after. "I beg your pardon?"

"Surely you know that Julian has no heir," Timoney said, as if this was a casual little conversation they could have been having at the sort of dinner party he despised. "He doesn't even have a distant cousin to step up and take over someday. I think he's desperate. Or maybe he simply doesn't care. I don't know. But whether or not I'm pregnant is no impediment, as far as he's concerned."

She even waved a hand at that, as if dismissing the whole topic. As if dismissing *him*. And then she rose to her feet with that innate grace that Crete had always found nothing short of mesmerizing.

Even tonight, when he thought he might implode with the rage that stormed in him, she was spellbinding.

But he shook off the enchantment when she went to move past him, very much as if she was headed for the door. Yet another unacceptable choice on her part in a series of the same.

Crete shot to his feet, then reached out to take hold of her arm, turning her back around to face him.

She had the temerity to look shocked.

"The matter of your possible pregnancy may not signify to your groom," he gritted out at her, and was dimly surprised not to find himself shouting. "But I can assure you, Timoney, that it is of critical importance to me."

CHAPTER SEVEN

"THAT MAY BE SO," she managed to say with what she hoped sounded like a great calm. "But I'm afraid it doesn't matter."

He looked astonished, taken back, and possibly outraged at the notion that *she* dared tell *him* that his feelings were not of paramount importance across the Commonwealth, if not the whole of the planet. He also looked, unusually for him, faintly disheveled.

Because he was Crete, more stunning than any one man had the right to be, that his hair looked like he'd run his fingers through it only made him look better. However impossible that should have been.

And Timoney kept telling herself all these ridiculous stories, thinking that she could handle this, handle him. Yet the look of surprise on his face didn't thrill her the way it should have. It made her want to make it all better. To jump into his arms and race him back to London. Anything to make him happy—

But then, she'd already tried that.

She had to take solace in the fact that however he felt just now at the prospect of her wedding in the morning—and she could see how he felt, written all over his face—it was nothing compared with the way he'd made her feel that last night in London.

There was a part of her that was already racing to tell her exactly how much of a fool she'd been to allow this to happen. Because now it was all brand-new again. The feel of him, deep inside her body. His mouth moving over her tender flesh. The reality of him, so strong and hard and solid, pressing her down to the ground—

Just thinking about it made her tremble, everywhere, as if it was that close to the edge all over again.

Timoney tried her best to tamp it down, because the longer she stood here, looking at his rampant male splendor—his talk of taking her back to London with him ringing in her head, more temptation than any woman should have to bear—the more she had to face the facts. Chiefly that she already regretted this.

All of this.

Because she'd made a critical error here.

She had come alive again, with him. As if she had never been anything but a rush of brilliant color and raw sensation. Her two months of gray were over. She could *feel* again.

Timoney felt gloriously *alive* from her hair to her fingers to her toes and back. There was an electric current sparking within her once more, making her skin seem to glow. Her bones seemed to hum inside her limbs.

And every place he'd touched, inside and out, blazed still.

There was no undoing that. She wouldn't *want* to undo it.

She told herself that it had to be better to take this memory with her when she sank down into the swamp again. And if somehow she couldn't freeze herself solid again, well. Julian could do what he liked with her body. Timoney would go off in her head, come back here, and that, too, had to be better.

This way she wasn't losing anything. Heading off to London with him again, on the other hand, was a recipe for loss. Would it be six months again? Less? And when he was done with her again, when he had truly destroyed her—again—what would she do then?

Maybe she shouldn't have indulged herself with Crete, but she would have a long, safe marriage in which to consider the matter from all sides. She might not be happy, but she had chosen her path. It wasn't a seismic event. Like meeting Crete.

Like losing him.

She told herself the choosing was what mattered.

"I do not think that you are understanding me," Crete bit out. His grip on her upper arm felt like a band of steel. And that, too, felt like a gift.

Timoney would hoard it all up, these excruciating gifts like too-bright treasure. And her hoard was what would make the next few years fly by before Julian tired of her. As she knew he would.

She couldn't wait.

"I think I understand you perfectly." She forced herself to meet his gaze again. "I just don't agree with you. I know that must be difficult for you, it being so rare."

Temper flashed over his face, and something in her seemed to roll over at that. Not in fear. Not in anxiety of any kind.

It was pure exhilaration.

Because the man Timoney had lived with in London had never let his veneer crack, even a little. There had never been a question that she might see beneath the masks he wore. The hard-edged businessman. The intense lover. The remote man.

This, too, was an unexpected gift.

"I am the bastard son of a man who could have taken care of me but did not." He bared his teeth at her. "You know this. You must also know that I would never, ever allow a child of mine to be raised apart from me."

Timoney couldn't let herself think about Crete as a child. It was too much. It had been bad enough to read those dry recitations of unfortunate facts in so many articles—but he had stood before her tonight and told her how little affection there was, how little kindness. She would dissolve where she stood if she let herself think about him as a small boy, surviving such coldness, and she couldn't afford that. He was a man who capitalized on the weaknesses of others, always. She admired that in him. It had made him who he was today, and she loved him.

But she couldn't allow him to use her own weakness for him against her.

"I'm sure you have nothing to worry about," she

told him, though she was not sure of any such thing. Her body had always seemed to delight in its irregularity. She did begin to wonder, as she watched that dark incredulity move across his face again, what exactly she was playing at here. "I don't think it's the right time of the month."

"Somehow, this does not comfort me," he growled at her, as if he knew exactly how unreliable her body was. To say nothing of her claims.

"I'm sorry to hear that," she said in as British a manner as possible. Which was to say, she made it abundantly clear she was not, in fact, sorry. "Not everything is comforting. Some things hurt, Crete, and they keep right on hurting. Time doesn't change them. Space doesn't change them. Sooner or later, you either die or you learn to live with them."

And she felt his hand contract on her bicep as he took her meaning.

She hardly recognized him then, his face was so hard. His gaze so cold.

"Was this your plan all along, Timoney? Is this some kind of sick revenge?"

She pulled her arm out of his grasp then, too aware that he let her do it. It was disconcerting.

"Did you know you were coming here tonight?" He only glared back at her. "I will take that as a no. And no, I did not, in fact, plot out some kind of revenge. I had no idea you would turn up here."

Not this night. Not ever.

Not even though she'd spent two very long months wishing fervently that he would.

"But now that this has happened, you are happy enough to capitalize on it, is that it?" He shook his head in a kind of awe. Not a good kind. "I had no idea you were so ruthless."

That was rich, coming from him, but she suspected he wanted her to lose her temper. One fire might lead to another, and then he would win. The way he always won.

"If you would like to sit down and answer more of my questions, fine." Timoney tried to look as if she was casually moving toward the door. Instead of what she was actually doing, which was making a break for it. "But if you're going to stare at me like that, as if you might at any moment begin to chew off pieces of me, I think I'll pass."

"You will not walk out that door, *Timonitsa mou.*"

The way he said that was alarming. She couldn't deny it. Every hair on her body seemed to stand at alert.

Especially because he didn't move.

As if he didn't *need* to move to cut her off. He was that sure of himself.

She told herself it was fear that raced through her, making her nipples harden into points and her core melt, but she knew better.

"I couldn't decide if I wanted to see you again or if I never wanted it," she told him when she reached the door. She put her hand on the latch but turned to face him because she felt she owed him this much. It was more consideration than he'd shown her—and she also needed to convince him not to press her.

Because her willpower to walk away from him and marry the man her uncle had picked for her was very flimsy indeed. "But I think that this has been good. It has eased something inside me, Crete. Though I doubt that was your intention, I'm thankful all the same."

"You are thankful," he repeated, his voice a dark and dangerous ribbon of sound that seemed to connect hard to all those places she was still trying to convince herself were fearful. And then set them all alight. "Oh, joyful day. You may be pregnant with my child. You insist that you will marry a man who disdains and disgusts you. But what can that matter when you are *thankful*."

Timoney felt as if her lungs were wrung out. She could only seem to take tiny little sips of air, and none of it seemed to get where it needed to go. Her hand ached, and she realized she was gripping the door latch far too hard.

But she didn't let go.

"Maybe he does disdain me," she replied, her voice not quite as steady as she would have liked, because she might have been ignoring his other points, but that didn't mean the blows didn't land. "But at least he's honest and up-front about it. Which is more than I can say for you."

Crete reared back slightly, as if she'd struck him. "Try not to alter history of which I was a part, please. I was never anything but honest with you. I *am* nothing but honest, and to my detriment." His hard mouth twisted. "Ask anyone."

"You may be blunt and direct when it suits you,

but that's not the same thing." She dropped her hand from the door and had the vague thought that she was making a strategic error, but she brushed it aside. And glared at him instead. "Are you ever honest with *yourself*?"

His eyes narrowed. And Timoney knew she shouldn't have let go of the latch. She should have left by now. She should have flung open the heavy old door, hurled herself out to the chilly hall, and then run all the way through this house until she could safely barricade herself in her bedchamber and count the hours until morning.

When you will do what? asked a sharp little voice inside her. *You will put on that dress you never liked but didn't wish to argue about? And then march down the aisle and shackle yourself to a man who thinks you're a whore?*

There was a sour taste in her mouth. She couldn't seem to stop flashing back to that particular look in Julian's eyes when he'd stood here before her, called her *my dear*, and called Crete a mongrel. She couldn't stop remembering the way his gaze had moved all over her, as if he was using his hands to find his way all over her body.

That was a preview. The voice inside her was certain. *And whatever made you think that because you've had so much good sex that you'll somehow be able to suffer through bad?*

And more, why had she imagined that she would be okay with that suffering? She didn't think Julian would hurt her. Meaning, she didn't think he would strike her. Yet it was suddenly occurring to her, much too late, that there was a vast gap between something that hurt—like a blow—and anything that was even remotely tolerable.

Sex had been a revelation. Having sex with Crete had altered everything. How she felt about her own body. What she did with it. How she viewed herself. She tried to imagine the same scene that had just occurred here on the floor of the conservatory, but with Julian rather than Crete—

Her mind balked.

Timoney hadn't been expecting revelations.

But she should have paid more attention to the cost of putting up with revulsion.

"Please," Crete said, still standing where she'd left him. Still seething. "Please do not lecture me on honesty. I am not certain that you have a handle on the meaning of the term as you prepare to walk into a wedding with another man, possibly pregnant with my child."

And this was not the time to think about what it might be like if she truly was—

It is not the time, she told herself sternly.

"Do you love me?" she asked him, her voice stark.

The way she had asked him once before.

Fatefully.

First she had said those words he didn't want to hear, and then, when he had coldly explained to her the usual consequences for that, she'd asked him straight out.

Because she hadn't believed what was happening. And more, she already knew the answer. Or she thought she did. And she'd been so sure that if she simply asked it, he wouldn't lie. That he couldn't lie to her face.

Not like that. Not to her.

But he had.

Crete had looked straight at her, straight through her, as if she was a stranger. And with no hesitation, he had said no.

Just that. Just the one word. *No.*

Timoney would have preferred it if he'd slammed his fingers into her chest, actually torn out her poor heart, and crushed it beneath his foot. That he'd done it metaphorically had left her gasping for air. Why not do it in fact and let the pain of it kill her?

Then again, it had. She just hadn't had the pleasure of dying.

Now she was too alive for her own good and her wedding was at ten o'clock the next morning.

And she hadn't run off to nail herself back into her coffin the way she should have when she'd had the chance.

Nor did she make a break for it now. She couldn't read the expression on his face any longer. It wasn't that cold, cruel mask from before. But there was nothing soft or loving about it, either.

Once again, she wished she hadn't asked.

"Do you love me?" he asked, and there was a dangerous edge to his voice then. "Does anything that you have done tonight feel like love to you, Timoney?

Because I will tell you, it feels a great deal like love to me. That is not a recommendation."

After the story she'd gotten him to tell tonight, he could not have delivered a more devastating slap.

Somehow, she didn't let it knock her flat.

"You were right all along," she said quietly, when she could. "We are better off apart."

Then, finally, she turned to walk away from him the way she should have done in the garden, but her fingers no longer seemed to work. She fumbled desperately at the latch.

And when the world seemed to spin out from her, tumbling around and around, she thought for a moment that she'd fallen.

It took her far too long to comprehend that he had come up behind her, spun her around, and tossed her over his shoulder.

"What are you doing?" she demanded.

She tried to brace herself against the wide wall of his back as he stalked through the conservatory. He swept up her cloak and draped it over her as she lay over him, then strode straight back out into the night.

The cold hit her hard, but mostly as a contrast to the heat of him beneath her. The cloak covered her and she was upside down, so there was no possibility that she could see where they were going—though she knew it was away from the house.

All she could do was hold on to him for dear life.

His strides seemed long. There was gravel underfoot, then grass.

She tried to roll off him, but his hand clamped down hard on her behind, holding her in place.

And, even now, making her melt all over him.

"Where are you taking me, Crete?" she made herself demand, because that felt like doing something. And surely she should *do* something.

His hand gripped her backside harder, the way he often did when he drove deep inside her. His shoulder was wide and sculpted beneath her belly, and she told herself the cloak was very warm and that was why she was suddenly too warm and given to squirm.

"Settle," he ordered her.

And he did not slow his pace at all.

"You must be mad," she threw at him. "You can't simply… What are you *doing*?"

"I should have thought that was obvious," he said, as he carried her off to the night. Walking tall and proud, as if it was his right, and gripping her backside as if he was claiming her. "As you cannot be trusted to make the right choices, Timoney, you are forcing me to make them for you."

Funnily enough, though she would have been delighted for him to make any choices for her that he wished a few months ago, she hated it tonight.

You mean you want *to hate it,* came that insinuating voice.

That made her something like desperate. "I beg your pardon. You have no right! Put me down this instant. *This instant.*"

She tried to throw herself to the side and he quelled it before she really even formed the thought. With a laugh. And the *quelling* made the core of her seem to hum.

"I cannot do that," he told her and if she wasn't mistaken, he sounded… at ease.

More at ease that she'd ever heard him before, in fact.

"What can you possibly be thinking?" she demanded, hardly able to hear her own voice over the clamor inside her, all of it spiraling around and around blooming into sheer desire between her legs.

"The time for thinking is over, little one," he told her, and if anything, his stride lengthened. "Now it is time for action."

"This is an abduction! You are *kidnapping* me!"

And this time, the hand on her backside smoothed over her curves, just enough to make every nerve inside her seem to dance itself awake.

Then shudder, like she was on the very edge of shattering.

"It is," Crete agreed, all dark male satisfaction. As if he knew. "You can thank me later."

CHAPTER EIGHT

THE LAST THING in the world Timoney wanted was to *thank* him.

Her pulse was a riot inside her. Her head was spinning, and not only because she was upside down. There was something buried inside her, something suppressed, that seemed to be storming its way out and she had no idea what might become of her then. She wanted to rip him apart with her fingers, to make him heed her cries—

Or that was what she told herself she wanted as he strode away from her uncle's house. Carrying her with him whether she wanted to go or not.

And she was terribly afraid that *thing* inside her, nearly free now, was a kind of triumph. Laced through with relief.

As if, despite what she might have said to him in the conservatory, she reveled in the fact he'd made this choice.

Freeing her from Julian and her uncle and the choices she'd made while grayed out and dead within. Without her having to make them herself.

Maybe you should thank him after all, that voice needled her.

The world spun all around again and she found herself on her feet, but only briefly, as Crete set about strapping her into the passenger side of the gleaming Range Rover he'd left parked haphazardly near the estate's lower stables.

He slammed the door and strode around the front of the vehicle. And it was only when he swung in beside her that Timoney realized that she really should have used this opportunity to effect her escape.

Because surely if she had an opportunity to escape and she didn't take it, that was a choice. Wasn't it?

But instead of hurling herself out into the night and running for the questionable safety of the house, she'd been too busy contemplating the fact that Crete Asgar had actually turned up out of the blue. Had kissed her silly, then made her sob and scream on the floor of the only room in that house that had always felt safe. And had topped all that off by abducting her.

The night before her wedding.

On Christmas Eve.

And by the time it occurred to her that she really ought to try the door and see if she could outrun him, however unlikely, he was already turning the car around and heading away from her childhood home.

With what felt like a tremendous amount of finality.

Not that she was required to accept that, she told herself stoutly. *He* didn't get to decide.

"This is remarkably childish, Crete," she said as he headed down the winding drive. The December dark pressed in all sides and his headlights caught the remnants of the mist as it still collected in the hollows. Making herself sound reasonable and rational made her feel, if not in control, at least not as out of control as this situation *should* feel. "What do you think is going to happen now? Do you think removing me from the house will fix anything?"

"It will fix one, pressing matter," Crete replied, his eyes on the road ahead. "This is something you should know about me by now, Timoney. I always put out the biggest fire first."

But she knew that wasn't true, because the biggest fire of all still burned inside her. She was beginning to understand that it always would. No matter how much ice she piled on top of it, or how much gray she wrapped around herself. The flames were only ever banked, never extinguished.

"Sooner or later, whatever madness this is will pass," she said quietly, because thinking about the fires within wasn't helpful. "What gives you the right to wreck my life in the meantime? You had the opportunity to stay with me forever and you chose instead to have me tossed out of your flat. You don't want this. You don't like to be told no, that's all."

And she hoped he never knew what it cost her to sound so *serene* when she felt anything but.

"Surely it's time to set aside all this drama." But she could see that despite that tone he used, as if this was all the deepest silliness, his hands were like fists around the steering wheel. "You were not tossed out into the street like so much rubbish and I believe you know this well."

"Was I not? I don't recall you being there as your men hustled me along. I was given two hours."

He muttered something in Greek.

"Two hours," she said again, more distinctly. "And it wasn't that I needed more time than that to pack, Crete. It was that my lover, whose home I shared, told me that he never wanted to lay eyes on me again. I understand that this may come as news to you, but for most people that is the kind of blow that it takes some time to recover from."

The real truth, she knew, as she looked out at the narrow lane that he was driving along now—and much too quickly—hemmed in on either side by the hedges, was that she wasn't recovered. She wasn't sure recovery was possible.

Wasn't that how she'd ended up agreeing to marry Julian in the first place?

She glanced over at Crete. His face was set in harsh lines, his lips pressed together as if he was fighting off some of those emotions he would claim he didn't have.

And this was the trouble. She didn't like the feeling that she'd actually hurt him. She loved him. Whatever else happened, that didn't change. That he wouldn't admit something hurt him didn't mean it didn't. She knew that. Just as she knew that all hurting him did was hurt her. Maybe that was love, too.

Because no one had ever said that love meant happiness. Or that joy didn't have a price. She had thought the price she must pay was Julian, but in many ways this was worse.

For it was sometime after midnight, she saw on the car's dashboard. Technically Christmas, and that made a kind of sense, because this was a bittersweet sort of miracle. She had never thought she would see Crete again, and yet he had appeared like a dream. He had swept in like the mist, told her things about himself he never had before, and the way they'd come together could only and ever be love, as far as she was concerned.

Whether he would call it that or not.

She wanted to think that it was anxiety inside her, carrying on, ordering her to leap out of the car, demand that he turn around, do something to make it clear that she intended to marry in the morning.

But she knew better. She was trying to defend herself against the inevitability of the next time he would leave her. She *wanted* to believe in this. She *wanted* this Christmas miracle.

All while she knew that he believed in Christmas and miracles about as much as he believed in love.

For some time they drove in silence. Timoney could feel some tension leaving her the farther they traveled from the house. From Julian and her unpleasant future. And yet the farther they traveled from her childhood home, the closer they got to London and the more a different sort of tension grew in her.

Mile by mile.

"You," Crete said, almost softly, if that was a word that could be used for such a hard man, "are the only person I have ever met who has never treated me as if I was some kind of alien."

Such a soft yet sharp spear, thrust straight through her heart. She folded her hands in her lap and stared down at them. "I don't think you're an alien. That would be convenient, wouldn't it?"

He let out a sound that she supposed was a laugh, though it seemed to curl around inside her like smoke and didn't help any with the weight of misery that seemed to sit on her then.

But she should not have felt miserable on behalf of her kidnapper. What was the matter with her? She ought to have felt miserable *because* she was being kidnapped, not because he might have tender feelings about it.

Something is very wrong with you, she told herself sternly.

Crete handled the country lanes easily, as if the towering hedges and slippery roads were nothing to him. As if the way the lanes wound this way and that was nothing short of soothing.

How she wished she could find a way to soothe herself—but she hadn't really managed that since she'd met him, had she? And she could hardly recall what had come before.

He made a low noise, as if he was coming to some kind of decision. She thought he sat a bit straighter behind the wheel. "You know my name is not actually Crete, do you not?"

"That is a wrinkle I did not see coming." Timoney frowned down at her interlaced fingers. "Though it would explain a lot if you had an evil twin. Did the bad version of you knock you over the head and lock you up somewhere? Is this the good version? I have a lot of follow-up questions."

He shot her a fulminating look, then returned his gaze to the winding lane.

"I was born with a proper Greek name," he told her, his voice a rasp across the darkness between them. "Adrastos Demetrios. My mother had many issues, there's no denying that. But she did not name her only son after an island."

And despite all the many articles that Timoney had ever read about him, she'd never encountered this little nugget of information. It seemed almost fantastical that he might have a name out there that no one had ever discovered. A secret name he was sharing only with her. Only now.

Something in her seemed to hum around the syllables of that lost name. Adrastos Demetrios. Him but not him.

Another gift, that voice within whispered.

"Crete is traditionally a female name," he told her. "It is also the only place in Greece my father's wife had ever visited. So this is what she chose to call me."

Timoney turned in her seat, forgetting her own concerns as she studied his proud profile beside her. "Do you think she knew that it was a girl's name? Does she speak Greek?"

"She does not speak Greek, no." His mouth curved into that shape that was not a smile. "But my father does. I myself did not learn Greek until I was in school and could choose my own elective courses. As you can imagine, Greek was not encouraged in the father's house. And so it was my Greek teacher who first told me that my nickname was usually only used for girls. I think she expected me to be horrified."

"But you preferred to defy expectations," she whispered. "As ever."

"I legally changed my name to Crete when I was eighteen," he told her in that same dark rasp. As if it was painful to tell her this. "Because it was the only thing my father and his wife ever gave me. And though they meant it as a mockery, I'm certain, I chose to claim it as a prize."

Of course he did. This proud, remote man. Timoney had never wanted to reach out to him more. It actually hurt to keep her hands to herself.

And Crete was still speaking. "But more than that, it was a challenge. Let them laugh at a man with a woman's name. Let them amuse themselves at my expense. It would only make it all the sweeter when I crushed them." He let out that laugh again. "And, indeed, it did."

And any remaining doubts Timoney might have had that she was head over heels for this man, despite everything, faded away then. Because when he told her such harsh things, such sad reminders of the brutal place he'd come from, all she wanted to do was wrap herself around him and show him at least one moment of softness. At least one small bit of something better.

Tears pricked at the back of her eyes. "I'm sorry that even your name is a battlefield."

"Everything is a battlefield, Timoney." His voice was low. Gravelly. "And I take a deep pleasure in winning these wars. It has been this way with everything and everyone, always. Until you."

Once again she felt winded, and she could feel the tears threatening to spill over. "That's not fair."

"Did you think this would be fair?" She only realized the car had slowed to a complete stop when he turned in his seat. His strong hand pulled her face around to his. "Love or war, it's all the same to me."

"You don't believe in love," she replied in a whisper, not jerking her chin from his grasp. Not fighting him.

"Maybe not, but I have always preferred war. It is simple. There are winners and losers. There is none of this mess."

"This is only as messy as you want to make it," she managed to say. "You could so easily have stayed away, Crete. You broke things off for a reason. You could have carried on as you have these past two months. What changed?"

"Nothing has changed." She thought she saw some kind of ghost in his gaze then. Or did she only wish she did? Either way he dropped his hand, though his gaze remained intent. "But you deserve better than Julian Browning-Case."

"Let's think about this rationally," she suggested, her gaze direct on his. "You carry me off like a caveman."

"Do cavemen drive Range Rovers?" His voice was arid. "I had not realized."

"Obviously there's a spark between us. I won't deny that. Let's say that I stay with you again. Or who knows? Find my way back to that listed house in Belgravia that you were so disdainful of earlier." She shook her head, still holding his gaze. "Sooner or later, it will be too much for you. Again. And by that time, perhaps, Julian will have moved on."

"Good," Crete growled.

Timoney sighed. "Julian isn't the point. If I don't show up at my own wedding tomorrow, my uncle will disown me."

"Is this a tragedy?" Crete demanded. "You'll excuse me if I do not weep. Whether your uncle disowns you or does not, all you will have to do is wait a few years for your trust to kick in. Is this not how it works to be an heiress?"

"You're talking about money, Crete. I'm talking about family."

"You don't even like your family." He sounded mystified.

"What does that have to do with anything? My aunt has her moments. And my cousins are perfectly unobjectionable." He had been honest with her about his name, so she swallowed, hard, and returned the favor. "And they are all I have left."

He shook his head, then turned his attention back to the lane before him. When the Range Rover began to move again, Timoney couldn't tell if she'd lost something or gained it.

"I know you don't understand family," she said, her gaze drawn back toward the way the headlights danced over the lane. The way the dark night held them fast in its grip, as if they were alone in all the world. Suspended here together in the quiet and the cold. "I don't expect you to. But until a few years ago, I would have told you I had the best family in the world. My parents loved me and I loved them in return. And I know that they would expect me to do whatever I can to maintain a relationship with my uncle and his family, no matter what."

"If your parents loved you at all, how could they possibly countenance your uncle's wish to sell you off to one of his cronies?" Crete made a dismissive noise. "A man who makes no secret of the fact that his only interest in you involves the marital bed. Was that what your parents wanted for you?"

Her parents seemed very far away tonight. But then, happily, so did any marital bed she might share with Julian. But what caught at her was that Crete had brought them up of his own accord. She couldn't recall him ever doing so before.

Much less speaking of love.

Her heart seemed to skip a few beats.

"My parents wanted me happy," she said quietly. She laced her fingers together again, because it was that or reach out to him and she didn't quite dare. "This is what I'm trying to make you understand, Crete. No matter what happens now, whether I am disowned or I simply go off with you for a time and come back to be married off to someone else, it's all the same, isn't it? I'm not happy. I'm not going to be happy. Because what I want I can't have. You've already made that abundantly clear."

"You don't know that."

But he drove faster, so that the dark and misty night seemed a blur on the other side of the windows.

"I do know that." She sighed. "I have no intention of playing war games with you. And you don't believe in love. Those are incompatible positions, Crete. You must know that."

"Compatible or incompatible matter little if you're carrying my child," he gritted out.

Her hands rested in her lap and she resisted the urge to touch her belly. To imagine. "And if I'm not?"

"Then you will come to a place of gratitude, I have no doubt, for the act of service this is," he said. With all his arrogance. "You are not required to suffer that man's bed. You are welcome."

Timoney kept her gaze on the dark blur of hedge and distant sky. "But I won't be happy, will I?"

Crete made a low noise. Disbelief. Temper. Some mix of both. "Are you suggesting that you would be happier suffering with that pig?"

And Timoney blew out a ragged sort of breath. "Julian could never possibly break my heart. He could only harm me in small ways."

"I think you underestimate him."

"But you, Crete." She frowned at him. "You want to drag me off and pretend that we can go back to some version of what we were? At what cost? I've already tried loving you enough for both of us, and that didn't work. Why should this?"

She thought she could hear his teeth grind together, so hard was his jaw then.

"Maybe it would be better if we postpone these discussions until such a time as we know whether or not you are to be the mother of my child." He bit the words out. "I suspect that will answer any questions you might have."

"Putting aside the fact that you haven't thought to *ask* whether or not I wish to be a mother at all, much less of your child, what do you plan to do?" she demanded. "Will you fly me off to one of your solitary islands? Will you hide me away so that I dare not make you think about the things you'd rather avoid?"

"What will be the point in that?" he hurled at her. "When you would only haunt me either way?"

For a long while, as he drove through the darkness, Timoney sat with that.

And wished—oh, how she wished—that it could be enough.

Her cloak lay over her like a blanket and she pulled it tighter around her now, letting her eyes drift shut.

Once, it would have been enough to imagine she might haunt him. Once, knowing she affected him at all would have felt like a prize. Worth whatever she had to do to achieve it.

But she knew better now.

Timoney would never think it was enough until he admitted that he loved her the same way she loved him. Without limits. Without sense.

Wholly, desperately, and irreversibly.

Until then, she did not doubt that he wanted her. But she also knew he wouldn't keep her.

So she kept her eyes closed and she let the rhythm of the wheels beneath her lull her into sleep.

Or into dreams, anyway, whether waking or not. Where she could pretend they might build a new life untainted by what had come before, or what she knew lay ahead.

Where she could pretend that love might finally be enough.

It was very early Christmas morning now, and maybe the true miracle was that she got this little space in between to imagine. To feel alive again. To remember the past without shutting down and to imagine the kind of future she knew they would never have.

To close her eyes in a speeding car and feel his presence all around her. To know, once more, the glory of his touch, and pretend for some little while that they could truly be together the way she'd always wanted.

It was a far better Christmas gift than she'd expected this year.

And Timoney would take it, for as long she could, before reality rained down upon her once again.

CHAPTER NINE

CRETE FOUND IT somewhat lowering that Timoney had actually fallen asleep beside him. He rather felt she should have been wide awake and on tenterhooks for the whole of the drive back into town, if only because *he* felt shot through with adrenaline.

As if he might never sleep again.

Still, when they arrived at his flat in London, he waved off the attendants in his garage and carried her into his private elevator himself.

And though her eyes fluttered open, he did not set her down until the lift delivered them into the stone foyer of his penthouse.

He opted not to examine the way he seemed to settle only when he carried her over his threshold, such as it was.

Then he found himself watching her as she blinked the sleep out of her eyes. Without looking back at him, she crossed the foyer and walked deeper into the flat. She didn't stop to turn on any lights and for some reason, Crete did not do it as he followed her. He was too busy watching her as she went. She dragged the bright red cloak behind her as she moved to the great wall of windows that looked out over giddy London, laid out bright and gleaming before them.

He was growing tired of the way it hurt him to gaze upon her when she was not even looking at him in return. She stopped at the windows and raised the hand that wasn't clutching the cloak to her. He watched as she pressed her fingertips to the glass, let out a sigh, and only then turned to look at him over her shoulder.

"This must be the most beautiful view in all of London," she said quietly.

Though it felt far more portentous than a simple comment on the view.

And Crete felt that it was some kind of surrender on his part to walk to her, still shrouded in the darkness—or revealed by it—but it was as if his feet did as they liked.

Or as if he could not stay away, a voice in him suggested.

Then, either way, he stood with her at the glass.

"Of course it is the best view of London," he said. "Do you imagine I would tolerate anything less?"

He was looking at her as he said that, not at the view. And not because he was stunned by her beauty, though he was. But because she smiled then, and it was a sad, small curve of her lips that he could not say he liked at all.

"I'm sure it cost you a lot of money," Timoney said softly. She turned to look at him then, and there was a starkness in that sea blue gaze of hers that brought that same ache on again, harder this time. "But you don't ever look at it, do you?"

They were no longer in the car, so he did not have to pretend that the road held his attention. He reached over and hooked one hand around her neck, tugging her closer.

"Is this another metaphor, Timoney?" Crete kept his voice far softer than that ache in him, or the drumming noise of his own pulse. His own need. "I'm growing tired of all these games you wish to play with words. Both you and I know what is between us. It is a mystery to me why you would pretend otherwise, but I have solved it for you. It is already Christmas. You are here. And if I have to tie you to the bed to keep you from racing back to your wedding in a few hours, I will. Happily."

He was fairly certain that the reason she glanced away was to disguise the flash of heat he'd seen in her gaze. But he thought it proved how magnanimous he was that he did not tip her chin up. He did not force her to show what he knew was there.

Crete only waited.

As he waited for nothing and no one else.

"You don't have to tie me up, Crete."

He couldn't read the tone she used then. He couldn't parse it, and that was unusual. Crete had long prided himself on being able to see beneath the words people used. To see to the heart of things, where most people were usually hiding their true motivations.

But this woman confounded him. If he was honest, she always had.

"Are you sure?" he asked, silkily. Because he could think of any number of reasons that tying her up seemed like a fantastic idea, and not a single one of them had to do with the vile Julian.

Or that abomination of a wedding that he would not allow her to go through with.

The lights of the city outside seemed to play in her hair the way the moon had out in the countryside. And he found himself toying with the thick silk of it, without even meaning to. Without knowing what he was doing until he was curling it around his fingers and letting it spill through. While the hand that cradled the nape of her neck seemed to absorb nothing from her but heat.

Crete told himself that she was a provocation, that was all. And he was a man who had never allowed a provocation to go unanswered.

Why stop now?

"You have me here now," she said after a moment, with a certain directness that pricked at him. Perhaps because it did not whisper to him of tying her up in a bed and making them both wild. "You've made it clear that I'm not to leave. At least, not until you've made certain that my wedding is called off. I could try to run but, chances are, you would catch me. Or have your security team do it." She lifted her chin. "What now?"

His thumb moved on her nape, up and then down. Again, of its own accord. And he felt how she shivered, though he wouldn't have known it to look at her, so well did she hide what he could feel with his own flesh.

And Crete could not help but feel a powerful sense

of loss, because once she would not have hidden her responses from him. Once, she had been all untutored enthusiasm, artless and sweet, running through his hands like sunshine.

He knew full well what had changed. And more, who had changed her.

But he concentrated on the heat instead. "Surely you and I can find a way to entertain ourselves, can we not?"

Again that smile, too sad for his tastes. "Is that what you want?"

Once more, Crete knew this was some kind of test. Like the stories she had demanded he tell her before. The answers she had needed him to give. Only this time, he had the distinct impression that this was not a test he could master.

And having her here again, in this space that he had always kept pristine, crisp, and utterly devoid of anything soft or even comfortable, brought it all back.

All of it, like a good blow to the head.

"You broke all the rules," he found himself saying, though he knew he should keep such things to himself. He had done his best to keep from saying such things for half a year while she'd lived here. He stood there, half in the dark and half lit up from London below, but all he could see was Timoney. "I do not indulge in public displays of passion in clubs. There's too much risk that it will all end up in the tabloids. But one look at you and it was as if I had no choice."

Her lips moved as if she meant to speak, but no sound came forth.

That was just as well, because Crete could feel a storm in him, gathering force. Driving rain, booming thunder.

Or maybe it was only his voice, telling her the things he had not told her the last night she'd been here. The things he'd had no intention of ever telling her.

The things he barely admitted to himself.

"There is an extensive vetting process," he told her as if he couldn't stop himself. He couldn't. "But I moved you in within the week. And the purpose of allowing a woman here is to make my life easier. So that I can concentrate on my work, give my all to my many business concerns, and have a woman here to fulfill my needs when and if I have the time. But you did not slot neatly into place here, Timoney. You... took up space."

This time her smile seemed something like rueful. "I suppose I did," she told him, her voice light but that intensity in her gaze. "But I had no choice. This flat is grotesque."

"I think you will find it is one of the most sought-after properties in London."

"It is grotesque," she said again, very distinctly, though her blue eyes gleamed. "Not only because of the fingerprints of too many mistresses before me, but because it might as well be a prison. Too much steel and concrete. Too many angles and cold expanses." She looked away as if she could see all the sharp corners and deliberately empty spaces without the lights on. "It's inhospitable to human life, Crete. I assume that's by design."

She was obliquely calling him an alien now, and it was astonishing to him, how deeply he disliked it. The whole world could line up to tell him how unnatural he was. How little he fit in. He took that as encouragement. As a challenge.

But it was different when it was Timoney.

Still, she needed to understand. Somehow, he needed to explain all of this to her. What it had really been like, those months she'd lived here. How he had felt so unlike himself. Careening from one meeting to the next and yet hardly paying attention. Instead of feeling pleasantly set, all of his needs taken care of in their appropriate compartments, he had rushed home whenever he could. He had changed his schedule so many times his secretarial staff had been driven round the bend.

Crete had changed his whole life. Worse, he had been aware of it while he was doing it, aware of every step away from the man he had always been before her—but he hadn't been able to stop. He hadn't *wanted* to stop.

Still, he had been horrified that last night, when she'd told him that she loved him—when she'd cried it out in bed as if she couldn't keep it in another moment—that his first reaction had been a kind of mad thrill.

Because he could not seem to get enough of this woman. Of the total disregard with which she treated this ascetic sanctuary of his. How she left her clothes scattered about, so that he found buttery-soft scarves in improbable pastels lying about on his cold marble, his brutally minimalist steel. She was fluffy and bright, and seemed hell-bent on leaving her careless mark everywhere she went. She left dirty dishes by the sink. She plopped down mugs of tea wherever she happened to find herself, wholly and utterly heedless of any rings of moisture she left behind.

His housekeeping staff had been relieved when she'd gone.

But he had discovered quickly that without her, this luxurious, aspirational flat felt more to him like a tomb.

"I don't like mess," he said darkly now, to her claim that this place was designed to be inhospitable. "I don't like complications."

"And yet you were singing the praises of war earlier, weren't you?" she asked, lightly enough. Though her blue eyes seemed dark. "I have yet to hear tell of any clean and uncomplicated wars, Crete."

"That very much depends on whether or not you are winning it, I think." His hands had moved now, without his knowledge. He was gripping her shoulders, holding her there before him, and he really could not have said if he meant to push her away or draw her closer.

He had never known.

"The trouble with you," he managed to grit out at her, though it seemed far harder than it should have, "is that you never fit here. You never slotted into place."

"I think I will take that as a compliment," she replied, as her chin inched upward. And the way her eyes flashed made him think he'd hit a nerve. "I was far too besotted with you to point out that no one particularly likes being *slotted into place* as mistress of the month. You do know how to make it all feel like a bit of an assembly line, don't you?"

"I do not recall you complaining about it."

She sighed. "I didn't, did I? But then, I knew I didn't fit in here, Crete. Much as I take that as a badge of honor, it only goes to show what I've been saying all night. Nothing has changed, or will. I guarantee that you will walk in here and find me far less elegant than required. Too messy. Too determined to not slot nicely into the little box you set out for the woman in your life. Eventually this will lead us right back to where we found ourselves two months ago. Why put ourselves through all that again?"

"I wanted to end things with you almost from the start," he told her, as if the words were being pulled out of him, backward. "Every day I would come home to you, determined that I would draw a line under it. Be done with it. Get my life back at last, so that everything might run smoothly again. That's how I like it, Timoney. Smooth, unchallenging, predictable in every way."

Her eyes glittered. "I can see why you stormed the family estate to abduct me away from my own wedding, then."

"And yet I didn't do it," he continued on, almost harshly. "Night after night, I didn't." He shook his head, almost as if he had lost this battle. When he did not lose. "Don't you understand, Timoney? You broke all the rules."

When all she did was present him with that smile again—so bittersweet that it made him wonder if he'd had a heart all along, for what else could ache like that—he did not wait to hear what other arguments she might mount.

Because there was only one argument that had ever mattered. Only one argument that ever could.

He swept her up into his arms again and this time got his mouth on hers, and he kissed the ache away. Again and again.

Until it made a new one.

Crete carried her over to the low, long sofa that she had often complained was the enemy of comfort and sitting of any kind. He broke the kiss, his chest working as hard as if he'd gone for a run, but he refused to analyze why it was he was so desperate tonight when he had already won.

He had *won*, damn it.

And this time, when she smiled at him, it was filled with heat and need, passion and longing.

Crete felt it echo in him like relief.

He set himself to the critical task of removing her clothing, at last. Finally, he tossed that cloak aside, with all of its yards and yards of fabric that had concealed her from his view on the drive here. Then he tended to the dress she wore. It was a pretty enough garment, but there was nothing on this earth as pretty as what he uncovered.

Timoney George, naked before him.

The way he always remembered her. The way he always wanted her.

"You, too," she murmured, sounding impatient enough to make the fire in him blaze higher.

Her hands moved to his coat and then the two of them worked together, with what he was certain was the same sense of urgency, to strip him, too.

And when they were finally skin to skin, he tumbled her down on that couch she'd always hated and exulted in the feel of her. Here where she belonged, after the longest two months of his life.

Naked in his arms, at last.

Naked and wrapped all around him, and the singular joy of it was nearly enough to send him catapulting over that edge.

For another truth he had not told her was that the mistresses of the month had never been like this. None of them could hold a candle to her. He barely remembered them. Sex had always been a pleasant release, but Timoney was something else again.

It was the way her body fit to his, as if they were a set of interlocking parts that only made sense when they were together. It was her scent like honey. It was the way she smiled at him, hot and knowing, when he groaned. It was the way she traced her fingertips down his back, as if making certain he was okay. It was a thousand little things and only one thing, in the end.

It was *her*.

He wanted to take it slow, but it was impossible.

There was a storm between them and Timoney liked nothing better than dancing in that rain.

While he liked nothing more than watching her dance them both into pieces.

They rolled, this way and that, until eventually she climbed astride him and took him deep into her body.

"Epitélous," he gritted out. *At last.*

The perfection of it. The slickness. That snug fit, so tight that everything else he was and all he felt seemed to expand in response.

She set their pace, taking him and teasing him in turn. Bringing them both to the edge, then retreating, until he couldn't tell if it was a game, or revenge, or some glorious combination of both.

And he couldn't care, not while he was inside her again.

Everything in him urged him to throw her over on her back and ride them both into oblivion.

But instead, Crete filled his hands with her round breasts. He pulled her face down to his to sample the bow of her mouth. He gripped her hips. And all the while he let her do as she would, drawing it out until it seemed the knife's edge they balanced on cut them both.

Deep.

And when he felt her go over, he watched it move through her. Timoney arched back, her hair all around her, beautiful beyond measure as she shook and shook and cried out his name to the steel beams far above.

Only when she slumped down against him, her open mouth to the crook of his neck, did Crete wrap his arms tighter around her and find his own, hard finish.

And it still wasn't enough. He was deep inside her, her wildflower honey scent all around him, and it still wasn't nearly enough.

When he could move, sometime later, he lifted her up again and carried her across the length of the penthouse toward the master suite. He ran her bath, then joined her in it.

And he took her there, too, sitting there behind her. It was a sweet, shattering joining in all that heat.

But that, too, wasn't enough.

Later, after he'd finally taken her back to their bed and tied her to it—as much to make a point as because it was fun—he gathered her in his arms when they had both finally exploded, and held her there while she fell asleep.

It still didn't feel like enough, but he let her sleep. He let her burrow her face against his shoulder and murmur what sounded like his name in her sleep.

Such provocation, but all Crete did was stay awake.

He didn't dare take his eyes from her. There was some part of him that worried that this was some rare dream. That he had never left the flat tonight. That Christmas morning was coming up fast and she would wake in that cursed old house, pull on a white dress, and marry that horrid old toad.

He stayed awake because he wanted this to be real, not a dream.

Because he was beginning to understand that when it came to Timoney, he would never, ever get enough.

CHAPTER TEN

WHEN TIMONEY WOKE, she knew exactly where she was.

She had dreamed that she was back here so many times in the past two months, curled up happily just like this. The heft of his pillows. The astounding softness of his sheets. The lightweight clasp and warmth of the duvet. The scent of him surrounding her, sinking into her, making her feel soft and molten and ready before she was even fully awake.

At first she didn't open her eyes. She simply let herself drift in the particular embrace of this bed she knew so well.

When she did open her eyes, it was to find that she wasn't dreaming, this time. She really was in Crete's wide platform bed, the way she had been so many times before. The way she'd been so certain she never would be again. It made her shake a little to find herself here. It made her feel a bit too raw.

She pulled in a steadying breath as she sat up, shoving her hair back. On the other side of the three walls of glass around her, it was still dark. Timoney pulled one of the almost scandalously luxurious blankets with her as she went, more so she could keep feeling it against her bare skin than any particular sense of modesty.

The room itself was as she remembered it. Profoundly stark, featuring only the imposing, masculine bed in deep gray linens against the single gray interior wall. There was concrete everywhere with steel beams above and London on three sides, right there on the other side of the private terrace.

When she had lived here, she had liked to tell herself that it was a kind of urban tree house, that was all. Made of concrete and steel instead of wood, but the same, really. It had helped her feel less dizzy, perched so high above the Thames and the streets below.

But that had only helped so much. It was still too far off the ground, too cold and impersonal, for her liking. She'd made the best of things, because what else was there to do? This was where Crete lived, so she had made her home here, too, however uneasily. She would have camped out in an actual tree house in a field if it had meant that she got to live with him, sleep with him, make love with him at will. She would have put up with any indignity.

Timoney told herself she ought to be embarrassed by how easily she'd surrendered herself to this dour concrete world of his. But even as she thought it, she was shaking her head. Because she hadn't really surrendered, had she? She had lived here, but she hadn't paid the slightest bit of attention to his rules, stated and unstated alike.

Because she had been so sure that she would win

him over. That she would introduce a little color into his life, not by actually coloring over his dark grays and steels and concretes, but by virtue of becoming that color herself. Timoney had danced naked on his excruciatingly hard sofas until he smiled, however unwillingly. She had painted the wall in his study and him, too, when he'd glared, affronted, at her make-shift mural. She had cooked elaborate, messy meals in his pristine kitchen, using up every pot and getting the ingredients everywhere. She had laughed when he'd scowled. She had imagined that she was the an-tidote to the rest of his hard, busy life.

In truth, she had taken pride in that role.

It had never occurred to her that it could ever end between them. That he would end it.

The overconfidence of virgins, he had said once. In a manner that had made it clear that it was not a compliment,

But Timoney had only laughed at him, then had crawled onto his lap in the back of the car they'd been in. *Entirely too overconfident,* she had agreed. *Shall I show you?*

She swung her legs over the side of the bed now, still too raw. And remembering everything too keenly. Even the height of the platform the wide bed sat on seemed to poke at her, casting her back into far too many memories.

It's like a throne for sleep, she had said once.

A throne for something, Crete had replied. *But not sleep, I think.*

And then he had demonstrated what it was for. Repeatedly.

Even thinking about the kinds of demonstrations he liked best made her shiver a little. She saw the strips of fabric he'd used earlier in a heap on the floor beside the bed and smiled. That was the thing about Crete. Whatever he dedicated himself to, he gave it his all.

Always.

She padded around the bare, imposing wall that served as a headboard, but Crete was nowhere to be found in the rest of the expansive suite. Something in her shifted uneasily as she looked into one room, then the next, but didn't find him.

Though she stood a moment in his study, staring at the mural she'd made him that she'd been sure he would have had repainted within twenty-four hours of her departure. It shocked her that it was still there, all the bright and garish colors she'd slapped all over the wall opposite his steel-and-glass desk.

Timoney didn't know how to feel about the fact the mural was still there. But it was nothing short of alarming that he wasn't at his desk. As far as she knew, the study was the only place he went in this sprawling flat of his when he wasn't making use of his bed.

And she found that she was...apprehensive as she went out into the rest of the penthouse. Had it already happened? Had he already changed his mind?

Just because she'd known he would, that didn't

make her prepared for it now that it had happened. And so soon.

Was he even now readying his vehicle to whisk her back to Oxfordshire and hand her off to Julian?

Funny, wasn't it, that she found that prospect nothing short of unbearable now.

Crete was nowhere to be found in the flat. But as she stood naked in the center of the great room, Timoney discovered that the relief she felt had only intensified after a very few hours of sleep. And it brought with it some clarity.

She did not want to marry Julian.

She did not want to experiment with his brand of marriage, much less what he would expect of her physically. Even if he tired of her in six months, that was too long. As she already knew from her time with Crete, six months could be a lifetime.

And imagining a lifetime with Julian made her stomach hurt.

She almost laughed at herself then, though it really wasn't funny. Even while she and Crete had still been in the conservatory, she'd been telling herself all kinds of stories. First and foremost, that it had been possible to imagine she could suffer through Julian's attentions when she'd still felt so dead inside. And then she'd tried to convince herself that she would somehow carry the much fresher memory of Crete with her, perhaps so she could retreat into her head while giving Julian what he wanted.

But now, only a few hours later, she couldn't understand how she'd managed to convince herself that such suffering was possible.

Maybe, something in her suggested, there in the unlit penthouse with only the relentless London gleam outside to light her way, *all you really wanted was to punish yourself.*

For giving so much of herself to man of steel and concrete, thinking that a few bright colors on a wall could make him love her. For falling in love with him when he was only having sex with her.

For letting down her lost parents by failing at happiness, and love, and hope. Again.

For that overconfidence when she should have known better. Shouldn't she have known better?

Because surely she should have learned something from losing them so suddenly. From everything that had changed afterward, irrevocably. How had she managed to throw herself at Crete the way she had, so appallingly *certain* that she could make the both of them happy, when she knew better? Happiness could be snatched away at any time. At any moment, like it or not. Life was all about the lie that it might last, but she knew better.

Timoney had known better—but her grief hadn't been enough to save her.

Not from Crete, but from herself and her own overweening confidence. Her abominable belief that her own feelings, her own heart, could make things end well.

When she knew they didn't.

She turned back around and headed for the bedroom again, thinking vaguely that she might as well shower, then get dressed again. Then she could wait for whatever next bombshell Crete would reappear to drop on her.

There would certainly be time enough for considering the ways she'd been punishing herself then. In the great stretch of *after* that would follow this one, last night. Where she could find a way to deal with how raw she felt that did not involve upsetting weddings, surely.

She vowed that she would make a point of it.

But when she made it back into the bedroom that was never truly any kind of a tree house no matter how dearly she'd wanted to convince herself, because it was really much more of a prison cell, she saw what she hadn't before.

Crete, who had not left her. At least not yet.

He stood outside at the railing at the edge of his terrace, wearing only a pair of low-slung black trousers, as if it wasn't December.

Then again, this wasn't just any grubby old flat and he wasn't risking hypothermia for the sake of showing off his sculpted torso to the uncaring night. The section of the terrace just outside the master bedroom was fitted with heated floors, making it far more inviting to make use of the sauna and hot tub nestled there, high enough above the city that there was no possibility anyone could be spying on what any resident here got up to.

Timoney dragged the soft blanket off the bed and

wrapped it around herself, then pushed her way out through the glass doors.

And she knew the precise moment Crete became aware that she had come outside to join him. She saw him tense, ever so slightly, and got to watch the muscles play all up and down the chiseled length of his back as she drew closer, the heated concrete warm enough beneath her feet to make the cold air feel like a caress against her exposed face.

It still moved in her like wonder that she had touched every part of what surely was the finest back in England. Worthy of being cast in bronze, at the very least. She felt that same old heat that never left her bloom hot within, making her thighs seem to whisper sensually as she moved. And the core of her pulse with need, as if it was new.

She came up beside him, but he did not glance at her. He kept that brooding gaze of his focused out on the city at his feet.

"You're really not good at this kidnapping thing, are you?" she asked lightly as the night air made her ears cold and her hair fly about. "I was left to my own devices entirely. I could have made a break for it while you stood out here, none the wiser."

She didn't expect uproarious laughter. Not from Crete. But he seemed extra grim, she thought, especially after everything that had come before this night.

"Do you wish to escape?" he asked, far too darkly for her tastes. "Have you woken with second thoughts?

And a renewed determination to sacrifice yourself at the altar of two old men's greed?"

That was a little too close to what she'd been thinking on her own. "And if I have?"

He pushed back from the rail but still gripped it. And when she glanced down at his hands, she saw that his knuckles had gone nearly white.

"Then I will be forced to disappoint you, Timoney. You will not be marrying Julian today. Or any day."

She could have told him how much her thinking on that had changed, but she didn't. She could have explained, talked about punishing herself, or even asked him why he hadn't erased the evidence of her terrible mural, but she didn't do any of that, either. Because he was straightening, then turning to face her, and the look on his face was…terrible.

It looked almost like passion, drawing him tight and taut.

But passion she could handle. Or she knew she would survive it, in one form or another, anyway.

Somehow, she knew it would not be as simple as that.

Timoney braced herself, for surely the look on his face meant that a cutting verbal blow was to follow. From a distance, she almost felt philosophical. How would he make it worse? He would have to, she assumed, to really make this hurt. He had devastated her last time. How would he—how could he—make that seem like child's play?

She had been so unprepared before. She'd been so in love that it had never occurred to her that anything could come between them. It was almost cringeworthy now to look back at how naive she'd been. She'd fallen so deeply and surpassingly in love with him. She had cheerfully offered up every part of her, heart and body and soul, with no hesitation and no catch.

The fact that it *could* end—that *he* could end it—had never crossed her mind.

Luckily, she was far more worldly and prepared now. He had seen to it personally.

So Timoney lifted her head proudly, tipped up her chin to take whatever he might toss her way, and told herself that come what may, she would be fine.

One way or another, she would be *fine*.

Eventually, something in her whispered.

"We should get married," Crete said, as if there was glass in his mouth.

As if the words shattered as he said them and were cutting into him as he spoke.

Timoney only gazed back at him while the December night slapped at her exposed face, certain she hadn't heard that correctly. "What did you say?"

If anything, he looked more in pain. Anguished, even.

"We will marry," he said, his voice like gravel. "That will put an end to all of this, I hope. If you must be trapped, Timoney, you might as well be trapped with me, don't you think?"

She was glad that she had thought to bring the blanket, not only to save herself from the chill of this Christmas predawn morning, since it seemed her feet had gone numb beneath her and she might never be warm again. But because it gave her something to grip as she tried to process what he was saying to her. Tried to make it make some kind of sense.

And came up with nothing, though her hands began to ache from the force of her clenched fists.

"Crete…" she began, though she hardly knew what to say.

Especially because, as reluctant and grim as he sounded—as clearly unwilling as he was—there was a part of her that didn't care about any of that.

Because she remembered that girl, only two months ago, who had loved him so wildly and so deeply that she had simply assumed it would end in marriage. Sooner or later. Because how else could it end? She had known, with a bone-deep conviction, that forever was the only possible destination for them.

And there was still some part of that girl inside her tonight, because she wanted to simply throw herself at him. To ignore all the warning signs and the red flags, his grimness and the things she'd learned these last months, and simply…say yes.

Because no small part of her wanted nothing more, ever, than to take this man however he came to her.

Just so long as he came to her.

But while it had been only two months since her last, awful night in this flat, it had been an instructive two months.

"This is what you want, is it not?" And he sounded even bleaker than before. "I will marry you. Then there will be no more concerns about appeasing your uncle. Whether he disowns you or does not will be a matter of little practical import if we are wed. Whatever olive branches you wish to extend to the rest of his family you can do without having to worry about his approval."

It seemed to her as if London was spinning all around them, but she focused on him.

"Why would you do this?" Her voice sounded far rougher than she wanted it to. It gave too much away.

"It is only a few years until you come into your own fortune," he muttered, seemingly to himself.

"It is five years, in fact." She tried to swallow, but her throat was dry. "Five years is a very long time, Crete."

He seemed to turn to stone before her. "Nonetheless, marrying me will solve all your problems."

"I must still be asleep," Timoney said after a moment, searching his face and seeing nothing but granite and reluctance. "And I don't mind telling you, I've had this dream before. Many times. So I can tell you what I've often told myself when I've woken up to find your proposals little more than wishful thinking." She had to clear her throat then. "You don't actually want to marry me. And martyrdom doesn't suit you at all."

He let out a bark of laughter. "I am many things, but I have never been a martyr."

"Then why pretend you want to marry me?" The words felt wrenched from her.

Because she still wished she could...just say yes. Come what may.

His gaze grew darker than the night around them. "If that is what it will take, then that is what I will do."

Timoney gazed at him for a long while, until it seemed to her that she was only hurting herself that way. She turned her head then, taking in the sweet stretch of sleepy London, here in the dark before dawn on this Christmas Day that she had expected to go very, very differently.

And later, maybe, she would explore all the ways that this moment, in many ways, had hurt her more than anything that had gone before. But she needed to make it through, first.

Somehow, she had to survive this, too.

She sighed, though she wanted to sob. She stood straighter, when she wanted nothing more than to collapse into a ball on the ground.

"I appreciate the offer," Timoney made herself say, though everything in her was a riot of a sharp, bright anguish. She wanted nothing more than to snatch her words back. Then answer differently. Just jump straight in, because surely, whatever happened, it would be worth it—she would have him in some way and that had to be better than not having him. But instead, she made herself keep going. She made herself do the hard thing. "But no."

He gazed down at her, a thunderous expression taking over from the bleakness. And that was better. More familiar, anyway. Because at least she recognized his arrogance.

"No?" he repeated, incredulous.

"No," Timoney said, more firmly. "I am not going to marry you, Crete."

The incredulity on his face became a scowl. "Why the hell not?"

And she couldn't keep track of the things she felt any longer. Because she felt too many things at once. Still the urge to sob, holding all the smashed broken pieces of her heart in her hands. But also, possibly, she felt the urge to laugh, too.

Because someday, surely, she would find all of this funny. This man, who no one said *no* to, clearly. The look of imperious astonishment on his face, as if he'd never heard the word before.

She supposed it was possible he hadn't. Not really. Not since he was a child.

"We've never talked about Christmas," she said quietly, her gaze still on the city streets far, far below. But she made herself turn then, to look at him. "I'm going to guess by the singular lack of anything even remotely festive in this apartment of yours that you don't care for the holiday."

"I don't like holidays." His scowl deepened. "Particularly Christmas. The only thing worse than festivities are forced festivities. Perhaps you haven't noticed, Timoney, but the whole of England appears to slide into a minced pie stupor come fall, and little sense can be had from anyone until the new year. It is tiresome."

She found herself smiling again. Not happily, perhaps, but still. It was a smile. "It's very easy to get caught up in all the trappings. Minced pies, for example. Festive decorations, the race for perfect gifts, carols and fizzy drinks."

"Do you require that I present you with gifts?" he demanded. "Perhaps you have forgotten who I am. Have an island. A fortune or two, if you wish it. It means nothing to me."

Timoney shook her head and held the blanket closer. "It's not about the trappings. I know you don't understand Christmas, and maybe you never will. When my parents were alive it was my favorite day of the year. And not because we exchanged gifts, but because we were all together and everything was as it should be. A fire in the grate. Happy songs in the air. Terrible jumpers and a proper home-cooked meal. Just us. Just *love*, Crete. All the rest we could take or leave, as long as there was love."

His jaw seemed more like steel than the railing he gripped. "Simply name the meal you wish to be served and I will make it happen."

As she supposed she should have known he would. He could buy her anything she claimed she wanted. He could send a text and buy out restaurants all over this city, even forcing them to open for him today. If he wished, he could do almost anything.

Almost. "I thought that with Julian it wouldn't matter, because I already felt so numb, so what was little more self-harm? But you saved me from that. And I'm grateful, I am. But now I understand far better than I ever could have before that Christmas, marriage, it's all the same, really." She shook her head, trying to keep her emotions at bay, because she couldn't quite believe that she was doing this. "It's not about what you can *buy*, Crete. It's about what you *feel*."

"Timoney—" he began, looking thunderous again.

"It's light and it's hope, Crete." Her voice cracked. That was how urgent this felt to her. "And you think those things are the enemy."

"I do not. Necessarily."

"You do." She didn't address the *necessarily*. She didn't have to. She could see it written all over his face, all his rationalizations and qualifications, and none of that mattered as much as what she was about to say. "You do, Crete. And because you do, that means eventually—inevitably—you'll think I'm the enemy, too."

And Timoney realized that some part of her was waiting for him to refute what she'd said…when he didn't.

It was amazing, truly, how much an already broken heart could still continue to break.

"You will say yes," he thundered at her. "You will, Timoney."

And she knew what he would do even as he did it. He swept her into his arms again, and carried her inside.

It was only back in the heat of his flat that she noticed how cold she'd become. When he laid her out on the bed and followed her down, and the passion she knew she would hold close to her heart for the rest of her life exploded anew.

He warmed her the way he always did.

"You will," he promised her as he drove deep inside her, making them both groan.

"I won't," she replied, wrapping herself around him, putting her mouth to his ear. "But I will tell you goodbye, Crete. Every way I can."

And that was what she did.

With every part of her body, her heart, her soul. Again and again, in all the dark before dawn they had left. Because she knew that once the sun rose, reality would reassert itself, as little as she might want it to.

But first it was this. First there was them.

First there was a small taste of forever that would have to last her in place of the real thing.

CHAPTER ELEVEN

CRETE DID NOT SLEEP.

He could not.

He stayed wide awake long after Timoney finally drifted off. She lay beside him, curled into him, her breathing deep and even. Sometimes she murmured wordless chants in her sleep, as if she was dreaming of giving long speeches. But all it took to settle her was to hold her close again.

Sometimes when he held her, she smiled with such pure, sleepy happiness that it pierced him straight through.

But no matter how he tried, he couldn't seem to sleep himself.

He left her reluctantly and swung out of the bed, noticing the first stirring of dawn in the sky outside his windows. As good a time as any to remind himself who he was, he told himself sternly as he moved back into the flat. He took a quick shower—cold—to reset. Then he threw on a pair of trousers and retraced the steps he'd taken a seeming lifetime ago when he'd decided to take that drive.

It had started in his study. He'd been catching up

on the never-ending fire hose of work projects that required his input or a critical decision to proceed. And privately, he could admit that he was no longer quite as driven as he'd been once.

Though that felt like a betrayal of the determined eighteen-year-old he'd been long ago, who had thrown himself so completely into his work that he hadn't known where one ended and the other began. It was all him. It was only him.

Until Timoney.

He took his usual seat at his desk but didn't turn his attention to the stacks of papers before him, the blinking light on his answerphone, or the many messages he'd been ignoring all night long. He didn't even crack open his laptop.

Instead, Crete found himself staring at the wall opposite him and the ridiculous mural that Timoney had painted there. It had been blank for years. Deliberately empty space before him to keep him from being distracted.

He'd flown home from a conference in Berlin that day and hadn't gone into his office the way he normally would. Instead he'd raced home to discover her here. She hadn't seemed the least bit put off by his reaction to the bold, bright colors she'd painted—or to her presence in what was meant to be his sanctuary.

You really need to think about brightening yourself up, she'd told him with that great, unearned authority of hers that had baffled him from the start. And bewitched him, against his will. *Maybe make that an action item in one of your meetings, Crete.*

You need to think about boundaries, he had growled back.

And the smile she'd given him had been pure wickedness. *Maybe you should teach me some,* she'd invited him.

He had. Oh, he had.

But what he hadn't done was take that mural down. Not even after she'd gone. And even now he couldn't seem to come up with a good reason why not. His staff had offered, repeatedly, and he'd simply waved them off.

And now he sat in his chair once again and stared at all the haphazard splashes of color, tossed this way and that as if she'd simply flung paint at the wall to see what might happen. Brilliant blues. Screaming reds. Sunshiny, buttery, happy yellows.

The bloody thing was an eyesore.

Crete found himself on his feet. He left his study and walked through the flat, turning on the lights as he went, though the sky outside was brightening and light was beginning to come in all the walls of windows.

It was one of the most sought-after spaces in London. It was the finest view available. That was why Crete had bought this place. But for the first time, he noticed what Timoney had been saying from the moment he'd brought her here. That it really was... institutional.

You are the richest man on earth, or close enough, she had said not long after moving in. *You can have anything you want, in triplicate. Why on earth have you chosen to live in this...prison?*

Her words seemed to chase him as he moved through his rooms. Rooms upon rooms, all of them empty, because the point was having them, not filling them. Concrete and steel in the place of furnishings, because he told himself he liked clean lines and no clutter, the better to focus. Selected works of art chosen not because they were pleasing to him, but because they were worth vast fortunes.

He didn't even look at them.

What Crete looked at—what he studied, day and night—was that mural Timoney had painted for him that would likely offend and horrify his art dealer.

And it all made sense to him now.

The problem wasn't the mural. He'd tried to convince himself, in these last few weeks, that he kept it on that wall to remind himself of the defacement he'd allowed. To make sure he never forgot how wholly he had abandoned himself for a woman.

Making him more like the father he had always detested than he found at all excusable.

But now it was clear.

Everything he did, everything he was, was a prison. This was a cell of many fine rooms and he little more than a prisoner of his own making.

He found himself standing stock-still in the center of the nearly empty great room his expensive decorator had assured him was the height of sophistication. Not that he'd cared either way. His only interest in sophisticated people and their elegant pursuits was in showing up to prove that anyone could buy the things they all held so dear.

That they could hate him all they liked, but he never went anywhere.

But he'd missed the fact that he'd made that…literally true.

This flat was a prison. His life was a prison. When he'd clapped eyes on Timoney outside that club, she'd been like a key in a lock he'd stopped noticing was there ages ago. She'd wedged open the door. And instead of finding his way out, he'd slammed the heavy bars into place again.

The word *prison* kept echoing in his head.

And it seemed perfect that he'd come to this realization while it was not quite daylight outside.

Because she had spoken of hope and light. It seemed he needed her to do that so that he could finally see all the bars around him. The ones he'd put there. Day after day, year after year. Building this cell and leaving himself here to rot.

Hope and light was a silly, soft sort of notion he would have laughed at, before her. He would have slept soundly, tossed her out the first time she'd left her things about, charged right on into the next project and the next and the next…

But now he understood.

Now he understood everything, and it was as if he was ripped wide open from the inside out, so that too much understanding poured into him, battering him.

Changing him.

Letting him know that truly, he had been changed for good long ago.

Outside a club, at a party he hadn't wanted to attend, when he'd caught eyes with a girl who'd looked like a moonlight over the Mediterranean.

She'd smiled at him and he'd never been the same.

And maybe it was finally time he stopped fighting that.

Crete was finally ready when she woke again. It was light outside and coming up on ten o'clock, when she was meant to walk down an aisle out in the country and hand herself off to a man who would stamp out every last trace of light in her as if it had never been.

Whatever happened here, at least he had saved her from that darkness. He could take some solace in that, surely, for there was no one alive who deserved to wilt away in the darkness less than Timoney.

He knew the moment she sat up in his bed, so attuned was he to the sounds in this prison of his. *Or perhaps it's the fact you've lived here for years but have never truly moved in. If you had bothered to put rugs on the floor there would be nothing to hear.*

Crete accepted that was true, little as he liked it.

He waited out in the great room, listening to the sounds she made as she moved around in the back of the flat. He heard the shower go on, then off some while later, leaving him with too many images of her lush body in hot water and slick with soap.

But today was not about his libido.

Or so he kept telling himself, until his jaw was so tight he was surprised it didn't snap.

Sometime later she appeared, her blue eyes still sleepy and her hair wet, buttoning up an old shirt of his she must have liberated from his wardrobe as she walked. Along with what he thought were a pair of his boxer briefs. Her favorite uniform, as he recalled.

As always, his heart seemed to swell at the sight of her. But today he didn't pretend that wasn't happening. He simply stood there and watched her come toward him, letting his heart do what it would.

And maybe because she was still half-asleep, her eyes lit up when she saw him the way they always had, before.

The way, he promised himself, they would again.

Because he watched the way she pulled herself back as she remembered why she was here today, and he'd done that. Crete knew he had. He watched the shutters close down her expressive face and knew that he was the only one responsible.

And God knew he couldn't bear the thought that any part of her should be dimmed.

But he didn't have too long to contemplate that because her eyes widened again in the next moment, as she came to a stop beside him and took in what he'd done.

"What… What is this?" she stammered.

He found himself scowling.

"Christmas." His voice was gruff. "Obviously."

Timoney moved past him, farther into the room. And he turned to look, too, wondering what she saw when she looked at his handiwork. This work of the few hours he'd had.

Because she had talked of Christmas, so he had ordered one up, paid dearly for it, and had transformed this room she'd had always hated.

Now it bristled with evergreen trees, all of them festooned with lights. So many lights it made the cavernous room feel warm and enchanted. It made this prison of his look the way he felt when he gazed at her.

The way he felt right now.

And it didn't feel at all natural to simply…let himself feel. Not to hide. Not to divert. Not to pretend it wasn't happening.

"Crete."

But the way she said his name was barely more than a whisper, laced through with wonder. Or what he hoped was wonder.

And he was ready when she turned around.

He stood there before her and though he had dressed at some point during his Christmas morning rush, he felt as if he had never been more naked.

"I do not want you to think that I am trying to impress you with what I can buy, *Timonitsa mou*," he said stiffly. "That is not what this is."

She looked almost stricken. Her hands moved as if she was reaching toward him, but she dropped them back to her sides. "Crete. I…"

But she trailed off when he shook his head. And he had the distinct impression that he looked more severe than necessary… Then again, he didn't have it in him to make this easy.

He didn't do easy.

There were some who had been born with that

sort of charm, but he was not one of them. Everything he'd ever gotten in this life had come from hard work. Day after day, year after year, when it yielded great results and, more important, when it didn't. He wasn't afraid of work.

In many ways it was the only love he had ever known.

But it was a cold love. A harsh love. It could give him a splendid prison and a life filled with only the finest things, but it couldn't make him as happy as a splash of yellow across a wall. It couldn't look at him with eyes brighter than the sky.

And it wasn't what he wanted any longer.

Crete had never faced a harder task—or a steeper mountain to climb, in his life of bounding over them like they weren't there—than this one.

"Your wedding was due to begin five minutes ago," he said, sounding darker than necessary. "I am surprised that no one has rung you, demanding to know your whereabouts."

She seemed to consider that. "Happy Christmas to you, too." And she didn't precisely smile then. But there was the hint of that wickedness he'd known about her. "And I imagine they have rung me repeatedly and searched the whole of the estate by now. What will all the abducting, I didn't have time to leave a note. Or fetch my mobile."

He studied her, telling himself to do this correctly. "Do you wish to contact them now and explain?"

Her chest rose and fell, hard, as if she was having trouble keeping her breath even. "I...do not." When he only waited, she sighed. "I suspect my absence will speak for itself. I imagine that Julian will think it's because I saw him in the middle of a dalliance last night, but that can't be helped."

"I can return you to your uncle's house, if you wish it," Crete made himself say. No matter how bitter the words tasted on his tongue.

She stood a little straighter then. "I do not wish it."

"Are you certain?"

"This is the first day of the rest of my life, Crete," she said softly. "There are a great many things I wanted to do with my life before I loved, then lost, then allowed myself to get talked into a wedding I never wanted. Before my parents died. Maybe I want to do some of them. All of them."

He nodded at Timoney's hands, and the ring she wore.

"You can start by taking that ring off." And he was not an uncertain man. As far as he was concerned, all he need do was think it and it became law, but this was Timoney. He cleared his throat, then forced out the unfamiliar plea. "Please."

It was distinctly unfamiliar, and uncomfortable, to admit to himself that he had absolutely no idea what she would do next.

Timoney blinked. Then she looked down at her own hand as if it surprised her to find it was connected to her. She frowned for a moment, then she wrenched the diamond off her finger. Then, holding his gaze again, she simply…tossed it.

Crete had never heard a finer music than the faint

clatter the ring made as it hit the floor, then skidded out of view beneath one of the trees.

"Did that feel good?" he asked.

And she smiled at him. That beautiful smile that had knocked his whole world askew the first time he'd seen it. And every time since.

"As a matter of fact," she said. "It really did."

So while she was still smiling, brighter than all the lights on these trees he'd put up just for her, Crete did something he had never done before in the whole of his life.

He sank to his knees before her. Then he reached into his pocket and pulled out the ring he had acquired by waking up London's foremost jeweler at the crack of dawn. On Christmas. And then making it worth the man's while to come here, bearing boxes lined with velvet, so that Crete might make his selection.

And no matter what happened next, it would be worth every last penny the man had wrung out of him for that service—simply for the look on Timoney's face as Crete knelt there before her.

"I wanted to give you Christmas because I want to give you everything," he told her. "I want you to do every one of those great many things that you dream about."

"Crete." His name was a whisper. "What are you...?"

But he couldn't think too much more about what he was doing or he wouldn't do it. He would retreat back behind his bars and live a life of cold steel and concrete. Darker and darker all the time. He might end up there still.

First, though, he would try to walk out of his cell, once and for all, and reach for the things he'd always told himself he didn't want or need, because they slowed everyone else down. Love. Companionship. The vulnerability of it all. The longing and the need and the perfect happiness of lying next to her in the dark, close and whole.

He had stopped holding out his hands when he was still a child. But hadn't his childhood taken enough from him? Two families. His name. His heart.

Crete held out his hands now.

And for the first time in as long as he could recall it, he let himself hope.

"I want to give you light," he told her, as if he was carving the words he spoke into the stone beneath them. "And I want, more than anything, to give you love. And all the hope you can handle. But I think you know how little I know of each. Light is one thing."

He couldn't look away from her. He didn't want to look away from her.

She stood before him, her hands over her mouth as if she couldn't believe what she was seeing. Wet hair and bare feet. Her face scrubbed clean. His boxer briefs.

Crete had never beheld more beauty. It filled him up. It coursed through his veins.

It made him believe.

"All I know of light or hope is you, Timoney."

He had never knelt before because it had always seemed like surrender to him, but he knew better now. He had never been more powerful than when he dared to do this. To hand over his heart to this woman, knowing full well that she could hurt him more, and more critically, than he had ever been hurt before. She could destroy him. But he did this anyway. "And any belief I might have in love, is you."

Crete held out the ring he had chosen, because it had reminded him of her. It was a precious moonstone, large and almost iridescent, surrounded by enough diamonds to sparkle the way she did.

"Are you…?" Her hands were still over mouth, so her words were muffled, but her eyes were bright. "Is that…?"

"I want to marry you, as I said last night," he told her. "But not to wait out your uncle or your money or whatever other nonsense I might have spouted. That was me trying to hide. But I do not wish to hide any longer, Timoney. I… I love you."

He thought she whispered his name.

But he pushed on, his voice growing rougher with each word, because he had said it. And now he needed to say the rest. "You make me imagine that I am a man. Not a mystery or a monster or an alien creature set down amongst these humans I cannot understand. With you I am only a man, flesh and blood and capable of loving you as you deserve." He shook his head as if to clear it. "I don't know if I ever will, but I know that I will start by setting aside all this anger, all this pain I have long tried to pretend was only fuel to me. I will let it go, Timoney. This I promise."

This time she said his name. He heard it perfectly.

"Because, *Timonitsa mou*, you are light and you

are hope, and there is nothing I cannot do when I put my mind to it. Only look around you." He kept holding the ring out between them, his gaze locked to hers as if he would never look away again. "If you give me the chance, I will spend my life trying to be the man you make me when I am with you. I will learn to be as you are, with the courage of a hundred fearless lions, prepared to fight for even as dark and twisted a heart as mine. And so sure, despite everything, that you would win. How could this not inspire me? I will dedicate myself to making you as happy as you can be, and making up for what I have put you through. I will leave my past where it belongs. Because what I want is the future. Every possible future. With you. And I promise you that I will love you, as best as I can, until I draw my final breath."

He realized his heart was pounding. His head felt alarmingly light. "If…" He cleared his throat. He dared to hope. "If you will have me."

And then he waited, his whole existence in the balance. In her hands.

For a long moment Timoney only looked at him. A great deal as if she was seeing a ghost.

And then his heart dropped, for her beautiful eyes filled with tears.

And he thought, *There it is, then.*

For there could be no arguing. There was no point in temper. It was one thing to bluster and carry on. He was good at that.

But it was another to offer his heart, unadorned, and have that be rejected.

Crete understood in that moment not only how it was that people died of broken hearts, but how easy it would be to succumb. Because how was he to go on with a heart that no longer beat?

But then, before he could even think about lowering his arms, Timoney's beautiful face broke wide open into that life-altering smile of hers.

Wider now. Brighter.

Then she was rushing toward him, hurtling herself into his arms.

Crete caught her, bearing her down with him onto the hard floor and turning so he could cushion her. She was so busy pressing kisses all over his face, his neck, that it took him a beat, then another, to hear what she was saying with every touch of her lips to whatever part of him she could reach.

"Yes," she whispered, fervent and fierce and sure. So very *sure*. "Yes, I will marry you. Yes, I will love you. Yes, Crete. *Yes*."

And so it was there, lying on the floor surrounded by his first Christmas ever and all the bars of his prison busted wide open, that he slid that ring onto her finger.

Then started his most important project yet: loving her forever.

Which, it turned out, he was as good at as he was everything else he touched.

Because Timoney was light. She was hope made real. He was grateful for her every day of his life.

But he was still Crete Asgar.

CHAPTER TWELVE

A YEAR LATER, to the day, Timoney George walked down the stairs of the house in Belgravia she and Crete had picked out together to marry the man who waited for her there at the bottom, in a grand hall thick with brightly lit Christmas trees.

She had never felt more alive.

"My love," Crete said, his dark eyes intent on her as she descended the sweeping steps toward him. "You are a vision."

And her smile was so wide she was afraid it might actually break her wide open. But maybe she wouldn't mind too much if it did.

This had been the best year of her life.

It had started in that cold, cavernous flat that he'd somehow filled with Christmas and it had only gotten better. Day by day.

Her uncle was still not speaking to her, but despite what her parents might have counseled had they been here, Timoney could not bring herself to consider his silence a loss. She had used Julian's behavior with the diplomat's wife as an excuse and Uncle Oliver had only sneered and told her to grow up.

Timoney felt that it had been a sign of how grown up she really was that she had not engaged with him any further.

Julian had been even more difficult. He had blustered and tried to bully her when she'd called him. Not because she'd wished to talk to him, but because she did not intend to hide from the choice she'd made. She had not called so he could soundly abuse her for the better part of a quarter.

Which he had done at top volume until Crete, who had been holding her in his lap while she sifted through the wreckage of the life she'd walked away from, jumped in. He suggested that Julian seek redress for whatever damages he felt he had faced through Oliver, as Oliver was the one who had set the wedding into motion in the first place.

And if you do not care for that solution, Crete had continued with a cool menace, cutting through Julian's outrage that easily, *I can assure you, this mongrel would be only too happy to let loose the full power of my legal team upon you.*

Timoney had never heard from Julian again.

Happily.

When she and Crete had gone back to fetch her things after New Year's, her uncle had quitted the house in protest. But her aunt had met her at the door. Hermione had insisted that Timoney and Crete stay for tea with her daughters, and had even, in an act of defiance the likes of which Timoney had never seen before, eaten a petit four.

Her daughters had been wide-eyed. Timoney had been filled with hope—for all of them.

Things had only gotten better from there.

She and Crete had looked for a place to live that felt like a home, and had settled on a house not far from the listed house she'd lived in before she'd met him, that he had once mocked.

And because they built what they had now around joy, anything was possible.

Anything was possible and nothing could take it away.

Every day that passed, the deeper it got. The better it got.

Crete learned how to delegate, turning over the parts of his businesses that no longer thrilled him to his fleets of underlings, all of them desperate to prove themselves. Timoney learned that when a person had been given everything on a platter, as Crete had once accused her, the best thing to do to live a meaningful life was turn around and start offering platters to those who might need them. She set up the George Foundation in her parents' honor, and by that fall, was ready to throw her first ball.

Where she and Crete had danced together, in public, for the first time.

She could still recall every moment of that waltz. His ring on her finger and his hand in the small of her back. His dark blue gaze fierce and proud.

And that crook in his lips that was only and ever hers.

That smile that would have told her how much he loved her—even if he hadn't spent a good part of each day making sure she knew exactly how much.

A favor she took great pleasure in returning.

"Are you ready, *kardia mou*?" asked the man who waited for her today, resplendent in a dark suit and unrecognizable from the Crete she had known before.

Because this Crete smiled. This Crete was transfigured by love. By joy.

By all the hope and light they could handle.

"More than ready," she told him, taking his hand.

And he led her into the room where their officiant waited.

A room filled with the life they'd built together. Art that made her heart hurt when she looked at it. Comfortable places to sit, to lie, to explore each other in every possible way. Rugs on their floors and happy plants.

The house they lived in together was filled with books. With laughter.

With enough love to light up the whole of London.

And often did, by Timoney's reckoning.

Today they stood in the middle of a beautiful Christmas and gave themselves to each other in a new way.

And after they said their vows—after Crete kissed her and murmured marvelously possessive words against her lips that she took pleasure in returning—he swung her up into his arms and looked down at her, beaming.

Not an alien at all, this glorious man of hers. But her husband now.

And more than that, too.

But she would save her little secret for later. After

they moved from this private moment that they'd wanted to be only theirs into the banquet hall where their friends waited. Her friends, that was, and Crete's half siblings, because this had been a year of new beginnings in every possible way.

Because joy made even the unimaginable possible, day in and day out.

They would feast and they would laugh. They would dance as husband and wife. They would toast their new life and ring out those Christmas bells.

And then later Timoney would share with him that there was yet another new life they could celebrate in six months' time.

"Hope and light," Crete said to her, like another vow, as he carried her into the hall to the sound of cheers within.

"Hope and light," she replied. "Forever."

But every part of her was bright and awake and alive now, and ever would be. Because Timoney knew that for them, forever was just the beginning.

* * * * *

COMING SOON!

We really hope you enjoyed reading this book. If you're looking for more romance, be sure to head to the shops when new books are available on

Thursday 25th November

To see which titles are coming soon, please visit

millsandboon.co.uk/nextmonth

MILLS & BOON

Coming next month

A CONTRACT FOR HIS RUNAWAY BRIDE
Melanie Milburne

'Could you give me an update on when Mr Smith will be available?'

The receptionist's answering smile was polite but formal. 'I apologise for the delay. He'll be with you shortly.'

'Look, my appointment was -'

'I understand, Ms Campbell. But he's a very busy man. He's made a special gap in his diary for you. He's not usually so accommodating. You must've made a big impression on him.'

'I haven't even met him. All I know is, I was instructed to be here close to thirty minutes ago for a meeting with a Mr Smith to discuss finance. I've been given no other details.'

The receptionist glanced at the intercom console where a small green light was flashing. She looked up again at Elodie with the same polite smile. 'Thank you for being so patient. Mr...erm... Smith will see you now. Please go through. It's the third door on the right. The corner office.'

The corner office boded well- that meant he was the head honcho. The big bucks began and stopped with him. Elodie came to the door and took a deep calming breath but it did nothing to settle the frenzy of flick-knives in her stomach. She gave the door a quick rap with her knuckles. Please, please, please let me be successful this time.

'Come.'

Her hand paused on the doorknob, her mind whirling in ice cold panic. Something about the deep timbre of that voice sent a shiver scuttling over her scalp like a small claw-footed creature. How could this Mr Smith sound so like her ex-fiancé? Scarily alike. She turned the doorknob and pushed the door open, her gaze immediately fixing on the tall dark-haired man behind the large desk.

'You?' Elodie gasped, heat flooding into her cheeks and other places in her body she didn't want to think about right now.

Lincoln Lancaster rose from his chair with leonine grace, his expression set in its customary cynical lines- the arch of one ink-black brow over his intelligent bluey-green gaze, the tilt of his sensual mouth that was not quite a smile. His black hair was brushed back from his high forehead in loose waves that looked like they had last been combed by his fingers. He was dressed in a three-piece suit that hugged his athletic frame, emphasising the broadness of his shoulders, the taut trimness of his chest, flat abdomen and lean hips. He was the epitome of a successful man in his prime. Potent, powerful, persuasive. He got what he wanted, when he wanted, how he wanted.

'You're looking good, Elodie.' His voice rolled over her as smoothly and lazily as his gaze, the deep sexy rumble so familiar it triggered a host of memories she had fought for seven years to erase. Memories in her flesh that were triggered by being in his presence. Erotic memories that made her hyper aware of his every breath, his every glance, his every movement.

Continue reading
A CONTRACT FOR HIS RUNAWAY BRIDE
Melanie Milburne

Available next month
www.millsandboon.co.uk

LET'S TALK
Romance

For exclusive extracts, competitions
and special offers, find us online:

- f facebook.com/millsandboon
- 🐦 @MillsandBoon
- 📷 @MillsandBoonUK

Get in touch on 01413 063232

For all the latest titles coming soon, visit
millsandboon.co.uk/nextmonth

JOIN US ON SOCIAL MEDIA!

Stay up to date with our latest releases, author news and gossip, special offers and discounts, and all the behind-the-scenes action from Mills & Boon...

 millsandboon

 millsandboonuk

 millsandboon

It might just be true love...